NUDE ON THIN ICE

It starts with a letter. Ken McCall is sunning himself in Key West with his current girlfriend, Betty, when he finds out that his old friend Carl has died. Carl's last wish was that Ken look after his wife, Nanette, a request which Ken is only too eager to fill. Besides, there may be a fortune to be had if he can just play his cards right. First he ditches Betty. Then, after a hot drive across country, Ken finds that Carl's New Mexico mountaintop mansion is in the midst of a record-breaking winter. He is warmed immediately by his welcome from a lovely young lady named Justine, who lives with Nanette and their surly caretaker, Elmer. Ken is beginning to wonder what he's gotten himself into, when Betty shows up in town. Ken's plans are going to hell fast when Justine comes to him with a plan of her own—for murder.

MEMORY OF PASSION

Bill Sommers has got it all. At 39, he has a beautiful wife, Louise, and a wonderful daughter, Lolly, and a successful career in commercial art. Oh, sure, maybe things aren't perfect between he and Louise, but that's life. And then one rainy night Karen calls. Karen, his lost love. Karen, his high school sweetheart. Karen, the one who got away. She insists they meet. Bill is too curious not to agree. But he's not prepared for the young lady who shows up, claiming to be Karen Jamais. She's got all of Karen's memories; even her looks, her moves, her delicious figure—and every bit of Karen's passion. But that went away 20 years ago! How can this be Karen, unchanged after all this time? It's like a wild, crazy dream. Bill is about to enter a hidden world of passion and violence on his way to fi impossible dream could actually com

GIL BREWER BIBLIOGRAPHY

Love Me and Die (1951; w/Day
  Keene, published as by Day Keene)
Satan is a Woman (1951)
So Rich, So Dead (1951)
13 French Street (1951)
Flight to Darkness (1952)
Hell's Our Destination (1953)
A Killer is Loose (1954)
Some Must Die (1954)
77 Rue Paradis (1954)
The Squeeze (1955)
The Red Scarf (1955)
—And the Girl Screamed (1956)
The Angry Dream (1957; reprinted as
  The Girl from Hateville)
The Brat (1957)
Little Tramp (1958)
The Bitch (1958)
Wild (1958)
The Vengeful Virgin (1958)
Sugar (1959)
Wild to Possess (1959)
Angel (1960)
Nude on Thin Ice (1960)
Backwoods Teaser (1960)
The Three-Way Split (1960)
Play it Hard (1960)
Appointment in Hell (1961)
A Taste for Sin (1961)
Memory of Passion (1962)
The Hungry One (1966)
The Tease (1967)
Sin for Me (1967)
It Takes a Thief #1:
  The Devil in Davos (1969)
It Takes a Thief #2:
  Mediterranean Caper (1969)
It Takes a Thief #3:
  Appointment in Cairo (1970)
A Devil for O'Shaugnessy (2008)

As Harry Arvay
Eleven Bullets for Mohammed (1975)
Operation Kuwait (1975)
The Moscow Intercept (1975)
The Piraeus Plot (1975)
Togo Commando (1976)

As Mark Bailey
Mouth Magic (1972)

As Al Conroy
Soldato #3: Strangle Hold! (1973)
Soldato #4: Murder Mission! (1973)

As Hal Ellson
Blood on the Ivy (1970)

As Elaine Evans
Shadowland (1970)
A Dark and Deadly Love (1972)
Black Autumn (1973)
Wintershade (1974)

As Luke Morgann
More Than a Handful (1972)
Ladies in Heat (1972)
Gamecock (1972)
Tongue Tricks! (1972)

As Ellery Queen
The Campus Murders (1969)
The Japanese Golden Dozen (1978;
  rewrites by Brewer)

Unpublished Novels
Angry Arnold
The Erotics
Firebase Seattle
  (Executioner novel, 1975)
Gun the Dame Down
  (You'll Get Yours)
House of the Potato
The Paper Coffin

Nude on Thin Ice
Memory of Passion

Two Novels By *Gil Brewer*
Introduction by David Rachels

Stark House Press • Eureka California

NUDE ON THIN ICE / MEMORY OF PASSION

Published by Stark House Press
1315 H Street
Eureka, CA 95501
griffinskye3@sbcglobal.net
www.starkhousepress.com

NUDE ON THIN ICE
Copyright © 1960 by Gil Brewer and published by Avon Books.
Copyright renewed 1988 by the Estate of Gil Brewer.

MEMORY OF PASSION
Copyright © 1962 and published by Lancer Books, Inc.

Reprinted by permission of the Estate of Gil Brewer. All rights reserved under International and Pan-American Copyright Conventions.

"Gil Brewer's Glands" copyright © 2014 by David Rachels

All rights reserved.

ISBN: 1-933586-53-2
ISBN-13: 978-1-933586-53-3

Cover design and layout by Mark Shepard, WWW.SHEPGRAPHICS.COM
Proofreading by Rick Ollerman

PUBLISHER'S NOTE
This is a work of fiction. Names, characters, places and incidents are either the products of the author's imagination or used fictionally, and any resemblance to actual persons, living or dead, events or locales, is entirely coincidental. Without limiting the rights under copyright reserved above, no part of this publication may be reproduced, stored, or introduced into a retrieval system or transmitted in any form or by any means (electronic, mechanical, photocopying, recording or otherwise) without the prior written permission of both the copyright owner and the above publisher of the book.

First Stark House Press Edition: April 2014

Contents

Gil Brewer's Glands by David Rachels 7

Nude on Thin Ice by Gil Brewer. 17

Memory of Passion by Gil Brewer. 141

Gil Brewer's Glands
by David Rachels

I.

He writes not of love but of lust, of defeats in which nobody loses anything of value, of victories without hope and, worst of all, without pity or compassion. His griefs grieve on no universal bones, leaving no scars. He writes not of the heart but of the glands.
—William Faulkner

Nude on Thin Ice (1960) and *Memory of Passion* (1962) rank among Gil Brewer's best novels, but they are not among his most read. In the main, this is because copies have been scarce. These novels have never been reprinted (until now), and used first editions have been priced for collectors, not for those of us who want to remove them from their mylar bags and actually read them. Many lesser Brewer novels are better known, buoyed by their initial popularity and subsequent availability in the secondhand marketplace. Before the recent flurry of Brewer reprints, the million-selling *13 French Street* (1951) was the Brewer novel that noir fans were most likely to have read, simply because cheap used copies were fairly easy to find. Unfortunately, *13 French Street* is not one of Brewer's better books. The novel's sex-driven plot may have thrilled readers in 1951, but today the book feels badly dated.

When Brewer died in 1983, his noir novels had all been out of print for more than fifteen years. The first reprint came in 1988, when Simon & Schuster packaged *13 French Street* with a much better Brewer book, *The Red Scarf* (1955). In fact, *The Red Scarf* has long had the reputation of being Brewer's best work, in part because it was anointed as such by legendary *New York Times* mystery critic Anthony Boucher:

> *The Red Scarf* is the best Gil Brewer novel I've seen: a short but full-packed story, pointed and restrained, of a Florida motel owner who sees a chance to cut himself in on some hijacked Syndicate money—an effective tale of an ordinary man trying to turn sharpie and destroying himself in the process.

Remove a few of the details specific to *The Red Scarf*, and you have the template for many great noir novels: an ordinary man sees a chance to cut himself in on some money, turns sharpie, and destroys himself in the process.

But *The Red Scarf*, however archetypal its plot may be, lacks the central element of a typical Brewer narrative: sex. Sex was Brewer's artistic obsession, yet *The Red Scarf* is almost sex free. Brewer constructs the novel's ordinary man, Roy Nichols, to be as sympathetic as possible. Desperate to keep his struggling motel afloat, Roy grabs the Syndicate money and takes great risks to keep it. Though he crosses paths with a gangster's moll, he does not fall into bed with her. He remains true to his wife, Bess. If Roy loses his readers' sympathy, he does so because his desperation for the money puts Bess in great danger.

Taken together, *13 French Street* and *The Red Scarf* might leave us with the impression that, although Brewer used sex to sell a million books, he did his best writing when he left sex out of the picture. *Nude on Thin Ice* and *Memory of Passion*, however, may leave us with a very different conclusion.

II.

Money. It could buy anything I'd ever want out of this life.
Gil Brewer, *Nude on Thin Ice*

At first, the plot of *Nude on Thin Ice* is all about money, but the novel's packaging was all about sex. Visually, no Gil Brewer novel sold sex harder than *Nude on Thin Ice* (excluding, of course, his pseudonymous porn novels of the early 1970s). The first edition's cover illustrates its title precisely: a naked blonde, down on her knees, covers her face with her hands while ice cracks beneath her. A damsel in distress, she awaits rescue and, presumably, seduction. But why would a nude woman be out on the ice? Above the book's title, the cover reads, "A red-hot hellcat in the frozen night—and murder on the prowl!" A weeping blonde on cracking ice would not seem to qualify as a "red-hot hellcat," but never mind that. This is about selling books, not logic.

Brewer's job was to write the books, not to market them or even to title them. But this did not stop him, of course, from giving them titles. On stray pieces of paper, he often brainstormed. On one sheet, he typed these possibilities for a manuscript he had recently finished:
DIE FOR ME
THE BIG SWITCH
SNATCH
THE WAY OUT
POSSESSED
NO EXIT
THE LOVELY LIE

DEATH FOR THE BRIDE
LIE WITH ME
MURDER ON THE MAKE
MY LADY WEEPS
FAREWELL TO EDEN
WAKE UP TO HELL
DEATH IS MY BRIDE
THE DEADLY TWIST
HONEYMOON IN HELL
THE DEVIL IS MY BRIDE
LOVE ME EVIL
THE ANGRY SIN
SATAN'S DOLL
TROUBLE IS A WOMAN
DEATH LIES NUDE
KISS MY SIN

Despite the obvious merits of *Kiss My Sin*, Brewer's publisher kept Brewer's original title for this book, *Play It Hard*. Usually, however, Brewer's titles were changed, and they usually became more sensationalistic. *Satan's Rib* became *Satan Is a Woman*. *Farewell to Eden* became *Hell's Our Destination*. *Haywire* became *Little Tramp*. *The Brass Moon* became *The Bitch*.

In the case of *Nude on Thin Ice*, Brewer's original title had been *Naked on Ice*. This change may be slight, but it is substantial. The novel's plot *does* feature a nude woman on ice (or, more accurately, a photograph of a nude woman on ice), but the ice is not thin and cracking, and the woman is definitely *not* a damsel in distress. In fact, she is a classic Brewer femme fatale, and her nudity represents not vulnerability but a temptation calculated to control and, if necessary, destroy.

The nude on the ice is named Justine, and she first appears in the novel's third chapter. At the start, *Nude on Thin Ice* shows a family resemblance to the sexless *The Red Scarf*. Like Roy Nichols in *The Red Scarf*, Ken McCall in *Nude on Thin Ice* is desperate for money, and he has the chance for a big score. But while Nichols is a good guy in a tight spot who needs the money to keep his dream afloat (a dream that he shares with his wife, no less), McCall is an unapologetic bastard who wants money because he wants money and for whom women are disposable objects.

The contrast is jarring, but as an artistic development, the progression makes sense. Bastard McCall, not devoted husband Nichols, is consistent with Brewer's view of mankind (and I do mean *man*kind), and from the start McCall is an unpleasant literary companion. On the first page of *Nude on Thin Ice*, he describes his woman of the moment, Betty Flanagan: "I looked at her. She wore a very tight and tiny two-piece orange swimsuit that inadequately covered the overplump body I'd been using as a forget-yourself machine." And then, on the next page, as he is dumping her: "Well, you have to treat them rough. [...] It was high time she got herself kicked. I'd been doing everything else to her."

The repellant McCall presents an artistic challenge for Brewer. He can make you care about what happens to a good husband, but can he make you care about what happens to a bastard? He relished this challenge, and he thought about it carefully, even compiling a list of principles for accomplishing it:

PRINCIPLES FOR MAKING UNSYMPATHETIC CHARACTERS LIKEABLE AND SALABLE*

1. Motivate his unreasonableness. Justify by showing why he feels as he does. Don't try to soften his Unsympathetic Characters Trait, but list reasons behind his feeling. Make reader feel Unreasonableness has basis as far as Unreasonable Character is concerned.

2. Let the Reader see Unreasonable Hero through Eyes more Tolerant than his own—the eyes of a good character in the story. Let this Sympathetic Character Understand your hero's unreasonable conduct sympathetically.

3. Let the Unreasonable Character suffer because of his Unreasonableness, let him suffer a great deal, don't relieve his suffering by allowing him to face any situation and win out. Let the Reader Feel that the punishment is Just. You win sympathy for Hero IF you make his suffering convincing. Let him Pay for his Unreasonableness.

4. Let your Hero be partially aware of his defection and Make him Try again and again to correct it, though he may fail.

5. Make your Unreasonable Character less unreasonable by showing that his Trait is Universal. Show that the people the Reader knows and likes may be very much like this character.

USE THESE PRINCIPLES NOT ONCE IN YOUR STORY—BUT AGAIN AND AGAIN, WHENEVER IT IS NECESSARY TO SOFTEN THE HERO'S UNSYMPATHETIC ACTIONS.

These principles, however, seem a better fit for Roy Nichols than for Ken McCall, largely because "unreasonable" and "unsympathetic" are not synonyms. At the start of *The Red Scarf*, Nichols is a sympathetic character, but

---

* This list was typed by Brewer on a single, undated sheet of paper. He may have written it himself, or he may have copied it from a how-to book. Brewer sometimes studied writing manuals and retyped key passages.

he becomes less sympathetic as his drive to keep the Syndicate money becomes increasingly unreasonable. But in *Nude on Thin Ice*, McCall is unsympathetic from the start, and this has nothing to do with his being unreasonable. "Reasonable bastard" is not an oxymoron.

If McCall ever gains reader sympathy, he does so because of Justine, the novel's femme fatale. At least one crucial principle is missing from Brewer's how-to list: An unsympathetic character gains readers' sympathy when he is in conflict with characters who are even more unsympathetic than he is. Before meeting Justine, McCall has already done his fair share of terrible things without a second thought. But when Justine has him in her orbit, he does things that give even a life-long bastard pause. At one point McCall narrates, "I did it alone, in my room, drinking brandy. There were all kinds of fear inside me, and I fought against doing anything, but I did it, just the same." He is working under orders from Justine now, and thus she has delivered the third item on Brewer's list: McCall is suffering, and readers will feel that it is just.

Of course, McCall's suffering will not necessarily cause readers to feel sympathy. Instead, they may feel a simple schadenfreude at seeing the bastard getting his due. "But it is *Schadenfreude*," wrote philosopher Arthur Schopenhauer, "a mischievous delight in the misfortunes of others, which remains the worst trait in human nature. It is a feeling which is closely akin to cruelty, and differs from it, to say the truth, only as theory from practice. In general, it may be said of it that it takes the place which pity ought to take—pity which is its opposite, and the true source of all real justice and charity."

Thus, if Brewer fails to make us feel sympathy for McCall, then maybe he succeeds in showing the truth of McCall's character. For if we feel pleasure in McCall's pain, then maybe Brewer has managed to make bastards of us all.

III.

What did those stupid knick-knacks called people know about certain so-called base instincts under the heading Sex? The preacher with his wiper still wet, because he hadn't had time for a shower—bells, you know, pulpit, you know, sermon, you know—standing there slightly above the congregation, some of whom had crabs, some gleet, some worse; every damned one of them knowing, and the preacher, too; standing there, yelling from a soft and attended throat, heart over-beating, "It's a sin—etc. etc.," while the choir boys and girls walked calmly, chaste, to their places—fingers still moist, eyes and life alert. Knowing, too.
Gil Brewer, *Memory of Passion*

The title *Memory of Passion* gives a fair idea of the novel's contents: the story of a middle-aged man who cannot let go of his past, who cannot stop obsessing over the great love of his youth. As far as this description goes, it recalls an earlier noir classic, Cornell Woolrich's *Rendezvous in Black* (1948), in which Johnny Marr clings to the memory of Dorothy, his dead fiancée. Dorothy's portrait is idealized and pure:

> You can't describe light very easily. You can tell *where* it is, but not what it is. Light was where she was. There may have been prettier girls, but there have never been lovelier ones. It came from inside and out both; it was a blend. She was everyone's first love, as he looks back later once she is gone and tells himself she must have been.

But this, of course, is not Gil Brewer's idea of passion. In *Memory of Passion*, Bill Sommers recalls Karen, the love of his teenage years:

> The broad mouth with those tender ripe lips, lips he'd kissed thousands of times. The faintly heart-shaped face, and that full, supple, absolutely marvelous body that seemed always drenched with desire—for him. And he for her. She had been the only woman in his life who had matched his sexuality. What they call a perfect match—on fire.

Johnny Marr clings to his romanticized memory of Dorothy in a romanticized way, keeping a nightly vigil at their meeting spot on the town square, waiting for a dead girl who will never appear. Bill Sommers, on the other hand, moves on. He marries, has a kid, and tries to salvage a reasonable facsimile of a sex life. In Woolrich a man can survive without idealized love, albeit miserably, but in Brewer he cannot survive without sex. He may have lost his "perfect match," but his glands require that he find a replacement sex partner.

When *Memory of Passion* begins, however, Bill's sex life is not good. On those occasions when he manages to get his wife into bed, their sex is "a fast lap of endurance into nothing." Thus, he is especially vulnerable to the strange phone call that he receives from a woman claiming to be his teenage sex match, Karen Jamais (name translation: Pure Never). If the woman on the phone were Karen, she would be about 40 years old, but Bill feels certain that he hears the voice of a teenager. And when they meet it *is* Karen, *young* Karen—or is it?—even though it makes no sense. Unfortunately for Bill, glands do not reason; they simply control.

Memory of Passion is divided into eleven unnumbered sections. Each section is designated with a line from the refrain of "Where or When," the first song in the Richard Rogers & Lorenz Hart musical *Babes in Arms* (1937):

It seems we stood and talked like this before
We looked at each other in the same way then
But I can't remember where or when
The clothes you're wearing are the clothes you wore
The smile you are smiling you were smiling then
But I can't remember where or when.

Some things that happen for the first time
Seem to be happening again
And so it seems that we have met before
And laughed before... and loved before
But who knows where or when!

As section titles, these lyrics create an ironic contrast, evoking the romantic world of Woolrich before we plunge into Brewer's world of sexual obsession. When Bill and Karen were teenagers, this had been their song. As a middle-aged man, Bill listens to "Where or When" obsessively and recalls Karen, "a memory that had been like one continual orgasm within his being for years."

In "Where or When," love at first sight becomes déjà vu: a couple who meet and laugh and love for the first time feel so perfectly matched that surely this cannot be love at first sight after all. They must have been together before. Perhaps they are equating their fantasies with the reality of this moment: if they have long dreamed of this day, it may seem to them that it has happened before. Their past was a hope, but their present is real. In *Memory of Passion*, Brewer inverts this relationship: Bill's past with Karen is real, but his present with her is only hope. This song that once spoke to their love (or, perhaps more accurately, to their sex) now speaks with even greater resonance to Bill's current fantasy. His glands tell him that he has met and loved this teenage girl before, even though his brain knows it cannot be true.

This premise would seem enough to carry the novel, but *Memory of Passion* turns out to be more ambitious. Possibly the novel's most darkly pleasant surprise comes early on when a third major character joins the proceedings: Walter Hogan, a sociopath who is stalking Karen. Prior to *Memory of Passion*, Brewer had already written one great novel about a sociopathic killer: *A Killer Is Loose* (1954), which Brewer himself thought might be his best book. In parallel with *The Red Scarf*, *A Killer Is Loose* is a sexless affair. It tells of an ordinary man trying to escape the clutches of a killer so that he can join his wife, who is in labor at the hospital. The novel's killer, Ralph Angers, has no interest in sex. His abiding obsession is building an eye hospital.

For Walter Hogan, sexual deviance and killing go hand in hand. As his character becomes integral to the novel's plot, lines from "Where or When" continue to appear as section titles, almost as if Brewer is unaware how the tone of the book has shifted. But while Lorenz Hart's romantic lyrics become increasingly discordant with the text, they also encourage readers to consider Walter within the song's frame of reference. As Bill perverts the song by making its sentiments purely sexual, Walter's presence suggests that the song's romanticism has no basis in reality at all. Walter may never have heard the song before, which is just as well. Hart's words would mean nothing to him.

In the end, Walter Hogan is Bill Sommers taken to the extreme. While Bill takes Karen as his ultimate sex object, Walter takes the female race as his sexual objects, to be used in succession and destroyed. Neither man can control himself. Bill, while he knows this cannot be Karen, nevertheless behaves as if it *must* be Karen. Walter, who shows discipline while stalking his victims, always loses control in the end. Together, Walter and Bill stand as Brewer's ultimate portrayal of the male condition. A horny sixteen-year-old male will always be a horny sixteen-year-old male, whether he becomes a married man or an itinerant sociopath. The calendar may say he has aged, and he may seem more mature, but his sexual monomania will remain.

Bill Sommers is 39 years old. When Gil Brewer wrote *Memory of Passion*, he too was 39 years old. Bill Sommers bemoans his personal fate for having "active glands." Gil Brewer bemoans the glands themselves and their power to control and destroy.

–September 2013
Lexington, Virginia

David Rachels is the editor of *Redheads Die Quickly and Other Stories* (University Press of Florida, 2012), the first collection of Gil Brewer's short fiction. He is a professor of English at Newberry College in Newberry, South Carolina.

Sources
"He writes not of love": William Faulkner, Speech at the Nobel Banquet, 10 December 1950. Nobelprize.org.
"*The Red Scarf* is the best": Anthony Boucher, "Report on Criminals at Large," *New York Times*, 21 September 1958, BR28.
"DIE FOR ME": Box 3, Collection 8184, Gil Brewer Collection, American Heritage Center, University of Wyoming.
"PRINCIPLES": Box 3, Gil Brewer Collection.
"But it is Schadenfreude": Arthur Schopenhauer, "Human Nature" in *On Human Nature: Essays (Partly Posthumous) in Ethics and Politics*, trans. Thomas Bailey Saunders (London: Swan Sonnenschein, 1897), 23.
"You can't describe light": Cornell Woolrich, *Rendezvous in Black* (1948; New York: Modern Library, 2004), 5.

Nude on Thin Ice

By Gil Brewer

PART ONE

Chapter 1

It was mid-January, but here in Key West, today was summer. Betty and I sprawled on the sun-palmed beach in front of the cabaña. We'd been staring at the blues and jades and grays of the water.
How could I tell her?
A white gull froze against the yellow sky.
The letter from Shroeder was a disease. I was a blocked somnambulist in the dark, juggling two sick dreams—one a red recollection of catastrophe, the other that drowning man's straw. In my mind, the straw was rapidly becoming a raft.
"Baby," I said. "Got something to tell you."
"Okay."
"Try to stay calm."
"So, I'm calm."
Her dark-blue eyes took on a forced gravity.
How to lie? I gnawed the inside of my cheek. How to tell her? It wouldn't be easy. It's not so easy to give the brush to a babe like Betty.
"Well?"
"Minute."
I lit a cigarette, musing all around this thing with a kind of quiet desperation, avoiding it, because to me it was a razor stroking thin-fleshed veins.
"Well, what is it?" she said.
I looked at her. She wore a very tight and tiny two-piece orange swimsuit that inadequately covered the overplump body I'd been using as a forget-yourself machine.
Two days ago that machine would have functioned. Not any more.
Not since yesterday, when I received the letter from Carl Shroeder out in New Mexico, forwarded by the lawyer who had settled Carl's estate.
Slip your panties to half-mast, girls, and lie quite still. Carl Shroeder is dead. But not his wife—not Nanette.
Betty was beginning to fidget. "Damn it, Ken. What is it?"
"I've got to go away."
She gave a sigh. "Oh, is that all? Listen, hon, I'm sick of it here, anyway. I'm game. Anywhere you want to go's jolly fine with me."
"You don't understand."
"Sure, I understand. Let's go back to Miami Beach, and have a ball." She

waved her hand. "This is for the gulls, Ken. It's too muddy. And I hate that seaweed. It's always getting between my toes."

"I said you don't understand." I looked at her, and tossed it into her comfortable lap. "I've got to go away—alone."

This time it reached her. Her face didn't change expression, but something smoked behind her eyes.

She said, "You mean all alone? By yourself?"

I nodded, flipped the cigarette toward the water.

"But you can't do that."

Well, you have to treat them rough. Like the man said: "A woman should be kicked regularly, like a Chinese gong." He was referring to wives, but we were registered at the motel as Mr. and Mrs. Kenneth McCall, even though her name was still Flanagan. It was high time she got herself kicked. I'd been doing everything else to her.

Betty was on her knees now, with her red-brown hair flopping around her face. Her full breasts joggled. There was a half-hurt, half-disbelieving look on her face.

"You mean leave me here—cold?"

"It's not so cold."

She began to pout. Then that went away, and you could see the anger come into her.

"Take it easy," I said. "You just stay here, and I'll be back."

I knew I'd never come back. I'd never see her again, but with what she had, she wouldn't be alone for very long.

"Ken. What's all this about?"

"Something came up. A big deal."

"A deal?"

"Yeah. I've got to leave right away. I didn't know how to tell you, Betty. I didn't want you to worry."

Her eyes lidded and she watched me, kneeling there that way. She had been a lot of fun. She had eased the forgetting of a good many unpleasant matters, mostly another woman, named Helen. She had more than served her purpose, and it was all over. Anyway, all I could think of was New Mexico, and Nanette, and other things.

"You're a stinking liar. You're running out on me."

"Have it your way. I don't want to argue."

"You lousy bastard!"

"Come off it, will you? How'd you make out before we met?"

"You stinking bastard!"

She just knelt there, calling me names. The anger kept spreading through her.

"Listen," I said. "It's a deal. For money, see? In case you didn't know, I'm almost broke."

"Broke?"

"Yeah. Crazy, isn't it? You think this could go on forever?"

"But you said—"

"Never mind what I said."

"A liar."

I stood up. The look in her eye was bad. I knew the type. She hadn't revealed it before, because we'd been having a time; but she would raise holy hell.

"Look," I said. I reached down and smoothed her hair. She snapped her head away. "Wait," I said. "Easy, now. I'll run back to the motel, get the Thermos filled with martinis at the bar. Then I'll come back. We'll talk it all over. I'll explain it to you. It could mean a lot to you, too."

She eyed me. She pushed the hair out of her eyes.

"You mean it?"

"I mean it."

"Okay."

"Be right back."

"Hurry."

You can bet I hurried. As soon as I got back to the room, I started packing the big old bombardier bag. I rammed my clothes into it any way they'd fit. With every move I made, I got more excited. The hell with Betty. I didn't even give her another thought; just get away. Get to New Mexico. Nanette.

I got out of there, slipped through the short alley off the court, and ran for the parking lot. This would be leaving Betty with a week's bill, but I knew she'd work it off one way or another.

The car was hot as a blister. It was a white '59 convertible Buick that I'd managed to pick up on a deal with a guy I knew in Fort Lauderdale. A nice pussy-wagon.

"Ken!"

Betty. I tossed the bag into the car, and didn't look her way till I got the engine started and was driving out of there. Then I looked.

"Ken! Damn you—Ken, stop!"

She had just scrambled up over the sea wall that led along behind the beach. Even at that distance, I could see those frantic eyes. She ran jiggling across the parking lot, waving her arms, bare feet tender on the sharp gravel. She stopped, reached down for a handful, and hurled it with everything she had. Gravel showered over the car and me as I swung into the street. I could still hear her yelling back there.

"Ken! Ken—"

In the rear-view mirror, I saw her running after me down the street. Then I couldn't see her any more, because I turned the corner.

For a tight second, I thought how all my life somebody had been chasing me—even at night, in my dreams, chasing me. So many things done to so many people. Sometimes it was as if they all chased me. Like right now, I'd sometimes have a flash of fear—someday they'd catch me.

I stopped at a service station on the edge of town, had the tank filled, and headed for Miami.

Chapter 2

Booming along the Overseas Highway, I picked stray pieces of gravel out of my shirt, and tried to avoid any thoughts of Betty Flanagan. She would be in a nasty snit for a time, but she'd get over it.

Clearing out of Key West was a relief. Free of Betty. I'd wanted to lay it on her a bit more gently than I had, but suddenly, getting away had been of primary importance.

I couldn't explain it, but a psychiatrist would have put it down as some sort of wild escape mechanism. And wild it was. Compulsion to get away, right then. On the beach there, with Betty, it had come over me like a chill. The same old excitement I'd contended with all my life. Pleasurable, too. The feeling was invigorating, like a new life.

I'd been living in Jackson, Mississippi, before I'd started this crazy tour of the Eastern seaboard, ending up in Key West with Betty. The letter had been forwarded from Jackson. I'd had no reason to hide my address.

There was a stilted note from the lawyer, a Devlin P. Montgomery, explaining things. And enclosed was the letter from Carl, written five months ago. It had kept me awake all night.

SANDIA LODGE, N.M.
August 13

DEAR KEN,

If and when you receive this letter, I'll be dead and buried, as they say—or, as I like to believe, balling it up with every vivacious devil I can get my hands on. And not giving any more of an inward damn here than I did there, where you are.

Is you still there, Charlie? Or will I meet you where I'm headed?

Not that I really believe in the Paradise of Hell, any more than I believe in the Hell of Paradise.

To get with it, then. Presupposing predilections to disaster, I'm penning this epistle. In other words, Ken, I've been assured by three heart specialists that the old crazy clock is running down; my ticker is no longer up to the tension of my spring. I've been warned to cut out my daily ration of gin—a quart, or over—by one harassed M.D., while another claims if I quit I'll surely croak in a matter of days. Either way, it's even money among what friends I have left that I'll blow this vicious Vale in six months. (I actually had to threaten bodily harm to my private quack to get him to admit this to me.)

Nanette does not know. She has stuck blindly—and I do mean *blindly*—by me through all the tattered travail of my existence. And that's what this letter is about. It—my death—will hit Nanette plenty hard. She's always banked in a broken safe—me—and if I know Nanette, she'll go all to pieces.

Now, since I always had too much loot, and you had none, I reckoned possibly you could use a couple grand. I'd like you to go to Nanette, and take care of her for a while; see that she gets over this troublesome time without eating four dozen sleeping pills. She'll do it, too!

I'm counting on you. Though she won't know, it'll be the only truly decent thing I've ever done in my life —or death, as the case may be.

Besides, you always had a yen for Nanette, right? And she had a certain sensitivity toward you. Help her, till she forgets.

There's more I should tip you to, but I'm beat, my left arm aches like hell, and I've got a hot date with a sweet tramp in Santa Fe.

Don't let me down.

Here's Hell!

CARL

Nanette. Nanette, the unattainable—as long as Carl had been alive. Only, it wasn't just Nanette. There are lots of Nanettes. Still there was that old feeling.

I drove along musing. The excitement inside me was devilish. It had seized hold of me when I got the letter, and I knew it wouldn't let go.

What I had in mind was nebulous. But the emotional excitement was very real. I was gripped by it; I knew I wouldn't deny it. It was like an old friendly fiend, eating at me, taking great hunks out of me, like a man-eating shark. It was not new to me. I was twenty-eight.

I had no plan. I knew in the back of my mind that this little adventure could lead to victory or disaster, but this time I felt I had to win. Opportunity was kicking madly at the door.

It wasn't just Nanette, though she might well enter into the program as a satisfactory form of entertainment. What interested me violently was the money. I knew there was plenty left. Carl was anything but a fool.

Adventurous, energetic and imaginative. Left a few million dollars to fool around with when he leaped astride his twenty-first birthday, Carl Shroeder had galloped off, pursuing a curious, indefinable hope nobody ever figured out. A dream. But he was nobody's fool.

Helen popped into my thoughts. For an instant, the nausea filled my chest, slipped like evil snakes into my mind. I fought it off. Helen. I'd thought she would become the sponge that would soak up the crazy part of me that went dashing off after glittering treasures. She had been that sponge, for a time.

I lit a cigarette, then gripped the wheel harder, pressed the accelerator a bit more. Wind buffeted the convertible top. Helen was gone, really. I didn't have to contend with her any more. Betty had helped with that. And now Nanette and Carl's death.... Helen was rapidly vanishing from my system.

I turned the car radio on, selected some way-out jazz, and turned the volume full up. The music roared out upon the sunny air. It throbbed inside me. I could think better when it was like that; allow the crazy catastrophe of existence to become a part of the music so it pumped through my veins. When the DJ came on between records, his voice was a blatant, raucous jumble of unintelligible sound—a man shouting over a PA system in a wind tunnel.

It pleased me.

I was on another crusade. The last.

If I could only take a plane, then buy another car when I arrived in Albuquerque. I didn't have the money. I would have to drive all the way across the country. Then I thought how I could sell the Buick, fly to New Mexico, and buy another car.

But I was attached to the Buick. I wanted this car. I would drive.

Besides, there had to be some sort of plan. I needed time to think. To map out the campaign.

The money would certainly be in a bank. A troublesome problem. Why in hell didn't people keep their money in a sock, at home?

I remembered Nanette, picturing her in my mind. Nanette, alone in that house among the Sandia Mountains.

For the first time, then, I began to wonder why Carl had written me. Why had I been chosen? Why, out of the tangled peregrinations of his life, had he decided to try to ease Nanette's dubious discomfort. How could he be sure she would feel as he thought she would?

Still, she must. Carl was seldom, if ever, wrong about things like that. Never about Nanette.

It didn't matter. I didn't care. He had written me.

But suppose she didn't give a damn? Suppose I couldn't swing it with her? I would have to feed her a good story.

I had to get into that house with her.

Fantastic? No, McCall, not so fantastic.

I stopped at the first large motel I saw, a place called the Pelican, made arrangements, and wired Nanette. Actually, she hardly knew me. All right. I decided to make the wire quite familiar.

NANETTE—ALL MY SYMPATHY OVER YOUR IR-
REPARABLE LOSS. HAVE COURAGE. I WILL SEE YOU
WITHIN A FEW DAYS. MY LOVE. KEN.

Then I thought, maybe she won't know who Ken is. I added my last name. I stood there, reading the wire before phoning it in, then started to write the address. Decided I'd better check it. That was when I remembered the letter.

I thought for a moment I would be sick in front of the motel clerk, on the fetching, thick-napped saffron carpet. Because in my mind's eye I saw that letter, folded and sticking out of a paperback novel, lying on the night stand by the bed back in the Key West motel.

I visualized Betty seeing it, opening the book, reading the letter with a kind of fiendish glee. I'd gone into Betty too deeply, told her too much, loved her too heavily, fed her too much wordage as well as yardage, planned with her too well.

The clerk at the Pelican was an obnoxious-looking slat of a possible female, with phony silver-blonde hair, completely plucked and redrawn eyebrows, thin, red-steel lips, and blunt, grubby-looking fingers. She wore a tight, red, one-piece jumper suit.

"Before I phone in this wire," I said, "I've got to make a call to Key West. Okay?"

She frowned. "All this calling is irregular."

I explained that it was an emergency, that she could check on the tariff with the operator.

"All right, bub."

I placed the call to the Key West motel. Steel-lips leaned broomlike against the desk and watched and listened.

"Yes," I said. "This is Mr. McCall." The woman who managed the motel at the other end of the wire went into a long tirade about guests who run off without paying their bills, but she was glad I'd realized my error and called. "I understand," I said to Key West. "I'm sending the money. I had to leave in a hurry—business. If you'll tell me the bill? I asked my wife to take care of it, though. Didn't she?"

"Mrs. McCall didn't go with you?"

"She—"

"She's certainly gone, you know?"

"Yes. You misunderstood. I sent her on ahead. She's visiting relatives."

"I see."

I knew damned well nobody could "see," but that didn't matter. "Listen," I said. "Would you please check something for me? I left an important letter in a book on the night stand in our room. Would you please send it to me in care of General Delivery, Albuquerque, New Mexico?"

"Certainly, Mr. McCall. Now, as to the bill." She told me what it was, while I held my breath, and perspired. I told her I would send her the money immediately. She said, "Good-by," and started to hang up.

I yelled, "Wait!"

"What is it, Mr. McCall?"

I told her to check on the letter. "I want to be sure it's there."

She agreed to check. I waited. Steel-lips eyed me with faint disdain, but did not move from her perch by the desk. The manager at Key West returned. I clung to the desk, knowing the letter would be gone.

"Mr. McCall?"

"Yes?"

"I have the letter. It was right where you said."

There seemed to be a big draft in my head. Then that went away. I slumped with relief. It had been a first error that had somehow miraculously corrected itself.

I mumbled a "Thank you, and good-by." She hung up. I handed the phone to Steel-lips.

"Monkey business?" she said. Without waiting for an answer, she checked with the long-distance operator. She wrote down the toll. I phoned in the wire to Nanette. Steel-lips checked with Western Union, just to make sure.

I staggered out of there, bought a bottle of whisky in a roadhouse across the highway, returned to the car, and headed for Miami.

My thoughts turned to the wire. The "have courage" bit, and the "my love," I knew would work. When people are in deep emotional turmoil, something like that plucks the strings of sentiment without their realizing it's phony as hell. Their critical sense is nil. I could visualize the teary film in Nanette's eyes as she read the wire. Carl had died seven days ago. She would just be truly feeling the sharp knife of his going.

Have courage, Nanette. Kenneth McCall is coming to your house.

All I could do was thank whatever gods might be for keeping Betty Flanagan from finding that letter.

On second thought, why should it matter? Betty was broke flat. Yes. But she had an international wiggle that could pay off very quickly. Anyway, why all the worry?

Chapter 3

Four days later, driving down Central Avenue in Albuquerque, I was shot absolutely to hell. I had driven straight past the Sandia Ridge Road, which led to Nanette. The Buick was beat, and I was beat. I was stifled from the car's heat. I had no clothes for cold weather. I was nearly broke—six dollars and forty cents remaining. I was sick from eating hamburgers, hot dogs and those fine prefabricated cheese sandwiches that are a part of our Great American Heritage, and from guzzling enormous quantities of coffee and whisky, and from no sleep, and from snow and snow and snow and ice and slush and the veritable hell of Route 66 in the crazy cold of an outrageous midwinter. I would remember Louisiana's bass-ackwards road signs, mixed-up detours, hub-deep mud, frozen red clods, and single-lane, two-way traffic until my dying day. Why I'd figured to save time cutting through that entertaining state was beyond me.

The Buick was heavily marked with signs of travel. The snow gods had unleashed the dark furies of storm. Mercury dribbled out of thermometers onto window sills. Dark streamers on newspapers read RECORD WINTER.

Ken McCall knows.

It was nine thirty in the morning. Completely enervated from lack of sleep, I'd begun to slip into a mood of depression. With the depression, my mind swung back to Helen. This only made things worse.

I checked in at a cheap motel. It wouldn't be smart to see Nanette, the way I felt. And before I saw her, I wanted to meet the lawyer, Devlin P. Montgomery, and try to wangle an advance on the two thousand dollars I was supposed to get for patting Nanette's head.

In the motel room, I took a scalding-hot shower, shaved, dressed, and phoned Montgomery. His secretary told me he was down in Alamogordo, and wouldn't return until the next day. "Whom shall I say called?"

I gave my name. "I'll check tomorrow."

I stretched out on the bed, poured a water glass half full of whisky, sipped at that, and smoked. Finally, I finished the whisky and just lay there staring at the paint-flaked ceiling, smoking. I needed sleep. I began to know I wasn't going to get any.

The excitement was too much. I was too close to it. It was as if my veins were tender; I could feel the blood pulsing through my body. I was alive to it. Even lying there on the bed, I couldn't stay still.

There was one thing I wanted out of life. I'd never been able to get it. I knew someday the right angle would show itself. *I wanted money.* It was that simple. I'd tried to get it every way in the books, but I didn't have the touch. It ate at me. It had always been this way.

Now I had the chance. And this game had to be played right. If I goofed this one, I was done. It was like a last wall to climb, something you knew and understood for a fact.

Not just a little money, not just enough to get along on. Not just a monthly allowance, like some dreamless people say they want. Not me. Not that way.

I wanted it big. If you have your health, and the right philosophy toward life, then money is the solution to everything. Enough money so you never have to think about it again. It was so bad I could actually see it, visualize stacks of it sitting on a table in front of me. Packs of greenbacks.

You think it can't be like that? Then you're nuts. That's how it was with me. *Money.* It could buy anything I'd ever want out of this life.

I lay there smoking, and twitching, looking back across the years, seeing myself as a kid, and knowing I had wanted it even then. It represented freedom. Freedom from the stink of how I'd been brought up, freedom from the sweat, freedom from the stomach-turning smell of poverty. When it was too hot, you could buy coolness with money, and if it was chilly, you could purchase warmth.

It could buy all the most beautiful women in the world—the luscious bitches I yearned for and could never have, because you had to have money to have them. You had to have it to throw away. You had to have enough so it didn't mean anything any more.

That's how I wanted it.

The instant I read that letter from Carl, I knew this was the chance. The cross-eyed gods of the universal cash registers had punched the No Sale key, and the drawer was wide open—waiting. All I had to do was reach in and take the money and fill my pockets.

Because I was too far along the road not to realize that you don't work for and earn the Big Money. You inherit it, or you steal it, or you wangle it; you play that gimmick when it shows.

I got up and began pacing the floor.

For some reason, Helen was mixed in with all my thinking. Maybe I would never forget her. The way she had been; the crazy, cockeyed way she had been. We'd never married, but she had been what they called my common-law wife. I could still remember her screaming at me, that final night when I tied her to the bed and ran.

"*I'll get you, Ken—I'll find you, so help me!*" Just yelling it, her face choked with blood; screaming it into the night. "*You'll never get away! You rotten thief! I'll find you, I swear....*"

Listen, McCall, I thought. Will you face it? Helen Ford was a whore. She was born a whore, the way life is born black or white or yellow or red, or cat or dog or bird or snake. She was mad because she thought she had wanted out of The Life, and she had saved her money and made it. But she was still a whore, and you know it, McCall, so quit stewing. She saved thirty-seven thousand dollars, which was hardly enough, anyway. She was mad because you helped her spend it. But you told her you loved her, and by God, you thought you did—until you got that money into a joint account and realized the truth. That she was a whore, and she would always be a whore.

It didn't help much, thinking like that.

Big Deal McCall. Draw out the thirty-seven thousand and play that hot system on the horses. Remember? It took less than a week, and you had about thirty-seven cents. Remember?

Why the hell hadn't she been able to understand? You've got to take a chance. All I'd wanted to do was run that thirty-seven grand into a real pile, because thirty-seven grand was nothing.

As I paced the floor of the motel room, it seemed crazy now. But not the way she looked when I told her. Not the way she had screamed at me after I tied her to the bed.

Women. Jesus Christ.

The one real woman you want just doesn't exist. She's a dream you have to live with. Reaching, reaching, reaching—but never touching.

Then, Betty—thinking of Betty made me feel depressed. She had been a sweet kid.

It was obvious I wasn't going to sleep. The suspense was too much.

The room had cost six bucks. I had forty cents to my name. The car needed washing and waxing. I needed at least a topcoat; all I had was a lightweight brown suit.

Well, the hell with that, too. If that's how it was, that's how it was. At least for the time being.

I got out of there, drove downtown, and checked at the post office. My letter from the motel in Key West was at the general-delivery window. I read it again, my hands trembling.

Traffic was heavy as I headed back up Central toward the Sandias. They looked cold as hell under a bleak blanket of dirty gray sky. Snow was falling in the mountains. Dust blew coldly in the valley. Sweet young university tail bounced, jiggled, and tittered in colorful groupings near the library, the park, and the university bookstore.

Nanette would be up there where it snowed, all alone in the big old house, musing on her past life with Carl. It had been short enough, and touched with calamity.

Then I got to thinking again. Suppose she's gone. Suppose she took off with his money. It could happen. Maybe she never received my wire. Maybe she would laugh in my face.

Outside of town, I drove up along the winding, cliff-edged main highway, Route 66, heading east again, until I reached the turnoff that went straight into the mountains. Snow gusted across the road. It was beginning to pack on the windshield. The wipers worked overtime.

When the weather got out of control, it always scared the hell out of me. You couldn't master the elements.

The road leading into the mountains was macadam, rather narrow, and very winding. The plows hadn't done such a good job of it, either. I'd been to Shroeder's place just once, and I knew I had to take a dirt road, and as I recalled, it went practically straight up for a time, rutted and bizarre.

I turned on the car radio. As luck would have it, Erroll Garner was playing *Caravan*, and I turned the volume full up and let it blast. How that man could play.

I drove. It got worse. The snow thickened, whistling around the car, a rushing white wind. A car nosed toward me, headlights like flickering matches. Then I passed a landmark I recalled, a restaurant and tavern to the right of the road, catering to cabins that clung to the hillside on the left, among dense pines, slate, and gnarled vines.

I kept driving, perspiring now, even with the cold drafts that fingered through the car. The wind grew worse, and the snow became thicker still. The radio blasted. Johnny Hodges winged along with *Ballad for Very Sad and Very Tired Lotus Eaters*, which was fine, but not conducive to any optimism at the moment. Besides, I had no lotus, and I couldn't take my hands off the wheel to change stations.

Tijeras Canyon. San Antonio. Cedar Crest. Cañoncito. And up there in the woolly wilderness, the Shroeder house.

I was on the dirt road now. Untouched by a plow. A car had driven over it, though, and I hugged the ruts, straining like hell to see ten feet in front of the car.

The road turned to the right, and I gunned it, standing practically on the rear bumper, fighting for every inch. Five minutes later, I roared into a windy glade, and saw the house humped against the swirling anger of the blizzard.

I drove to the broad gallery fronting the rambling structure, and parked. The radio kept on blasting. I sat there in the black-white blindness, listening numbly to an insane hillbilly outfit, and some dame shrieking about her lost sombrero. Finally, I gathered enough of my wits to shut off the radio and the engine. I sneaked a long pull from the whisky jug of under the seat, lit a cigarette, took three drags, and got out of the car.

The wind nearly knocked me flat. My cigarette was gone. I ran sideward toward the porch; slipped and almost fell on the snow-banked, ice-packed steps; slid across the porch to the door, and began to hammer on it with my fist.

"Hey!" I yelled. "Nanette!"
The door swung open.
"Hello?"
A shapely young girl with strange greenish eyes and long pale-blonde hair stood looking at me. She couldn't have been more than than eighteen. She wore tight-fitting black woolen Capri pants, and a thin, tight jersey with a turtle neck, and tiny golden slippers on her tiny feet.

I had never seen her before.

"Nanette's sleeping," she said. She spoke very softly against the rushing winds. "I'm Justine. Won't you come in?"

I went in.

Chapter 4

The first door opened on a small storm vestibule. It was windless and cold. She closed the door and looked at me. "Are you selling something?"

She had the damnedest eyes. They were very steady, and she looked straight at me with a kind of boldness I'd never experienced before.

"In this weather?" I said.

She shrugged. "You never know."

"Guess that's right."

She didn't take her gaze off me. There was something lazy and distracted about her. She was considering something else as she looked straight at me. There was a go-to-hell look, behind her eyes.

Hers was no stereotyped beauty. But it was very lush, and it was very much there. Very much sexual, and bold, and it came through so strongly and quietly, that I didn't know what to say to her for a moment. She was a waiter; she had lots of time and knew it and didn't care. She didn't smile. She just stood there, and I could see the perk of her nipples through the thin black jersey. She was one of those immediate hell-raisers with the pulse beat, yet she gave the impression that she wouldn't give a goddamn if you dropped dead at her feet. She would probably just quit looking at you, step over you, and walk back inside the house. I had never seen anything quite like it.

I said, "Can't we go inside?"

"I don't know. Who are you?"

"I'm Kenneth McCall, a friend of Nanette's. I wired her I was coming."

She tilted her head back slightly and blinked. "Oh. It's you. All right."

She turned, opened the large, heavy, plate-glass-paneled door, and stepped into the hallway beyond. I followed her. She wore nothing under the tight black Capri pants, either. They were skin tight, and she was shaped for everything. She moved it plenty as she walked, silently, lazily. Small, yet lush. She was very choice. Only remote. There was the feeling she would spit on you. There was the feeling you wouldn't care if she did. There was a voluptuousness about her, from the fine soft pale thick blonde hair to the tips of her golden-slippered toes.

Maybe I was going crazy. McCall, I thought, the trip was too much for you.

She closed the door, leaned against it for a brief instant, watching me soberly, then turned away and moved off down the hall.

"I suppose you'll want to see her."

I didn't say anything. I just followed along again, staring. Some far-out jazz drifted softly through the house, from somewhere impossible to pin-point.

"Things have been a little wild," she said. "Dig?"

"I suppose—"

A stairway was at the end of the hall—broad, with a curving banister, the steps thickly carpeted in black. The plush, sprawling interior of the house was furnished with sprawling plushness. Carl had owned other homes, but this one, left him by his father, was his eventual favorite. He called it his getaway cave, and finally moved into it for good. It was warm inside, and there was an odor of slain flowers that made me think of coffins and funeral services, though I felt sure Carl had been cremated, which was what he had wanted. The house was shadowed and very still, save for the quiet, delicate, very intricate phrasing of a tenor sax, the inspired bump of a bass, the strong yet almost tender poetry of a chorded piano.

The girl paused by a broad archway that led down into a sunken living room I remembered. Most of the furnishings of the house had been changed since I'd been here four years ago, but everything was of the same remarkable hugeness—deep, soggy leather; thick, rich upholstery; and soft, dark, opaque draperies. The paintings on the walls had not been changed, but the collection was enlarged. They were mostly abstractions, action paintings. The intense and abysmal world of Jackson Pollack. Then there was Picasso. Giuseppe Capogrossi. Ibram Lassaw. Sugai. Afro. Davis. De Kooning. And many more. On the wall just beside where the girl stood was an eye-jarring display, hung with erratic subtleness, faulting all laws anent picture-hanging, the paintings wild and unwild and interesting—seven water colors by Henry Miller. I eyed them with strange envy.

"Do you paint?" the girl said.

"I used to."

"It's the one thing I ever wanted to do," she said. "Creatively, that is."

"The one thing?"

I looked at her.

She said, "What I meant before. Carl is dead, you know. It's rather strange with him dead. Sometimes I have a feeling he isn't really." She hesitated, staring directly at me with those damnable eyes. "Carl's the kind of man takes real long in the dying. A real bastard. You know?"

She turned and moved down the three broad flagstone steps into the living room.

"I like you, Mr. McCall. Coming?"

"Yes. I see. Okay."

"Now's a good time to listen for the sound of one hand, Mr. McCall."

I had no idea what the hell she meant. Maybe she was crazy. The atmosphere of the house had changed with Carl's death. A bright new knife had sliced, with corrosion under the gleaming blade.

We passed through the huge room. I noted that the enormous fireplace still blazed away. They kept a fire burning all winter, night and day. The telephone was on the mantel, beside a row of six crystal oil lamps, the latter for emergency light, in case wires blew down during a storm.

There was a sense of doom. It was something you couldn't read, couldn't decipher. Too much, I thought, not knowing what "too much" meant. It was as if the place held its breath. It was crazy, maybe like that moment just before the explosion when the nightmared gymnast is shot from the circus cannon. What did he feel at that moment?

Ken McCall knows.

We entered another long, narrow room and I saw Nanette. A man sat shoulder-slumped on a broad studio couch, and Nanette looked at him, propped on one elbow.

The man saw us, leaped up, heavy smoke from a cigarette in his lips swirling about startled, heavy features.

"Aunt Nanette? Someone to see you," the girl said.

Nanette fell back on the couch and said, "Who?"

The man continued to smoke his cigarette without taking it from his lips, dragging at it deeply, blowing smoke out in loud gusts.

"It's a Mr. McCall."

It was then I saw Nanette was drunk.

The man seemed to hesitate a moment. He was heavily strung together, tall, with long arms, wearing khaki work clothes. A black wrangle of hair fell over his brow, above dark, sunken eyes. He needed a shave. There was something peculiarly strained about him, as if full of an ever-present anger. He stood, the eyes watching me, puffing, puffing at the wagging cigarette.

He turned, said something briefly, quietly to Nanette, and walked fast in a sort of quiet lunge toward a door at the far side of the room.

"Elmer?" Justine said.

He did not stop. He opened the door, vanished, closed it quietly behind him.

The girl, Justine, shrugged. She looked at Nanette, who stared at the ceiling.

"Hello, Ken," Nanette said.

Again the girl shrugged. Abruptly she, too, turned and left the room, going back toward the living room we had just left.

It was very silent, except for the music coming from some unknown quarter of the house. Suddenly that, too, ceased.

Nanette Shroeder lay quietly staring at the ceiling. The silence was a dark shroud.

"Nanette?" I said.

She did not speak. There was very little light in the room. A lamp with a blue shade cast curious glows across her body.

"Nanette."

Still she said nothing.

I recalled the brassy highlights of her hair. I remembered how I had pictured her, in a bright, flower-print dress, gay, touched with laughter, her slim body a whip of energy. I remembered the sparkle of her eyes, the open, frank smiling of her lips.

She rolled on her side and looked at me.

"Good to see you, Ken."

"Yeah. Me, too."

I stepped nearer, then paused.

She didn't have the stares, anyway. Not at me, anyway. This was different. She spoke to me, her face turned toward me, but her eyes regarded a distant corner of the room, as if she saw something intensely interesting there, yet was devoting her entire attention to me. It was disconcerting as hell.

But that wasn't it; not that alone. Something had happened to Nanette. Something beyond her husband's death, certainly. Carl's passing hadn't done this to her, whatever it was.

Then it came to me. All the lights had gone out in Nanette. Somebody had switched them off. It was as if she had misplaced her soul, and didn't have the energy, or will, to find it again.

I suddenly wanted to leave this house, fast. I didn't, though. Somehow, you never do. It's so damned easy to ignore wisdom when it whispers.

Chapter 5

"Ken," Nanette said. "Come here, and sit down by me. It's been one hell of a long time."

I went to the couch, sat beside her. I could smell gin. She wore an expensive crimson peignoir, with black and gold threads running through it. It was nearly completely transparent. She wore nothing beneath it, and didn't seem to give a damn about her rather abandoned position. It was as if she dismissed her body as inconsequential. It was anything but. She still possessed the sleek, racy lines I recalled. It was only in her face that the strangeness showed—the averted eyes, the bitter lips, the curious unhealthy pallor.

I remembered sharply why I was here.

Old Ruthless, Heartless McCall.

I didn't feel heartless right then. It was more a sensation of wonder, of astonishment.

"Ken, how are you?" she said.

I heard a rustling step behind me—a kind of dragging and a tap, and at the same moment, dry, high laughter, like the windy whisper of crisping leaves.

I turned, frowning.

A very old man stood there watching us, staring with rheumy eyes, his withered form and shrunken ocher features subtly crouched over a knobby black cane. He was clothed neatly but ludicrously in a finely creased burnt-orange gabardine double-breasted suit, with a black silk shirt and a white tie. He was something straight out of a comic magazine, and all he needed was a bomb, or a hypodermic needle.

The hiss of laughter ceased. "Did you lay her yet, sonny?" the old man said. His voice was like a sick sparrow. His eyes seemed to gleam and fade with distant light, like a wind-washed candle.

"You get the hell out of here, Jack!" Nanette said. She slammed the couch with her hand. "Get out!"

The old man rapped his cane on the floor. "You tell me how it was, sonny," he said in that breathless whisper. "We'll swap stories. I got some good ones. You come an' tell me how it was."

"Jack. Get out of here."

The old man looked at her and grimaced. Then he turned and stumped from the room. He moved stiff-legged, propped over the tapping cane. He vanished through the far door where the other man had gone.

Nanette's hand touched mine. "I'm sorry, Ken. That was Carl's father. You never met him."

She really startled me. "But I thought he was dead. Carl said he was—" I still looked at the door where the old man had vanished.

"Everybody thought so. Now you know." She sighed. "It was Carl— But I don't want to discuss it, Ken. Not now, Don't talk to me about it."

She wasn't looking at me. "Take it easy," I said. "I'm here now, and I want you to take it easy."

"Easy to say."

"Nanette. Who was that other man?"

"Elmer? He's worked here for a long, long while." She paused, and for a moment, I didn't think she would continue. She seemed to be thinking. "His father worked for Jack, years ago. Elmer Nash has almost become one of the family."

"I see."

"He takes care of the place. It would go to rot, otherwise. He's never had anything. Just us, I guess. He's rather—well, protective, if you know what I mean."

"I don't think I do."

She twisted on the couch, still not looking at me. I looked away. She said, "Elmer works terribly hard. I've never seen anything like it. He's devoted. He loves to hunt. He knows every inch of this country. I'm telling you this because I think you should know. I mean seeing him around the house, so on. You know what I mean. He's such a tireless, strong worker. And so steady."

I looked quickly at her. She immediately averted her gaze. I had the impression she'd been watching me. I didn't know what to do, or think. A feeling of confusion came into me. Again I had the urge to leave the house at a dead run. It was that bad. But I sat there.

Nanette turned her face away, toward the wall, and began muttering. I caught a word here and there. She was cursing.

She turned to me again—her face, anyway. Her eyes searched the corner of the room. It was a hell of a thing.

"I'm drunk," she said. "Plastered. I can't talk now. Find Justine. She'll show you your room. Get some rest."

"All right."

She looked at me for the first time. It was the look of a frightened rabbit. She looked away. "I know why you came," she said. "It's no use."

"How do you mean?"

She did not speak. I tried to get her to speak, but she wouldn't. I looked down at her. The long, racy legs. The triangle of pubic hair. The flat belly. The breasts. The face. She had her eyes closed now. A strand of hair was in her mouth and she was gnawing on it.

There was a fluffy white coverlet at the foot of the couch. I shook it out and spread it over her. She seemed to recoil. "Beat it, Ken. Will you, please?"

I walked away. In the arch that led to the other room, I turned and looked back. She was weeping.

The girl was seated on the flagstone steps that led from the hall into the room.

"You met the old buzzard," she said. "I could've stopped him, but I figured you might as well see him."

"Yes. Nanette said you'd show me a room. I'm beat."

She stood up, watching me with those eyes again. "Don't you wonder who I am, Mr. McCall?"

"Call me Ken."

"Don't you wonder?" She moved closer to me and laid one hand on my arm, her fingers faintly squeezing. She looked up at me, and slowly ran her tongue across her lower lip. She spoke very softly. "Don't you wonder, at all?"

"Yes."

Still she did not smile. "I like you, Ken," she said. "I don't think I'll tell you just yet. Who I am, that is."

I said nothing. Neither did she. We stood there like that. Suddenly, she bent her knee and brushed it against my leg. She released my arm, turned, started away.

"C'mon," she said. "I'll show you upstairs."

I followed her. Outside you could hear the wind. It seemed very far away. She hummed quietly. I couldn't take my eyes off her.

She paused on the first landing, and turned with one hand on the highly polished mahogany railing. She looked at me soberly for a full five seconds. Then she turned and started up again, still humming.

"Here you are," she said. "The guest room."

She held the door open, and I stepped quickly past her into the room.

"I cleaned it for you," she said. "It was very dusty. Seldom used, you know."

"Thanks."

"Don't you have any bags?"

"One, in the car. I'll get it later."

"Is that all? You're going to stay, aren't you?"

For the first time, I detected a note of urgency, or maybe even fear, in her tone.

"I think so. I shipped some other things."

This seemed to relieve her.

"I knew you were coming," she said. "I've been waiting to meet you. You were a good friend of Carl's."

"Yes."

"Won't you call me Justine?"

"All right, Justine."

"Thanks, Ken. I like how you say my name."

"Fine."

She pulled the sweater down tightly over her breasts, the red lips very sober, the eyes watching. She didn't move then, just stood there, staring at me.

"What's the matter, Ken?"

"Nothing."

"All right. Listen, if you need me, I'll be around. I'm always around. Okay?"

"Okay. Justine, how did Nanette take Carl's death?"

"You thinking about Nanette?"

"No. I mean yes. That is, I'd like to know."

"I see. I'll tell you later. Why don't you get cleaned up? You need some rest. I can tell."

She turned and closed the door, and I heard her move down the hall, humming.

I looked at the room.

Chapter 6

I was a fine McCall, I was.

There was a series of Japanese ink-brush paintings on the wall. I stared at them for a time, trying to connect myself up again. They only seemed to take me farther away from myself, into a strange and believable mist of white air where people walked with birds across unseen clouds.

Listen, I thought. You've stepped straight into some kind of mucked-up psychiatric ward where the doe is out to lunch. Perpetually out to lunch.

So let's have it, McCall. Brace! Stiff upper! Suck that gut! I turned and sagged around the room, shooting a glance at the closed door now and again, wanting to leave the room, go down, and get my one bag. I felt naked this way, vulnerable—as if it were a cell. You've got to at least have a toothbrush and a pair of socks to make it home.

The hell with it. I went downstairs at a sort of shambling dog trot, beat it outside. The car was gone.

I stood there in swirling snow, feeling my ears and nose freeze. The tracks of the tires were still discernible. I followed them through the violent eddies of snow. They went along the front of the house, then turned into what was probably a drive when it wasn't snowing, and followed the side of the house. House? It was a god-damned mansion, that's what it was. It seemed larger even than I remembered. It was an amazing place. As I traced the tire tracks, I couldn't get that Justine out of my mind. She clung there by her long fingernails, with her eyes watching. And I knew she'd been trying to say something with her eyes, only I didn't want to admit to myself what it was.

There was a five-car garage. The Buick was parked just in front of an open stall. I could hear somebody inside the garage. Maybe the mysterious Elmer. I reached into the car and hauled out the good old comfortable brown canvas bombardier bag, and took off through the skirling whiteness toward the front again. I had the feeling that spectators were watching from all the windows.

I went inside, held my breath, and beat it down the long hall and up the stairs to my room. Inside the room, I dropped the bag and stood there breathing heavily, feeling as if I'd escaped, somehow, the whole hell of the Spanish Inquisition. Modestly.

There was a large, fuzzy, white-covered contour chair over beside the bed. I put the bag there, opened it and began taking out clothes—what there was, that is—then just slumped on the edge of the large bed holding a pair of wrinkled and ragged tan slacks and staring at the floor.

My mind began going around. Carl, Nanette, Jack the Cane, Elmer, Justine, Justine, Justine—Devlin P. Montgomery—yes—and then the sudden, ever-sickening memory, Helen, and the topping on the sour pudding—Betty Flanagan.

I threw the slacks down, walked the room and came back and sat on the bed. There was a bookcase against the wall, and the gleaming cover of a paper-bound book caught my eye. I grabbed it up.

The Zen Teaching of Huang Po.

Very interesting. I opened the book and began to read, fighting to close my mind against my thoughts. What the hell was this Zen? Somewhere I'd heard something.

The music started again. It sounded like Charlie-Bird. I looked around. The jazz was piped into the room; maybe piped into every room in the house. A neat, small hi-fi enclosure was on top of the bookcase. The volume was too high. I stepped over and turned it down.

Touching the knob, I thought of Justine. She was at the other end of the wire.

I went back to the bed, and looked into the Zen book. Questions and Answers.

> Q: What is the Way and how must it be followed?
> A: What sort of *thing* do you suppose the Way to be, that you should wish to *follow* it?

I sat there. The music cascaded softly into the room. I looked out one of the two tall windows, sided by thick black draw drapes. The drapes were open. Outside, night was closing down, very early with the storm. I saw a black bird fly past, pumping through the snow.

I felt Nanette's eyes staring at the corner of the room as she faced me.

I read again.

First, learn how to be entirely unreceptive to sensations arising from external forms, thereby purging your bodies of receptivity to externals.

Was Justine an external form?

I knew my receptivity to her.

I tossed the book down. Old Zen Master, how do you become unreceptive to Justine?

Thoughts of the money came down over me like a wet dredge.

Carl Shroeder.

We had known—

There was a knock on the door.

"Yes?"

The door opened and it was Justine. She held the door partway open and leaned loosely against the jamb, watching me, and with the sober red lips—the mouth darkly crimson, not a pout, not an un-pout. I sat there on the bed and stared back at her. I realized my fingers were clenched into the side of the bed. I released my hold. She saw me do this.

"Are you all right, Ken?"

"Sure."

"Wanted to tell you Elmer put your car in the garage. But I see you got your bag."

"Yes. Thanks."

"I suppose the way Nanette is—I suppose it startled you. She's in her room now, trying to sober up. She spends a lot of her time in her room. She doesn't go out much, any more. Of course, Carl used to insist she snap out of it."

"She been like that long?"

Her eyes lidded. She shrugged.

"Who are you, Justine?"

She watched me, flicked her upper lip with her tongue. She released the door, and stretched the sweater down over her breasts. Then she reached up with both hands and squeezed the pale silvery-blonde hair away from her head, and let it fall thickly sprawling to her shoulders. "I don't think I'll tell you yet."

"Are you an external form?"

She didn't move an eyelid.

She said, "It depends, Ken." She rubbed both long-fingered, silver-nailed hands on her thighs, her legs pressed tightly together.

"Jack," I said. "The old man with the cane. What about—tell me about the old man."

"Not now. Don't talk now. I'll tell you later. Why not just look at me? You like to look at me, so look at me."

My heart moved heavily.

"Think I'll try to rest," I said.

She closed the door and went away.

Carl Shroeder.
Justine.
Nanette.

Carl Shroeder. We had known each other for six years. I hadn't seen him in four. But you think, corresponding as we had, that you know what's going on. You don't.

He had told me his father was dead.

"*My father died and left me all this god-damned loot,*" he'd said. "*I am trying to spend it. My father, the old son of a bitch, was left it by his father. So it'll take two generations to spend it, because the old son of a bitch just didn't have the kind of zip it takes to go through the kind of fortune he started out with. He tried hard as hell, but he had a friend who was bugs on investments, so forth, and he couldn't get through the money. He plowed it plenty, but he couldn't spend it all, even with the monkey glands. He was tentative, I think; reticent and the node of carefulness was still on his brain. Damn the investors. Spend the loot."*

The thing was, Carl later told me he had some of the "node," or whatever the hell it was, that he hadn't found out about until then. He'd tangled with the investments, too. In a quiet way.

Only Carl's father wasn't dead?

It was six years ago, yes. In Vegas.

I remembered the letter. I got it out and reread it, and read that line that had meant nothing to me until now.

"...There's more I should tip you to, but I'm beat, my left arm aches like hell, and I've got a hot date with a...."

More he should have tipped me to! Christ. I had to find out if there even was any money left. Maybe I was scrounging round in the bottom of a barrel.

No, McCall. You know better. And, anyway, there's the two thousand. Hell with the two thousand.

I remembered something out in the hall; I'd seen it when I'd come up the stairs the last time. Now it registered.

I went and carefully opened the door. All was quiet. I stepped into the hall. It was a broad landing above the stairs, larger than a good-size room, with an immense stair well. The stairs curved up, the railing snaking all the way around. The landing was thickly carpeted, naturally, so everybody could pussyfoot around the joint.

I hurried past a thick, heavy, scraped-leather lounge that was about eight feet long, and reached the gleaming black cabinet. Probably ebony. A fist-large carved ivory Buddha on a jade base set jolly-giggling and serene on the polished cabinet top. I opened a sliding door.

It was packed with bottles. I grabbed the first at hand, then an old-fashioned glass from a glittering stack, and headed back for the room.

I drank the brandy, smoked a cigarette, and lay there on the terrific bed, regurgitating the past six years.

Before Vegas, I'd been hung up, and was clouting cars for a guy in South Carolina. It was peanuts, as usual, but it was bread, as they say. It just wasn't always martinis. Then the old compulsion to go. Maybe it was a good thing, maybe the gods had me fingered in a kind way. Because the guy I'd been stealing the cars for, and who sold them in Florida, where I brought then, was nailed, screened, and tossed into a particularly nasty slammer. The only thing that seemed to burn him was he'd lost his floor plan. He'd wanted to go straight.

B.H. Before Helen. Now it was A.H. Ah, hell.

So then I bought a car, clean, and made my getaway.

You poor McCall. I made the gas-station route all across Tennessee, Mississippi, and on west. Arkansas, still hitting the gas stations; fifty bucks, a hundred bucks, two hundred bucks, six bucks, and not even with a gun. I never wanted a gun. I'd mud-up the plate, turn my jacket inside out, roll my pants up a couple notches. And I only wore white socks on that trip, along with a black Homburg I'd found in a street in Chattanooga, and the black bandanna over my face. I figured, why show them what you look like? It's stupid. I'd walk in, holding a jack handle, and tell them. I was always a big bastard, six three, and heavy across the shoulders and chest, so they listened. I'd get myself all worked up, act crazy, like Billy the Kid. Storm them. Before they knew it, they'd parted with the lining of the cash-register drawer. Pull the phone then. Lock them in, and powder. I always parked away from the station, so they couldn't catch the make of the car. A mild sort of McCall crime wave. I didn't care about prints. I was one of the lucky. Nobody had my prints, not ever. No Boy Scouts, no baby-hand-on-memory-paper, no Government crap, no war, no nothing. Just McCall, like a bird.

Flee.

Then, in Oklahoma—it was Cherokee or Waynoka, I forget which, near the Cimarron, or the North Canadian—it was raining, and some cowboy made the plate. I'd been stopping at libraries all along the way, because I liked to read, and I always thought if I just hadn't stopped. I know it was the cowboy. On a horse, right along where the Shell station was, at three in the morning. What in hell he was doing out there in the rain at three o'clock in the morning on a white horse is more than I ever figured. Maybe checking his marijuana orchard.

So they chased me, and I cracked the car up, but I lost them. A cruiser and a motorcycle. I buried the hat, and all the white socks, and the license plate. I wiped the car clean. It had stopped raining.

On the road I caught a ride with a very cool cat in a cherry Lincoln Cosmopolitan, and he was very cool indeed, but warmed up after a time. He was headed for L.A., which was fine with me.

He was a compulsive talker, but I finally went to sleep, until I felt the hand. Then I knew. He said he'd wanted to make sure I was comfortable, and suddenly he wasn't a cool cat any more. So I decided to pile out of the car, only it was raining like hell again, and we were someplace in top Texas wilderness. So I let him argue and argue for a long time, till after daylight, tirelessly, his head snapping around on the starched white collar, until I couldn't stand it any longer and asked him to stop the car. He did, still talking, and I got out and he drove off, maybe still talking, and I picked up with a truck and a driver with stomach trouble who was an expert on the Government, and we went all the way across New Mexico that way, right past the turnoff to Carl Shroeder's place.

I remembered, sipping the excellent brandy and smoking, with the music from Justine flooding the room softly. Thelonious Monk was playing *Monk's Blues*.

All my life it had been like that.

Except that that was the last time I ever stole anything—blatantly. My nerve went. Something happened. It was too risky, and it was stupid, because it was the big money that counted. I'd been a damned fool, but lucky as hell with those gas stations.

McCall, I thought, you've got to make it this time. Sipping the brandy.

I had thirteen hundred dollars when I hit Vegas, and a new suit. I met Carl Shroeder. I was mistaken for him. Everybody said we looked a lot alike. We were both drunk, and he had these two live ones, dancers, strippers from one of the clubs, and they were high on Mary Jane and what-else, so we started out, balling it like maniacs.

"I'm a married man," he kept saying. "I'm married. I'm a married man. I got a wife." Till I finally said, "I don't believe it."

He was a good guy, but crazy as hell; actually he was shot, even then, but he just went on and on, like sometimes a busted tire will, until it finally blows. One time he urinated all over a slot machine. He thought he was in the men's room. It was getting pretty bad. Lots of people watching him, and we had to run for it, the girls running with us giggling like the fiends they were. Nice fiends, though.

But he had the habit. I mean, it was getting on to Christmas, and in the hotel lobby they had this huge Christmas tree sticking clear up to the first floor mezzanine, with lights and all kinds of decorations, and presents wrapped for the guests, and so forth, and we were sitting up there drinking, waiting for the girls, and he just went and stood on the railing, teetering, swaying, and peed down on the Christmas tree, with everybody looking up in astonishment, and wild surmise.

That's how it was. That's the kind of guy Carl was, evermore.

So I said, "I don't believe it. You haven't got a wife." So nothing would do but I meet his wife, which I wanted to do anyway, being broke. I had to get out of Vegas somehow.

He drove his Cadillac. No sleep. Unable to eat now, either; just guzzle, driving all the way to the place here in the Sandias. And Nanette was something then, bright and cheery, and there was something between us. I stayed on for over a month. Carl kept right on raging. He never stopped. He would fold and sleep, then begin again. Nanette said he was suicidal. But he was kind to her; he never dragged the other women into her bed, that is.

But it got tangible between Nanette and myself. I had to get out, so I left.

Carl and I corresponded. Then I saw him again two years later in Quebec, and we pulled the same crazy whingding as in Vegas, on and on. Only he was worse; his memory was bad, he blacked out and still went on and on, a battle-scarred wreck, but with this insane zest for living and laughing it up. He wasn't psychopathic, just very humanly crazy. Not psychotic, either. I saw Nanette again in Quebec, but not to speak to. She got off a train as I got on another. She was coming to pick him up and take him home. He told me that was beginning to happen a lot lately.

We wrote back and forth. I think it was a kind of purge for him, telling me all the things he did—collecting paintings and junk, flying here and there, all over the world—and I was with Helen, and figuring ways to make the thirty-seven thousand grow.

Until now. In this house of doom.

I lay there on the bed, poured more brandy, and drank it. As I started to light a cigarette, knowing I was a bit high, I heard a noise by the door. Then there came a faint rap.

"Yes?"

Nothing.

I got up and went over there. Something was on the floor. It had been poked under the door. I quickly opened the door and looked out into the dying light of the hall. Nothing.

The music suddenly switched to straight drumming.

I lit the cigarette, closed the door, leaned down and picked up whatever it was.

It was a Polaroid snapshot, clear as a crystal, glossy and gleaming.

Justine.

She was posed on her knees, facing the camera, leaning back on outstretched arms. The sober look was there, the eyes watching, and she was stark naked, kneeling there in the middle of a small, frozen stream.

Naked on the ice.

The music ceased. Somebody was approaching my door.

Chapter 7

Whoever it was rapped lightly on the door.

I felt trapped and guilty. I made a dash for the bed, trying to think where to put the picture, and stabbed it into the leaves of the book on Zen.

"Who's there?"

The door cracked open. "It's me, honey. I remember, we never even kissed hello."

Nanette pushed the door farther open, and stepped into the room. She was worse off than before. All I could think of was Justine. The snapshot had triggered something I'd felt ever since I'd met her, only a short while before.

Nanette still wore the crimson gown.

"Also," she said, her voice faintly thick-tongued, "you oughta go down and get something to eat, Ken. I won't be downstairs tonight. I'm just too damn' plastered for words. I am. But you better go an' get something. I'm a fine hostess, I am."

She started to lurch. I caught her. She fell against me, looking up at me. She reached up and rubbed her finger across my lips.

"Sweet of you to come, Ken. Been so longish. We nearly had something, didn't we? Back then?"

Here I was thinking about Justine, when it was Nanette who had the money. And that's what I'd come for. And to top it off, Nanette was a lush, and she was the kind of female lush I had an aversion to.

McCall, I thought, you're losing your grip. Get with it, McCall. Make it look good.

"What're you thinking, Ken?"

"Thinking about you."

"That's nice."

Her breath gassed me. It was real long on gin.

"Ken? You think I shouldn't be acting this way, with Carl dead only a few days?"

I shrugged. She clung to me. Her hips were resting against me. Her eyes were dim, dreaming maybe; they seemed to dip in and out of comprehension. You could actually see it. You could see her remember and forget, realize and drift off again to wherever she spent her time.

"I'm free," she said. "At last. You know?"

"No. I don't think so."

She turned suddenly and sneezed. It wrenched her loose all over, and she clung to me. Then she looked at me again.

"Carl left me quite a lot of money, you know. Not as much as he might have, because he worked so hard to spend it. But plenty. Plenty. So I'm free that way, too. See?"

"I'm happy for you, Nanette."

She blinked at me. "Are you, really?"

"You know I am, Nanette."

I stroked her back, her arms, and thought of Justine.

She said, "About Carl's father, Jack. He's been in and out of sanitariums for a long, long time. Carl got him to sign everything over to him a long while ago. But he took care of him."

"Carl told me he was dead."

"Yes. That's the way he wanted it. I never questioned Carl too deeply, you see. It wasn't wise. He wanted his father dead. So that's the way he told everybody, see? Jack really is dead—in a way, I mean." I thought she was going to cry, for a moment. But she didn't. Then she looked wild. "I can't stand it!" she said. She thrust against me. She clung to me. "That crazy old man! I can't stand anything any more."

I stroked her back.

"You're as lovely as ever, Nanette."

"Liar!"

She pressed against me, looked up, smiling. "Kiss me, Ken."

I kissed her. She was kind of wild with it for a moment, then she drew away, looked at me again.

"Wait'll I sober up, Ken."

I pulled her to me. She shook her head.

"Ken," she said. "You be careful with Justine. You stay away from Justine, hear? I mean it."

"Who's Justine?"

"You know god-damned well who she is. Just stay away from her."

"I meant what is she to you?"

She paused, shrugged away from me. "Justine is one of the relatives. I'd better go lie down. See you later."

She started toward the door. I went after her. This was ending on a wrong note. She whirled, suddenly.

"Thanks for coming," she said. "When I received your wire, I knew I'd been right."

"What do you mean?"

"I know why you came. I know Carl asked you to come, didn't he? How much did he pay you to come and look after me? Well, I don't need looking after."

"It's not that. But maybe you do need looking after. You've got things wrong. I just wanted to—"

"Stow it, Ken. You can stay as long as you like—but stow it."
"Nanette. Baby. You're wrong as hell."
"All right. I'm wrong, then."

I forced myself to kiss her again. She moved against me, and ran her fingers around the back of my neck.

"All right, bucko," she said, and left the room.

I closed the door and stood there, gnawing the inside of my cheek. Then I lit a cigarette, and cursed quietly, harshly.

I'd lost an inning, all by my lousy self. I began to pace the room. I couldn't control the way I felt. The itch for the money was stronger than ever. And the only way to get it was to get Nanette first. It was obvious.

Be practical, I thought. Marry her. It's the only way. Get her off the sauce, and she'll be a beautiful woman again. She's beautiful right now.

But she's wise. Wise to the fact that Carl sent for me.

If—so what? Maybe I could work that to the good. I could say he'd sent for me, that I knew he was dead, that I'd always longed for her.

I ground the cigarette out in the ash tray by the bed, on the night-stand. It was too crude. I wasn't thinking right. The place had me all screwed up. Damn that Justine.

I poured another drink and drank it.

It's a gamble, McCall. The biggest gamble of your lousy life.

I was standing there somehow with the photo of Justine in my hands, staring at it. I put the picture back in the book and went downstairs. Halfway down, I heard the phone ringing. Somebody answered it. Justine.

I was on the first landing as she approached the stairs. She saw me, paused.

"Ken? You're wanted on the phone."
"Who is it?"

She shook her head.

I hurried down the stairs. She leaned against the wall at the foot of the stairs, watching me.

"Ken? Did you like the picture?"
"Yes."
"Thought you would."

She turned and went up the stairs.

I went over to the blazing fireplace. My hand trembled faintly as I took the phone down from the mantel. I said, "Hello?"

It was the lawyer, Devlin P. Montgomery. He was calling from Truth or Consequences, downstate; from a pay phone. He came on fast and rather loud. He had a deep, smooth voice, and he was glib.

"You're McCall?"
"That's right."

"Kenneth McCall?"

"Right."

"Montgomery here. My secretary called me. She said you'd stopped by the office. I left word, just in case. I'm driving back to Albuquerque."

"Must be rough. The roads."

"Foul. I want to see you in the morning, first thing, Mr. McCall."

"Fine. I'll be there."

"You'll get your two thousand dollars."

"Oh?"

"That's what you want, isn't it?"

"I don't get you."

"Don't snow me, McCall. I know all about you."

"That's fine."

Something was happening inside my gut. It was something I didn't like.

"Where are you staying, McCall?"

"Right here, Montgomery."

"I mean, what hotel?"

"No hotel. I'm staying right here."

"I don't think that's wise."

"Sorry."

"McCall. You take a room at a hotel. I can suggest a good one. The—"

"I told you I'm staying here. With Nanette."

He thought a moment. I could hear him breathing over the wire.

"Now listen, McCall. She's rather mixed up. It's difficult."

"Well, don't you worry your head about it."

Pause.

"All right," he said. "See me first thing in the morning. Say nine."

I started to say something bright. He'd already hung up. I replaced the phone, went out into the hall.

"Ken?"

It was Justine. She was leaning over the stair railing, looking at me. She smiled. Her breasts, in the tight, thin jersey, thrust over the railing. The smile went away.

"I fixed you something to eat. It's on a tray, in the big room there."

"Thanks."

She began to slide down the railing, watching me, with the pale hair thick and soft around her shoulders.

Then she paused again.

"Nanette came to see you, in your room," she said.

"Yeah."

I stepped closer to the stairs. We were face to face. She was whispering.

"What did she tell you?"

"Told me to stay away from you."

"Are you?"

"Am I what?"

"Going to stay away from me?"

She reached out and laid her palm against the side of my jaw. Her palm was very cool.

I heard a gentle tapping. The old man came through a door at the foot of the stairs. He wore a white robe now, corduroy. He paused and looked at us in the dim light from a very dim chandelier in the hall. There was no expression on his face. He was mouthing something, gumming his gums. He looked away, and rapped off, bent over the cane. He turned to the left, off the hall, and vanished into a darkened room.

"Poor Jack," Justine said.

Her hand still lay on my jaw.

I reached up and touched it, then held her wrist.

"Ken," she said. "Go eat something."

She pulled her hand away.

It was like a crazy dream. I kept seeing that photo of her, naked that way, looking at me.

I turned.

"See you in a little," she said.

She went upstairs again.

In the other room, only one light was turned on. It cast a yellowish glow on a roomy leather chair. There was a coffee table in front of the chair, with a linen-covered tray on it.

I went over and sat down and lit a cigarette.

Now, why in hell had Montgomery gone to all the trouble of phoning me? His secretary must have told him I'd call him in the morning. And why was he concerned about my staying here?

Music began playing again, coming from somewhere, permeating the atmosphere like poured emotion.

It was very soft, very distant.

I looked at the tray and uncovered it. There was coffee in a silver pot, a small, juicy-looking steak, creamed potatoes, peas, corn bread, and apple pie.

I looked around the room.

Just the very quiet music. The silence, except for occasional cracks and snaps from the fire in the big old fireplace. A huge log burned slowly. The crystal oil lamps twinkled and sparkled up on the mantel, throwing flashes of lively light across the large, heavy beams on the ceiling. Outside I could hear the sound of the wind, of snow against the house.

I had to eat. I picked up the napkin, and stopped.

Another Polaroid picture lay under the napkin. It was a close-up. Just her face, with the sober mouth, and the eyes staring out at me. The lips were faintly parted, the eyes slightly lidded. It was as if she were begging for a kiss, or more, and it was one of the sexiest damned pictures I'd ever seen. Horizontal calisthenics showed in her eyes.

I stared at the steak, but it was a long while before I was able to eat anything. The food was cold by then.

That night they chased me.

They were everywhere, and they were all chasing me. I knew they wanted to kill me. All through the night, I ran and ran, trying to avoid them. I could feel their hot breath on my neck. Sometimes their hands brushed against my back, fingers clutching. They didn't speak. I didn't know who they were, just that I had done something to all of them; I knew they deserved to catch me. The fright was terrible. Sometimes they surrounded me, coming at me from all directions, eyes like fire. I only managed to evade them by leaping over them. My leaps became weaker. I was just making it.

I woke in a drenched sweat.

I finally slept, lightly.

Chapter 8

I came awake early and was outside the house by eight o'clock. It had ceased snowing, and the country was terrific to see—the heavy weight of the snow on trees, the drifts, the smooth whiteness. As I walked around the house, scuffing through the heavy blanket of last night's fall, I wished I had a coat.

I had to see Montgomery.

A car had already been out of the garage. There were fresh tire tracks, and the snow around the garage entrance had been cleared.

The door where the Buick was stood faintly ajar.

I stepped inside, started around the rear of the car, and walked straight into a fist. It was the man called Elmer.

He slugged heavily, coming at me in a snarl of fury, savagely, gasping, with obvious pent-up emotion, and the necessity inside him to maim, or even kill.

He wore a heavy red-and-white Mackinaw, and yellow pigskin gloves on his fists. We stood between my car and another, the make of which I couldn't catch at that moment, and fought. Silently. I realized he was using everything he had, and he was a powerful man. I couldn't seem to touch him right, him wearing that damned thick woolen Mackinaw.

I was fogged from his first blow. I struck for his face, managed to catch him with a right across the side of the head. It jarred him. He fell back against the other car, his booted feet scraping the cold cement of the garage floor.

"You get the hell out of here!" he said.

"Hold it. What's all this about?"

He came at me again, head down, in a violent rush. His head got through my guard and smashed into my solar plexus. He ravaged my back with his fists. I brought my knee up and caught his chin, then slugged him twice across the side of the face, feeling the hard bone of his jaw. It didn't faze him.

"You leave her alone!" he gasped.

"Who?"

"Nanette, that's who!"

Again he rushed me. We stood face to face and fought now, and I sensed the wild, animal-like anger in him. I tasted a rush of blood in my mouth. His face was a grimace of effort and strain, the eyes near-maniacal.

I saw the fist coming, tried to feint, and goofed. I sprawled backward, fogged good and proper now; my head smacked something and I sagged to the cold cement.

I could hear him breathing, but I couldn't move.

"You leave this house," he gasped. His words came down to me from far away. "You leave now, and you don't come back. You don't even say goodby. You just leave."

"Up yours," I managed, fighting to get to my feet.

I couldn't stand up. I heard him walk away.

Finally I got to my feet, turned, and stumbled out of the garage. There was no sign of him. His footprints led toward the rear of the house, into the trees. I ran, following them. But they mingled with other footprints made this morning, and I couldn't tell where he'd gone.

Blood dripped from my face to the snow.

I went to a small gallery at the back of the house and tried the door. It was locked. I started to turn, and the door rattled, then opened. It was Justine.

"Ken, what happened?"

I was mad as hell. "Just some playful snow funning," I said. "Nothing like it for an appetite. Where the hell's Elmer?"

"Elmer? I haven't seen him. Did he do this?"

I didn't even look at her. I walked fast out of the large, gleaming kitchen, and down a hall, and found my way to the front stairs. I went on up to my room, and looked at my face in a mirror in the adjoining bath.

The cut was inside my mouth. I rinsed my mouth with cold water, and it finally stopped bleeding. All the time I kept cursing him, and wondering at him, too. But he hadn't really hurt me. It had been a lucky punch. Then I remembered smacking my head, and felt it, and it hurt like hell.

I went back into the bedroom, sat on the bed, lit a cigarette.

"Ken?"

She stepped inside and closed the door and leaned against it.

"Take a drink," she said. "Take a good one. It'll make you feel better."

I did that. I poured brandy into the sticky glass on the night stand, swallowed it and stared at her. Then I poured another drink and drank that. On an empty stomach it was a lot of brandy, and I began to feel it, quickly.

"Better?" Justine asked. She moved slowly toward me, then paused halfway to the bed from the door. She wore a Mack shorty nightgown, a piece of breathless fluff with tufts around the edge that brushed her bare hips as she moved. She kept watching me, fiddling with one corner of the gown. She was a knockout. The beautifully shaped legs were faintly spread as she stared at me. From what I could see, she didn't wear the shorts part to her outfit.

"This Elmer," I said. "Who the hell is he?"

"Never mind now," she said.

She took another step toward me.

"Ken, where were you going?"

"Had to run downtown."

"I want to go with you."

"You can't."

"Your suit's all spotted with blood."

"I can't help that."

"I'll go with you. I know where there's some of Carl's clothes. You could wear them. You haven't anything to wear, Ken."

I couldn't speak, looking at her. She stepped closer, not smiling, just watching me that way. Then she moved until I could smell her perfume, and her legs touched my knees, where I sat on the bed.

"Ken."

I suddenly reached out and ran my hands up the backs of her legs, up along her smooth thighs, and stood up against her.

It was as if somebody were torturing her. She gave a kind of groan in her throat. She began to twist and writhe, and I began to want her more than I'd ever wanted any woman.

Her whisper was hoarse. "Feel me—feel me!"

My fingers sank into her buttocks. She strained, arched her back, and I kissed her on the mouth and she sucked at me, tonguing, and for that brief instant we were like two raging maniacs.

I pulled her around toward the bed.

She gave a catlike squeal and yanked away, pushing, cringing, and ran for the door. As she opened it, she said, "Not now." She said it like a small child. For a moment she looked almost childlike—the strange, sensual, hurt-sad twist of her red mouth. And the driven plea of her eyes. At the same time, it was a kind of joyousness, and I suddenly knew she had the power to drive me crazy.

I went after her. It was as if she were clothed in a tender nerve sheath of lust.

She didn't move.

"Don't," she said. It was close to fright.

I paused.

"I mean it," she said. Her breasts rose and fell, the hard nipples poking the thin, silky gown. She had both hands cupped between her legs, her thighs clamped tightly together. Abruptly she gave a deep sigh and leaned back against the jamb.

"Come," she said. "I'll show you where the clothes are. Then I'll dress and we'll go into Albuquerque." Her eyes were veiled now.

I felt as if somebody had slugged me below the belt.

"All right."

She gave me a quick, mechanical smile. "I like you more and more, Ken."

We stepped into the hall. I had to touch her. I reached out and ran my hand down her back, and felt her move against my hand slightly. My fingers brushed the thick softness of her hair.

A door across the hall slammed.

"Nanette," Justine said.

At the same instant, I saw the old man standing at the far side of the landing, wearing rumpled black pajamas with gold and silver and green dragons sporting on the jacket. He rapped and rapped the floor with his cane. He was laughing, by the expression of his face, but all you could hear was an almost soundless keening wheeze.

Justine gave me a quick glance. "Be right with you, Ken," she whispered. "I'd better check Nanette."

She hurried across the landing to the opposite door, opened it, and went inside. I heard her say something, but couldn't catch what it was.

The old man looked at me. He gummed his gums, standing silently now. Suddenly he turned, rapped swiftly toward the head of the stairs, and went down. He moved with frightening speed, shuffling slippered feet. Going down the stairs, he kept glancing up toward me. I could see his jaded, rheumy eyes and ancient face pass between the white rails; it was like those old moving-picture books we had as kids, where you riffled the pages and dogs and people ran and leaped and laughed, and French can-can dancers kicked and kicked. Then he was gone.

I started back toward my room.

Justine ran across the hall to me.

"Follow me, Ken."

"Nanette?"

"It's all right. I explained about Elmer. She's going to speak with him."

We came to another door. She looked at me, and there was something sly in her eyes, as if she knew something she wasn't telling me. Then she touched me quickly, lightly with the backs of her fingers. "She didn't see anything."

I had the impression she was lying. But now we had a secret. Now the slyness had begun.

She opened the door. It was a long, large closet, and with the opening of the door a light had come on. It was hung with rows of suits, jackets, coats, slacks, by the dozens. Shoes on a canted rack lined the floor along the wall.

She said, not looking at me, "I can still feel your hands."

I wanted to touch her again. I reached for her, knowing it was crazy.

She slipped past me, and moved away. "Find something to wear. Be with you in a few minutes."

Okay. I tried to treat it nonchalantly, but these were still a dead man's clothes. Did you ever wear a dead man's clothes? All right. For some reason, this faintly bugged me. But I finally found a suit that fit, and an expensive lightweight topcoat. After dressing, I stood in the hall and stared at Nanette's door. I wanted to speak to her, but I couldn't. There was an evil feeling about the whole thing.

The hell with it. I decided to head for town. Without Justine.

I made it outside, and plowed through the snow around the side of the house. There was no sign of Elmer. I swung the garage door open, climbed behind the wheel.

Justine was slumped at the opposite side of the seat.

"I figured you might try to go alone."

I didn't say anything.

"Carl's clothes fit you perfect, don't they?"

I still said nothing. I sat there, staring at the horn button, then turned on the ignition, started the engine, and backed out of there.

"You're an awful lot like—Carl."

I drove around the drive, trying to keep in the other car's tracks. It was a cold morning. My face hurt a little from where Elmer had hit me. The inside of my mouth was sore, and my head ached.

Then I saw him, standing by the corner of the house, watching as we drove off. He did not wear the Mackinaw now. His hair blew in a faint wind. He was smoking a cigarette. There were dark shadows where his eyes should be, and I thought, he looks like Death, standing there.

I guided the car, slithering and lurching, down the hill to the main macadam road which had been partially cleared by a plow. A fine snow was beginning to sift from the skies again.

I took a few quick glances at Justine. She sat at the far corner of the seat and looked straight ahead.

She wore nylons, black spike-heel pumps, a tight red woolen skirt, and a fur parka-type coat, with a dark fur collar that ran around her neck and under her chin. She was bareheaded, with the thick pale-blonde hair splayed down over the fur collar. She was very beautiful, sitting there. She wore brown mittens, and carried a red leather purse. As I looked, she crossed her legs, and the taut skirt slipped up over her knees. Something about the way she sat, the way she looked, made me catch my breath. I couldn't help but wonder who in hell she really was.

I had the heater going now and I switched the radio on, softly.

"What's with this Zen?" I said. "There was a book—"

"I know," she said. "I'm just playing with it. Carl was studying it. He kept saying if he could ever attain Satori, he'd have everything solved."

"Satori?"

"Enlightenment." She paused. I thought she wanted to speak, so I waited. She finally did. "Just before he died, you know, I was with him. The thing was, he said he'd always had enlightenment and hadn't realized it."

"I don't understand."

"Oh? Have you a cigarette, Ken?"

I gave her one. We drove on in silence. Now was no time to pump her.

Her skirt kept sliding up on her thigh. I thought of Nanette, and remembered the money, and gripped the steering wheel a little harder. It didn't help.

We didn't speak the rest of the way into town.

"I'll have to let you out some place. You can't come with me. I'll meet you later."

"Okay. Any place will do."

I stopped in front of an Indian trading post, with *concho* belts, obviously fine pawns, and strings of silver and turquoise and colored beads in the window display. "Pick you up here in say a half-hour?"

"Yes." She slid across the seat toward me, flipped her cigarette out the window. She came to her knees on the seat, and moved against me, planting her mouth on mine, all tongue and heat. She was bold with her hands. Abruptly she broke away and opened the door, scurried out of the car. She ran across the street. I watched the bright scissoring of her shapely legs, the way a streak of sunlight caught her hair.

Montgomery's secretary was a middle-aged, dark-haired woman wearing a brightly printed dress. She had rather intense dark eyes, and smiled all the time. It was a pose to get things over with fast.

"Mr. Montgomery won't be able to see you. He's busy. He left you this, Mr. McCall."

I opened the long envelope. There were two thousand dollars in cash, all in hundred-dollar bills. There was a brief note. *"McCall. You can go home now. D. P. M."*

I saw his office door. "He in there?"

"Yes, but—"

I went to the door and pushed it open.

Chapter 9

"I was listening on the intercom," he said. "I figured you would come in."

"Yeah."

He was alone, behind his desk. The office itself was rather old and beat, with that mid-thirties look about it. Maybe he worked hard and didn't care about plush appearances. There was a carpet, but it was a hard, flat, colorless carpet. The desk was large, but it was the old golden oak, plenty scarred. There was one of those shiny black leather couches, taut-springed, with a bulbous leather headrest. The old office couch of long, long ago; you knew it would squeak like stricken birds—very large birds. The bookcases had the same old look. The filing cabinets were long since outdated. There was an oil stove in the corner of the room. Thin, dusty, sun-beat saffron draperies clung to the old green-black shaded windows.

Montgomery stood up behind his desk. He was a young guy, maybe twenty-six. He was big, like Superman, but he had the same mild look about him. He wore a single-breasted gray suit, with a dark maroon tie. His eyes were very mild, under neatly brushed sandy hair that lay flat on his skull. His mouth tried to smile. Underneath all this, you had the impression he was trying very hard to do something he disliked. How in hell had Carl got mixed up with him?

He came around the desk. "You're unimpressed," he said. "You wonder. I'll explain. This was my father's business. I've taken over. He was a very old man, and he didn't like change. I haven't got around to change yet."

He had a faint accent, but I couldn't place it. It could merely be some sort of a colloquial pickup.

I said, "You had charge of Carl's estate?"

"Yes. But I'd rather not go into that with you. There's no need, you see."

"You know what Carl asked me to do?"

He waved one hand. "Certainly." He gave a tiny laugh through his nose, which naturally was supposed to dispense with the entire matter. "You understand, I really have no bone to pick with you, McCall."

Now it was "McCall" again.

"Maybe I can dig one up," I said. "Why do you want me to leave town?"

He crossed his arms, leaned back on the desk, and regarded me with his finest courtroom scowl—the ruminative, "Now, ladies and gentlemen of the Jury," stare.

"McCall," he said quietly. "There's simply no need to go into that, either. You know as well as I do that there's no need of you staying around here."

"This tells me nothing."

"All right, then. Plainly. You're much like Carl, whether you realize it or not. Mrs. McCall's welfare is certainly, to a degree, under my disposition." He cleared his throat. "You'll only make her worse by remaining. Certainly you realize Carl had no judgment regarding things like this. He was a willful child, aimless, without roots." He shrugged. "Really, Carl was as crazy as a bedbug."

"I see."

"Mrs. Shroeder is in a bad state over his demise. She realized he had to go, the way he was living, but nevertheless, it was a shock to her. She always somehow imagined he would outgrow his nonsensical stage. He never could, of course. She's in a state of shock. She'll get worse with you around. I've spoken to her on the phone."

"I see."

"Good. Then you'll leave, right away?"

"No."

He gave a sigh, put his hands on the desk, and stared at me. He seemed rather nervous, despite his measured calmness. I had the feeling he wanted to yell.

"What did she say on the phone?" I said.

"She was distraught. She said you reminded her of her husband, but that you were an old and good friend. She didn't want to hurt you. She didn't know what to do. I said I'd take care of it."

"Then you both knew I was coming? That Carl had asked me to come?"

"That's right."

"Who's this young girl, Justine?"

He blinked. "Just a relative. She's staying over for a short while. I wouldn't get mixed up with her, either, if I were you."

"Why?"

"Let's say she's rather young. Eh?"

He moved around the desk again, and sat on his creaky old wooden desk chair. It was a gesture of dismissal.

"I'm staying on with Nanette, at the house," I said.

He looked up at me. "We'll see what we will see, McCall. Now, if you'll excuse me? I'm quite busy."

I went on out of the office. The feeling about this whole thing was very evil. The secretary said nothing, and she was no longer smiling. She'd probably been listening on the intercom, too. A snappy twosome.

I took the elevator down, walked through the short lobby. There was an auburn-haired girl standing by the magazine rack, near a small coffee shop.

"Hi, Ken."

I stopped dead. For an instant it just didn't register. I couldn't believe it, yet there it was. Betty.

Anxiety spread through my blood like a shot of H. I wanted to bolt. The reaction was very strong, and very bad, on top of everything else. Somebody had cut the string on the hanging sword. You watched it fall at your head.

I must have looked like a yokel ogling a side-show peeler just as she snatched the G string. I could not speak.

"I've been waiting for you," she said. "For three days. I knew you'd come eventually."

She looked slick as all hell; polished, neat, and with that feminine deadliness that can drive you nuts. They work on it till they get complete control of the situation. There's no use trying to break them down then. They've made it.

She was like steel. It was in her eyes, and in her voice, and in the fine, shining look of her. From the sparkling ankles to the expensive-looking crink of a hat. She looked sexy and untouchable, the way they can look if they want. She looked expensive.

"Did you think you could ditch me like that, hon?"

I still said nothing. I tried a game I knew wouldn't work. But I had to try. I walked briskly past her toward the entrance. She let me get out onto the windy, dusty sidewalk before she spoke. And she didn't speak softly. She took two sharp clicks after me, and said, brightly, "Then, Ken, I'll see you up at Shroeder's?"

I stopped. The wind blew. An Indian in a cheap department-store blanket slipped past, wearing a black hat. I turned and looked at Betty.

She stood there, watching me, a faint curl at the corners of her red lips.

I went after her. I was half nuts. I knew what she was, then; I recognized it, because I'd seen a lot of it. This god-damned world was populated ass over teakettle to the hilt with sparkling parasites—diamond-bright babies and diamond-bright boys.

A guy walked out of the building. In the coffee shop, a waitress saw me and stared. I didn't give a damn.

I grabbed Betty. "You bitch!" I said.

The guy paused and turned. He looked at me.

I shoved her back into the building foyer, toward the magazine rack, thrusting her one-two-three with my arm, with my fingers gripped into her arm. I shoved hard.

"Here, here," the guy said, closing in, blundering.

I looked at him, and said quietly, "You want to keep your teeth?"

He turned and walked away. Through the window over the magazine rack the waitress watched.

I shoved Betty into the magazine rack, wanting to hurt her. She tried to keep her balance and stepped on magazines, slipping. Her expression didn't change.

"I read that letter, Ken," she said. "I flew out here, caught a plane in Miami. I passed you in a taxi on the Overseas Highway. You think I'd let a bastard like you know I had any money?"

I kept pushing her back against the magazine rack, flooded with thoughts of Nanette and the money, and Justine; all of it mixed up in my mind.

"You're not running out on *me*," she said. She was nuts.

I held her tightly, and told her to her face, "You come near me, you crazy bitch, and I'll break your god-damned jaw. I'll wipe your nose right off your face. You want that? You think I won't?"

She watched me. Not a change in her expression.

"Get it," I said. "Get it straight."

I was shaking like hell. I gave her a brutal shove, and she sprawled fanny first, legs high, down against the magazines. Her skirt was up to her neck. She lost her hat. It rolled out across the lobby, and a guy came near to stepping on it. He looked at me, then at her. Then he walked straight out of the building.

She lay there with her skirt up, wearing frilled red-and-black panties, and sheer nylons gartered high on her tanned thighs. She lay there and just looked at me and didn't change her expression. It bugged me. I turned and got out of there.

In the street I paused. I went back. The waitress was on the phone at the end of the counter in the coffee shop. Betty was getting up. She was on one knee. I picked up my foot and gave her a push. She went flat again.

"Remember it," I said.

"I will, Ken. I will."

She untangled herself from the *Post* and *Look* and *Life,* and came to one knee again. I heard a siren.

I took off. The car was a few steps down the street. Running, I glanced back. Betty was outside, on the walk, knocking the dust off her hat. She walked away, still looking as expensive as ever.

I hurried to the car.

Justine sat there, watching me. I got under the wheel, pulled out and drove down the street. A cruiser passed me and slowed. I kept going.

How in hell had Justine found the car? If she'd seen Betty—What had happened was bad. Everything was going wrong, and I was still nowhere.

"Who was she?"

Justine's voice was like still water.

"Who?"

"That woman. The one you were talking with."

Maybe she hadn't seen anything. We'd been inside the building foyer for the most part.

"Wanted to know directions. A bum. Drunk."

"Oh. Well, this is quite a drinking town."

I began to breathe easier. But only for a moment, and it was completely minor compensation. I felt sure Betty wouldn't go to the police. That would be senseless. I wasn't sure of her game, but it smelled. I *was* sure of that.

Maybe I'd thrown a scare into her. Yeah.

"I could do with a drink," Justine said.

"We're going back home."

"I'd still like a drink."

I reached under the seat, uncapped the whisky, and took two healthy swallows. Then I passed her the bottle.

"Thanks, Ken. You're a funny guy."

She slugged at the bottle. It showed practice.

There was this lousy frustration all through me.

I glanced at her. She had her coat off. She wore a thin white sweater. The tight red skirt was hiked up over her knees again. When she threw her head back, drinking from the quart bottle, her breasts stood out, and she wore no brassiere. It was all I could do to drive the car. She had me going right in the midst of everything.

It can be like that. But the thing was, Justine was a hell of a lot more than just any dame with a sexy shape, and I was beginning to realize it more and more. That was the hell of it. I didn't want it this way. Just the same, there it was. There was no fighting it off, either. It was like being tied hand and foot, sinking, sinking into deep water. A crazy, excitable, desperate feeling.

I was plenty nervous from what had happened. There was the gooky way Montgomery had been. I couldn't figure him. And what the hell could I say to Nanette? She was hip to too much. I had to do something. I wasn't going to let the whole thing slip through my fingers before it had even begun. Too much was at stake.

Justine spoke. "I suppose you're wondering how I happened to be in your car?"

"I never wonder about anything."

"Like hell. I followed you. I knew where you were going."

"I see."

Everybody knew everything but me. I was blind, deaf, and damned near mute. What was left of my mind was so muddled I couldn't scheme. When you can't untangle the angle in a deal like this, you're dead.

I looked across at Justine. She was sucking on the bottle again. Some of the whisky ran down her chin. She gave a little giggle and wiped it away on the back of her hand with a little-girl gesture, and glanced at me from the corner of her eye. She began to look younger and sexier. I wanted her.

This was crazy, maybe, but it was how I wanted her. Knowing. Strong as hell. Wanting to lay her, wanting to tell her all sorts of insane things, wanting to kiss every inch of her lovely body, to hold her, smell her hair and her armpits. Crazy? No. But it was all the way. Wanting everything about her—everything. Wanting to kiss her fingers—wanting her the way you want a woman in the first fires of what they call love.

"Justine. You going to tell me who you are?"

She nodded slowly, holding the bottle, sticking her tongue down its throat. "Later, though," she said. "I want to show you something first."

She was watching me. Something came into her eyes. She slipped across the seat and lay lightly against me, her leg touching mine. Hell, I thought. Hell.

She took another nip from the jug. I told her to watch it. "You didn't eat any breakfast."

"That's when it's good. I love it. I like to get high. Best of all, I like good marijuana. The flower, you know. I really like that. I like what it does to me. I feel really good then—better than with this."

We were in the University Heights section. Cold winds gusted across the street, carrying sand and dust, and there were darkening clouds up in the mountains. It would be snowing again up there before long.

"You remind me so much of Carl," she said.

"You don't remind me of anybody I ever knew," I said.

She took my right hand, laughing faintly, then turned very sober as I glanced toward her. She opened her legs a little, pulled her skirt up, and laid my palm on her bare, smooth thigh, above the taut roll of her stockings. She pressed my hand there, tightly, for a moment, then put my hand back on the steering wheel. It was a hell of a thing, and I was crazy for her. She did not pull her skirt down.

The radio played softly. The car was warm.

She spoke, nearly whispering. "D'you like that?"

Traffic was heavy, but I drove fast. In my head I was wild. The street was wet and covered with mud and slush.

"It felt good to me," she whispered. Then she said, "Ken," snuggling against me. "Do you believe, on such short notice—I mean, we've only known each other a couple of days. D'you think anyone could love somebody else? I mean, like really love somebody else?"

"Yes," I said.

I wasn't thinking. Not giving a damn, either. All of it mixed interminably with Betty and Montgomery and Nanette and the money I had to have, and god damn it, was going to get. Only here she was, beside me. And I knew she was everything I'd ever wanted. The dream. Even with her cockeyed ways and her crazy Polaroid pictures. There was something screwy about that—lying naked on the ice, leering out that way. But something soft about her, too. Something good. Something the very best.

We skimmed through town, up into the canyons, and I turned off on the ridge road.

She just lay there against me. She didn't speak. Every once in a while, she would sort of squirm closer against me. Then I heard myself speak, almost harshly.

"Let's park some place."

She snuggled some more. "Yes, Ken. All right. But not along here, please. I've something to show you, remember?" She paused. "You know, you remind me terribly of Carl. You're so much like him, in so many ways. He told me all about you. I guess you were the only friend he ever had, who he could depend on. I've thought about you so much." Again she paused, snuggling some more. "Just drive right by the turnoff to—Carl's. Just go straight on, like a bird. I'll tell you when to stop."

"The roads may be bad."

"I know this country, Ken. Don't worry."

Like a bird, yet.

Chapter 10

The dark clouds made it seem like dusk, but there was a luminous quality to the snow—fine snow, like powdered sugar dusted across the landscape. We had passed the turn-off to Nanette's and had come far into the mountains on a deep-cut dirt road. It curved to the left and began to slant down, then it took a still sharper dip.

"Park here," Justine said.

I stopped the car.

Some one hundred and fifty yards or so ahead, the road rose gently, then dipped and turned inward upon itself. In the declivity you could see the road again, flattened now, between two rows of battered and ageless adobe houses. From a few of the houses thin smoke fingered the air, then wisped away on the wind. Chickens ran in haphazardly walled and fenced yards. A burro stood tail to the wind, like a statue. A brightly colored blanket flapped sullenly against the side of one house.

Behind us, on either side, and beyond the small village, it was rather thickly forested, the trees rising toward the peaks, the peaks themselves lost in snow and cloud, barren and remote. But where the handful of one- and two-room houses stood, I saw only one tree, a skeletal twist of dead despair.

People lived here. You did not see them. But you knew they existed. Even the snow did not cling to that barren, rocky, hard-packed, dusty earth.

"Nobody will bother us here," Justine said. "Nobody travels this road. A few cars in the summer. None in the winter."

"But people live down there."

"Yes."

"How do they get to town?"

"They don't."

I looked at her and instantly we were clinging together. It was like some sort of savage fight.

"The back seat, Ken. The back seat."

We scrambled, tumbling over the back of the front seat, still fighting to come together, and I saw her eyes, smokey, hot, and the red wound of her mouth, and dimly realized the bottle of whisky had tipped over on the front seat and was gurgling slowly, and didn't care. Nothing. Just Justine.

Animals. We didn't speak. She made sounds like an animal, and I suppose I did, too. Her head flung back in a kind of agony, the wild tumble of her thick pale-blonde hair, mouth and teeth obscene, and the hot, fierce readiness, the tearing at her black lace panties.

"Never mind—just—!"

Her fingers dug at me, raking my back, and the music swelled and swelled like a balloon overhead, with the whisky still gurgling slowly. She choked in whispered Spanish: *"Prisa! Prisa! Cuánto me alegro! Prisa!"*

The balloon burst.

For a long moment it was like warm rain. Then it was silent, except for a radio commercial—a potato-mouthed announcer seriously discussed primal man and the sweat glands, and the marvelous discovery of a fabulous new underarm deodorant.

Justine had done a bit of yelling. She'd carried on in Spanish, and one of the words was something like *morir*. It reminded me of death. I wondered what she had said.

We lay there. She was an amazing creature, and I knew she was what I'd always wanted. The thing in my mind was I didn't want to lose her, ever. This thought was paramount. I must never lose her. I had hold of both her wrists in a tight grip.

She had a strange, sad expression. She pulled away, brushed my lips with hers, leaned over the front seat, and came back with the bottle. There was still about a quarter of the whisky left. She drank, sank back looking at me.

"You love me," she said.

"Yes."

"I am the same," she said.

I don't know, it was like a kind knife, the way she said it. Her voice was soft, warm, and each word was like a kind knife, and I knew I must never lose her. I had never before felt anything exactly like this. It was a wild, uncontrollable need. To grasp at everything about her, to have her always, and to know everything about her. Love, to me, had always been nothing—a word, nothing more. Now I knew it was much more. I tried to tell her.

She listened, and said nothing till I had finished. Then she said, "It is the same with me."

"What did you say, in Spanish?"

"Not Spanish. It was Mex."

"Mexican?"

"Yes."

"What did you say?"

She touched my face with her finger tips. Her eyes were veiled with long lashes. Color had come to her cheeks. "I wanted you to hurry. The first time—it was—I can't say. I said how glad I was."

"There was something else."

Her eyes opened wide, regarding me soberly.

"No. Don't ask me."

"It was something like *morir*, something like that."
"Don't ask me."
"Please?"
"I wanted you to— Listen, Ken, do you like my hair?"
"Yes."
She kissed my hand.
"Justine, what was it? What did you say?"
She spoke with her lips against the back of my hand. "I asked you to kill me."
We sat there. Then she said, "Let's not talk about that. Sit up, look over there. Quickly, Ken."
I looked where she pointed. The snow was increasing slightly, but I could still see the adobe houses. One of the doors had opened and a fat, native-looking woman had emerged. She stood in the front yard—huge—wearing a red blanket. Her hair was gleaming black, tied down flat against her head. She was feeding her chickens, throwing seed from a shawl about her waist. Silver-and-torquoise jewelry gleamed on her wrists.
"You see that fat woman?" Justine said.
"Yes."
"She lives there," Justine said. "She's feeding the chickens."
"Yeah."
"Look at her closely."
"Can't see too well."
"She is my mother."
I stared at the enormous woman in the red blanket, watched her feeding the chickens in the thin snow. She threw a last handful of corn, looked at the sky, wiped her hands on the shawl, and waddled back into the adobe house. The door closed.
Justine said, "Yes, Ken. She is my mother. Carl Shroeder was my father. You see?"
"Quit joking."
"I'm not joking. She really is my mother. I had to tell you."
I stared at the adobe house through the increasing fall of snow. Now and again wind lashed heavier flurries past my vision, blotting out the houses.
I looked at Justine.
"Look, Ken—here."
She drew close to me, and pulled her hair taut against her skull with one hand. "Look closely, Ken."
I did as she asked. You could see the black roots of hair, close against the skull.
"I purposely haven't dyed it recently. I haven't touched it up, because I wanted you to know. My hair is very black, Ken."

"You mean, Carl was—she—? That woman, down there? You're actually her daughter?"

"Yes. You still love me?"

She waited. She waited like a little girl. Maybe she thought I would boot her tail out into the snow.

I said nothing. The wind and snow increased now, and the music played softly, swelling from the radio. I took her in my arms and told her nothing mattered, and her hot nakedness stirred against me. Her eyes were wide and blank. There were tears behind her eyes.

I kissed her breasts, telling her over and over that this could never matter to me.

She whispered "Ken!", her eyes startled, and at the same instant I heard something and felt the shadow. "Ken!"

I whirled, staring. Elmer Nash stood at the car window, watching us with wide, bright eyes. He cursed, said something about Nanette.

For a moment, I felt ridiculous. My pants were off. I was sitting there in my shorts.

"I'm going for the police, McCall!"

I sprang for the door, knocked it open, and leaped outside into the driving wind and snow. Nash turned and started running away from the car. I took three bounds, and tackled him. He went to his knees, twisted toward me, chopping at my head with both hands. We came to our feet, wrestling, sliding on the snow, falling back toward my car.

I knew the man's enormous strength, and tried to take care this time. Even so, he seemed worse now than he'd been in the garage that morning. He kept cursing, but most of it was unintelligible. His fists were bare now. He wore only a heavy gray shirt. Corded trousers were bound in high-top leather boots.

I heard Justine yell something from the car.

He caught me a hell of a crack across the side of the head. There was abrupt jubilation on his face. He followed the blow with a rain of punches that drove me backward. I stumbled past the convertible, trying to hold my ground, unable. Snow lightly covered the hard-packed dirt road and it was slippery. My feet slid crazily. He came at me, bulling savagely, in a running crouch. I let him come, set my feet, and swung a right from the ground. It broke through his guard and slammed against his throat. I thought I had him.

He shook his head as I came at him again. I got three good ones in against his heart, but then his strength returned. Abruptly he came at me, leaped into the air and drove his feet against my chest and groin.

The pain was like white light. I doubled and fell sliding backward across the road, into a ditch. I couldn't move. I lay there doubled up, groaning. It felt as if my chest was smashed; my gut was tied in knots. The pain was worse than I'd ever known.

I tried to get to my feet, digging my fingers into the snow and dirt as wind and snow drove down across me.

Nash turned and started stumbling back up the center of the road, along the slope. He was slipping with each step, his leather boots skidding.

Then I saw Justine at the wheel of the convertible. The engine roared to life and the car shot forward viciously. She was yelling something again.

"Justine—stop!"

My call smashed back into my face, driven by the wind, drowned in the insane roar from the car's engine. I fought toward Nash, but couldn't move.

He stopped, flung up his hands, and screamed, just as the convertible smashed head on into him. His scream sliced through the wind, and I saw him bounce back, flung by the impact from the car. Still the car came on, tires biting, and again it smashed into him. This time, he vanished under the front bumper, disjointed, like a dummy. She drove over him.

I heard her applying the brakes now, and saw the convertible slide faintly sideward down the slope, then come to a gentle stop. I managed to get to my feet, lurched across the road, and stared down at Elmer Nash.

His head was crushed. No feature was left. His skull lay red-white against the bleeding snow. His chest was torn open, and broken ribs thrust out like splintered white wood, the dark blood mixing with the bright-red blood from exploded lungs.

I knelt in the road.

"Nash—Nash!"

I heard her running along the road. She paused beside me. I felt her standing there, and then I saw her feet.

"Nash," I said.

He was dead. I knew he was dead. I couldn't believe it, though. I didn't want to believe it. I knelt there and stared at him, stared at the dead mass of crushed body lying in the cold, reddening road.

"Ken?" she said softly.

I continued to stare.

"Ken?"

I looked up at her.

"Don't worry, Ken. It's all right. I'll explain. This is the way I wanted it. It's just right. Believe me, it's just perfect." I watched her. I knelt there, propped with one hand on the road beside the body. I couldn't look away from her. She was watching me, soberly. And I knew it was as if it all had to be this way, from the start; it had been coming to this.

She watched me soberly, blinking as the wind drove across the road carrying gusts of snow. My right hand, on the road, felt warm. I looked down. It was covered with blood. I leaped up, staring at my hand.

PART TWO

Chapter 1

My pain was hellish. It came in driving waves, sweeping up through my body. I looked up at the dark sky, then at the surrounding country. Snow blew into my open mouth. My mind refused to function. I could only think one thing.

"We've got to reach the police. We've got to tell them—somehow explain this."

"No."

I quit looking at her, moved to the side of the road and wiped my hands, washing the blood off with snow. I glanced over at her.

She stood above the body, her hands clasped, staring at it, wind and snow frothing her hair around her head.

The pain in my lower abdomen was awful, dull and pervading now. I began to feel the cold, the wind, for the first time. I went back to Justine.

I had no idea how she'd come to do what she had. But I knew she must be muddled in some way. I knew, too, that we had to reach the police, and explain this thing—immediately. It kept coming to me, how you shouldn't touch the body; shouldn't move it. My imagination worked overtime. I was scared, plenty. It had been straight murder. All I could think was that *that* had to be somehow explained away.

Death, like this, frightened me. And the unleashed storm only made it worse. I felt panic gnawing inside, and there was no way to combat it.

Could somebody down among those adobe houses have seen what happened, heard Nash's maniacal scream as the car smashed into him?

With the panic was a sense of helplessness.

"Justine."

She stared at the body. She seemed hypnotized.

I took hold of her arm. She turned slowly and looked at me. "Justine, we've got to explain this to the law, don't you understand? It's plain murder. It's got to be explained so it won't appear to be murder."

She began slowly to shake her head. "No, Ken."

I took both her arms, shaking her, the panic getting worse. "Yes," I said. "God damn it! You don't go around killing people. That's one thing you don't do."

Standing there in the snow and wind and gathering murk, with the bloody, smashed, and cooling body at our feet, desperation took hold. The whole thing was insane; me standing there in my shorts, half freezing, shivering; the whole damned matter was insane.

"Ken, I told you I loved you. I mean that. I do."

"Never mind that now!"

"I've got to mind it. I've got to tell you. We're not going to any police, understand that. Get it through your head. I said this was perfect and I mean it. If you try to go to the police, I'll fix it. I mean that, too." She paused, standing there, watching me with the sober eyes. "I'll say you raped me. I mean it, Ken. That you raped me, that Elmer was suspicious, and he caught you at it, and you fought. I'll tell them you managed to get the best of Elmer, you knocked him down. I tried to stop you, but you got in the car and drove into him—that you killed him. I'll say it. I mean it."

"Justine!"

"They'll believe me, Ken. I'm known around here. They'll believe anything I tell them. Listen, Ken, I'm sixteen years old—just to start with. And Nanette will go along with what I say. She'll tell about the fight this morning. I told her Elmer and you fought because Elmer thought you were after me. I reassured her then—but I'd straighten that out, believe me."

I held her, staring at her.

"They'll believe, Ken. Because Daddy told me what a nut you are—just like he was. And he told me lots of the crazy things you and he did together. And, Ken, I've got all your letters, the ones you wrote Daddy. I know you stole cars, and I know you did lots of things against the law."

I dropped my hands. I was half frozen now. I looked at the body, then at her again.

"Now, you listen, Ken. I've got a good idea why you came here in the first place. Not just because Daddy asked you to. Why should you do that? I bet you came here because you saw a chance to get some money—you probably figured you'd make Nanette, maybe talk her into going away with you. You'd have your hands on money. But you listen—it wouldn't have worked anyway."

I said nothing. Wind moaned down across the foothills, and snow curled and chewed at us like harsh sand.

"You're in this with me, Ken."

"In what?"

"I hate Nanette," she said. There was an awesome bitterness in her tone. "She was the cause of Daddy's misery. You listen, Ken. Elmer Nash was with her for a long time, and they've been loving it up for a long time. They've been like a couple of snakes. I even saw them! Before Daddy was ill."

"That can't be right."

"It *is* right. I tell you, I saw them. But you'll believe it—just listen. Nanette drew all the money out of the bank. It's in currency. I don't know what kind of excuse she made for doing that, but she did it."

Despite everything, I felt my heart quicken. Then that feeling went away, because here was the body, and here I was, in the middle of everything with everything getting progressively worse every time Justine opened her mouth.

"There's not time to go over it all now," she said, "but Nanette and Elmer were going away. They were going to leave the old man—Jack, Carl's father—and me, and just go away, together, with that money. And, Ken, I have a paper, witnessed, written by Daddy, telling that I'm his daughter, and it'll stand up any place. Nanette knows about it, but she can't find it 'cause I keep it hid. So they were planning to go away—anywhere—change their names. I'd never have that money."

"All you'd have to do is show that paper."

"Don't you see!" She stamped her foot on the road. "Are you blind? As long as Nanette's alive, she has control of the money. If I showed that paper now, maybe I'd get some sort of fool allowance, but that's all."

I didn't even think about what she was trying to say. "Justine, we've got to get out of here."

"Don't you see how horrible it is? It's crooked and deceitful."

"Yeah."

"You're going to help me."

I shouted it: "We've got to get out of here!"

"First, we've got to get rid of Elmer's body."

"Get rid of it?"

"Certainly. They aren't going to find his body, Ken."

"What the hell do you mean? We can't get rid of the body. That's crazy."

"Crazy or not, that's what we're going to do."

I thought maybe I was nuts. I started toward the car, paused, looked back. She hadn't moved.

"You beginning to get it, Ken?"

I stared at her. She was insane. She had killed a man in cold blood and now she stood there asking me to help her hide the body.

"You can't hide the body," I said. "Somebody'll find it."

"You're beginning to understand," she said.

"I don't understand a damn' thing!"

"I know right where that money is," Justine said. "I've had it in my hands. See?"

I stood there with both hands over my face. My teeth chattered, and I was freezing. The winds were even worse now. Snow boiled madly in the road, hooding the road from cut to cut. I thought for a moment I really was going to flip. O my god, not this, I thought. Not this, McCall. Not murder.

Chapter 2

Ken McCall knows.

"First, learn how to be entirely unreceptive to sensations arising from external forms, thereby purging your bodies of receptivity to externals."

I stared at the body which had attained its own strangely perfect Satori—the enlightened and unreceptive body of Elmer Nash.

We went back to the car, and drank some of the whisky. I put my trousers on, and the topcoat. I could still feel the vanquished stickiness of blood on my right hand. I looked at her, at her excitement, at her eyes, and her body. I took another drink, finishing the whisky.

I began to laugh. It burst past my lips. She stared at me, then she began to giggle. My laughter ceased abruptly.

We didn't speak for a time. She tugged at my arm and we walked up the road through the streaming snow, toward the car parked nearly at the top of the rise—Elmer's car. It was a black Cadillac sedan. Not Elmer's car; one of the family cars.

"Well?"

"We've got to park the car in the trees, off the road, Ken. Till we come back for it, after we get rid of the body."

"Will you for chrissake stop saying that."

"All right."

I drove the Cadillac. We backed up the rise, and suddenly she said, "Stop. See that wash?"

Through the snow I saw a small arroyo. A trickle of water came down through rocks. It was flat.

"Back in there."

"Somebody will see the car."

"I told you nobody comes past here."

"Elmer did."

"We've got to hurry, Ken! We've got to get back to the house. Nanette will get suspicious."

I began to laugh again. It ceased, though, before it really began. It wasn't real laughter; it was a kind of throttled choking.

"You're so much like Daddy. Really you are."

I didn't say anything.

"Ken, back the car in there."

I sat there. I stared at the snow through the windshield. "I can't."

She turned on the seat and began to pound at my shoulders with both tiny fists.

I backed the car into the arroyo. We nearly got stuck a couple of times, but the Cadillac had a big, powerful engine, and we made it around a bend, under some trees. The car was well hidden.

We got out, not speaking, and walked back down the arroyo, through the snow to the road. Then we went down the road to the body.

"Bring your car up here. We've got to put him inside."

I brought the convertible up, backing it to where Justine stood by the crushed body of Elmer Nash.

"Do you have a blanket, or something like that?"

"No."

The snow whirled crazily. It whirled whitely and crazily inside my head, and the whole world whirled with it. I felt dizzy and blinded. The whisky helped. The emotional upheaval was very bad, and that tended to raise hell with things, too.

"We'll have to use your coat."

"Why?"

"Because! We can't get any blood in your car. You never know. Don't you see?"

"Yeah." I took off the coat.

"You'll have to put him in the trunk. I'm not strong enough."

I turned, holding the topcoat, Carl's topcoat, and stared at her in the whirling white now.

"If you were strong enough, you'd do it?"

"Certainly."

I opened the trunk of the car. I knew I was going along with this. I saw absolutely no way out. And at the same time, I kept thinking crazily of Justine herself. I honest to god didn't want to lose her. Maybe I was mad.

I stood there, staring into the darkness of the trunk, smelling the odors of rubber and dust and oiled steel, and I thought for a moment I was going to cry. I stood there watching snow whirl into the trunk, eddying madly, and remembered all the newspaper stories of crimes, and all the books I'd read of criminal case histories, of murder. Everybody's read them. But here I was. Ken McCall.

"Hurry up, Ken."

I stood there. And through all the nightmare it came to me lightly, like a feather, tickling the top of my brain. *McCall*, the talking feather said. *McCall, all you've got to do is drop the coat, close the trunk, get in the car and drive like mad. She can yell rape if she wants. Or she can hide the god-damned body herself. Because, McCall, this isn't in your line. Not murder. Not the real thing. You're just a joker, McCall, don't you see? You can maybe ship out of the country—anywhere....*

I turned and looked at Justine. I thought of the money. I thought of the things she'd said, and the things she'd left unsaid, and of how it had been with her in the car. She watched me soberly, the wind blowing her hair, and it was curious how she looked at me.

"All right," I said. "Get out of the way."

I approached the broken body.

We backed up the rise with the body in the trunk, and Justine directed me. We drove back, and turned off on another road, and drove a few miles to a deserted mining town. An old ghost town. It was called Golden. She said some Indians still lived there, and there was a store, but nobody would see what we were going to do.

We turned up across hard ground, following what she said was an old trail. We drove into the hills.

"People sometimes come back here," she said, "but nobody will ever know. It's perfect. You'll see."

"Okay."

She snuggled against me.

The snow was very bad now. I mentioned it briefly, because I was afraid of getting stuck in the snow.

"We won't. It's just right. It'll erase all tracks."

Finally she said to stop.

"See, out there?"

The foothills rose, nearly hidden by the driving snow. Around us there were very few trees. It was a kind of level mesa, with very small humps of hills that looked almost man-made. There were black spots in the snow. Suddenly, I realized the black spots were holes. We were parked right near one. The snow curled over the lips of the holes.

"Those are mines," Justine said.

I'd always imagined mines entering the sides of mountains. She explained it wasn't always that way. The gold miners used to dig straight down; just dig a god-damned hole, straight down.

We got out and looked. I tossed a pebble down one of the holes, standing well back. The pebble fell for a long time, then bounced off a rock 'way down there. Then silence.

"See?"

"Yeah."

So I got the body out of the car and started toward the hole, at her direction. I stopped, dropped the body, and stood there.

"I can't do this!"

"You've got to." She was almost serene. My head ached. I wanted to get drunk. There was no solution.

She began to drag at the body. The coat slid off the crushed head. One arm dragged stiffly across the bitter ground. I grabbed the body and ran, pulling it toward the hole. I felt like a maniac. I was nearly at the edge when the curled lip of snow fell off. Stones and gravel cascaded downward. I went kind of crazy then, and just seized the body and hurled it at the black target. The coat flew off and fell down. Elmer Nash started to slide feet first, his stiff arms and clawing hands dragging at the snow, the broken skull showing.

He slid slowly over the edge. I thought he would never go. Finally, he vanished with a last bloody, agate-eyed, broken-necked glance at the white void of the world. I heard him strike and fall and tumble amid a roaring shower of gravel. Then there was only a minor sifting of sand, trickles around the edges.

I stood there, in the silence. In the blowing cold, I was covered with sweat. She had hold of my arm, pulling at me.

"We've got to hurry, Ken."

"All right."

"He's buried forever. Perhaps he's not alone."

Already, I saw, snow was beginning to cover the bare gravel and earth around the mine shaft that had been dug sometime in the previous century.

We got in the car.

We came back out of the hills, and down onto the dirt road that led through the ghost town of Golden. Remains of old buildings hulked against the snowfall. Wooden sluices still stood where they had been built years and years before. I saw the remnants of a cemetery, what was left of miners' homes, now only foundation stones, well scattered.

"Make it as fast as you can, Ken."

We drove through the snow. At last, we reached the arroyo where the other car was parked.

"Now," she said. "I'll drive your car, Ken. You drive the Caddy. Follow me. But when I turn in by the house, you wait down the road, behind the pine trees. Watch the house. You can see it fine from there. Watch the window on the second floor, at the back, nearest the road. I'll signal you. When you see me open the window and wave, you drive the Caddy into the garage. I'll meet you out back."

I looked at her, said nothing. She was very beautiful. She must have felt something from the way I looked because she moved swiftly, came into my arms. "Oh, Ken, Ken," she said. "I love you so."

I held her there, smelling her hair, my face buried in it.

"Ken. We'd better go."

"All right."

I released her, got out, walked up along the arroyo. The stream among the rocks was deeper now. Maybe the Cad would get stuck. I found the car, slid under the wheel, gunned it, and drove lurching without a hitch out onto the road.

Justine drove the convertible away immediately. I followed her. I felt numb. My mind refused to function. All I could see was the body of Elmer Nash sliding into that black hole, and the way his dead eyes had flipped up at the world.

I stopped the car by the pine trees, and watched Justine drive up toward the house. In four or five minutes, the window opened on the second floor. She waved. I could just barely discern her through the thickly falling snow.

I drove up the steep driveway, like a motorized somnambulist, and parked the Cadillac in the garage. I got out, closed the door. The convertible stood there, looking peaceful and not at all like a death wagon. I checked the trunk quickly. There was no sign of blood.

Outside the garage I saw Justine standing on the back-porch steps. She made a circle with her fingers, motioned me in, then vanished through the door. By the time I was in in the kitchen, she was gone.

I walked down the hall and stood in the open door where I'd first seen Nanette, lying drunk on the studio couch.

"Well, hello there, McCall."

I stopped dead in the shadow of the doorway. Devlin P. Montgomery was seated on the edge of the studio couch. I just stared for two or three seconds. My heart thumped so hard it pained.

"Hi, Ken."

Nanette was sitting in a chair across from Montgomery. She looked quite fresh and nice, wearing a crisp black smock, clasped with a gold brooch at the throat. She was at least partially sober—something like her old self in that brief instant.

Montgomery looked exactly the same as he had in the office. Doubtless he'd come out here to discuss me with Nanette.

Nanette smiled. "Have you been out in this horrible weather?"

"Had to run downtown."

Montgomery raised his eyebrows. I kept trying to think through the smudge of my mind. I didn't recall any car parked in front of the house. I might have missed it, because I'd driven along the outer drive, intent on making the garage fast.

Montgomery cleared his throat. His eyes were fishy.

I was plenty rattled.

"Oh, Ken?" Nanette said. "Did you happen to see anything of Elmer outside?"

"No. No, I didn't."

She frowned. "I'm awfully sorry about what happened this morning. I wanted to speak to him about it, but I haven't been able to find him."

"He's probably around," Montgomery said. "He's always around." He looked at me, then at Nanette, then at me again. His eyes were shrewd to the point of superciliousness. "What happened this morning?"

"Nothing, really," Nanette said quickly. "Just a misunderstanding."

"Misunderstanding?" Montgomery said. "What kind of a misunderstanding?"

"It was nothing," I said.

"How do you mean?"

"Really, Dev," Nanette said. "Nothing at all. Forget it."

Montgomery pursed his lips, watching me.

The son of a bitch was a digger, a curious, poking bastard.

"Nan," Montgomery said. "I insist you tell me. If something happened, I'd like to know about it."

On top of everything else, I suddenly realized I must look a hell of a mess. And that god-damned Montgomery had me going.

"Well," Nanette said, "if you must know. Elmer and Ken had a set-to."

"Set-to?" Montgomery scowled deeply. "I don't follow you." He kept watching me.

Nanette said, "They had a fight."

"A fight!" It was as if he'd witnessed a nuclear explosion down the street. "What about? Why did they fight?"

Nanette shrugged and stared at her fingers.

"Nan," he said. "Will you please explain this?"

I began to back away from the shadow of the door. "See you later," I said. "Think I'll go clean up. Had a flat on the way home."

Montgomery glanced quickly at me, then lunged around on the couch, staring at Nanette. "Now, Nan," he said. "You tell me all about this. I insist."

I moved away, went to the hall and headed for the stairs. Justine was coming down. I felt dizzy again and my head throbbed. I didn't know what the hell to do about Montgomery. I reached for Justine as she passed me on the stairs. She held up a hand, whispered, "Not now—don't talk now," and hurried on down.

I went up to my room, closed the door and went over and sat on the bed. Thoughts rushed through my mind nightmarishly, like a speeded-up movie. I couldn't stop it.

What was Montgomery thinking?

I stared at my hands, and recoiled. A dark, flaked smudge of blood was on the back of my right hand. I leaped up and ran for the bathroom. I scrubbed at the blood harshly, hearing myself breathe in wild gusts. Even when the blood was gone, hands completely clean, they still felt sticky, dirty.

I tore off my clothes, Carl's clothes, hurled them to the floor, and got under the shower.

I turned the water on full blast and let it drive against me. I stayed there for some time, the water drumming against my head.

As I stepped from the shower stall, the bedroom door opened. I heard it close.

"Ken?"

Justine.

Chapter 3

"Ken?"

"Be right with you."

I used a thick towel briskly, wrapped it around my waist and stepped into the bedroom. She stood by the door. She had brushed her hair; it was thick and foaming around her shoulders. She wore a white satin Oriental-type gown that reached all the way to the floor, with big gold straps where it was fastened. Her lips were very red, and the tips of her fingernails. I'd never seen anything so beautiful.

She did not smile. She locked the door.

"Nobody will bother us, Ken. Nanette and Montgomery are downstairs, talking."

I said nothing.

She moved toward me. As she moved, she began undoing the fastenings on her gown, reaching down and flipping it open from the bottom up to her throat, watching me. She was completely naked beneath the gown.

Something happened to me. It was the culmination of fright, perhaps; what we had been through. The need to escape, if even for a moment; the need to forget what had happened.

There was something of deadly earnestness in her face, in her eyes, in the crimson line of her full, damp lips. Her lips were faintly parted. I could hear her faint breath. I dropped the towel and put my arms around her, under the gown.

"Oh, god, yes, Ken."

I peeled the gown off her, hurriedly, in a sudden panic of need. It fell at her feet and we came together, stumbling toward the bed. A strange brutality was in me. I wanted to rape her, to hurt her.

Instantly, I realized she was the same.

We were together in mutual want, fighting to wreck and smash, to annihilate what had happened out there in the white remonstrance of winter.

It was a stretched and red-hued time of shudderings and shiverings; of gasps and efforts to reach closer to each other than we possibly could; of desperation and a furious, brutal resolve in both of us to wipe out whatever had happened before; of plungings and lungings and utter seriousness, with no laughter, but with jerks of half-spoken words, of pleas, and cutting hates. Of grasps and digs and sobs, all melded together in vicious taking. A deadly serious purging, with wild kisses and probes; an untame, vain, crazed savagery, in an obvious effort to explode, disintegrate, vanish.

As savagely naked as the hopelessness itself.

We lay still, clutched in each other's arms, panting, still faintly stirring, then spent.

Slowly, I began to hear the wind outside, feel the bursts of snow against the windowpanes.

"You're all sweat," she said. "You dripped sweat all over me." She rolled away, stood up beside the bed. "Be right back."

She went to the door, unlocked it, and vanished silently, swiftly out into the hall.

She returned in a moment with a bottle, locked the door, ran to me, and sprang upon the bed. She sat cross-legged, facing me, and opened the bottle. She drank deeply, then offered it to me. It was straight rye, and it began to work quickly. I drank a lot, as fast as I could. Then I looked at her.

"Justine. There's no one like you."

She half smiled. "You mean in bed?"

"Yeah. That's not all of it, but that's what I mean, right now."

"I should be. I had a good teacher."

"Yeah? Who?"

"Daddy. Carl. My father. I always called him Daddy. He was the first. He was the only one, other than you."

I stared at her.

"Shocked?"

I couldn't speak.

Abruptly, she twisted and let herself down across me on the bed, nuzzling my neck with her warm lips. Her hands caressed me. "You're so much like Daddy. I love you, I love you."

She kissed me on the mouth. I lay there like the tomb.

"Ken, would you mind if once in a while I called you Daddy? I mean just in secret? Between us? Would you mind, Ken? Please—please say you won't mind!"

She held herself up, staring down at my face. Her eyes were almost insane with pleading.

"Please, Ken! Say you won't mind!"

Chapter 4

I continued to stare at Justine in a kind of awe.

Then I heard Nanette call.

"Ken? Ken? Somebody wants you on the phone. It's some woman. Ken?"

Justine sat up. She sat on the edge of the bed, watching me. She was very beautiful with the suddenly frightened eyes, not because Nanette had called, but because of what she had told me and asked me.

I called, "All right. Be right with you."

I heard her walk away down the hall.

Had she heard anything? Could she possibly have heard what Justine said?

Justine clutched at me as I tried to stand.

"Tell me—tell me, Ken!"

I ran my fingers through her hair. "All right," I said.

She fell across the bed on her back and stared up at the ceiling. Her lips were parted. It looked as if she might be smiling.

I slipped on a pair of trousers, a shirt, and shoes. I looked at Justine. Then I went to the door, unlocked it, and hurried down the hall. My mind whirled. I only half realized I was headed for the phone, that somebody wanted me, some woman. All I could think of was Justine, and what she had said.

"I had a good teacher."

"Who?"

"Daddy."

"Daddy who?"

"Carl-Daddy—that who!"

I found myself at the foot of the stairs.

"She wouldn't give her name, Ken."

Nanette stood down by the hall door. I heard Montgomery say something, but I couldn't see him. Nanette laughed brightly, turned, waved to me, and disappeared into the room. I went into the front room, picked up the phone and sat on the wooden bench in front of the fireplace.

"Yes? This is Kenneth McCall."

"I'm coming out there."

It was Betty Flanagan. I went absolutely sick. Something about the way she said it, the shock of hearing her voice, of her saying those words, knocked me into a bad state. "You hear, Ken darling? I'm coming out there."

"Hold on. I can't talk now."

"I don't give a damn whether you can talk or not. I said I'm coming out there. You can go to hell, you son of a bitch!"

She was crocked, not bad, but nasty-crocked. "I'm coming out there, by god," she went on. "I'll clobber you if I get the chance, you bastard, so don't turn your head on me."

"Betty. Take it easy. I can't talk."

"I don't give a goddamn. You'd better talk, and fast!"

I tried to think. My mind was black sludge.

"Who was that sweet little bitch you had in the car?"

She'd seen Justine. She must have seen us when we drove down the street. We had passed her, and she must have seen Justine.

"Nobody."

"Nobody, my—"

I hung up. I sat there, perspiring, staring at the phone. It rang again immediately. I picked it up.

"Nobody, my ass!" Betty said.

Nanette stepped into the room. I motioned her back with one hand. She frowned and looked hesitant.

"It's for me," I said.

She flapped her hand and vanished into the other room.

"You're damned right it's for you, darling," Betty said. "Who was that you spoke to? Nanette? That who?"

I lowered my voice, speaking in a whisper. "I'll meet you," I said. "I'll meet you some place and explain."

"Talk up. I can't hear you."

"I said I'll meet you some place. Where you staying?"

"You'll come and see me? Why?"

"I can't say now. Just tell me where you're staying. I'll meet you tonight. Get there as soon as I can after dark. It's something—I can't tell you now. Trust me, honey. Believe, will you? This is important. It's big. It's important to you." I really laid it on. And it got her. It always got her.

"You mean it?"

"I mean it."

She lowered her voice and began to whisper herself. For chrissake, she was flipped, too.

"All right. If you're not fibbing, Ken."

Not fibbing!

"I'm not fibbing. Where you staying?"

She told me. It was a big motel on the east end of town, not too far away.

"You'll really come? Tonight?"

"You know it."

"Oh, god, Ken honey. I'm sorry, if I— I didn't—"

"Forget it. Got to go. See you."

"Ken, do you still—?"

"Yes. You know it." I hung up, and sat there sweating all over, wringing my hands and gritting my teeth, staring at the god-damned telephone as if it might leap up and crunch me to bits in its black teeth.

She couldn't come out here. Not now. Not ever. I put the phone back up on the mantel, started to get up from the bench, then sank back again. The heat from the fireplace was furnace-like. A black dizziness came over me, and my head whirled. Then, through the whirling, came the problem of Elmer. It hit clear and hard, like a hammer. They would know Elmer vanished. But he couldn't just vanish. He had to be explained away. Because if he just vanished, then there would be questions and a search, and all hell might break loose.

I found myself running up the stairs.

"Ken?"

It was Nanette. I stopped, looked down over the banister. She stood in the hall.

"Anyone we know?"

I shook my head. "No. No. Friend of a friend, back East."

"Oh? Long distance?"

"Yes." Naturally it had been a station-to-station call, so I was all right there.

"Don't forget," Nanette said. "We've got to get together and talk soon. I feel much better."

I nodded. "Yep. Sure. We sure will." I motioned toward the room where Montgomery was. "Soon as he goes," I whispered to her. "Okay?"

She winked, turned, and marched back to Montgomery.

I raced up the stairs, across the landing, and into my room. Justine had not moved. She was still stark naked, lying on her back across the bed.

I forgot everything then. Just Nash—Elmer Nash. I closed the door and locked it.

"Justine, listen. We've got to explain Elmer's disappearance."

"Yes, Ken."

"But, how. I'm a dope. I didn't think. We've got to do something, and fast."

She propped herself up on one arm. "Calm, calm—I already thought about that. I know just what we'll do."

"You know?"

"Yes, darling."

I slumped on the bed. I took the bottle off the night stand and took three long swallows. The whisky hit bottom and growled.

"I began thinking about it right after he was dead," Justine said. She sat up, slid over beside me, and took my hand. She held my hand to her lips and kissed it, and nuzzled it, watching me all the time.

I sat there. I thought of what she had told me about herself. She'd slept with her own father. Obviously it was done. You heard about such things. But I'd never run across it, and certainly not like this. The thing was, she had liked it. And it must have happened often.

To each his own is a good policy to remember.

I looked at her. I knew I still wanted her, the same as before. So maybe I was debased, too, in a way. At least, there were people who would think so. But it didn't really matter.

Yet, there it was. I would look at her curiously forever. But what was forever? With me, with what was happening, what was forever? I knew now that I had become a part of whatever this house stood for. The feeling of doom that I'd felt when first stepping into the house—I was a part of that now. I held some of the secrets.

She whispered it. "Daddy?"

I damned near jumped out of my skin. It was like being blown up. I sat there beside her, looking at her. She held my hand, nuzzling it, kissing it, watching me with those eyes. I sat there and I thought about the money, and how close it was getting. I remembered what we'd done with Elmer Nash, and my insides twisted a little. And I looked at her, at the soft sweetness, at the sugar softness that was mine. I looked at the thick, soft hair, and felt the soft, lush body next to me, and I could feel her love. Justine's eyes looked at me, and I could feel what was behind those eyes. The touch, the promise, the happiness, and the contentment.

McCall, I thought, you are stark, raving mad.

I thought of the way she said things—"Daddy?" Timorously, you might say. Not quite sure, but full of hope, you know. Like a little girl. That was it.

Then, I thought, god damn it, okay. So it's Daddy, so what? Lots of babes have called you Daddy. But they didn't mean what she means.

Then I thought, my god, maybe they did. Psychological, you see. Maybe some of them meant it exactly that way. The id guffawing through a conventional giggle. It could happen.

Well, I thought, I'll be damned. But I tried to think of it the other way. That's how I would think of it. Like that. Daddy.

I was flipping; gently, gently flipping. That was the trouble. But I began to understand about Carl now. About his crazy tearing around, and why he had more or less committed suicide. I thought I understood some of it, anyway. I could be wrong. It was damned easy to be wrong.

Labels, I thought. Small, printed absurdities.

I drew her close and kissed her. She smiled at me. I thought about what I'd been thinking about.

Daddy's baby, I thought.

Good god, McCall. You crazy bastard. I picked up the bottle and took a good long drink, then set it down.

"You said you had something worked out," I said. "What is it?"

She got up off the bed and ran jouncing across the floor, not at all timorously, and picked up the white satin gown. She fumbled with it, shoved her hand in a pocket and came up with some folded paper. She dropped the gown again, came over to me, and unfolded the paper. It crinkled in her bands.

"Ken, this is something Elmer wrote. It's a letter to his mother, so he must have a family somewhere. I didn't know about that."

"What the hell do we want with a letter to his mother?"

"To copy the handwriting. You're going to use it as a sample. Don't you see, Ken? It's perfect. I thought about it when we were out there, in the snow. I knew we had to figure a way. Because he couldn't just vanish. It has to be explained."

I watched her, feeling very strange.

"Do you see?"

"Yes," I said. "I thought the same thing." I paused, and then said, "Justine, have you ever thought how it will be if we're caught?"

"I don't think about it. It won't happen."

"I see."

"Besides, Ken. We haven't even begun yet."

Something came into her eyes, that deadly earnestness again. "There's a lot has to be done yet. That's why we've got to get this done right away. You've got to copy Elmer's handwriting, and write a note of some kind, from him to Nanette, saying he's going away. He should say in the note that he couldn't face her to tell her. He's got a job somewhere in the East—I think that's good. Put sentiment into it, but no mention of what's been going on between them. Make it short. Tell how he knows if he faced her to tell her, he'd never go. But this is his one chance to break loose from the work he's been doing. He never really liked it. He's going to take the chance. He won't tell anybody where he's going in case it doesn't pan out. But when it does, he'll write."

"But he'll never write."

"Naturally."

I swallowed that and said, "Shouldn't he say something to Nanette? Since they've been—"

"No. That troubled me, too. But just leave it. She can think whatever the hell she wants."

"But the money. She drew it out. They were going away together. You said—"

"Ken. She'll *wonder*. Sure she'll wonder. But what the hell good will it do? She can't tell anybody."

"Why not?"

She shrugged. "She just wouldn't. And to anybody else, it's a perfectly legitimate note."

I kept trying to think. "His clothes!"

"I already thought of that. I packed them, the first thing. We simply have to ditch them."

I took the letter from her, and looked at it, read it. It was brief, and unimportant. It was obviously a chore, his writing to his mother. The weather was fine, but cold and snowy. He felt fine. He hoped she felt fine. He looked forward to spring. He was eating well. He hoped she was eating well. He realized he didn't write much, but she understood. He realized she couldn't write much, but he understood. It was a bunch of crap. But it would serve its purpose. There was no address, and no date on the letter.

Justine started to put on the white gown. Again, in the midst of everything else, I felt a strong, hot lust for her. Her large white breasts were in the way as she tried to fasten the gown. She caught my eye, hesitated. I took her in my arms, feeling her body all over, and she took two or three deep breaths, her lips pressed into my neck. She spread her legs, moving her body against me and I slipped my hand down between her legs. She gave a brutal moan.

"Wait, Ken. We can't, not now. There's too much to be done." She backed toward the door, fastening the gown, her face flushed. "I'll bring you Elmer's paper and pen."

I turned away from her. I couldn't even look at her, the way I felt.

She left the room. I stood there, gradually calming down. It was really something, the way she affected me.

Something else was in my mind, but I couldn't tell what it was yet. I just stood there, looking at the dead man's letter to his mother that I'd dropped on the floor. I picked it up and reread it, feeling nothing, only realizing I was ignoring what was in my mind.

Justine returned with a cheap pad of paper and a gold fountain pen. The fountain pen was very old.

I took the pad and the pen. Then it hit me. What good did it do, killing Elmer Nash? What good did his being gone do? It put Justine no closer to the money. That god-damned money. Why, hell, if—and then I knew.

I knew as sure as hell.

Looking at Justine, I couldn't believe it. I couldn't believe that I was somehow a part of it. But there it was. It had to be. There was no other way. I looked for an out for myself. There was none.

Justine watched me with those eyes. She was smiling faintly.

"Ken," she said. She almost whispered it. Her tone was harsh, close to obscene. "I know what you just thought. I read your mind. I'm positive I know."

I was like a rock; like something that had been carved from enduring stone centuries ago and was still standing here. I heard my voice. It was a hoarse croak, as if someone else had spoken.

"You're going to kill Nanette," I said.

She looked straight into my eyes, her expression very sober. "Yes, Ken. That's right. How else could it be? I'm going to kill Nanette, and you're going to help me. It will be a poetic accident," she said. "For me, really, it will be the sound of one hand."

Chapter 5

Weird Chinese music began to filter softly through the speaker in the room. It was an offbeat plucking of discordant minor strings, nothing else. Just that.

"I put on a tape," Justine said. "Do you like it?"

I said nothing.

The music *plinged* and *planged* and *plunked* and *clunked*.

"I think it's very interesting," she said.

I threw the pad and pen and letter on the bed, stepped up to her and grabbed her by the shoulders. I shook the living hell out of her. All the time I shook her, those eyes watched me, the head bouncing around on the shoulders, the molten mass of blonde hair tossing.

"We can't do it!" I said.

She did not react.

"We can't!"

I felt an abrupt anger, and struck her across the face. A red welt of blood showed beneath the skin. I twisted, hurling her. She sprawled, stumbling, fell against the bed and slid to the floor, watching me. She did not speak.

The music *plinked* and *planked*. It was insane.

"Ken, honey?"

I took a step toward her. She lay back against the edge of the bed, seated on the floor. One delicious thigh poked through the slit of her gown.

"Ken? Think about it."

"How much money is there?" I heard that, too. That was me talking.

She said, "Nanette drew out exactly four hundred thousand dollars. There's more. I know there's more, but that's what she drew out of the bank. At least, I think there's more."

"Four hundred thousand dollars?"

"Yes, Ken."

"It's in this house? You've seen it?"

"I've seen it. I've counted it."

"But how could she draw out that much? Without questions, I mean. Four hundred thousand dollars."

"Exactly. Listen, Ken. If you have money, they don't ask so many questions. They can't stop you if you want to draw it out. She drew it out quite a while ago. Like I said, I don't know what she told them—but believe me, it's there. I checked again last night."

I couldn't even speak now. I paced up and down the room, and I kept seeing all that money. It was crazy as hell, the way I felt.

She sat there, watching me, and began to stroke the inside of her right thigh with the palm of her hand, her eyes misty and distant.

She spoke softly, distantly, against the weird *plinking* and *plunking* of Oriental strings. "I never had anything, Ken. I never had anything, except Daddy. He was wonderful to me; you'll never know how good he was to me. So tender and wonderful." She paused, then went on. "For a long while, I never knew he was my father. But he would come and see me, I remember. So long ago. I lived out there, where we were, Ken. I lived in that house, where you saw my mother. She was very beautiful once, Daddy told me. She wasn't always fat like she is now. And he would come and play with me. He taught me everything I know, Ken—I never went to school. He taught me English, so I could speak. He taught me everything. Crazy things, too. He was interested in lots of crazy things, you know."

I stood there, listening, watching the way she stroked her thigh with her palm, up and down, up and down, sensually, slowly, her eyes raptly peering inward on something darkly sweet and forever distant.

"You didn't hurt me when you hit me, Ken," she said. "Daddy used to hit me sometimes. But he never hurt me, either. We tried—you know—him spanking me, like that, but I never got too many kicks out of that. Neither did he, really. We just tried it. We tried a lot of crazy things."

The house seemed to grow darker still, and the music flowed on endlessly.

"I'm a half-breed," she said. "A half-breed Mex. A breed, you say. Daddy always said that makes you healthier, better in every way—stronger. Do you like black hair, Ken? I have very black hair. Someday you'll see it all black. If you like it. Do you like it?"

"Yes."

"Really, Ken, you know, I'm a true Indian. I mean my mother was a real Mexican Indian, because— Daddy told me all about it." She hesitated, paused in the stroking of her thigh, then began again. "It will sound strange," she said.

I was as rapt as she was now. It was something like moving slowly, without walking, skimming through the earth, down and down into dark caverns.

"He found my mother 'way down in the mountains, in Mexico. She was very beautiful, and he brought her back here, to that 'dobe house, where I was born. Daddy was there. He supervised the birth. It was an arrangement; he arranged the whole thing with my mother. She speaks very little English—just a few words."

"What do you mean, 'arrangement'?"

"My mother—me. So that when I was old enough, he could have me. I was twelve when it began. He said someday he wouldn't be here, that some other man would have me, but that he would at least teach me everything there was to know. And he did. And now, you're that man, Ken."

I said nothing. She looked up at me with those eyes.

"Nanette never knew," she said. "Nobody knew, except the witnesses who signed the paper and everything. He brought them from someplace else. He was very careful. He said when he died I should come here, and show Nanette the paper—prove to her who I was. So I would always have money enough. So until he died, I lived in that house you saw, with my mother. Of course, Daddy used to take me places. We went everywhere. We went to Europe, to Africa, to India. We were always together." She paused. "When I told Nanette, she—well, she changed. I mean, I came and told her even before Daddy died. I knew he was going to die. His heart was all worn out. He was tired. He told me he didn't really care if he lived any more. He said he'd lived just as much as he could, and there wasn't anything left, anyway. He really lived, you know. I mean, he just never stopped, even for a minute. He said he didn't regret anything—nothing he'd ever done. To a lot of people it just seemed like he was tearing around, a playboy like. Only it was his life. He lived it as he pleased."

"Yeah."

"And I found out what Nanette was doing with Elmer Nash, and everything. Daddy liked lots of variety with his women. He said the code people are forced to live under is utterly stupid. But anyway, Nanette couldn't give him any children, but he wouldn't divorce her. You know what?"

"What?"

"He said I was the best of them all." She giggled. "Nanette like to flipped. She just like to flipped her silly lid."

I took her hand. "Justine?"

"So I'm just a relative living here. I'm Daddy's brother's daughter. I'm here because my father and mother were killed in a plane wreck. Only"—she giggled again—"Daddy never had a brother."

"Justine?"

"Yes?"

I leaned toward her. "You killed a man," I said.

"Yes. I don't care."

"And now you want to get rid of Nanette."

"We must."

"What about Carl's father?"

"I don't know."

We looked at each other. There was a drowsiness, a laziness about everything.

"Justine?"

"Yes?"

I leaned still closer. She put her head back on the bed, watching me. Those greenish eyes watching me.

The music went on and on, strangely discordant, seemingly pagan, ringing and singing out of the ageless, living past.

Chapter 6

I wrote the letter.

It took less than an hour to master Elmer's handwriting and turn out a passable note to Nanette. I did it alone, in my room, drinking brandy. There were all kinds of fear inside me, and I fought against doing anything, but I did it, just the same.

By the time I finished, I was pretty high. I took the letter Nash had written to his mother, burned it, and flushed it down the toilet.

Every damned thing I did seemed like an inexorable step down a long, gleaming corridor with carbon steel walls that brushed my shoulders on either side. The corridor was absolutely straight. It was bright and white with an unknown suffusion, but I couldn't see the end. It just went on and on, with a curious and deadly unconcern, because it was somehow alive, sealing up behind me; disdainful, bizarre, obsessed.

I kept seeing Elmer Nash's smashed, bleeding body; the broken skull, the white shards of ribs, the bright-hued lung blood, the eyes flipped up at the world as he dropped....

With the letter folded in my pocket, I tried to find Justine. I couldn't. I didn't even know where Justine's room was. I prowled the house, but there was no sign of her.

For the first time, I realized I was hungry. There was nobody in the kitchen and no sign of a cook. I wondered who did the cooking?

I kept thinking about that amount of money, and it dug into me harshly. There was the money and there was Justine. They balanced together, and they were an excitable weight. I could actually feel the beating of my heart, a heavy thudding against my ribs. A strong urgency was taking hold of me, sinking its teeth in. I knew I would go through with this thing. I didn't give a damn what happened—only I knew that was a lie, because I had to keep telling myself I didn't give a damn.

I forced myself not to think about the law. I'd never been caught at anything. But I'd never been mixed up in anything like this. And the feeling would come over me. It came over me now. If I'd been sleeping, it would have been another nightmare—being chased and knowing I'd be caught, by all the hands and all the unknown faces.

The law. It had always been there, in the back of my mind. It was like knowing all the time you'd be caught. I knew I could never live behind bars. What we'd done, and what we were going to do—well, you seldom lived behind bars for long.

Justine. Every time I thought of her, there was a subtle explosion in my veins. It was fire, the way I wanted her. It was worse, having her, knowing I could have her. Knowing that if I just did what she wanted, got away from this house —yes. With that money played right, we'd be set for life.

Only—Nanette. The old man, Jack Shroeder. How?

I forced my thoughts away from that. I suddenly remembered: maybe I could paint! I could paint pictures, the way I'd always wanted but never had done. Only at odd times. It was maybe the one honest thing I could talk about and really mean what I said. I remembered how every time I ever painted, I could lose myself in the colors squeezed out of the tubes; how it was tremendous kicks to take up gobs of mixed paint and lay it on canvas with a brush, or a knife, letting whatever was in you come out in color and design. There was a wild kind of satisfaction in painting that I'd never found anywhere else. I remembered times when whole days went by like a blink, and I'd paint on into the night by lamplight. The excitement was very real. I'd get carried away with all that wonderful color and what took place on the canvas.

One time I'd rented a small cottage over on Cape Hatteras, near the inlet, and there was this girl in New Bern, and we'd get together, and I always played it straight with her. I tried to recall her name and couldn't. I felt a sensation of loss. But that cottage. I'd painted like a demon, covered every wall in the place with canvas after canvas. It was wonderful. Swimming every day in the ocean, and with the girl, and with the crabs biting our feet, and the way she laughed. We always swam in the raw, and maybe she understood me; I never really knew. Because I never understood myself. The crazy thing was, that whole summer and 'way up into the fall—till I couldn't stand it any longer and was going broke anyway—I'd financed the whole thing on legitimately earned money. I'd worked for nearly a year heaving crates in a warehouse.

God, yes, I thought, pacing up and down in the big front room of the Shroeder house, with the fire blazing away in the fireplace. And then I remembered how it ended. How that girl, whoever she was, had been the only person ever saw my paintings. And how I told her—it was October already—that it was all finished, I wouldn't see her any more. I had to go away. She argued with me. She said the paintings were good. But we carried them out to the beach, and burned them.

I stood in the big room staring at the fireplace.

We burned them all. Every last one. She wanted just one, but I wouldn't give her any. They had to be burned. She kept telling me they were fine paintings, and when they burned, she cried. She wept, sitting there on the cold sand of the cape, with the cold, dark Atlantic out there—it must have been some time past midnight. She said I'd done something evil, burning them. They made a big fire. People came and watched, standing in groups in the windy, sparse brown grass and the sand. Nobody said anything. I told her good-by, that I'd see her. But she knew it was really good-by. And I packed and left that night, and never saw her again.

"Ken?"

There was a kind of cramp around my heart. Justine came up to me.

"You finish the letter?"

"Yes."

"You've been drinking a lot. I can tell."

"What of it? Okay. What now?"

She looked up at me, and smiled, and all the other went away, like blowing out a candle. She still wore the Oriental robe of white satin.

"Nanette's in her room. Hurry, come on."

I followed her upstairs. We turned to the right, and through a door that led down a narrow hall toward the rear of the house.

"I want to see the letter before we put it in Elmer's room."

"Okay."

I followed her through the dusky hall watching the way she moved, the flow of her hair, everything about her. And I knew she was mine. It was like fire.

I closed in on her, held her by the waist, and walked pressed in against the thrust of her buttocks, kissing the back of her head. She took my hands and, still walking, held them up on her breasts. Then she paused at a door and turned her face up to mine. We kissed. She drew away.

"Not now."

"All right."

She stood with her hand on the doorknob.

"Do you still have any reservations?" she said. "About what we're going to do?"

"No. We're going to do it."

She opened the door. "This was Daddy's room," she said.

It was like stepping directly into another world. The moment the door closed, we were in another century, on another planet. It was phony, maybe, but it was a dream, and the phoniness didn't matter.

The room was immense. In the center, a gnarled oak tree grew, perfect and complete, leaves and all, under a vast skylight. It grew from earth and moss, bordered with rocks and slate in a varied pattern on the floor. It was not full-size, of course, but it wasn't a complete dwarf, either.

"The tree is Japanese," Justine said. "It's very old. They prune and root-prune, and so forth—it's a science. This one's special. Not like the little ones. But it never grows any larger. Still, it's perfect."

"Yes."

"When Daddy was alive, Nanette never entered this room. I don't know about now. I don't keep it locked, or anything. I suppose I should."

There was a huge Pollack drip painting on the far wall of the room, a sort of cross between "Full Fathom Five" and "The Deep," which were my favorites, it seemed. It was a tremendous painting, and it seized you and you didn't fight, you just dove headfirst into the depths of color, and drowned in fear and joy and apprehension and a kind of wild, fight-less series of culminations, maybe like Burroughs staring at the toe of his shoe, endlessly, endlessly, not even nodding, just caught up endlessly, in Tangier, in opium.

"I like it, too," Justine said. "I don't get it, but I like it. I think."

I said nothing.

You could die in the damned thing. Or you could live.

There were other paintings. The furniture was of black leather, even the bed, which was under the Pollack painting. There were no rugs on the heavy planked floor, which had been painted black at some time or other, and was well worn with walking. Another wall was covered with hi-fi controls and equipment. A tape slowly revolved, and I saw where the music came from. Most of the rest of the wall space was covered with books, a collection of pornography probably equaled in only a few places in the world. I glimpsed titles supposed to be impossible to come by. But there was every type of literature, all vitally interesting stuff. At the head of the bed, as I walked around, I saw a lot of books on Zen Buddhism. I picked one up, opened it, and stared at blank pages.

Justine giggled. "Daddy had them printed himself."

"I don't get it."

"If I were an old Zen Master, I'd beat you with a stick, or something. Maybe sick a dog on you." She giggled again. "That's what Daddy told me when I said that."

I riffled the pages of the book. On a few pages there were periods, in the center of the page. Just a dot. Or an exclamation point. One page toward the end of the book had a tiny word printed. I squinted, to read. It said, "Shit." I closed the book.

"Hurry," she said. "Let's see the letter."

I handed it to her, and as she read, I continued to look around. There was a well-stocked bar, a typewriter on a small table, uncovered, except for dust. Not a sheet of paper, or pencil, or eraser. Just the machine. There was no ribbon in the machine.

I began to feel strange and wanted out of the room.

"It's perfect, Ken."

"Then let's go. You stay here? In this room?"

"Yes."

Once out in the hall, I felt better. But then, what we were doing returned with a rush.

"Let me check on Nanette," Justine said.

She went ahead, and I started down the stairs. Before I'd reached the foot of the stairs, I heard her racing after me. She had the letter in her hand.

"It's all right," she said. "Nanette's asleep."

We went down and on through the house, to the back. Off the kitchen was another hall. It was very dark, and smelled cold and damp. At the end was a door. She opened it and we stepped into a small room. Elmer's room, obviously.

It was very plain. A bed, a couple of chairs, a bureau, a closet, and a small desk with some science-fiction magazines stacked on it.

"What about his clothes?"

"They're in your car, Ken."

I began to feel a slight nausea again. The pent-up feeling of excitement came back with a rush.

"You'll have to go out and bury them someplace. It's the only way."

I remembered I had to see Betty. "All right." I couldn't tell Justine about Betty.

"Listen," she said. "We'll leave the letter on the desk."

"Why not out in sight?"

"This way, *I'll* find the letter. It'll be best, see?"

I looked at her and experienced that same strange awe. And at the same instant sensed rather than heard a dry, wheezing sound, coming from behind me. I turned, fast, knowing what it was before I saw him. Jack Shroeder, the old man with the cane.

He had on a flatly pressed blue serge double-breasted suit, with a red flannel shirt. The collar of the shirt was much too large for his scrawny neck. He frowned, staring quizzically, almost comically at me, rapping the cane on the floor.

"Carl," he said to me. "Carl, I want you to run into town and pick me up a case of applejack. I've had a hankering for some time. You do it right away." He started to turn back into the hall, his cane tapping, then he whirled on me again. "You aren't too drunk to drive, are you, Carl?"

I couldn't speak.

"Jack," Justine said. "You'd better run along now."

He stared at her, tapping and tapping with the cane. His eyes were coated with a sort of yellow skin, but life still gleamed there, faintly flickering.

"You just don't give me any sass, you cute little devil. I've got my eyes on you. I been watching the way you hey-hey around here. Carl gets me that applejack, you can come and have some with me." He winked, his lid sticking a little. Then his face went blank. His mouth came open, chin dropping to his crumpled collar. He slapped the cane against the floor and shouted in an old, dry, choking voice, "Where the hell's Emmy?"

"Emmy was his first wife," Justine said. She stepped past me, took the old man's arm and started him down the hall. "You better go lie down awhile, pop. You've been hitting it too hard lately," she said. "Okay?"

The old man rapped and tapped with his cane, wagging his head from side to side, gently cursing under his breath. Justine let him go. He wavered and staggered on down the hall, humped over the cane.

She came back to me, and we looked into the room. We glanced at each other. The letter was on the desk. She turned off the wall switch, and closed the door.

I'd been hungry. I wasn't any more.

I had to see Betty. I had to get rid of Elmer Nash's clothes. Something began to come up inside me then, a kind of strong will, a demolishment of everything, and I wanted to get all of this over with as quickly as possible. Even Nanette.

"What are we going to do with the old man?" I said.

"I don't know. We've got to do something."

"How's about showing me that money?"

"Not yet."

"Why?"

"Ken, you've got to take Elmer's clothes and bury them."

I'd have to discourage her if she said yes, but I had to ask her. "You coming with me?"

She shook her head. "I'm cook in this house. Nanette will want to eat, I think. And the old man's always starving."

"You—cook?"

"I didn't want anybody else in the house. They had a cook, but I fixed that. It was okay with Nanette."

"Then maybe I'd better take off."

"Yes."

I kept looking at her, and wanting her with this hot feeling. There was nothing I could do about the way I felt. I knew the money was mixed up in it plenty. I'd wanted that kind of money all my life, and here it was. And here was the girl, along with it. It sort of swamped me, I guess. I took her in my arms, but she was stiff, and nervous.

"Daddy," she said. "Not now. We've got to take care of things first. There'll be plenty of time for all the things we want to do—later."

"Yeah."

She kneaded her loins against me for a second, kissed me quickly on the chin, then broke away.

"You'd better go, Ken."

"All right."

"I'm going to start getting Nanette drunk," Justine said. "I've got an idea."

She was cold as hell. A coldness came into her eyes, and she was far away, in her mind. You could tell that easily.

I told her good-by, and tried to kiss her again, but she wasn't having any—not till I'd done what I had to do. Then I realized I was trying to put off what I had to do, so I went on down the hall toward the stairs. Justine vanished toward the kitchen.

If I got hungry again, I could get something to eat in town.

I drank a full glass of brandy in my room, shaved and dressed, then went out into the hall. I opened Carl's closet again, and found another topcoat. It was a gray-and-black check.

I went back to the room and stood there for a time, not thinking, not anything. Just experiencing a touch of excitement and fear. Just knowing I was in it, up to here. And that I wanted it that way.

Music poured softly from the speaker. I stood in the midst of it. Then I had an idea, thinking about Betty. I went and got the two thousand dollars Montgomery had given me, took his note out of the envelope and put the money in, and put that in my jacket pocket.

As I stepped out of the room, Nanette crossed the hall toward me. She was dressed in black. A tight-fitting skirt, blouse, and jacket, with black pumps and sheer black stockings. She looked all right, not soused badly, but she'd been hitting the jug.

"Ken. We haven't even talked. Let's sit down for a minute."

She went over and sat on the big couch on the landing. She patted the cushion beside her, and crossed her legs. I sensed something coming, but I didn't know what. It got me going a little.

As I sat down, I thought again how I'd just come to this house for a try at something, and now look. And the try had been aimed at Nanette. I didn't give a damn about Nanette now. Not a damn. Just Justine.

"You going out?"

"I've got to run downtown."

"I see."

She was chilly. There was something about it.

I sat beside her at the other end of the couch, with plenty of room between us, and turned toward her. She turned toward me, hitching one knee up a little, rather careless about her skirt, too. Not that it mattered. But she seemed to be trying to show her leg without being too open about it. Just the same, she made it clear that she was showing her leg. Some women can do that, and still retain that strange appearance of decorum, or modesty, or whatever. They ignore everything, talking with only their lips.

Nanette was concentrating, though. It was obvious. She'd planned the whole thing. It came across like a movie scene. She just dropped it like a bomb.

"Ken? How long are you going to stay here?"

It hit me straight in the teeth. It was like ice. I didn't say anything for a time. She just sat there, looking straight at me that way, with her leg hitched up a little, and her eyebrows, too. It was the coldest damned look any woman had ever given me. Really glacial.

"I mean it, Ken. How long is this going to go on?"

"I don't think I understand."

She laughed. She just laid her head back against the couch, and opened her mouth and laughed like hell.

Chapter 7

Her laughter ceased.

"Excuse me, Ken. I couldn't help it. The laughter, I mean. I just couldn't help laughing."

There was nothing to say to that.

She turned still more toward me. "But really, Ken, you aren't fooling me, you know."

"I'm not."

"Nope. Not a speck. I know Carl left a letter for you when he died. I know what was in the letter. I know you collected your two grand. So aren't you happy?"

I began really to look at her now, and the hate began to come up in me. It wasn't exactly hate; just a heavy dislike. She was acting like a beautiful bitch, which maybe she was. What the hell, she didn't have to throw it in my face.

I kept looking her over. I didn't find anything I liked particularly. I'd once had some crazy plans for her, but she was no longer included. That is, not in the way she might like to be if she knew the whole score. The hell with her. I hadn't believed she could be like this. Then I knew she was trying to make me mad, make me say something, maybe make me mad enough to leave the joint. Well, she could go spout up a rain pipe.

"You're such a fool," she said. "So much like Carl, and he was just a born fool. You know that? Why, you even look like him. You think I give a damn about him dying? I don't. Just understand that, will you?"

"Sure."

"Do you take me for a fool?"

"No, honey. That's something takes cultivation."

"Glad you realize that, at least."

"Glad you're glad."

I knew I was smashing something, but I didn't give a damn.

"Well, then." She glanced down at her knee, and began rolling the hem of her black skirt back and forth on it. Then she began wrangling with her kneecap. She looked over at me again, half smiling. It was the knowing half smile; the subtle super-supercilious smirk of a smile that was supposed to make you turn red, then white, then get up and run and fall over your feet, and crawl the rest of the way out of her sight on your hands and knees.

I just sat there.

She cleared her throat. "Really, Kenneth McCall. I can actually read your mind."

"Why don't you rent a tent?"

She blinked. If she wanted to play, I didn't give a damn about that, either. I figured maybe that last glass of brandy helped, but whatever it was, the hell with Nanette Shroeder.

Her eyes got just a little narrow. Not much. She wouldn't let it show that much. She had to preserve her discretion.

I got up, walked across the landing to the liquor cabinet with the jolly little Buddha on top, got out a bottle of something, poured it into a highball glass, three-quarters full, and carried it back to her. I handed it to her with a slight bow. She took it, saying, "Well!" with her eyes and lips.

"You look strangely pallid," I said. "This'll help."

She watched me. Then she threw the drink in my face, holding onto the glass. The drink ran down and dripped on the rug. I licked my lips. It was whisky.

"I didn't really care for any," I said.

I took her glass, went back and refilled it, drank it, filled it again, returned and handed it to her once more. Then I went and sat down on the couch again, and looked at her. I pursed my lips. I got out a cigarette, did not offer her one, lit it with a match and tossed the match on the floor, still burning. It finally went out, but it left a small black smudge.

I was getting higher by the minute.

I actually thought about giving her a good roll, right there on the couch, just for the hell of it. Maybe it would do her good. Then I thought, why waste the energy?

Instead, I said, "Are you through yet?"

"No."

I said nothing, watching the glass of whisky, and I spotted something. This gal was on the high road. She kept trying to hold the glass braced on her thigh, but it shook in her hand, just the same, and it didn't shake because of any irritation over me. It shook because she wanted to drink it.

"Go ahead," I said, pointing my cigarette at the glass. "I'll close my eyes."

She actually snarled. It was nothing else. It was a half loose-lipped, half tight-lipped snarl. She raised the glass and gulped it down.

We sat there. That jolt reacted so fast it was comical. She got all bright, and her eyes began to shine. You'd think she'd used a needle in a vein, it was that fast, and that interesting.

"Well," I said. "You could've taught ol' Carl something."

"Humph," she said. "I did teach him. Where you think he learned to drink? He never touched a drop till I got him going. We were married very early, you know, and he was the athletic type. He wouldn't even touch beer."

"My, my," I said.

"So, now, Kenneth. When are you leaving?"

The evil, frightened feeling began to come up in me. I tried to stay level, but it wouldn't work.

"I've got to run downtown at the moment," I said.

"You know what I mean."

I felt nervous. I got up, went over, and took the glass from her hand. At the liquor cabinet, I filled the glass, returned to her, and she took it with a bitter face.

I sat down and smoked, waiting, wishing, knocking ashes on the rug.

"Must you do that?" she said.

"Yeah. I must."

"Did you think you'd be able to make it with me, and get your hands on what's left of Carl's money?"

"It was the general idea, Nanette."

We had come to terms. The terms were lousy. They would be better. Inside she made me seethe. She would find out.

She waved the glass and spilled a couple of plops of whisky in her lap. She took a long, big-mouthed drink, brushed at the spots with a lazy backhand.

She was getting potted.

"Ken, darling," she said. "I want you out of here tonight. I don't want you hanging around."

I stood up and looked at her. She was half shot. I buttoned the topcoat, said, "See you later, Nanette," turned, and headed for the stairs. If she'd known how I felt, she might have laughed again, right then. I mean I was scared.

"Tonight, Ken," she called. "I really couldn't stand it any longer. I mean it."

I looked at her from the head of the stairs. There was a brass urn with some cabbage leaves growing in it. I flipped my cigarette into the urn, then went downstairs.

Justine was starting up. She paused, half ready to speak. She must have seen something in my face because she turned and ran down the two or three steps, and waited. Seeing her did plenty to me. It was the knowing she was mine, the being in this house, and everything. Like a shot in the arm. I felt off my rocker. I knew I was kind of tight, but seeing her raised hell with me right then.

I nailed her by the elbow at the foot of the stairs, pushed her though the door into the hollow darkness of the hall, and held her tight.

"We've got to do something. You've got to do something, right now," I said. "We've got to get moving."

"I am, Ken." She gave a little giggle. "I'm on my way up to see Nanette now. I'm going to wake her up—"

"She's awake." I told her the score.

"It's perfect. I'm taking up Elmer's note."

"I thought you were going to stage a search."

"This is better."

"Okay. Maybe." I tried to make out her features in the darkened hallway. She thrust her hips against me, moving it around.

"You wait just a sec or two, and see what happens."

"Maybe nothing'll happen."

"Maybe not. Anyway, you've got to get rid of those clothes. Now, Ken! Let me go!"

"Okay."

She went through the door and I listened to her going up the stairs. I waited. A kind of breathlessness came into me. The whole thing was revolving around me, but I was spinning in the opposite direction.

They were arguing up there.

I heard a shuffling noise coming from the other end of the hall. Then a dry wheezing. I couldn't see anything. I plastered myself against the wall. It was that old man again. I could smell him. And then came the tap-tap-tap of the cane. I held myself tight up against the wall, hearing them arguing up there.

"Oh, hell," Nanette said. "I don't give a goddamn what you've got to show me!"

"You'll care, all right."

The old man paused in the dark of the narrow hall. I heard him hold his breath. There wasn't a sound. He was listening, and I could picture his face in my mind, with the ears sticking out like those old gramophone horns, really tuned in. Then I knew he wasn't listening to what I was listening to—he suspected somebody else was in the hall.

We both waited, holding our breath. He finally began to wheeze and whistle like an old bellows, gasping for breath. But he didn't move. The son of a bitch just stood there, and I couldn't even see him. Then he began to curse very softly, muttering, and spitting in the dark. It was some of the foulest cursing I ever heard. Nobody touched him, the way he went at it.

"I know you're there, Carl," he said. "I know damned well you're there. You an' that gal making hey-hey all the time, like you do. Think I don't know, Carl? Think I don't know my own son?"

It got me just that much more. I felt like reaching out and twisting his rotten old neck.

They were still at it up there.

Apparently Justine still hadn't shown her the note.

"Son?" the old man said. "You aren't dead, are you? They been fooling with me. Your old gran'pa made a lot of money, and I couldn't spend it, but you been trying to, haven't you? Only you haven't spent it all yet, have you? So you aren't dead, are you?"

I didn't say anything. There was just the old man's voice coming from close to me in the dark of the hall. Then it began to come closer and his feet shuffled, the cane tapping.

"Son?" he said. "Carl, my boy. Do your old father a kindness and fix him up with a nice woman, will you? I've plumb got a hankering, Carl. It isn't right you should coop your old father up like this. I'm a bit erratic, I admit. But it still isn't right."

I gave a cold shiver.

Right then, Nanette yelled upstairs. She'd read the note. She said something sharp to Justine. Then I heard her heels hit the floor. She was running for the stairs. It was Nanette, because she took longer strides than Justine.

The old man moved like grease toward the hall door. I saw him go out into the main hall. I went after him, passed him, and went down the other hall toward the kitchen. I turned off into the room where I'd first seen Nanette, and waited.

The old man said something to Nanette. She cursed him, then came sailing past the door where I stood, and went on down the hall. I went into the hall. Justine was coming down the stairs.

"Take off, Ken—right now."

I stood there, looking down the hall toward the kitchen, and where Elmer's room was.

"Ken! I mean it—hurry!"

"Yeah."

Nanette came back down the hall, saw me, but didn't react. She went plowing through the door, careening a little, and on toward the big front room. I heard her dial the phone.

"Who's she calling? Who in hell would she call?"

"I don't know. Ken, you've got to go."

I remembered Betty. It was like gall in my throat.

"Dev? Dev, is that you?"

"Calling Montgomery?" I said.

"Get going, Ken."

I took off. I went back through the kitchen, and out to the garage. The goddamned convertible was loaded with suitcases. There were three of them. When I got in, that convertible was loaded with fright, too. Then I got out again.

Shovel. The stuff had to be buried. It was the only way. In the darkness he began to follow me, pacing after me on the cement floor—Elmer. I imagined it, but it was real, too. It was bad.

I found the light switch, and turned it on. There was a stack of shovels in the corner of the garage, but they were all snow shovels. I scrambled around, and finally found a long-handled digger under a bench. I got that in the convertible and backed out of there. It was snowing lightly. I left the garage lights on.

Now, driving away, that money really began to sing inside me. I don't know. Every time I got behind the wheel of a car, like this, when there was excitement mixed up in it, I really swung.

But there was too much else. There was Montgomery. What did she want to call him for? What could he do? I couldn't figure it.

Then there was the clothes-burying deal. And then Betty. And Justine would be expecting me back soon. And Nanette had said, tonight you've got to go. Well, she knew damn well I had to come back for my clothes.

And anyway, she was drunk.

I hit the main road and started off toward Albuquerque. I had to pick a spot. I kept thinking of that hole where Elmer Nash lay, down there in the black. I wished I could throw his clothes after him. It was too far to drive.

Then I knew it wasn't too far.

I stopped the car and just sat there. I thought I was going to burst wide open, or maybe bawl, or just sit there and yell like a crazy man. That's how I felt. My mind kept whirling. I couldn't make it stop. I was dizzy and half crazy.

Then I thought, McCall, you're half drunk, that's all that's the matter. Relax, McCall. You're going too fast. You're worried, and things are getting a little out of hand, is all. Calm down, and you'll be O.K.

So I sat there in the night with the snow lightly coming down, and smoked a cigarette. It didn't do a particle of good. I looked back toward the house, but couldn't see anything. Just the snow lightly whirling out there.

What is it like to be in the middle of a black dream? Ken McCall knows.

I drove about three miles and spotted a turnoff that went up toward the peaks. It was a dirt road, but it had been partly cleared by a plow. The snow was still falling very lightly, and with the snow you could make out things, more or less. I drove for a while on the first road, then saw a gully cutting up toward a hill.

I stopped the car, got out, and had a look up the gully. It turned into a glen, widening, then finally narrowing and getting very steep.

I went back and got the shovel and the three suitcases. But I couldn't carry the three suitcases and the shovel all at the same time. Panic began to nibble at me again. Suppose somebody came along here. A Ranger, or somebody. I leaned against the car and lit a cigarette, then dropped it and stepped on it, and tried to think.

In the trunk I found a piece of old clothesline that was all chewed up; I'd used it for a tow job back in Florida. That made me think of Betty again.

I fastened the three suitcases together, picked up the shovel, and dragged the suitcases behind me. It was pure hell just getting far enough away from the road. But once I got into the glen, it was better. The snow was smooth, and I just dragged the suitcases along, all the time thinking, the ground's going to be harder than rock, McCall.

Finally I stopped. A trickle of water ran in the glen. I knew if I could get to above the rock, maybe the ground world be fairly soft near the water.

I started out again. I was on ice most of the time. My feet slipped, and it was a pure bitch. At last I got on the rock, and hauled the suitcases and the shovel up, till I was on a small stretch of level ground. I couldn't go any farther, or I wouldn't have the strength to dig. I tried to get close to the water, but it was all frozen up there. The wind was blowing tight and cold.

I sank the shovel into the ground. It was hard, but it chipped away, and before I knew it, I was going good. It surprised the hell out of me. I kept working, and the hole enlarged rapidly. I didn't stop for anything. I began to sweat, but the physical labor was good. Somehow, it made me forget. It cleared my head and took away some of the anxiety.

I kept right on digging even when I figured the hole was large enough. I didn't think anything for a long time, just dug. And then it began to take me back. I went back in a flash to some time in my childhood out in Washington state, just digging. I couldn't remember what it was, or anything, but I remembered digging. It was so similar, somehow. And I felt relieved, because my mind was 'way back some place where it had been good. Certainly, it must have been winter.

I stopped.

It had been winter, all right. We had lived on a little farm, not far from the Canadian border. I remembered, all right. I'd been helping to dig my mother's grave.

I jammed the suitcases into the hole, covered them, and stomped it fast and tight. Then I scraped some snow over the ground, all the time remembering. There was a kind of rage inside me. It was as if I buried my mother all over again, with the suitcases. It was so damned long ago I couldn't even remember why she hadn't been buried in a cemetery.

I walked away from there. Away from the past, too.

When I reached the car, I heaved the shovel into a ditch across the road. I looked at it, lying there. I went over and got it and carried it back and put it in the trunk of the car. Because somebody would miss it at the Shroeder place. And somebody would find it. And then they would find the goddamned clothes.

Then they would crawl down the black hole and find Elmer Nash. They always did. Somebody always saw you. They always found everything. I knew they would. But I had to go through with it.

I headed for town.

Betty was waiting. It was a rambling, large, very modern motel—real tourist bait. She had a plush room.

At the door, she said, "I didn't think you'd show, Ken."

I grinned and said, "Old man surprise."

Chapter 8

She sure as hell wasn't smiling.

"Got here as soon as I could," I said.

She closed the door behind me, and it was like stepping into another world. A world I was familiar with. I stood there for a moment, and couldn't figure it, then I realized I was back in a normal place, where people were just people. My kind of people. It was damned strange.

"What's the matter, Ken?"

She was leaning against the door. She was all dolled up, and really looked great. She came back to me, and it was the way it had always been with her, and with all the others, down the road of my life.

It was in the way she stood there, and in the way I felt about it. It was in all the clean shining modern touristy phoniness, and it felt good. Every bit of it felt grand.

"Why are you looking at me like that, Ken?"

"You look nice," I said. "You really look good to me, Betty."

I swear to god, she blushed.

She had on this shining green dress; it was iridescent, and it clung to her shape very softly. You knew it would be soft against your hands, and that it would slither against her body, that she would slither around inside it when you took hold of her. Her hair was brushed to a coppery sheen, and her lips were plump and red, a very dark red, to go with her hair, and the smile was in her eyes. She wore tiny gold earrings, and a gold snake bracelet on her right forearm, and a gold chain around her waist, making her waist very slim, which it was, anyway. The neck of her dress was a slit, clear to her waist, and her breasts thrust smoothly, and you knew there was very little under that dress except glorious woman. She wore sheer black nylons, and tiny black pumps with plastic toes. She looked wonderful.

"You keep staring at me. Why?"

"I want to. I like it. You look wonderful."

"You hit me. Why did you hit me?"

"I'm sorry. I mean it." I took a step toward her.

"We going out?"

"No."

"Well, then, give me your coat."

I took off my coat and threw it over a chair. Then I stepped up to her and took her in my arms, conscious of the cleanliness of the motel room, and then very conscious of her. The dress slithered just like I'd figured, and I felt her all over, sliding my hands up and down and all around, feeling how it slithered, and she gave a little moan and began to cry.

She shoved me away.

I walked into the bathroom, washed my hands and face, dried and stared at myself in the cabinet mirror. I looked okay, and I felt okay. I straightened my tie, went back and looked at her room again.

She hadn't moved. She wasn't crying. She was standing there, watching me, soberly.

"Ken," she said. "I don't—"

"How's about a drink."

She practically ran. She bounced across the room, and fixed two whiskies over rocks and handed me one.

"Nice room."

"I think so," she said, sipping. The ice clinked. I remembered the ice in the glen. I remembered the ice in the Polaroid snapshot of Justine. I drank the drink straight down, went over and filled the glass to the brim and drank that, and filled it again and drank half.

There was just some very dim, pinkish, indirect lighting up around the walls of the room. I put the drink down and went over to her and started feeling her again. It was marvelous how that dress felt, and how she felt through it. She began to squirm.

"I'll spill my drink."

I took her drink and put it on the table.

I held her close and began nuzzling her ear. I said, "I've got something cooking, Betty—something big. I couldn't help what happened. You shouldn't have come here, you know."

"I know," she said.

She didn't know what she was saying. I could tell. She wasn't listening, or anything. I had her skirt pulled up and I put my hands on her. She was naked underneath, just a silky slip, and the bare flesh of her.

"I'm hot—I'm hot," she said.

She began to move against me. I put my knee between her legs and she opened them, moving against me.

"Oh, Ken—Ken," she said. "Oh, Ken, honey—"

I wheeled her around and moved her back toward the big bed. She fell on her back on the bed and pulled me with her. She wriggled up on the bed a little, reached down and yanked her dress up to her neck. Her eyes slitted, and she was grabbing far me.

"Oh, honey—I've been going crazy. I was afraid to hope—it just—hurry! Honey! I never—!"

Well, right then was when it all went to hell.

The whole god-damned world just shuddered and heaved right over my head, with Nanette and the old man, and Elmer Nash, and the clothes, and the snapshots, and the music, and Montgomery, and everything else. And I saw Elmer Nash lying in the road with his broken face, and the ribs sticking out and the violent snow.

"Ken—Ken!"

And then it was just Justine and the money. Like that. I couldn't explain it, not ever.

"Ken, honey!" She kept grabbing at me. She was violent, savage.

Just Justine. Justine and that money. I could only see Justine. It was as if Justine stood by my shoulder, watching, waiting. I could see her plain as hell—the beautiful thick wealth of hair and the wonderful small wonderfulness of her.

I stood by the edge of the bed, staring down at Betty Flanagan. Just staring down at her that way. She tore at her dress, gasping—wriggling out of her dress and slip, there on the bed, till she was nude, with only her sheer black stockings and the black garter belt on, lying there, utterly wild and abandoned, still clutching at me, and grabbing, and saying, "Ken—Ken, honey—" only with a kind of startled expression on her face, and something almost like fear in her voice.

I stood there and zipped up my pants and fastened my belt. Then, sitting up on the bed, she grabbed me. I put the heel of my hand on her forehead and gave her a shove. She sprawled back on the bed.

"Easy," I said. "Just take it easy, will you?"

She lay there, watching me. I turned and went over to the door, then came back, and stared at her and lit a cigarette and blew smoke at her, and stared at her some more. She was beautiful.

The trouble was Justine, and the money, and Killer McCall. That was it. Killer McCall. Sure.

I reached into my jacket pocket and brought out the envelope with the two thousand dollars in it. I took the money out of the envelope. She watched me all the time. I fanned the money like a deck of cards; all in one-hundred-dollar bills.

I threw the two thousand dollars down at Betty. The money fluttered and flopped on her bare body, falling on her breasts and belly and thighs.

"What's all this?"

"You recovering? It's yours. I told you I had something. I'm sorry about right now, how it was, but I've got a lot on my mind."

She picked and plucked at the money. It looked like more than it was. It looked like a lot to her. She might have a little money, but it was damned little, I was sure of that.

She sat up on the bed again, pushing her hair out of her face with one hand, plucking at the money with the other. She sniffed it, and rubbed it between her fingers.

"It's real. It's yours."

She turned and stared at me with a fistful of the money. "Mine? I don't understand."

I talked off the top of my head. "You go back to Miami," I said. "Tonight, if you can. I'll be in touch. Better yet, you go down to Key West, to the same place we stayed. Then I'll know just how to contact you, see? And you wait. It won't be long, and we'll be together again."

"But—Ken? Tell me what it's all about."

"I can't."

"Please, Ken." She came to her knees, still holding a handful of the money. "Ken"—eagerly—"tell me what it's all about."

"No," I yelled it at her. "I can't tell you!"

She sat back and turned her face away.

I looked at my feet. One of the hundred-dollar bills was on the floor by my right foot.

I picked it up and put it in my pocket. It made me feel good. Then I came around and sat on the bed, took hold of her ankle, pulled her over till she was seated beside me. She had hundred-dollar bills stuck between her legs, and plastered to her belly, and everything.

I put my arm around her, and felt of her left breast, and gave her a kiss. I mean, she meant nothing to me—nothing at all. All I could think about was Justine. It was the god-damnedest thing I'd ever experienced. I wanted to get back to Justine. She was all that mattered.

"Will you do as I say, Betty?"

She hunched her shoulders, holding some of the money, plucking at it in her lap. She looked down at the money.

"C'mon, Betty. Please? Do as I ask? It means everything to us. I can't possibly swing this thing with you around. Just knowing you're around upsets me. Can't you understand? Please, Betty—try to understand." I talked softly, and directly.

"Will you, Betty?"

She was pouting. "You love me?" she said.

"Yes. You know I do. It won't take me long," I said. "We'll be together in no time, and we'll have plenty of money."

"Money," she said.

"What's wrong with money?"

"Nothing's wrong with money."

"Well, then?"

"You don't really love me."

"Certainly I love you."

"If you loved me—"

Well. She looked at me with her mouth half open, and money stuck all over her, and her eyes half-lidded that way. I held her tight, and closed my eyes and thought of Justine. I rolled her over on the bed and laid her.

"Now do you believe me?"

"Yes."

"You feel better?"

"You're wonderful."

I peeled a hundred-dollar bill off my chest, and stuck it on her left nipple. She began to laugh. She hugged me and rolled on me and off me, and laughed. Then jumped off the bed and bounced lustily over and got our glasses, refreshed them, and brought them back. Some of her heat was drying and the hundred-dollar bills fluttered around her like leaves.

She handed me my drink and flopped beside me. I had to get out of there.

"Will you stay all night?"

"I can't. Not possibly. I'd love to, Betty—you know how much I want to be with you. But I can't. Besides, I won't feel right till you're back in Florida."

She sipped at her drink.

"Try to go tonight, huh?"

"Okay."

"Listen, I've got to move. I was supposed to meet a guy. It was part of the deal."

She nodded, sipping and smiling. "Okay."

I kissed her quickly. "Better get dressed," I said.

"Okay."

Chapter 9

It was snowing a little harder. I drove as fast as I dared—I drove faster than I dared. Too fast. I hit the ridge road, and it seemed as if I were crawling.

It had to happen tonight. Whatever it was, it had to happen tonight. It was still very early. I checked the time—not even eight o'clock yet. It seemed like midnight. I needed a drink badly, but I needed Justine more than anything.

I was about a quarter of a mile from the Shroeder place when I saw the car loom up in front of me. It was parked diagonally across the road. I slammed on the brakes. The convertible fish-tailed on the humped, iced macadam. I somehow kept it under control. I saw a man standing in the wash of my headlights. The convertible kept sliding, and slid slowly to a stop about five feet from the car.

Somehow it reminded me of how this very same convertible had slid down the dirt road after striking Elmer Nash. With Justine at the wheel.

The car was a big sedan, shining in the steady, light snowfall, headlights tunneling the darkness into snow and pine trees.

I got out. "What's up?"

"McCall?" It was Montgomery. He strode toward me and stopped, and stood there.

"What the hell do you want?"

"You're not going back there. I mean it, McCall. I didn't want any scene at the house. Nanette is bad enough as it is. So I've been waiting. She said you went downtown some place. Where've you been? I knew you'd be back soon. You can't stay away, can you?"

He wore a hat, and a heavy overcoat with the collar turned up. He wore leather mittens.

I didn't say anything. I turned and started to get back in the car. He nailed me.

He grabbed my shoulder and hauled me around and swung at me. We both slipped and sat down hard on the iced macadam. We looked at each other.

"You son of a bitch!" he said. "You're not going back there."

"What's in this for you?"

"Nothing. I'm just telling you. I'm her friend, and—by God, you're not going back there!"

He got to his knees and tried to leap at me, and slipped and fell flat on his face. I got up slowly and started for the convertible again. He came at me in a kind of crazy, slipping, oggle-eyed rush, with the headlights from the convertible playing on him and the snow swirling around. He slipped again, just as he reached me, and fell sprawling into my legs and we both went down. The road was a sheet of ice.

We tangled and fought, and rolled against the car. He was kind of sobbing out loud, and cursing at the same time, and he had these thick mittens on, so he couldn't hurt me at all. And his overcoat was so thick I couldn't hurt him, either. It was like kids, wrestling in the snow, all fury and gasps and flying arms and hollers, with nothing really happening. I couldn't figure him.

"I'm going to call in the police," he said. "I mean it, McCall. I told Nanette I would. And this time I'm going to."

He swung a hell of a one and caught me on the shoulder, then slipped and slid backward right off the road into the ditch. He sat there and looked stupid and shocked for a minute, then tried to get up, scrabbling at the snow. But he kept slipping back into the ditch.

He'd hurt me a little and I was mad. I managed to get up and ran crazily at him, and felt myself falling as I dove at him. I hit him.

I hit him smack in the face with the top of my head. It stunned me. I lay there in the snow, looking at the sky. Then I rolled over and looked at him. He was out cold.

I got up and carefully walked over to his car. It was headed toward the ditch at an angle. I put it in neutral, released the hand brake, and started to push it. But it rolled off the road into the ditch, plowing into the snow. Both headlights were buried, but they kind of haloed around the fenders in the snow.

He still lay there in the snow.

I walked very carefully back to the convertible, got under the wheel, very carefully started it up, very carefully turned the wheel and straightened the car and went on down the road.

The anxiousness was all through me.

I parked out front and went inside the house. It was quiet as hell. No sounds at all, just the wind outside, rising, blowing through the trees and battering the sides of the house. The snow had let up suddenly. Only a few sparse flakes drifted on the cold, dark wind.

"Justine?" I called her name softly.

No answer.

I went into the big front room. The fire in the fireplace blazed, throwing wild shadows across the walls and the big, beamed ceiling, playing across the draperies. I headed out into the hall and turned toward the stairs.

I called for Nanette this time. Still nothing.

The house was strange. The night was strange, with the wind and the mountains out there. On the first landing I paused by a large window and looked outside. You could see the night howling through the mountains, and the snow sides convulsing through limber limbs of trees, and the inky, starlit sky. I laid my palm against the cold windowpane, and felt the cold sharply. Standing slightly away from the window, the pane was jet black. You had to press your face against the pane and cup your hands to really see out there.

Looking out, at the corner of the house, I saw the garage lights were still on, faintly illuminating the snow. But there was nothing out there. Just the wind-filled empty blackness of the night, like in that old poem, where it's a black vacuum, but the wind blows and blows.

I went on up the stairs. A dim lamp burned by the couch on the landing, and streaks of light glowed across the ebony liquor cabinet and the swollen belly of the Buddha, glittering on bottles and glasses.

I walked soundlessly on the thick carpet to the hall that led toward Justine's room. In a way, it was good to be here. In another way, it was evil as all hell. It was quiet. I felt alone. I turned down the hall.

For the first time, then, I realized music was playing. It was very soft. So soft you almost had to strain to hear it. The wailing of a tenor sax, nothing else; just that sax, beetling like lazy black wings in and out and up and down.

I reached Justine's door, rapped lightly. Nothing. I tried the knob. It worked.

The door opened, and I stepped inside. Blue light shone from the rocks and moss under the oak tree, shining up into the tree, so the leaves appeared to be silvery and white and bluish, and the music sifted among the leaves.

I stood there for a moment. It felt cold in the room. The leaves seemed to move faintly. I glanced up and saw the night sky and the bright stars through the skylight. A cloud like spun white spiraled across the sky. The music soared, the sax wild now, momentarily insane with beauty.

I noticed the skylight was opened a crack, which accounted for the chilly sensation.

I went back into the hall and closed the door and walked quickly to the outside landing again. I started toward my room, then paused. I heard something in Nanette's room.

It was Justine, giggling.

She stood by Nanette's bed.

The room was done in pink. The entire room was a pink nest of curls and curlicues and ribbons and bows and pillows and tufts and wafts and wifts. The rugs were pink on the gleaming hardwood floors. The wallpaper was pink with pink designs and the ceiling was pink polka dots and silver-pink shadows. The big mirror on the dressing table was pink-tinged. It was a very pink room.

Justine giggled.

Nanette lay sprawled on an enormous pink bed. Even the wooden parts of the bed were pink.

Nanette lay on the bed, arms sprawled out, one leg on the bed, the other hanging to the floor. She wore the same red gown I'd first seen her in when I'd come to the house. She apparently had been undressing. One stocking was still on, the other hanging from her toe to the floor. Her mouth was open, and she breathed heavily. The fingers of her right hand jiggled nervously.

"She's out—she's passed out."

Justine was in black. She had on the tight black Capri pants, and the black turtle-neck sweater. She looked absolutely wonderful to me. Wonderful and evil, and I liked it, every bit of it.

"Drunk?" I said.

"Yes. And a little something more. I put sleeping pills in her last two drinks."

"What?"

"I busted open some capsules, and put it in her drinks." She came running across the room to me, looked up at me, with her hair moving around her shoulders. Her eyes were very excited, but her mouth had that curious sober expression that got me deep and hard.

"Ken, I know how we're going to do it."

It was as if a chill came into the room, from nowhere. I felt it on my back. It was pure excitement. The need.

"How?"

"We're going to stuff her with drinks, with sleeping pills in them. Enough to kill her. She's half dead now."

I felt the chill again. I stared at Justine, and wondered how she could act the way she did, and then I began wondering about myself. Then I quit wondering, because it had to be done, and she was right. Tonight was the time.

"Listen," I said. "I saw Montgomery." I told her what happened down the road.

"It's perfect, then."

I walked over to Nanette and looked down at her, then away. Justine was watching me.

"You don't have to worry," she said. "I'll do it."

"How'll you get it down her?"

"I'll get it down her. She's still half awake, lying there. I'll bet she even hears us. Watch her fingers. See them move? But she can't do anything, and she knows she's going to die and we're going to have all that money."

She spoke softly, coming toward the bed.

"You hear that, Nanette? Damn you," she said. "We're going to kill you. And you can't do a damned thing about it." She leaned close to Nanette's face and said, "We're going to kill you and take all your money, Aunt Nanette. Aunt

Nanette—you hear me?"

She started to shake Nanette, and I felt something in the room. I turned and the old man stood there. He was watching us.

Justine hadn't seen him.

"...going to get rid of you, Aunt Nanette."

"Wait," I said.

The old man's eyes were big and round and very wise. Justine turned and saw him and clamped one hand to her mouth.

"Jack," she said through her fingers.

The old man still wore the blue serge suit. He rapped the cane hard against the floor, just once, turned, and shuffled crazily out the door. I went for him fast, but the door slammed, and a key grated.

He stood outside the door and yelled in a quavering voice. "I'll stop you, Carl! By God, you won't do it—by God, son—I'm calling the police."

"Get him," Justine said. "Get him, Ken."

I fought with the door, trying to open it.

"He's locked the door."

I glanced at Justine.

"You've got to stop him."

And right then was when I knew everything had to stop. I had to stop the old man, and I had to stop Justine, and I had to stop myself. Everything had to stop. I realized I was drunk, and going along with murder.

I felt half crazed. I yanked and twisted at the door. I felt a savage helplessness, and I could still hear the old man's quavering voice.

"Ken. Through that closet."

She pointed to a closet door.

"It leads into another room. You can go through that way."

I ran for the door.

Chapter 10

Well, the Devil is an old man, too.

He's anybody.

I shot through that closet into another room, and clawed my way through shadowed darkness and starlight toward the outline of a door. I heard Justine behind me. I smashed into a chair and made the door, flung it open and ran out into the hall.

"Ken—Ken—get him—"

I reached the top of the landing, and saw him down there. He was just taking off from the foot of the stairs into the hall. I ran down the stairs as if they'd suddenly become level ground. I came around the landing, past the black window, and headed straight down, running like hell.

I didn't think. I was too scared for that. I just ran. I had to catch him.

I yelled it. "Jack Shroeder!"

He didn't stop. He kept going. He was in the big front room. I made the hall, slid and damned near fell, then raced for the room after him.

"Police!"

He was yelling a lot of stuff, but that was the only word I caught.

I came through the archway and he was already over by the fireplace mantel. He was a little short. He was reaching up, clawing for the phone, craning his neck back at me. There was a roaring fire in the fireplace.

"Stop," I said. "Wait."

His hand missed the phone by a mile. It snagged one of the kerosene lamps and it fell, and he caught another and that fell, and he kept clawing and another fell and they all crashed and broke around his feet and oil splashed and he was a sheet of flame. Flames roared into the room, and he screamed. He clawed wildly and more lamps fell. His cane was on fire. He flamed like a flare. He clawed every lamp off the mantel, clawing in flames for the telephone. The lamps shattered on the stone hearth. Kerosene splashed and ate lazily across the room, and he turned screaming and started to run in circles.

"Don't touch him!" Justine said.

I tried to get at him. The old man screamed and screamed. I couldn't touch him. I tried to run at him, thinking maybe I could knock him down and save him that way. But he was too hot. He burned and crackled and he ran from me with a sudden childlike agility, as if all the stamina of his youth had returned.

The room was already burning. Draperies were going up. The rug flamed, furniture blazed. Jack Shroeder ran for the archway and collapsed.

Justine had hold of my arm. She was saying something, but I didn't know what. I grabbed at a drape that hadn't caught fire. The heat blasted at me, and I could hear it start to roar.

"Don't!"

I threw the drape over the old man, and fell on it, trying to smother the flames. But the cloth caught fire in a savage burst. It combusted right in my face.

I leaped back, and ran for the hallway. Justine was with me. I stood there and watched him burn. He danced, lying on the floor, with the flaming ember of the cane in his flaming hand, his face on fire, his entire body swathed in yellow fire, scrabbling on the floor, yelling, and then he stopped.

"The money, the money," Justine was saying. "Quick. Upstairs."

And I knew. Yes, the money. This was it. From then on, I took over.

I had to get the money. And there was damned little time. That big room was roaring like a furnace, and fingers of fire seethed into the hall.

She was already halfway up the stairs. I caught up with her.

"We've got to drag Nanette to the stairs," I said. "It's got to be that way."

"Why?"

"So it'll look as if she tried to get down—heard the fire, or something—this whole place is going up. Where's the money?"

We raced up the stairs, and into Nanette's room. Justine went under the bed and came up with a shiny black steel suitcase.

Four hundred thousand dollars.

"This is it," she said. "Always kept it right under her bed. A real nut."

"Get going," I said. "Run for my car. It's out front."

"This is too heavy for me."

"Run."

"But I've got to get some things of Daddy's—"

"Get the hell outside!"

She started toward the bedroom door, lugging the suitcase. I could hear the fire roaring. I got to thinking, we won't make it, McCall. This place is old. There's a big wind outside. It'll go up like a shingle.

Then I was dragging Nanette toward the stair landing. I got her to the head of the stairs.

"Ken—hurry—the hall's burning!"

I didn't know what the hell to do. The whole world had gone mad. I picked Nanette up and got her half over my shoulder, and started running down the stairs, and I knew I was going to save her, and I tripped and she went flying.

She went straight down the stairwell and landed in the side hall, kind of on the back of her shoulders.

I was down there beside her before I knew it. The place was burning like crazy now. Flames roared, searing the walls. It began to stink with the heat, and bellows of smoke rolled yellow and thick and choking.

"Nanette!"

She was dead. I started to pick her up again, but she was dead. Her head hung at a crazy angle. Her neck was broken. It was a hell of a thing.

I got up from my knees, and ran.

I caught Justine. She was trying to make it for the front door, which was out of the question now. Sheets of white flame licked like huge tongues across the ceilings and up the walls, and the oil paintings burned, spitting and flaming.

I grabbed the suitcase of money, and Justine's wrist, and yanked her down the side hall. We stumbled running out through the kitchen, and into the back yard.

"The car," I said. "As fast as you can run."

"What'll we do, Ken?"

"Just get to the car."

We came around front. The fire was through the walls now, and in the windows, like madmen with torches. The sky was clear, there was no snow, and the wind was strong. It was bitter cold.

We reached the convertible. I tossed the big steel valise in the back seat, got Justine in and slammed her door. I raced around and slid under the wheel. Then I took one last look.

You could hear it. It was almost human, and it was a lot like distant guns. The whole place would explode in a while. I started the engine. We got out of there fast.

I knew exactly what we had to do.

We hit the macadam road, and I turned left.

"Ken—where you going?"

"First, to your mother's." I tried to explain. "We'll leave the suitcase at your mother's. Okay?"

"Yes—yes."

"Then we're going into Albuquerque. We're going to a movie."

"We can't come back on this road, Ken. And we can't possibly make it through the Sandias in wintertime. I'm telling you. We can't."

"I've driven through the mountains once, long ago. I can do it again. We've got to do it."

"We can't make it. Not at night—not in the winter."

"We've got to."

I had the convertible at seventy and I just held it there, ice or no ice. It was a race with time. We had to be long gone before the fire trucks got up here in the mountains. The way the roads were, it would take them some time, and they had a long way to come.

"You'll have to sneak the suitcase into your mother's house, somehow."

"She won't say anything. That much is perfect."

She shut up. She didn't say anything more. I turned on the radio, got some music and let it blast. It helped. It drowned some of the other out. But then Justine reached over and shut it off.

She slid across the seat and huddled against me.

"Nanette was dead?" she said.

"Yes."

"And Jack's dead."

"Yes."

"We've got her money," she said.

"Yes. All we've got to do is get to town the back way, and then come home. You see?"

"We can never make it, Ken."

I found the back road to the adobe village.

I could smell smoke on my clothes, but I wasn't burned. I kept seeing that old man burning, and running and yelling. Suddenly I stopped the car, got out and ran for the ditch, sliding on the snow. I was sick. Justine didn't get out or anything. I was very sick in the snow. The night was all around me.

I came back to the car, and drove fast again. She didn't say anything. I kept thinking about that old man running and flaming, and then the way Nanette had looked with her neck broken, and I knew she was burning now. And I thought of Elmer Nash down in the dark old mine.

"We're nearly there," Justine said.

We came down the incline and around the curve, and I slid to a halt in front of the dark adobe house.

"I'd better go in," Justine said.

"All right. But hurry—run!"

She looked at me soberly, just staring at me for a moment. Then she opened her door. I got the suitcase and handed it to her. She dragged it toward the front door of the adobe house.

"Okay," she said, coming back. She jumped into the car and slammed the door. "It's all set."

She snuggled over against me. "Daddy," she said softly.

"How can I short-cut back to the road?"

She showed me. I turned left after a couple of minutes of fast driving, and we came onto the main road again.

We nosed north toward Santa Fe. I knew how rough it was going to be, and I knew we might not make it. But it was the only chance we had.

For a little while, it wasn't bad. Then we began to see signs.
PROCEED AT YOUR OWN RISK!
BEWARE FALLING ROCKS!
ROAD OUT!
I simply ignored them. I had to.

We went through forest, and the roads were bad, but somebody else had been through. We went up and up and up, and then we were on the bad part. Nobody had been on these roads. The cliffs sledged up toward the sky on one side, and straight down to darkness on the other. But the drifts hadn't piled up. It was too windy up here. Just ice and snow and rocks. I drove as fast as I could, but that wasn't too damned fast, and we had a long way to go. I was driving against time. And they were chasing me, all right. I could feel them....

The road was narrow. It was just a gouge in the mountain side, falling off to nothing. It went up and up, and around the sides of peaks, with the edge off to nothingness. Then it began to swing down, and I just said to hell with everything, and drove. Neither of us spoke.

She sat tight up against me and every once in a while, I felt her tense, and tremble.

Somehow we made it.

By the time we reached the turnoff, near Bernalillo, and headed back toward Albuquerque on Route 85, I was soaked with sweat and still trembling from what we went through. Justine hadn't moved.

This highway was clear. I put the pedal to the floor and held it there. It was starting to snow again. The sweat began to cool and dry, and I felt the cold. But the trembling didn't stop.

I turned and got on Fourth Street, and we came roaring into town.

It was getting late.

My teeth were clamped together and my jaws ached. The muscles in my arms ached. But somehow, seeing the lights and getting into town helped. There was a feeling of safety. It was false, but it was there. Buildings and people and streets and cars. It changed how I felt.

We grabbed a parking place on Gold across from the courthouse. Wind and snow came down. I switched off the ignition.

"Come on. Let's go."

"I don't even have a coat."

"Oh, God."

This was bad. She had to have a coat. I still wore mine. But if she didn't have a coat, it would look like hell. I couldn't even think.

She began to see how she had to have a coat, too.

"What'll we do, Ken? What'll we do?"

It was the first time I'd ever seen her rattled.

"We'll find a coat, that's what we'll do. Come on," I said.

We got out of the car. Every time she spoke, I told her to be quiet, so I could think. We headed over to Central and up to the movie.

"Now," I said. "Listen. We're going in there. You go first, then I'll come in. You wait inside, in the dark. No. You go directly to the women's rest room, see? It's up to you. You've got to get a coat. Some woman'll take her coat off. They must have to." I had her by the shoulders, right there on the Avenue, shaking her. "Do they take their coats off?"

She was nodding and trying to make it look all right.

I quit shaking her. All I could think was, we've got to go back to that house, and she's got to have a coat. Else they'll suspect. As if they wouldn't suspect. But maybe they wouldn't.

"All right," I said. "Go."

She started toward the bright marquee. She stopped. She turned.

"I haven't any money."

Christ. I remembered. All I had was some small change, and—no, I didn't even have that. I just had a hundred-dollar bill. That's all I had.

"You've got to wait here." I explained it to her. "I'll get change in a bar some place."

So far nobody had paid any attention to us, but there were plenty of people on the street. We huddled in the doorway of a jewelry shop. She was cold, I could tell, but she was a knockout to see on a winter's night, all in black with that hair foaming around her shoulders. She just kept nodding like a little girl, looking up and down the street.

"All right, Ken. Hurry!"

So I cut across the street toward the first bar I spotted. I went inside. It was a dark place and it was packed, so that helped. I acted a little drunk, and ordered a double rye, and paid with the hundred. I didn't give a damn what he did. It would have been perfectly all right with me if he shortchanged me. He didn't. He looked at the bill, then at me. He shrugged, and gave me the change.

I gulped the drink, and left fast.

He would remember that one-hundred-dollar bill.

I cut back over to the jewelry store. Justine was gone. I had a momentary panic, then spotted her over by the theater. I motioned to her. She came back, and I handed her a wad of money.

"See you inside. Get that coat."

She went. I waited. Then I went over and bought a ticket, trying to hide my face as best I could, and went inside. I waited in the darkness and avoided the usher.

I got over by the women's lounge. There was no sign of her. The audience laughed now and then. I didn't give a damn what picture was on. The panic was in me bad now.

I waited and waited, and she didn't come. I waited for half an hour. Still she didn't come.

I was sweating again. And shaking. I couldn't stop how I felt. Finally I started toward the women's lounge, planning to walk right on in. Just as I reached the door, it swung open and she came out with a coat over her arm.

"I got the coat."

"Let's go sit."

We went and found a seat and huddled together.

"It's a nice coat," she said.

"Great."

"It's black. It fits, too. I tried it on. Maybe we'd better get out of here. They might watch for it."

"Study the picture," I said. "We've got to leave when it ends, and it's going to end any time." We huddled together and I whispered close to her ear. "We've got to know what the movie's about, see? We came here over an hour ago. It's got to be that way."

"All right, Ken."

I caught the story line, finally. And the feature ended.

"Now we go."

"We just got here. I'm not really warm yet."

"We go, anyway. We drive home now."

We got in the aisle. A couple of ushers were flashing flashlights at the people who were leaving. It was the coat. I knew damned well it was the coat.

"Give me the coat," I said.

I took it and as we pressed up the aisle, I threaded it around my middle, under my topcoat, and buttoned my coat over it. Stout fellow, that McCall.

We got out, and I pulled her to the right. I laughed and talked loudly about the picture. People stared. I wanted them to stare.

We went up the street, and turned right. I gave her the coat and she put it on fast as she scuffed along.

"Okay," I said. "We go back to Central now, and take a walk, and drop in at a bar."

"That's the best news yet."

Suddenly it was nothing. I mean, it was what it was. We came back onto the main street, and crossed, and started down along the sidewalk, and it was all okay. We'd been to the movie, and we were going to stop and have a drink before going home.

"Relax," I said.

"I am, Ken."

"How you feel?"

"I feel fine."

We walked along.

We went into a bar and sat in a booth. It was warm and cozy and people laughed, and joked, and drank. We did, too.

"Fun, isn't it?" she said.

"Yeah."

I drank a lot. Everybody was laughing. We laughed.

For me, you could say it was the last time.

Chapter 11

The place was a black shambles. What was left.

Little spouts of smoke.

Fire trucks. Police cruisers. People. Cars. The area was crowded. It had been a terrific fire, got completely out of control. The place had burned to the ground.

I'd coached Justine. She acted perfect.

We showed all the necessary shock, and Justine cried fine. Then, after she cried, she put on a scene. She flipped. She brought it out plain, and made it loud, and everybody heard her. We had decided it was the only way.

They took her to one of the three ambulances that had come up, put her inside, and gave her a sedative.

She was a little girl. Carl Shroeder was her father. "Daddy," she said.

But that wasn't all she said. She started to rave, and she really tore her hair. It was about the money. It was her money now. She wanted everybody to know it. She made it loud. She said she'd kept quiet as long as she was going to, now that she couldn't hurt anybody.

They got her calm. She talked, but she was calm, and she was a terrific actor. She was so terrific it frightened me.

It was the sheriff who finally nailed me and started questioning. Most of it had been haphazard up till then.

"Mr. McCall?"

"Yes."

"I'm Sheriff Watkins. Walt Watkins. This is a terrible thing."

"Yes."

He was all bundled up, with a Stetson hat, and boots shining, and a sheepskin coat, with his gun belt and holster and forty-five right outside, where you couldn't miss it, and his bright, gleaming badge outside, too, on the sheepskin coat.

He was a big man, with a florid face, and he smiled when he talked. He smiled all the time. It was some kind of nervous affliction, but it raised hell with me.

The eyes, and the smile. Showing the teeth, you know.

We stood by his car, in the cold wind and snow, and stared at the blackened remains of the house. There were crowds of people who had driven up from town. They were still using the hoses, playing water on the smoking embers.

"You knew the Shroeders?"

"That's right, yes. This is awful. It's terrible. We went to a movie, you know. Justine and I."

"Oh."

"Christ, it's awful."

"This—uh, Justine. Says she's Carl Shroeder's daughter. Claims she has a paper to prove it."

I nodded. "It's true, all right."

He shook his head. "I knew Carl. He was a son of a bitch, for sure."

I didn't say anything.

"You been here long?"

"No. Only a few days." I explained all about how Carl Shroeder had written me, and asked me to come and comfort Nanette. It was the thing I worried about most, but it had to be brought out into the open. "Devlin Montgomery can tell you all about that," I said, feeling my throat constrict. Because Montgomery could raise absolute hell, and blow the whole thing.

"Monty. I know him. Knew his father, too."

"That so?"

I was looking over Sheriff Watkins' shoulder toward the house. I looked straight into Montgomery's eyes. He stood back there by a group of people, watching me. He just watched me. He wasn't wearing a hat, and he looked half frozen. His face was pale in the lights that were trained on the area.

Watkins hitched at his belt, then lifted his Stetson, and set it straight. Really straight. He kept on smiling with his teeth.

"McCall?"

"Yes?"

"What's with you and this girl—this Justine?"

"How do you mean?"

He gave a snort through his nose, glanced over toward the ambulance.

"Anybody with half an eye—" he said.

"Half an eye, what?" I said.

"Okay, then, McCall. It's okay. You were at a movie, right?"

"That's right."

"Well, stick around, anyway. There'll be an inquest, I think." He smiled brightly.

"You found bodies?" I asked.

"Yeah."

"What did you find?"

"The old man, and Mrs. Shroeder."

I didn't speak. I stared at the ground, remembering.

"It's plain, all right. We got it pretty well figured already."

"That so?"

He nodded, grinning. I saw Montgomery coming our way, very slowly.

Watching me, all the time. He looked as if somebody'd shot him in the stomach.

"Pretty damned plain," Watkins said, grunting it out. "The old man must've tried to get to the phone. The phone was on the fireplace mantel and he upset an oil lamp. Way we figure, Mrs. Shroeder, now, she was drinking. Could she have been?"

I stared at the ground. "She was drinking," I said. "That's why we went out tonight. I mean, she was pretty bad off. Ever since Carl died."

"We know."

"It's bad, all right." I rubbed a hand over my face, thinking in a bright flash about that steel suitcase, and at the same time my skin crawled because Montgomery kept coming closer and closer, working his way through the packed and soot-blackened snow.

Watkins said, "I've been to the house. Saw those lamps, the way they kept 'em on the mantel. We figure, from what we found, the old man upset a lamp, and set fire to the place. Mrs. Shroeder probably was upstairs. Looks as if she fell. Going to try an autopsy. Not much left, but maybe they'll be able to find out whether she was really loaded."

"Take my word for it," I said. "There was nothing I could do. I tried to make her see reason."

"Yeah. Only thing, we can't figure who the old man was. Known to be around the place, but nobody knew who he was. Not really, I mean. Fishy, you know?"

"Not any more." I told him who the old man was.

Watkins shrugged. "I figured that," he said. "I figured it." He turned and saw Montgomery. "Hey, Monty. Over here."

Montgomery trudged through the packed snow and came up to us. He looked at me, then at Watkins. Montgomery looked sick. I'd never seen a man look so sick.

"Trying to get some facts," Watkins said. "Anything I can get will help."

"I understand," Montgomery said.

Montgomery's coat was burned round the edges, and his shoes were muddy and soaking wet.

Watkins mentioned what I'd told him about the letter from Carl. "That right?" he asked Montgomery.

"Yes. That's quite true," Montgomery said.

Watkins grinned, and scratched his face. "Thanks." He nodded at me. "Stick around for the inquest," he said. "Pretty sure there'll be one. Just to clear things up, you know?"

"Sure."

He walked off, around his car. Justine was out of the ambulance. She stood looking at the house. I didn't know what to do.

"I want to see you," Montgomery said.
"You're looking right at me."
"Take a walk with me."
"I'm pretty busy."
"You'd damned well better!"

He had a point. He didn't even bother to see if I was following, just turned and walked down to the road. I passed Justine, and caught her eye, and shook my head faintly. She got it, and turned away.

I thought I heard Montgomery say, "Bitch," but I couldn't be sure.

I followed him. We walked down the road past lines of cars, with people returning to them now, starting engines, getting ready to go home.

We got to a car. "Get in," Montgomery said.
"I like it out here."
"Get in my car."

I got inside and sat there, waiting. I watched him cross around front, slide under the wheel and slam the door.

"Where's the money, McCall?"

I stared at him.

We sat there for a full minute. He was twisted in the seat, watching me. Now and then, somebody plowed past us, walking and gesturing, talking loud to somebody else. And through all of this, the panic ran like a thin steel wire. I was scared to rock bottom. I wanted to be with Justine, anywhere but here. But I couldn't be with her. It would look bad. It looked bad now. She'd acted all right while I'd been able to hear her. But what was she saying now? Suppose our stories got mixed—and they would. I knew it. Was Watkins questioning her? Certainly he was questioning her. I felt the whole thing crumbling around my head.

I was looking straight at Montgomery and he just went nuts, sitting there. He blew his stack. I'd never seen anything like it. First he began to shake, then he started pounding his hands on the steering wheel, and then he wept. He cursed and shook and wept, and it all came out, choked and garbled.

"That's my money!" He said that over and over. "Mine, you hear? Nanette's and mine!" I felt a strange dark laughter, deep inside.

He was crazy for a while, telling me how he and Nanette had loved each other for a long time, and that ever since I'd come, he'd known what I was here for. He seemed to know a lot about me. He told a lot of things, choking over it. "She couldn't stand that slimy old man—the way Carl had him staying there. She was sick with it—I tell you, she was sick with the whole works. The way Carl acted—the women he'd bring around. And then Justine. She could raise a stink any time she wanted, and we knew she was up to something. And Nanette hated her—hated the sight of her. So we planned it all out. It would be so easy, and not really illegal, or anything—not really." He kept choking, banging the wheel. "Nobody could understand. She had to get away. So we decided to take all the money, and just go—go away some place, and be together—change our names. Nobody'd ever know."

He told it all, because there was nothing to hide from me. He was too sure about me. He was positive about me. He was right about me.

"She had the money right there in the house. I told her not to do that. Good God, I told her over and over. That bitching girl—" He paused a moment, unable to go on. The man was sick and driven. I understood him, but not his insane display of emotion. I guess it could be that way, though. But it was comical, too. Except for what hung over my head. The whole bloody world hung over my head, with knives in their hands.

"McCall! Where'd you hide the money! I'll find it, McCall—where is it?"

"I sure as hell don't know what you're talking about."

"Liar, liar, liar!" He yelled it in a strangled whisper, beating the steering wheel. Then he stopped and swallowed. "Justine. I know it was her. She was getting snotty and wise. Justine and you—" Then he beat the wheel some more. The dark laughter kept coming up from deep inside me. "That Nash. We were going to pay him off—"

"Why?"

"Because he caught on. He was blackmailing us. He knew even before Carl died. He wanted to go to bed with Nanette. But he left a note tonight—I saw it. He didn't take the money, either. He went away. Must've got scared."

I didn't speak. I'd recalled something in my favor, Justine's and mine. I had our ticket stubs from the movie, and they might help. I checked my pocket, and they were there. I'd taken hers when we were seated. A tiny hope. But the usher could have seen us, marked the time when we came in. If he was asked, he might remember.

"You son of a bitch," Montgomery said softly. "You and Justine. I know who she is, Nanette told me." He balled his fist, and whispered it: "McCall—where's that money? I've got to have it—I've got to!"

"I should think, with all this love stuff and everything, you'd be mourning for Nanette."

He choked and swallowed and sat there.

"What about the old man?" I said. "What were you going to do about him?"

"The state would have taken care of him. We weren't worried about Jack Shroeder. My God, he drove us nuts. And we weren't worried about Justine, that bitch. We'd just go. Then Nanette would stop her damned drinking, too, because it was just that house—that awful house, and Carl, and the old man, and Justine—everything. But we wouldn't hurt anybody—we'd just go. What difference?"

"There's a difference now, isn't there."

He beat on the wheel some more.

He said it tightly, softly. "I know you've got the money. They didn't find that steel suitcase. There would've been something left. Of course, nobody knew about it. But I looked—my feet are burned from looking. But I'll keep looking. I'll never stop looking. By Christ, you killed her, didn't you. You killed her and the old man, too."

"Why don't you tell that to the law?"

He paused, breathing hard. He could never tell anything.

"You're crazy as a bedbug," I said. "I'm leaving."

"You can't leave. McCall—where's that money! I've planned. I've got debts. I never wanted to be a stinking lawyer. Just because my fool father—I hate it—I hate it, I tell you. McCall—"

I reached for the door.

He grabbed my coat, gripped it tightly, pleading. "McCall. Have pity. For God's sake. I've got debts, I tell you. I can never pay them."

He could never tell anything, either. He never would. He couldn't blame me for anything, or Justine. If he said anything, he could easily involve himself. If he really spoke up, so could we. He couldn't say a word. And there was Elmer.

I couldn't help myself. I looked at him. "I know where Elmer is," I said. "Would you like him back here now?"

His eyes were big and round and frightened. Elmer knew everything. Elmer could tell everything. Elmer could nail him to the post. The only thing he could never know was that Elmer was in a deep, dark hole. Yes. We had all the cards in the deck, where Montgomery was concerned. I began to feel a bit light with that. It became plainer and plainer to me. There wasn't a damned thing he could do.

But Watkins, all the others—they could do things.

"You heard Justine," I said. "She's claiming the money in the bank—"

"You know damned well it's not in the bank!"

"You heard her. She's next of kin, all that."

"McCall. You know that money was in that steel suitcase, in Nanette's room, under her bed."

"Oh, come off it. You're acting stupid. What money?"

"Four hundred thousand dollars. That's what money. It's everything, too—nothing left—nothing."

"You couldn't touch it anyway, Montgomery. It all goes to Justine. Get it through your head. Anyway, how would she know it was under Nanette's bed?"

He began to scream softly. He kept it up. I began to laugh.

"Why don't you blow your brains out?" I said.

I kept laughing. I opened the door and went outside, still braying to myself.

Well, donkeys bray, too, you know?

They held an inquest. I stayed at the same motel where Betty had been, and I was scared. I was never so scared in my life, because so many things could happen. I sweated and worried and waited, knowing it would end for me. I stayed half crocked most of the time on what was left of that hundred-dollar bill. That was the only money I had.

Just to bring my spirits up, I checked, and sure enough, Betty Flanagan had left for Key West, Florida. That was fine with me. I even phoned her one night, collect, and talked with her, and told her not to worry, that I'd have everything straightened out soon.

She said, "I know you love me now, Ken, darling. I just know it. I'll never forget that last night. Hurry, darling, hurry—it's swell down here. And there's no more seaweed, either."

"Be seeing you, doll. We'll have a real blast."

The inquest was a big zero. A farce. The damnedest thing. They checked, of course, which was routine. I gave Watkins the ticket stubs and he grinned and showed his teeth. But nobody remembered anything. It was mad. The bartender didn't recall that hundred-dollar bill. A patrol cop remembered our car, that was all, parked across from the courthouse. And we were seen drinking in the bar later on, and at the movie. It was smooth.

I just said to hell with everything, and let her rip. I consorted openly with Justine, as it were. What the hell, I was all she had left in anybody's eyes, and I was very kind to comfort her, you know?

She put on a terrific act all over again when it was revealed that Nanette Shroeder had drawn all the money out of the bank. What negotiable stuff was left went to cover bills.

A zero.

There was nothing to point a finger at us.

Montgomery was around, and he was drinking a lot. He looked bad. He tried to talk with me a couple times, but I just walked away. The poor bastard was positive. He knew that money existed, and he wanted it. And there was nothing he could do. Absolutely nothing.

Well, I began to get the hots for Justine all over again, like new. Maybe it all did something to her. I mean, she looked better than ever. And we had the money. And how we laughed at Montgomery and his problem.

"You're so wonderful," she'd say to me.

"You, too."

"You really love me, I know that."

"We love each other, baby."

All I kept thinking was, after a while—after a while, we'll just go away. We'll spend the money. Maybe invest some of it, so we'll always have plenty. No gambling—at least, not too much. Just a ball. A balling time. That's all I thought.

We'll just wait awhile. Then we'll have a ball.

PART THREE

Chapter 1

The fact is, all sorts of fools bray.

You see, four years have gone by now, and I have yet to see that money. The money, or the steel suitcase. It's something, all right.

As I write this, I keep wondering what I'll do next to take up the time. There's so much time. It's a trying problem.

Four years.

Oh, I paint. I try, that is, but the spirit isn't really with it, any more. Something's lacking. Something went out of me four years ago.

I have a room of my own here. There's not much in it, but it's a room of my own. I built it myself. Justine won't let me have a door on it, but it's a place where I can get off by myself.

"I want to always be able to see you," she said. "So I don't want you to put a door on your room. It's all right for you to have a room like that. But a door would trouble Mother, too. You know how she is."

Yes, I know how she is. Doors trouble her. Mother.

That great mountain of sunburned flesh under a never-ending red blanket that is seldom washed. And the black hair.

Of course, Justine's hair is all black now. It took some time to grow out, but it did. After four years, a lot of black hair can grow out.

Mother.

Justine calls me Daddy, of course,

What can you do?

It's mixed up, you might say.

One of the things that bothers me is the smell. It's very strange and you can't escape it. Maybe it's the adobe brick. I'm quite a hand with adobe brick now. As I say, I built this room that I'm writing in. And I built a sort of hen coop for the chickens, out of adobe. The few people around here thought I was crazy—Pedro, and Juan, and Maria, and Carlos, and the rest.

But I've come to like them, in a small and wondrous way. They're very friendly. They want to be helpful. That's the only problem.

I built an outhouse, too. They didn't use one before, you know. It's a sort of throwback situation. You might say we live rather primitively.

Of course, I thought of running. I probably wouldn't have, but I thought of it. Justine said something, though. She just said it once. "You wouldn't ever leave me, would you? Because I'd tell everything if you did. I'd want to die. I wouldn't care."

It was never referred to again. I wouldn't have gone, anyway.

I watch her a lot. You might say I watch her all the time. And she watches me.

"Now, Daddy. You won't let me out of your sight, will you?"

"No, baby. I won't."

Then she giggles. It sounds strange coming from that short fat girl with the oily black hair; most of her talk sounds strange. I guess it just naturally would. She's really very intelligent. It's just the idea, when you see her. I mean, I've seen her for a long time, and I can't get used to it.

Montgomery drives out here every few days. Oh, yes. He parks in the dirt street, in the blinding sunlight, and sits in his car and stares. Sometimes I sit on the front threshold and stare back. He narrows his eyes and watches. He watches Justine. He comes out and just sits there in his car. He keeps hoping, I suppose. He used to speak threateningly. He doesn't say anything any more.

Montgomery's changed a great deal. He spends most of his time cadging drinks down on First Street, in Albuquerque. He doesn't work much, and his car is old.

Sometimes, in my room, I think about Zen, and how it might help me. But nobody could ever get beyond the way Carl understood it, and put it on that blank page in his book. I think I understand that. But it doesn't help. Not really.

And sometimes, I think of Betty. More often than not, I cry when I think of Betty. I can't help it. One of those things. I can remember every wonderful detail of that last meeting at the motel. The luscious, slithery feel of that green dress against her ripe young body. The body that will never get fat and have rich, oily black hair. And I remember the cleanliness of that phony motel room. Phony. Oh, hell, there's no point even in writing it down.

Sometimes I hike over to Golden, and stare at the black mine hole where Elmer lies. His bones, that is. It doesn't do any good.

I didn't know it at the time, but I buried his clothes in a park—a picnic area. Someday somebody will dig up his three suitcases. They won't mean anything.

Justine said, "We'll just have to put the money away, Ken. Maybe later on we can use it. But, you see, they know we haven't any money—I'm not supposed to have any."

So I can't have anything. Not even cigarettes. I manage, what with these friendly people, but it's rough. Let me tell you, it's rough.

She said, "Someday we'll have a ball." Then it got so, after a time, she began worrying. "We've got to use it very sparingly, if at all."

We don't even use it sparingly.

I couldn't change her mind. I knew where it was then, all right. But one night when I got drunk and went to get it, it was gone. I don't know where it is now.

But I watch her. I keep an eye on her. Someday maybe she'll slip. I'll find it. The thought keeps me going, you know.

I found out about the pictures, the Polaroids. Carl took them of her. He had a thing about her being naked on ice. In the summer, he'd put ice in the bathtub. Then she would sit on it for him, and he would take pictures of her, and things.

She has a lot of those pictures. A whole basketful, that she'd kept at her mother's here. I look at them once in a while, for the hell of it. It's something to do.

She forgets. Sometimes she asks me, "Daddy, would you like me to get some ice? I'll bring the camera."

We never get to town. We have no money. Where the hell would she get the film?

I tell her, "No, Justine, baby. Not now."

She likes me to call her Baby.

I just watch her. She's changed a great deal. Someday maybe she'll make a slip. It's got to be around here someplace.

Montgomery's out there again. I just saw him drive up. He's sitting out there, watching. Things are piling up. It's beginning to get me.

What can you do?

THE END

Memory of Passion
By Gil Brewer

"It seems we stood and talked like this before...."

1

The phone rang.

"I'll get it, Louise."

Anyway, his wife was halfway upstairs, on her way to dress for the Wednesday night booze-fest over at the Thomases. Louise had a minor obsession about wanting to answer the phone. It wasn't really compulsive, though.

"Hello?"

"Hello, darling."

He hesitated, frowned. "Who's speaking?"

"You're sweet. You never forget."

"Look. Who is this?"

"All right, darling. I'll play. 'Who is this?'"

Louise lightly snapped her fingers from the stairway. "Bill?" He glanced at her and she lifted long gracefully arched eyebrows in question. He shook his head and motioned her on upstairs. She turned and went up, using both hands to unzip the snug back of the white linen dress she'd worn that afternoon, revealing a smoothly curved bare back, her full blonde hair catching soft highlights from the hall lamp.

The girl on the phone possessed a gentle, lyrical voice.

"I'm sorry," he said. "You have the wrong number."

He started to hang up.

"Bill? Please, cut it out."

He shifted the phone to his other hand.

"Come on, now. Who is this?"

The girl laughed lightly. "I suppose we might blame it on the connection." He sensed she was quite young, whoever she was. And, though you could never go by such things, probably pretty, with a voice like that. It almost seemed... but, no. It was impossible. There were just certain nuances that seemed to bring someone to mind. He did not know who.

"Thinking?" she asked.

He knew he should hang up. It was stupid, just to stand here, like this. He had no idea who it was, and whoever it was, she obviously had the wrong number.

"Okay," he said. "I give up. Who are you?"

"Guess."

For some reason, this didn't irritate him. He had nothing to do but wait for Louise to dress. She was invariably slow. All he had to do was slip on a jacket. He quickly tried to think of all the women he knew, but none sounded like this girl. Yet there was that curious feeling he should know who this was. He thought of Louise's friends; tried to come up with something. No dice. He could hear her breathing faintly at the other end. Of course, there were a couple of practical jokers among their friends. Helen Solby? Helen might… no. The Solbys were in Rochester over the weekend.

"Afraid I'll have to give up."

She laughed again, very lightly, and not at all disturbed. It was the kind of laugh two people shared when they were on intimate terms, and knew exactly what each other was thinking. He was a sensitive person. He got this.

She said, "Shall I hint?"

He glanced toward the stairway, then at the clock on the mantel above the enormous fieldstone fireplace across the living room. 7:45. He had half an hour.

"Okay," he said. "Give me a hint."

Games, yet. Probably those three martinis speaking.

"Remember April?"

"Certainly, I remember April. This is April."

"Oh, Bill. I know it's April. Isn't it always? Well, then—the mailbox—in the rain?"

"What mailbox?"

Her tone softened. "You know." There was a bundle of sex tied up in the way she spoke, no mistaking that.

"I sure don't know," he said.

"Let's skip it. Honey, I miss you so. I mean, even an afternoon away from you. Every minute is hell. And then, when I'm with you—it's just sweet hell, all the time. I love you so damned much. I'm like a fuse burning."

He savored the words and realized she spoke truth. It wasn't froth. For God's sake. Either that, or she was an accomplished actress. Actress? Selma? Selma Williams? No. Selma was over at that crackpot reducing academy on Lake George. Reducing her alcohol intake.

He stared scowling across the room at the predominantly red and yellow oil painting resting on the large display easel. He always kept one painting in the living room on the easel; the one he was currently engaged with; his noncommercial work, his playtime. He carried it to the studio out back each morning, and returned it each night. After that, anybody could have the damned thing… but…. "Bill?" the girl on the phone said. "Please. Say it to me—please. Tonight?"

"I'm going to hang up."

"Eight-thirty, then?"

"Sorry. I've got to hang up."

"Go ahead."

He did.

He stood there. He took out a cigarette, glanced at the stairs again, lit the cigarette and walked slowly across the room toward the painting on the easel. He took a long drag on the cigarette. The painting was coming along damned well. A break from the usual run of commercial stuff, and the post-mortems, as he called them. Damn. Painting pictures for people of their deceased kin from photographs, sometimes from ancient tiny snapshots, had developed into a whale of a business. Paid well, but what a bore; just because he'd done one for a friend. Nobody could ever say that word-of-mouth publicity wasn't the most thorough.

The phone jangled.

He moved over, picked it up, said, "Yes?"

"Bill?"

The girl again. The same soft, gentle voice.

"Okay, honey," he said. "Who are you?"

Her laugh was more a whisper of secret revelation and desire.

"I'm Karen."

"Karen?"

"Yes."

He didn't know any Karen.

"Bill?"

"Yeah." She had his name, but she could have found that in the phone book.

"Eight-thirty? Same place?"

"You have the wrong number. I'm telling you. Sorry, but you'd better check it again."

"Eight-thirty. What would you like me to wear?"

That last was almost an insinuation. Again, for a scant instant, it seemed... somewhere, some time.

"Listen," he said. "Wear whatever you like. Maybe a diamond in your navel? Now, so long."

"So long, darling. See you soon."

He hung up and stood there with his hand on the phone, the cigarette between his lips, smoke curling pale blue-white up across his face. He squinted dark eyes.

High school kids. Pranksters. He'd heard about them pulling similar stunts. Another few martinis and he might have taken her up on it, just to call her bluff. That would be good. Then, he thought, Sure, and probably get stomped, or whatever it was they did to you.

Only, the way she'd spoken.

It had been just as though it was absolutely real.

To her.

The room was large, and expensively furnished, with lots of color, and for deep comfort. The lighting was indirect for the most part; a soft suffusion.

He continued to stand by the phone. Then, suddenly, he turned and headed out through the large archway into the hall and started up the stairs at a half run.

Brother, he thought. Meet me at eight-thirty. I'm Karen, and I love you....

He stopped abruptly. He reached for the polished bannister, gripped it and stood there like stone.

Karen.

A chill spread across his shoulders and his heart began to pound. He heard Lolly, his daughter, nearly eight, now, singing with a nutty children's record in her room. He heard Louise in the bedroom closet, hangers scraping.

Karen.

There had only been one Karen. That was—how long ago? God. April. The mailbox. This was insane, completely insane. He stood there, a tall man, on the thin side, with a shock of black hair touched sparsely with nearly indiscernible gray flecks, straight black eyebrows, deep-set dark eyes, a strong nose and chin. The mouth, right now, was drawn and set. He wore dark trousers, a white shirt, a dark tie. His large hand grasped the stair railing.

Memory poured through him. Again that chill spread through his shoulders.

"In the rain."

What was it? Nineteen thirty-seven? Thirty-eight? Thirty-nine? Say, maybe twenty-two years ago.

He thought of her sometimes. More often than he cared to admit, maybe. But.

He took his hand off the railing, and actually forced a laugh. Turning, he jogged rapidly downstairs, through the hall, and back into the kitchen. He took the bottle of Gordon's Gin, poured some into a glass, added a little water at the sink, and drank it down.

He set the glass beside the sink. There was no light on in the kitchen. He came back through the hall and started upstairs again.

"Eight-thirty."

All right. Forget it. It was nonsense, and he'd always been taken too much with this particular bit of nostalgia anyway. He knew it. Whenever he thought, remembered, strange things happened inside his chest.

Sommers, he thought. This is rotten coincidence. Will you get off it?

He paused on the top landing.

First of all, Karen would be thirty-nine years old, the same as himself. Well, actually, she was three or, four months older than himself. Good God. April, again, her birthday, month, anyway. But that had not been the voice of a thirty-nine-year old woman. It had been the voice of, say, a fifteen-, or sixteenyear-old girl.

The feeling was all through him.

He had to shake it off. He turned to the right along the landing, walking on soft-napped, deep tan carpet. He paused at his daughter's door, glanced into the room.

"Hey, there!"

"Hi."

A lot like her mother. Blonde, full of quickness—oftentimes too much—and questions; bright as the devil. Kind of pixie-like, too. Very sweet of voice, almost too sweet. You wondered half the time if she weren't kidding the hell out of you.

She was bright-eyed, in white pajamas, with red and blue clowns on them, and she wore tiny red slippers.

"What you doing?" he said.

"Planning my career."

"I see. What've you selected?"

"Not 'selected.'"

"Oh? Okay."

"It's a toss-up."

"Between what?"

"Not between—among. Daddy, don't be such an utter poop, will you, please?"

"So, now I'm a poop."

She twisted on her bed in the pink room with the dark blue ceiling covered with planets, constellations. She lay down and turned away from him, blonde curls snarling like springs on the pillow.

"A square poop," she said.

He glanced at his watch. "Mrs. Martin'll be here soon. And we have to scram, remember? You treat her right?"

"She's a square poop, too. A very bad case."

"All right."

He left her door and went to the large front bedroom Louise and he shared. As he came into the room, Louise wore a pair of extremely scant red panties with a black lace frill, stockings and shoes and nothing else. She was just fastening her right stocking top to the garter. She glanced up, frowned faintly, then looked down at the stocking again.

"Who was that on the phone?" she said.

"Wrong number."

"But you talked."

He shrugged, sat on the bed, and looked at his wife. There seemed to be about her a more than usual lush sexuality, and something stirred in his loins.

He reached out and ran his hand down the back of her thigh, along the smooth bare flesh. She was slim, well-bodied, with small firm breasts possessing inordinately large nipples. Nothing covered her breasts at the moment.

She gave him a cool, faintly annoyed look, then moved over to the dressing table. He watched the way she moved. The phone call was a troublesome thing in his mind.

"You have damned gorgeous legs, you know that?" he said. She watched him in the mirror. He thought she was going to speak, but she didn't. She turned and looked at him. Her lips seemed a bit mushy, the way they got sometimes.

He wished things hadn't been going as they had of late. Maybe if… it might help wipe out that feeling inside him. He motioned to her, feeling a faint sense of guilt.

"I'm not your whore," she said. Then, she covered that. "Anyway, we've got to get ready."

They stared at each other, without expression.

There had been a lot of strain between them lately. He hadn't been able to pin-point it; a growing apart; when he wanted her, she was swiftly, intensely busy with something. Or it was a fast lap of endurance into nothing. When the probable light showed in her eye, her actions, her late close-to-inhibited approach (directly opposed to her true character of utterly uninhibited response to personally triggered emotion, or otherwise; the old hot savage sock of direct need, of honest lust) he was somehow always deep in truly concentrated work; a deadline to meet.

Once she'd said, "I'm beginning to think you paint with your penis."

She knew otherwise, but there was the feminine trick of the bright and brittle knife.

He'd come back at her fast. "Maybe you'd like to try a brush? Here's a beaut." He tossed her the largest, fattest oil brush he had. Then he tackled her, and they curled into a ripe throbbing mangle on the floor. That was some time ago. It had been good. But that was some time ago.

Now, she was busy, too, with this, that, the other; Parent's and Teacher's, and Lolly only just starting. And the garden club—other phony clubs, none of which she fitted, truly. What rot. And he with his painting. Degree by degree, less and less need to speak to each other, to partake of the other's thoughts or wishes. Somehow things were getting off the rail. Then he saw something, felt it. This moment. Like husbands and wives everywhere; immediate touchy problems were forgotten in the co-comprehension of body need.

One of those things.

He knew it wouldn't change what was happening.

But it was there. He might have been anyone. She, too.

She started past him. He caught her, put his arms around her hips, kissed her belly, recalled the "diamond in your navel," and looked up at her. She parted her lips, showed him her white, immaculate teeth.

"We don't have time," she said.

She pressed against him.

"Quick. Close the door," she said. "Lock it."

He did this, returned in a swift movement and held her in his arms, kissing her, gently moving his hands over her body, then using more force—wanting to speak through a shuttered mouth.

"Wow," she said softly.

He recognized it as a personal response, like maybe to a knowledgeably turned bed-post. But for that instant, too, it enhanced things. Because his was the emotion of memory.

He kissed her breasts, the nipples, felt them harden. He began stripping her pants off. She was breathing rapidly, her eyes bright with eagerness. She had an almost pure oval face, and a normally pleasant mouth which at this moment was twisted with lust, teeth tight.

"We'll have to hurry," she said. "Hurry...."

The doorbell rang downstairs.

"Mrs. Martin," he said, feeling the first seeping away of emotion, knowing suddenly that this time, this moment was abruptly precious to them both, that it might ignite a certain reasonable understanding, the beginnings of what they'd had before.

"Oh, God damn her!" Louise said.

He caressed her. She clung to him, her body moving, lips parted.

The doorbell rang again, insistently. Feet pattered in the hall.

"Hey!"

It was Lolly.

"I'll let her in," Lolly said, and the feet scampered away.

It was gone.

"We can't—not now," Louise said.

She wasn't looking at him. She reached and quickly pulled her pants up, snapped them at her waist, smiled.

"What is it the French say?" she said. *"C'est la vie!"*

There was nothing to say to her. The shade was drawn, perhaps fastened more securely than ever. He went into the bathroom.

He had tried kidding her. He had tried lots of things. In front of the bathroom mirror, he straightened his tie. Twenty-two years?

The brick-bat of recollection.

Something thick, like intense anxiety moved inside him. He cleared his throat.

The one chunk of heady nostalgia that remained; the one strong chunk that would never go away. The memory that clung and festered and prowled the nights with him sometimes; a memory filled with regret, always touched with the desperate urgency of the impossible... like the impotent athlete, alone in an expensive suite with a hundred-dollar-a-night call girl. For him, Bill, what was lost was lost.

Yes, he thought. You cannot retrieve those lost years, that one lost love you were more certain about as each year trod upon the next—the one you tossed away, let go to the winds like lint from a favorite pocket. The mistake you lived with.

He came into the bedroom. Louise was slipping into a dark sheath dress. He slapped her across the red panties.

"I'll go down and fix a couple drinks," he said. "Everybody'll be looped, anyway. May's well get a little start."

"All right."

She wriggled into the dress, watching him, cool-eyed.

2

It was a lousy evening from the start.

It grew progressively lousier.

He had things on his mind; things he couldn't shake. The way he figured it, twenty-two years was far too long to carry a burning pine-knot that gave off a cold flame. You'd have to be real neurotic... well, that's how it was, then.

But, this thing tonight. It had set him off.

He was making too much of it.

A shock, that was all.

Only he couldn't shake it.

He got away from the others at the party. Nick and Elaine Thomas owned a large home with a pool, heated, and shielded by screen and small thick cedars, and Elaine, who was guzzling some sweet wine, kept insisting everyone go for a swim.

"Who cares? This is our house—Nick's and mine! We wanta go for a swim, we'll go for a swim. You don't have suits, the hell with it. We'll go in the raw. Let's make this a real party. Let's make it a weekend. Been so long since I was to a real party. For cryin' out loud!"

Elaine Thomas was an extremely sexy redhead; in her way very hard, and also very sentimental. Nick owned the one large lumber mill in Allayne, so they were well off. Neither Bill nor Louise knew many of the people who were there. As a rule, Nick's parties swung quite well. But this was one of those other parties; everyone spontaneously conscious of its failure, the inadequacies of response; everybody on the verge of resembling cornered rats, watching, drinking too much in an effort to create an already buried and unmourned inevitability.

Some of the men kept urging Elaine toward the pool, hoping against all probability; it could mean resurrection of the dead.

Bill knew she would eventually strip and go into that pool. She had to. Elaine was like that. One more drink of over-sugared grape would do it. He was willing to bet she would strip to the buff. There would be furious argument. Nick would get huffy. Tomorrow Elaine would weep on the phone to Louise—and others.

The phone.

An Erroll Garner record was on the stereo. *Moonglow.* That didn't help, either.

Bill poured a substantial drink of gin and found an empty bedroom. He sat on the edge of the bed. The damned music was piped into every room in the house. That had been one of the tunes… not *the* tune. Bad enough, though.

He drank the gin.

He kept hearing her voice over the phone.

Abruptly he got up, just as a strange, willowy, dark-haired girl fumbled into the bedroom. "Watched you, honey," she said. "Watched an' waited." She came toward him. "Got key to door—"

"Not now."

He went out and found Louise. She was dancing with a strange guy. He motioned to her. She looked stunning, eyes bright, and the black sheath fit her fine figure like black devil's flesh.

"Going to walk on home." It wasn't far. "Not feeling so hot. You stay, come home in the car when you feel like it."

He knew there would be some argument. There was. But it was false. She didn't want to come home, now. Things were beginning to swing a bit.

Elaine was undressing frantically by the pool. Nick started toward her, stolid, determined, glass in hand. Elaine rushed it, trying to laugh, stripping her clothes off. She was down to orange-colored scanties.

"You're all a bunch o' cowards!"

Louise's voice was strained, her lips tense. "All right, Bill. I'll be along. I'll cut it short."

"Don't. Have fun. I just don't feel so hot. Go on back and dance with handsome Dan, there."

"Crazy," she said. "You know? His name is Dan. He's from Tonowanda."

Everybody cheered. Elaine had her scanties off and she was gifted with an enormous patch of flaming pubic hair, thick and startling; large enough to plant flowers in. Georgia soil. She had come from Atlanta, originally. She went into the pool with a thunderous splash, shrieking, and immediately was possibly the sanest person at the party.

Nick walked solemnly, stolid, square-faced, arm-swinging through the glass doors toward the group gathered watching the happy, winey mermaid.

"Last one in's a rotten egg!"

3

April.

He tried to force it from his mind. He walked along the elm-shadowed streets, inhaling spring, feeling it all, remembering. He thought of Louise. Loved her, didn't he? Whatever you call it. What do you say to that? Quit paralleling, Sommers. She's your wife and she'll remain your wife.

And there's Lolly.

Lolly was right. I'm a square poop.

They had been married eleven years. When they'd met it had been a fiery thing, and they were married in three weeks. He'd met her in Chicago, through a musician friend. A drummer with a solid beat. Already, then, he'd been doing commercial art work, and had given up on all the dreams. You're not Picasso, Sommers, or Pollack, or much of anybody, so relax. Now, he worked on order, through a New York agent. He'd discovered his rut, clotted, too, from rim to ditch with other dreamers. He painted his dreams on the side.

Not bad, either, Sommers. He'd taken some prizes, not just local, either. Sold some of the "good" stuff. He was hung in three notable galleries.

The screwy thing was, Louise had originally come from Allayne, too. *The town.* The place. She'd left early in life, and hadn't known Karen or any of their present friends. And when they'd returned here to live, all the old crowd was gone. That had been one hell of a long time ago. Changes.

Yeah.

Something else; he hadn't known he'd married considerable wealth, until Louise's father died and the will was read. Her father had been wise with investments, after making a killing with a string of hamburger-heavens. He'd sold out, and now... well. Louise had been an only child.

People always gave him a second look when he said he was a "painter." He never used the word artist. Anyway, word had it that Louise provided the money, inherited, and he made a pretense of providing. He told himself he didn't care, not any more. But early parental traps, religious extremes of early youth—these still hampered, though he dismissed them intellectually, detesting the thought that such myopic hell should have been imposed upon himself, along with the thought that it might, would, be imposed upon this new generation. Not Lolly, by hell!

Karen.

It was a bad thing. The nostalgia was really on him. Why had that crazy girl phoned? Why hadn't she had a name like Mary, or Gladys, or anything. Just not that one.

Maybe she did have such another name.

It was going to rain. He could smell it, walking along the quiet streets, the trees moving high and soft against the uncalm sky.

Well, he was the age for it. A sentimental, nostalgic old square poop, up out of the thirties, still hearing Benny Goodman—dragging the whole thing along with him. Christ. He couldn't think of anything but Karen. Memories surged and swamped him.

The way she looked. The way she spoke. The soft brown hair with the auburn richness; the deep blue eyes, always smiling, but somehow sad, too. The broad mouth with those tender ripe lips, lips he'd kissed thousands of times. The faintly heart-shaped face, and that full, supple, absolutely marvelous body that seemed always drenched with desire—for him. And he for her. She had been the only woman in his life who had matched his sexuality. What they call a perfect match—on fire. Just a touch, a look.

Everything about her. The way she walked. The touch of her hands. The complete giving, understanding they'd had. Nobody could ever be like Karen.

But, Sommers! Every Bill had a Karen, and every Karen had a Bill.

Yeah? He didn't believe that.

And he couldn't dismiss, laugh off, even lyingly, the memory of this Karen.

But good great Christ. That was all the way back into the late thirties. High school days. Fifteen, sixteen, seventeen... and then....

Hell, they laughed then, people. Now, the young kids married and nobody laughed. Except with them.

He grunted, almost to the house now. He lit a cigarette.

Maybe everybody had times like this. When they remembered. He'd used to think you forgot, with time. It didn't work that way. Maybe you remembered too much, old pal; maybe you'll see the men with the white coats... the way you're remembering.

It started to rain, very softly; just a mist, full of April and promise (to somebody else), the air cool, still touched with the breath of a lingering winter.

Wouldn't know it, but there'd been one hell of a snowstorm, the last of March.

On the corner, the way they'd often met, under that big old elm, by that mailbox—both probably gone by now. Over on Lewis Street, near her home.

The way she would walk up to him. If it were raining, she wore a light transparent raincoat, with a hood.

"Hi."

"Hi."

Never any baloney, not from her; never anything to make him feel uncomfortable, like most women. She played it straight.

The long kiss, then, with the streetlamp gleaming not too brightly, light flickering through the small rain, among the slow movement of the elm, the shadows that were theirs, whatever they might be.

He hurled the cigarette away, and crossed the lawn toward the house. As he opened the front door, he recalled Mrs. Martin. She would be here. Good, solid, plump Mrs. Martin, a widow. The sturdy baby-sitter. Well, she could run along home, now. He'd pay her full time, of course.

He knew what he would do. He would get drunk.

Weak people get drunk.

What else?

Strong people go fishing.

Strong people face things healthfully, with a hook in the stomach of an undersized sunfish.

Or they are intensely assuming and myopic-brained; unimaginative unlovelies, academically unsmart, even stumbling wildly like drunken Paul Bunyans over their own myriads of star-spangled inhibitions that grow out of their heads on strong poles for all to see and some to admire, while at the same instant attempting with near belligerence to solve vociferously what they believe (know) are flaws and faults in some happy complex being whose fin has happened to be snagged, and who hangs around momentarily because the situation is entertaining, enlightening, real, and he might discover something, though it's doubtful because he's traveled the road— when he was eleven, twelve, thirteen.

Nope, Bill thought, not all strong people.

Labels and categories be damned.

Get drunk, then, and remember it all, and then try to forget how he had met that girl from Portsmouth, and told Karen flatly, believing it at that moment, that he no longer loved her, wanted her. And he had never again seen the girl from Portsmouth; she was married a week later to a carnival roustabout, and he never even recalled her name. Karen was gone. Then he was gone. Forget all that.

How he had hurt her. He knew. And himself.

Maybe paint? It might work.

Mrs. Martin was eating peanuts, crunching away, and watching TV, from the couch. Loretta Young. There were tears in Mrs. Martin's eyes, behind the gold-rimmed glasses. She looked as sturdy as ever, though.

"I don't feel so hot," he said. "You'll be able to go home."

She gave him a look. The money.

He paid her.

"You have a nice time, Mr. Sommers?"

He shrugged, wishing she would leave.

"Lolly been okay?"

"Sweet as ever. She's a sweet dear. Never any trouble."

I'll bet, he thought. He felt impatient. He watched her start for the hall closet, her umbrella, raincoat, all the rest of her paraphernalia.

The phone rang. Stiletto.

He stood there and stared at the ringing.

"Shall I take the call, Mr. Sommers?"

"No. Thanks."

He picked it up.

"Bill? I just wondered—you're late."

"Yeah."

"Please, did something come up? Will you be there?"

He thought fast. Her last name. That could help clinch it.

"What's your last name?"

"Darling, what's got into you?"

"What's your last name!"

"Jamais."

Something inside him drowned. That was the name. There was one other thing; something he would not mention.

"All right," he said suddenly. "Soon as I can get there."

"Hurry. You know how it is."

"I'll be there."

He hung up, turned and hurried into the hall. Mrs. Martin was opening the front door.

"Wait," he said. "I find I have to go out, after all. Do you mind? Sorry. I know you'd like to get on home, but something's come up."

She beamed under the black hat, in the heavy coat, with the big black shopping bag filled with God only knew what, the umbrella.

"It's perfect," she said. "I'll be able to watch the show finish—and there's another right after I'd like to see. I'm a regular TV fiend."

"Great."

He went to the closet, snagged his trenchcoat off a hook, ripping the strap, and without another glance at Mrs. Martin, left the house.

This would be good. He'd go to the corner on Lewis, by the mailbox, where they'd always met. Naturally she wouldn't show—she couldn't.

He didn't have the car. Damn.

Still, he hadn't had a car twenty-odd years ago.

Sommers, he thought, you're a crazy fool.

Well, if there were no real complications, it might be a strange piece. He got to thinking that way, and it felt good. The way things were with Louise.

Only, the way it was—it was really strange.

These thoughts began to filter away. It was the night, the feeling of the night, and memory.

He walked hurriedly down the street through April.

4

She wasn't there.

For an instant he experienced jubilance.

But, then, there was just too much of everything.

The mailbox was still here, big, snugged in against some bushes by a fence, just as it had always been. And the elm tree, though it seemed to have grown some. Not as much as he might have supposed. Maybe it was another elm tree. The streetlamp, there it was, glowing dimly through the gently tossing limbs. Christ, maybe they hadn't ever even changed the bulb. The sidewalk was still flagstone, gleaming dully from the April rain. Not really rain, just a lazy misting from the sky.

He was breathing heavily, taking in considerable emotion with one sock, and he had walked fast some twenty-five blocks, across streets he hadn't been on in nearly that many years.

She wasn't here.

He could not explain what he felt; something between sharp exasperation, anxiety, and relief.

Anyway, it wouldn't be the Karen he'd known.

He heard a soft noise, looked up, stood there.

She was coming toward him. There was the mild, and—to him—sexy rustle of the transparent raincoat, and the hood, and the light from the streetlamp shopped honestly among the dark hair curling from under the hood.

She came up to him. "Hi."

"Karen?"

She smiled. She moved into his arms.

"We looked at each other in the same way then...."

1

He was, at that moment, sixteen, seventeen, standing here holding Karen, and the future was still an easy promise. The night came down around them.

Her body pressed tightly. Her raincoat was open, and he felt the thrust of her thighs, her breasts, and the faint abrupt aphrodisiac of perfume he knew so well. Hers.

The moment shattered him.

Her lips were near his. He looked into her eyes, and they were Karen's eyes. Those were Karen's lips. This was Karen with a dew of sparkling rain on her hair. The vital, urgent appeal of her body was Karen.

Abruptly, he grasped her shoulders, held her away.

She smiled, her hips swinging toward him.

Her voice appealed. "Kiss me. It's been so long."

His throat was thick with emotion—sudden confusion. Everything about her was his memory of Karen. The sound of her voice. The feel of her. Her hands on his arms, then against his chest; the way she looked at him from the deep blue eyes, and the happy-sad turn of her broad, full, red lips.

Only this was not Karen.

He wanted it to be, Christ knew, right then.

But it was somebody else.

Something in his mind said, *"Let it ride—let it ride."*

Not so simple.

Yet....

He looked at her. She at him. Her lower lip more and more took on that elusive turn of sadness, of hurt, of a confusion that resembled his own.

With one hand, she reached up, swept the rain-hood off her hair, tossed her head slightly, watching him.

And it was Karen's hair.

He wanted her. He wanted her so violently it ached. He wanted to erase, drown, obliterate.

He trembled all through his body. Desire raged.

"Who are you?" he said.

"Bill." She slowly moved her head from side to side. "I'm Karen."

Any normal person can misplace his senses momentarily.

"It's been a long time, hasn't it, Bill? A very long time."

Her voice was lyrical, gentle. For an instant, she averted her eyes, then looked at him again, searchingly, just as Karen had always done when she was about to say something that was difficult to say; something that hurt her while denying truth.

"Please, Bill. Don't feel so bad. I know how you must feel. I've felt bad, too. But what's done is done—I've long ago forgiven you everything. What we had is something we'll always have, now. You can't just throw something like that away." She paused. "Isn't that right?"

Be realistic, he thought. But the thing was, all the emotion he'd ever had for Karen in the long ago—and it was a veritable furnace—was this much more real now, this much stronger because of the past itself. There had been all through the years the knowledge that this was gone; that he had lost this, destroyed it. A violently wonderful sexual thing between them, and everything that went with it. The touch of her, thought of her, even, and his blood streamed unappealed, enfusing like rock that vital point of life. It had happened now. And she knew it.

Now it was here; what he had lost, destroyed. A kind of culmination of everything, like drowning in a sudden inconceivable explosion... and at the same time knowing it was unreal.

Yeah. Only it was real. Because there she was.

He wanted to grab it, hold it, go to hell with it; wherever it led; regrasp and hold the cracked dream of the past... dismiss forever the impossible fact—make that fact real.

Here she was; dream tendrils, red regrets, saying, *"Kiss me. I forgive you."*

The backs of her fingers brushed his fly. "You haven't changed, honey. But, take it easy—for now, huh?" She reached up, ran her fingers through his hair, smiling. "I feel the same way, you know. Remember the time in the laundry room?" She smiled. Her tongue tipped her lips. "You said then, it would burn forever. I guess you were right. But let's work up to things. There's so much else, too. So much time. A lot of knowing."

He glanced down. She even wore saddle shoes, silk stockings, white ankle socks. The weather was still chilly. That's what they'd worn, hadn't they? But....

She had on a soft skirt of thin woolen material, a light-colored sweater, with the white round collar of a blouse showing around the neck. A tiny beaded pin of some kind was on the neck of the blouse. He recalled the pin.

Everything?

A soft April wind palmed the street, fragrant yet with winter's traces, new green life, and rain.

He damned it. He damned it all.

"Let's walk, Bill—huh?"

She took his arm.

The night was mad.

He yanked his arm away. The words burst from his lips, full of anger now. "Who are you?"

She smiled, then looked puzzled.

His voice was rough. "I want to know. I've got to know. The hell with the rest. Who are you!"

2

She reached into a pocket of her raincoat, took out a wallet, opened it and withdrew something.

"Look," she said. "You haven't changed so much. I thought you'd put on a lot of weight, but you haven't."

It was a small snapshot. He stared at it under the flickering streetlamp.

A photo of himself. Young. Maybe sixteen, seventeen; a sweater, slacks, books under one arm. He was standing by a tree.

"Remember when I took it?" she said.

Karen's hobby had been photography. He remembered the picture. It wasn't dog-eared much; there was only a single small crack at one corner.

He thrust it back in her hand and she put it away.

"You didn't take that picture."

"No. But I might have."

"What's your name?"

"Karen Jamais. Look at me. Kiss me. Hold me. See if I'm not."

"Where'd you get that snapshot?"

"I've had it a long time."

"What the hell are you trying to do?"

"Come back to you. The way it must be."

He had a strong impulse to walk away; a stronger one to hold her, pull her skirt up, take off her pants, and the merry hell to everything. He seethed in confusion. Not the question of whether or not she was whom she claimed to be. Rather what to do about her.

But—she was so like Karen.

"Look, honey," he said. "How old are you?"

"You know. Sixteen—going on seventeen."

"That snapshot was taken twenty-two, twenty-three years ago."

"So?"

"I'm thirty-nine years old."

"That's right. But, d'you feel thirty-nine, Bill? You sure don't look it."

He stared at her. She had to be perfectly sane, whoever she was. She couldn't look as she did and be mad. Yet, all of this was mad.

And yet, in a lot of ways, it wasn't.

"Let's walk, Bill. Like we used to."

All right, he thought. Be crafty.

"Where'll we walk?"

"I can't stay long tonight. You know how it is. Let's cut up through the alley, here. We can—we can stop in old Flannigan's garage, for a minute—just a minute, though. I know what you want to do—and so do I. But not now."

He stared at her, remembering.

"We could walk around the playground. Then I have to get back."

"Back where?"

"Let's not talk about it. You know."

She tugged at his arm. Her full hip brushed his. They passed the mailbox and moved slowly through the darkness of the alley. There was the sound of trees, the wind.

To the left the dark garage yawned, where Mr. Flannigan kept his car. He was always out late nights. He and Karen used to stop here for a short kiss... sometimes more. Once, even….

"You want to stop a minute?"

She turned slightly, her body tightly brushing him.

She held to his arm. The rain had ceased, but overhead a low ceiling of darkness writhed with Spring. Somewhere out on Main Street a car's horn bleated.

They were by the garage doors. There was an odor of damp earth, and her perfume.

She swung around and pressed against him, moving her hips faintly, tightly. Her face was a blur. She looked up at him.

The ache was crazy.

"God," she said. "That feels good. Even if we can't, right now. Oh, good—good."

He kissed her. He slid his hands under the raincoat, pulled her to him, feeling the surging contours of her back, the touch of her hair, her hot lips opening under his, softly, and there was the urgent, wild need. His hands tore up under the sweater, the blouse, slid all around and he held one large breast, felt the hard nipple. She moaned faintly. He was back there—back with Karen. His hands slipped down, and he pulled her skirt up, feeling her full straining thighs. He gripped her buttocks with both hands, suddenly realized she wore no pants. They strained against each other and she reached for him, between them, with a throaty moan, their mouths still together, tongues working.

Suddenly, she said, "No! No—not now—here!"

At that same instant, he thrust her away. Her skirt was caught for a moment up around her hips and he stared at her. Then she gave a twitch and the skirt fell; she pulled it down. He looked at her eyes; they were swimming.

She moved against him again, half sideways now. "You're in a bad way," she said, touching him. "Easy, darling—it'll keep."

He couldn't get his breath. Her words came in short light gasps. Her lips looked bruised.

Doomed? Great Christ.

She watched him.

"Darling," she whispered.

Enough. He wanted to seize her, crush her, take her; talk wildly about everything, tell her a thousand things.

She watched him patiently. "I'm not going away," she said. "It'll be like always; any time, anywhere. Just, not tonight." She hesitated, pulled her raincoat around her. "Think of something else."

He could still feel the violent surge and seeking of her lush body; the knowing way she had come to him; how she had touched him.

"You knew another Karen," he said.

She nodded.

"Say it, then. Say it!"

"I knew another Karen."

"Where is she?"

"Dead. A long time now."

He still wanted to just take her. He knew he could.

He knew he would wait.

"When did she die?"

"She didn't exactly die."

He went a little crazy, right then. He grabbed her arm, swept her back and forth roughly. She continued to half smile at him. When he moved his hand, his hand touched the strong thrust of her breast. He ceased. Again he wanted to turn and walk away. He couldn't. He was trapped, just as if she had her legs locked around him—their brains fused.

"Who are you?"

"I'm Karen, Bill. I've come back. I'm never going away again. We'll never be apart again. We'll always be together. When I lived, I knew another Karen. She often spoke of you. But you see, she gone now—she's dead."

"Where was this?"

"Never mind. She's dead."

"When did she die?"

"She didn't, exactly. But it was three years ago. She took her life. It was very sad. I don't like to even think about it. But you should know, I guess. She—she took sleeping pills, but they didn't work right. So, then... they found her. I found her, really, and told them. The police, that is. I went to her place, to talk, and she'd hanged herself."

He stood looking at her, hearing a soft wind.

He sensed a kind of petulance in her tone, now. "She was a good friend. I was alone—so was she. She had never married. She was terribly alone, Bill. She spoke of you. But, you see? Something happened."

His voice was harsh. "Where're your parents?"

"You know I haven't any. Daddy died, and I never saw my mother. No one's left. Just me."

He was even more abrupt. "Where was all this?"

"I won't tell you, so don't ask me. But that's how it is."

He stared at her, wanting more reaction, wanting something he could nail down; reality.

"So, now I've come back to you. I'm Karen. I've come back." She touched his arm with her fingertips. "You may as well believe it, Bill."

He thought he heard somebody in the alley, in the shadows. A footstep? He listened intently, positive. Just the wind, now. A car passed down on the street, under the elm, where the mailbox stood.

The sexuality that seemed to emanate from her was overpowering, to him. He reacted almost violently, every time she moved or spoke. He thought of Louise and life was a blank. Lolly.

She said, "You love me, Bill—and I love you. You know how it is. It was all a mistake—all these years. You know that, too. I've come back to you. It had to be this way."

"I'm married. I have a child. Damn it, talk sense—you don't talk sense, I'll...."

She broke in, "And you will, too. But it's all right. It doesn't matter. I'm yours. It has to be that way."

He blurted it. "You're Karen's daughter!"

She laughed shortly. "Don't be stupid."

"You've got to be."

"I'm not. I'm Karen."

He reached for her, meaning to grab her, but didn't touch her. "It's nuts. You go on home, whoever the hell you are. Forget you saw me. I've got to get home."

"I understand. That's all right."

He was perspiring, shaken. It was like throwing a baseball at a cement wall, and suddenly the wall becomes a limp sheet, quicksand—enfolding the ball, taking everything away, making it aimless. He didn't know what to do. It was easy to say she was out of her mind, but that solved nothing. The hell of it was, he had the deep itch to play along. He wanted her desperately; certain visualities of mind that he hadn't had since Karen, had returned, strengthened with years of defeat.

He had to leave immediately.

"When you kissed me," she said softly. "I came."

Jesus. Karen, all over again.

He paused, thinking again he heard something in the shadows of the alley. Of course, it was nothing.

She didn't seem to hear anything.

"I have to go, too," she said. "Kiss me, now?"

He turned abruptly, started away.

"Bill?" She took a few quick steps after him. He turned to her. "I was listening to our song," she said, "all afternoon, today."

"Yeah? What was that?"

"*Where or When*," she said. "See you, darling."

That damnable tune, those words. It had never seemed to have meaning—yet he, too, still listened, listened.

She turned and started down the alley, through the shadows. He watched her go, the way she moved. Karen.

He moved up the alley to the street, turned left and began walking briskly toward home.

He knew damned well he would see her again.

He knew it couldn't be helped.

Suddenly he wanted to turn and run back to her, make her tell him everything. Somehow, he knew she had told him everything.

For a while there he'd almost been caught up in it; caught like herself.

Base instincts? Hell. There was everything else, too. What did those stupid knick-knacks called people know about certain so-called base instincts under the heading Sex? The preacher with his wiper still wet, because he hadn't had time for a shower—bells, you know, pulpit, you know, sermon, you know—standing there slightly above the congregation, some of whom had crabs, some gleet, some worse; every damned one of them knowing, and the preacher, too; standing there, yelling from a soft and attended throat, heart over-beating, "It's a sin—etc, etc.", while the choir boys and girls walked calmly, chaste, to their places—fingers still moist, eyes and life alert. Knowing, too.

Direction. Want.

He wanted that girl. She said she was Karen.

Well, why the hell not?

Only, what to do.

Louise, he thought. Lolly. He would go home. The whole business would end. It was crazy. Anyone would tell him that—save for a few untouchables who had made their way to God.

Then Karen was dead?

Questions beat at him.

A cruising cab. He shrilled at it, hadn't shrilled in years, either; tongue doubled back and down against the teeth—another banshee, more than wailing.

The cab braked happily, made a skilled swift U-turn. He gave his home address, slid in on the seat.

He didn't even know where she lived.

But she knew where he lived.

That picture, too. She'd looked like Karen, talked like Karen. Said she was Karen.

Blackmail?

What else?

Don't be stupid. A sixteen year old girl?

3

The young man in the alley watched them part, from deep in the shadows. He stood quite still in the black shadows of the garage. It had been close. They'd almost come into the garage. Jesus, what the hell would he have done then?

Just stood here, he thought. What else?

He stood now, absolutely motionless, containing his breathing as well as he could, and watched her come slowly back down the alley.

Why had she met him? That old guy?

Crazy. Real crazy. Wow.

He watched her legs move, and imagined the ripe body under the raincoat and the skirt. The long nylon stockings that reached high up on her thighs. The black garters biting into the soft plump white flesh. The tiny frilled white panties.

They had almost... but he hadn't been able to see very well. Probably a good thing, too. But the way they went at it there for a few seconds.

Something welled and wrung inside the young man.

He wished he could just burn the clothes off her with his eyes. Of course, he had watched her dress, and everything, but he could never get enough of seeing her. Jesus, what she did to him. She flipped him, completely. He was off his nut, the way she had him.

Not really—not yet.

She passed the garage, walking slowly, the raincoat rustling, her hair picking up tiny little lights from the streetlamp on the corner.

Now. Now, he thought. He could just drag her into the garage, into the darkness, and... and rip off her clothes. He could have her, the way he wanted.

But that would end it. Right there. He knew that. It had happened before. It was all over then. Really, it wasn't over until afterward.

Once he got her.

He had to have her.

He knew he would. But the thing was to prolong it until he couldn't stand it any more; absolutely couldn't stand another minute of it. Then, it didn't matter. Then just let it bust wide open. Jesus, the things he thought when he looked at her, whenever he saw her, thought of her.

Take it easy, he told himself. Man, you'll turn into a real joker and tear this thing—you'll smash it.

And this is the best. This is the best you'll ever get your hands on. You never saw anything like this, did you?

There was that one in Chicago. But, Jesus, even she didn't touch this. This one was all over pure plump ripe and ready.

He could tell when they were aching for it, just aching, seething inside like he seethed. He knew. He could tell. He knew plenty about this one. Man, what he knew about this one. What she did. All alone in that room.

Okay. Get going. And don't follow too close.

He stepped into the alley. She was just rounding the corner down by that mailbox where they'd stood for so long.

What the hell kind of crap was she giving that poor bastard? He'd looked out of his frigging head. Looked as if he wanted to cry, a couple times, there. A real joker. A square if he ever saw one.

Man, she wasn't square. What a bitch!

His hands were sweating, and something else had happened, but the hell with that. Sometimes that's how it was. He couldn't control himself at all. Anyway, it didn't matter. Dig, you blind crazy bastards.

He was a lion, wasn't he?

She sure dressed funny, though, like tonight. With those crazy shoes and those crazy white socks. He liked her when she had on a good tight dress. Those white nylon dresses, they fit her plenty tight, and they showed a lot, too. When she wore them, you could see the pink-white of those thighs right through the dress, and all.

He paused by the mailbox, under the drifting shadows of the elm and the streetlamp. She was headed down toward the main street, now. Not the way she'd come. Well, it didn't matter.

He stood there watching her. Let her get about a block ahead of him. He could just watch her from that distance, and imagine. Because he knew what he'd come home to.

And the eventuality.

The thought wrung him.

Take care, man. You'll just flip like a busted bongo.

He was neatly dressed. He was always careful of that. It counted plenty. He wore a dark single-breasted suit, white shirt, dark tie. His shoes were well-polished, and he carried a lightweight plastic raincoat over his left arm. He wore a dark straw pork-pie hat with a broad maroon band. That set things off, that hat. He took the hat off, waiting, and mopped his brow with a clean white handkerchief snatched from a breast pocket. He had thick, close-cropped blond hair. His face was square and tanned, the eyes a pale blue; very open, frank eyes. Of medium height, strong shouldered, he stood there, waiting.

Nothing square about you, man, he thought. Hip, that's the word for you. Hip.

His name was Walter Hogan.

That was his name this time, in this town.

It began to rain now, the mists changing into a slow warm spring rain.

Walter Hogan slipped on his raincoat and started down the street, keeping pace with Karen Jamais.

He wanted a cigarette. It could wait.

Play it cool. Straight down the line.

4

As Walter Hogan followed the girl along the streets, wild things passed through his mind. Intense schemes, plans. Intense livings. Dreams and wishes. Imaginings.

With the girl.

How it would be. Exactly what he would do. He varied the effects, varied the drama of the culmination.

He played with thoughts like this all the time, letting it build good and solid. It was all right, because he never depended on the schemes.

The secret was not to have a scheme. The minute you made a perfect plan, you made an error. He knew this. He'd had enough experience, from coast to coast, hadn't he? Hell, man, that was for damned sure. Plan all the hell you want, but never figure to use a plan.

He had tried it. And something always went wrong. You plan, and then some fool thing would change it, right when it counted. Things couldn't go to the scheme; you fouled everything up if you tried it that way. He knew.

Like the time with that broad in Kansas City. Jesus, and what a piece she was, too. But he'd made plans, and stuck to them, trying to force everything to come out the way he'd dreamed it up. And he blew the whole thing.

Because something always went wrong.

If one tiny step went wrong in the plan, then the whole thing was shot to hell. For some reason. He didn't exactly know why.

So, plan and scheme all you want, Walt, he thought. But when it hap-

pens—let the Devil take the reins.
　Then it would be right. He knew. He really knew.
　Sometimes the way his heart beat, he thought he would die. Like now.

5

　It was an old three storied house, with an attic, too.
　He had the room directly over hers. In his floor, up over the foot of her bed, was one of these old-type ventilators. It resembled an old floor register. Only it wasn't. There were black cast iron gratings on her ceiling, and on his floor. There had been some baffles in there, but he had taken those out weeks ago.
　During the daytime, or when he had lights turned on in his room at night, he kept a small throw rug over the ventilator. So if she ever happened to look up, she couldn't see anything but blackness. And with the lights out, it was all right, too.
　In fact, during the daytime, if he couldn't stand it, when he had to look at her or flip completely, he pulled the shade on the single window in his room and covered the window with a blanket, then removed the rug.
　And looked.
　Like right now.
　She was a little difficult to figure, though. This one. She did strange things, sometimes. She acted strange. It seemed to him. She never went anyplace. He couldn't quite dig her, really. Well, time would do the job.
　He lay flat on the floor, his face pressed against the cold cast iron grating and watched her undress.
　He lay naked on the floor.
　Soon she would be naked, too.
　Then....

"But I can't remember where or when...."

1

Bill Sommers finished the gin and tonic in his bedroom, then stripped naked, and headed for the bathroom. He was covered with a film of perspiration, and the whole business had him dizzy. That was a mild word for it.

He turned on the shower, adjusted the taps, and dodged under the spray. He slid the glass paneled door closed.

Too hot.

He turned it to cold; plain cold.

For the moments that the water beat upon him, drenching his face, needling spray brisk and powerful, the evening dimmed.

Louise wasn't home yet. Still, it wasn't late. He had let Mrs. Martin toddle on home. It seemed strange so much had happened in so short a time. It was only a little after ten o'clock.

He soaped briskly, turned the shower on full, and let the spray blast at him. He wished he could just stand in the shower forever. While the water boomed and drummed against his head, he didn't concentrate. It would take an effort, and he'd rather not make the effort to remember—much rather not....

The instant he stepped out of the shower, everything returned with a crushing blow to his psyche. He seized a thick towel and attempted to rub it briskly away with that. He splashed rubbing alcohol on his face. It did no good. Suppose she phoned again? Louise mustn't get messed up in this.

He thought of Lolly.

He was like an aching, ignorant adolescent.

The medicine cabinet mirror wasn't fogged because he'd used cold water. He stared at himself, sourly.

"Look. You really haven't changed so much."

He leaned forward on the sink, till his nose nearly touched the unforgiving glass.

He spoke in a harsh whisper. "But she isn't Karen!"

Hell. Stand them all on their heads, the man said. Maybe some guys could do that. He could do it with some women. But there was a mark of derivation. In this case, the derivative equaled the sum of truth. And the truth was quite obvious.

He stared at himself in the mirror. There had been the time, a while back, of the mustache, and after that the mustache and the beard, then just the beard, then the mustache again. Then he'd shaved the whole business off.

Not because of the conventional fears. Piss on them. But because it was something to do.

Such a small thought. Such enormous impact when realized.

What would she have thought.

Already he was registering himself, his thoughts, against her summation.

You fool. She wasn't Karen. She's a girl and looks practically exactly like her, acts like her, speaks like her, knows things. How did she get that way. She knew too much. Too damned much!

He hurled the towel savagely into the sink. It made a soft inconsequential sound.

He really hadn't changed much. Not inside, either. He was a bloody monomaniac. How had he been able to do his work—as he had done. Because that memory was always there; ripe and waiting, with the absolute knowing she would return, that sometime, somewhere, he would see her again, tell her his mistakes, and she would know. When he thought like this, there was no Louise, no Lolly. Just himself, and Karen, as they had been. He knew how long ago that was. But memory was one thing—practicalities something else. In the mind of a psychiatrist, he never had regressed, he'd just never grown, in that one area.

Bull.

Where did she live.

What was she doing now? This instant?

What about boy friends. Certainly, a girl as winsome, as sadly beautiful as she—a perfect mark for the wise guys—must have a brisk, sardonic herd tumbling after her heels.

Heels, hell.

He didn't like the thought, somehow.

He knew he wasn't thinking sensibly; the way one was supposed to think. But how often did something like this happen to a person?

He stomped into the bedroom, snapped open a bureau drawer, grabbed a pair of white shorts and put them on. Then he found a pair of khaki trousers, and rammed his feet into the legs. Starched. Damn that laundry. He'd told them a hundred times not to starch his goddamn' trousers. He worked in them. It took a full day to make them comfortable, and besides, though he liked them, their cool quality, their lightness, the starch brought back World War Two, every time, and suntans in Texas, before—long before the invasion. The ETO.

Not long after Karen. He'd been really torn up at that time. So, what the hell do you call this?

His zipped his fly, rammed his hands in all the pockets and tore the pockets loose from the starch. All of his khakis were paint-stained, because sometimes a paint-cloth wasn't handy, and he worked in a sort of dynamic frenzy, as a rule. The splotches of color that the laundry could never erase were predominantly brown, from washing.

He was known for working with all the variants of red. Alizarin was his favorite. The things you could do with alizarin crimson. He could sit all day just mooching the marvelous stuff around on canvas board.

He snatched up his glass and went downstairs at a run to the kitchen. He uncapped the bottle, poured the large highball glass half full of gin, plopped in an ice cube from the flooded bowl, splurped in some quinine water.

This was no ordinary mess. For damned sure.

He drank half the glass, gulping it, uncaring that it was barely cool from the single dwarfed ice cube.

Plan. He had to plan something.

He kept jerking his mind back to the fact that she was not Karen.

Dead? Sleeping pills. Hanged. By her own hand.

It didn't jell.

It was stupid, he knew. You were supposed to get over these things. How many men, women, walked the streets, befogged by memories? Damned few, certainly, if they had any sense at all.

But the fact of tonight.

Maybe he was crazy. *Maybe!* You just didn't love a person, after not even seeing them for this length of time.

And she was gone. Dead.

Yet—damn it, he had kissed her, tonight.

He walked through the hall, turned left through the broad arch into the large living room. The TV still glared soundlessly at him like a bright-eyed compulsive fiend. He swatted the knob and the light went out.

There'd been no TV, back then. Just….

He looked across the room, down beyond the fireplace, at the hi-fi; Louise's pride. His, too, shrug, as a matter of fact.

Blackmail? No. It just didn't seem right.

His glass was empty.

He walked past the hi-fi components, set on shelves, snapped on the amplifier and the record player, then went fast to the kitchen. Three ice cubes, the bottle of gin, and he uncapped a bottle of quinine water, then returned to the living room. He sat on the floor, poured a drink, drank it, the ice cubes banging his teeth. He began desultorily checking endless sheathed LP's. What a mint of loot was tied up in them.

Indirectly, he knew what he looked for; he didn't even let the thought touch his mind. It wasn't among the LP's. He got up, went to the large cabinet of 78's, ignoring the classics, fingering old albums.

His hand brushed it quickly enough, quite blindly.

Where had they all come from? A special album, full of this meaningless, sentimental old tune. He took out one, the one, and put it on the changer. The B. G. Trio, with Martha Tilton, nineteen thirty-seven.

He sat, listened, drank.

"...*clothes you're wearing are the clothes you wore... things that happen for the first time....*"

He drank. Finally he put on an Art Tatum platter, and listened to cascading notes. He didn't need words.

There had been others. *Once In a While*, and *Stardust*. Particularly *Stardust*. Yes, that's right.

Where or When....

Jesus Christ, would he go mad? A sentimental old poop of a square if there ever was.

Over and over Art Tatum fooled around with *Where or When*, and Bill drank, and lay back on the floor, swimming in it. He knew he was very drunk and it was a good feeling; mellow-sad yesterday yesteryear drunk.

The phone crashed upon a certain night.

He knocked over the highball glass. Gin, water and ice cubes slopped across the carpet.

2

"I had to call you," she said. "I wanted to say goodnight."

He sprawled on the couch with the phone. "Karen."

"I can hear the music. I listen to that tune a lot."

He spoke sharply. "The music doesn't matter. You can't call here. Get that straight. No more."

She said nothing.

"You hear me?" he said.

"Yes, Bill. Anyway, it won't be long and we'll be able to sit and listen together. I'm lying in bed," she said. "I don't have a stitch on. Remember how we used to talk on the phone, and I wouldn't have anything on, and the things you used to say? When I think of it, now. What if the operator heard? I haven't even any covers on—just lying here."

"Don't call here again. Ever."

"Your wife, you mean?"

"Yeah, yeah—my wife. That's only part of it."

She broke in. "Don't worry about your wife. It'll just be you and me in a little while. That's how it was meant to be."

He groaned inwardly. "I've got to hang up." Didn't she know what she was doing to him? Just the sound of her voice? Jesus Christ.

"Goodnight, darling. See you tomorrow. We'll work it all out."

"Listen, will you!" He tried to think of something to say, the right thing; all he thought was of how she had looked, the urgent feel of her body, the realization of a memory that had been like one continual orgasm within his being for years.

Her voice was almost a whisper. "Tell me goodnight."

"Yes," he said. "Goodnight." Christ.

"Be thinking of you—all night—like this, right now—"

Click.

He slammed the phone in its cradle, got up and lurched over and picked up the gin bottle, then returned to the long couch, and flopped heavily.

Yes, surely, kids having love affairs in their teens—they must behave much the same. But with Karen and himself, it had always been one sweet hot long drench of desire and appeasement. He could recall times beyond counting, the absolute concert pitch of always and the progressively mounting culminations that never gave any signal of an ending—had never ended.

Everything else, too. Everything.

Maybe he was gifted with too strong a memory. Baloney.

With Louise sex had always been good, but never like the other. And actually, with Louise, what else was there? Nothing to depend on. No balance of likes. Always the petty arguments, the for and against this and that. There had been many women.

Yet, just this one stood out, burning. Not alone with sex, then, but with everything; consuming him. But, just the same it all hinged on that volcanic get-together. Anyone who said sex didn't count, or that it only had its place and time, cut-throat, was stupid and a liar. It lived in everything that was worthwhile, and it lived like an all-knowing eye in every person's mind. Maybe it was just that some persons thought they had a headache. A shame.

And more and more the newspapers recorded the fact that these headachy persons, somehow notoriously politicos, lawmakers, surrounded by other headachy persons controlled the American sheep, slowly, surely herding them with twisted crooks back and back toward the dark ages, toward the ignorance instead of the light—out there.

He no longer read newspapers. It was altogether too sickening, too destructive to hope.

You're a great big dumb nut of a square poop, Sommers.

As bad as the rest. Living on memories, like canned peaches, or something.

For twenty-odd years, whenever he thought of Karen, that same strong desire surged within him. It had never lessened. And now this girl.

All right, Sommers, face it. You're mad.

But he knew the truth. The truth was that Karen and he should have married. It was one of those terrifically cockeyed honest-to-God chemical precipitates of real magnetism. You see it, sometimes. A guy and a gal. Then they marry, and as husband and wife, forever full of surprises for each other, they go sailing through life with the continual hots for each other, and no one else matters, or can ever matter.

You have that, you've got all there is; you'll make what you want. There'll always be bread, because it doesn't matter if there isn't.

The man who said "You can't live on love alone," was bruising his knuckles, trying to say something, and he'd never had that thing. Once you've had that thing, you know, even if you've lost it. You'll always know—you'll die knowing you once shot for the moon and made it, but fell off; but that you could have remained there.

Well, he had even tried to find her a couple of times, but not hard enough; he didn't know then. There had been no trace.

He tipped up the bottle of gin and gulped it down, swallow after swallow.

You, Sommers. You destroyed it; for that little blonde witch from Portsmouth. You were crocked. She was all sweetness and malarky, and you laid her within an hour after you met her, and a week later she was married.

Undying love.

Not that Louise wasn't a fine wife.

But, face it. Karen was the one for you, Sommers.

Man, was he drunk.

Louise should be home.

The music roamed the April night, the house, the room.

"...*we looked at each other in the same way then....*"

Karen. Dead.

He had to find out, now. He had to know.

3

Louise was pretty well in the bag when she came home. Handsome Dan, as Bill had called him, had been after one devil of a lot more than a dance. That was for sure. She had torn a stocking and stretched a strong bra to prove it. What a nut, that Dan. But a sort of sweet nut, at that.

She leaned against the outside of the house door a moment. Might be a good idea to fix her lips. He'd been like a seventeen armed gampus with ten mouths and an early mating itch, in the bedroom, there, when she'd gone to use the john.

Waiting in the shadows.

She chuckled softly. Oh, well. She'd fought for her honor, pretty much, hadn't she? And all that...?

As if it really mattered.

Next time, maybe la-de-da!

He'd been a skirt puller-upper, too, and fast as lightning. She thought of a more apt simile, but shoved it from her mind with a smile, straightened her dress, fixed her lips, touched her hair, blinked her eyes rapidly.

Toujours gai, she thought. *There's a dance in the old dame yet.*

All right. So, I drank too much.

But that Elaine. She was too much. Nick hadn't been able to do anything with her, the poor dope. She'd finally managed, too; into the pool, kersplash—in the raw. Nick gave up and retired to a lawn chair, and it was chilly out there, too, drinking by himself. She was sure a big busted bitch, that Elaine.

Handsome Dan from Tonowanda hadn't missed a thing.

Maybe, even... well, she'd find out. Tomorrow the phone would ring and Elaine Thomas would be a very sad pulsing hangover, indeed.

She went inside and closed the door.

What the heck? Every damned light in the house on, and the hi-fi blasting.

Sure. You might know. That tune, too.

Where or When.

She knew plenty, guessed, that is about....

She saw Lolly. Lolly was seated halfway down the stairs, on a step. Her eyes were half closed, and she was all folded up into herself, hair limp, lips puffed.

"Lolly." Louise hurried up to her. "What're you doing here?"

"How do you expect me to sleep with all this going on?"

"All what?"

"Please. It's just daddy. That same song, over and over. If he'd just change it I could stand it."

Louise glanced at her watch. It was quarter to three.

"Come on, now—up to bed. Snappy, like."

Louise guided the limp staggering Lolly up to bed, trying not to stagger at all herself.

"Now, you go to sleep."

Lolly looked up at her from the bed. She spoke matter-of-factly and plainly to the point. "You tell him to just turn that thing off, and go to bed. I'm sick and tired. I need my sleep."

"Yes, Lolly. 'Night."

"G'night."

She went downstairs.

Bill was on the couch, cuddling the bottle of gin. She plucked this from his hand. It was empty, and he was out cold, and that tune powerfully streamed through the well-lighted house. The ash of a cigarette was a long gray worm on the carpet. She brushed it. Now it was a long black worm.

She snapped off the hi-fi, and stood there a moment.

Every once in a while, something like this happened. He'd start playing that damned record, over and over, and his eyes would be far away. Where? Who was she? Louise knew very well it was a woman, and she sure must be some memory, because sometimes Bill would turn into a regular zombie. And he didn't have any affair going at the moment, either. She felt certain of that.

Of course, he'd come home early. But, no. That hadn't meant... well, it meant this.

It simply must be a memory.

Must be some memory.

Didn't the big stupid fool know everybody had memories?

It would be just like him to be in love with a memory.

She went around the house, turning off lights.

How long would this go on? As long as they'd been married, it had been that sloppy tune. Every now and then. She even knew enough never to touch that one album of records. How she knew! The first time she'd taken it down and started flipping through it, he'd acted as if she were chopping his soul with a double-bitted axe, or something.

She'd caught on, right away.

Sometimes, when she felt hellish, she'd wait till he was near her by the record shelves, and then she'd finger that album, start to take it down. Then glance at him. Boy. What an expression.

"Come on, you drunk. Get on your feet."

He finally came awake, and they moved upstairs together.

"Have nice time?"

"Yes."

"Nice. Good. Great."

"You?"

"Fell sleep."

"With all the lights on and a fifth of gin in your belly, and records playing all night."

"Records."

He turned abruptly, and lurched down the stairs, and she waited, hearing him fumble, and put away the record, then the album.

They got to the bedroom.

"Shall I help you undress?" she asked.

"Don' be foolish."

He managed to undress, managed to get out of the khaki pants. He got in bed and stared at her as she slipped her dress off, She was conscious of the torn stocking, and stripped it off immediately.

"Good time at the party?" he said.

"Yes, darling. I told you."

"Good. Great."

He was asleep.

She stood in front of the full length mirror on her closet door, kicked off her other shoe, stripped the other stocking off. Then she took off her bra. Not so bad, she thought, holding them in both hands. She ran her hands over her hair, then hooked her thumbs in her panties, and took them off. She stood nude before the mirror. She smiled at herself. She wiggled a little. Pull in your tummy, that's right.

She giggled softly, gave a couple flicks with the backs of her fingers to the triangle of curly hair up between her nicely shaped thighs, then turned and moved with a broad, accentuated hip-sway to the bathroom.

Shower, she thought. I'll feel better.

She paused by the bathroom door, glanced back at her husband.

He was snoring, his dark hair a snarled thatch.

Poor old boy, she thought. Who is it you dream about? Did she live here, in this town, where you grew up? Could it be that long ago?

Worse still, does she still live here?

Artists. Even commercial artists; though Bill certainly had dreams, and he did good so-called serious work. Maybe someday... but artists. What a crew, and Bill was tame compared to some. And writers. The creative instinct; never a truer word was spoken. She remembered a writer friend of Bill's. During the first five minutes after meeting him, he'd devoted himself entirely to her, then he'd tried to rape her on the spot, right in front of Bill. And all Bill had done was continue to smoke a cigarette, then ask if anybody cared for another drink.

A bunch of bastards, that's what.

She stuck her tongue out at him and headed for the shower, wagging her round behind, and thinking of Handsome Dan from Tonawanda. He'd had the creative instinct, and he was a boat builder.

Damn it, she thought. I should've stayed.

4

Bill sat in the studio with a broad background brush in his hand, staring ruefully at a vast expanse of naked white canvas board.

His head throbbed. There wasn't a precious drop in the house. He'd have to run downtown and have a few hairs of the dog, and buy a couple jugs.

He stared at the white expanse.

Louise had acted a little cool this morning. Well, it was nearly nine-thirty. He should've slept till noon.

He stared at the white expanse.

For God's sake, all he had to do was create a kind of modernistic glass of grape juice, with beads of cool sweat on it, and maybe a hand reaching for it—and maybe a couple of thirsty looking mouths. Okay, what'll it be? Kids, back from play? Mommy in the kitchen. Or a man and his wife, with fiendish eyes. Or a young boy and girl, maybe after a hot session on the living room couch, so she'd just fixed cool, refreshing grape juice in the kitchen…. Oh, yes. He remembered, all right. Karen. The kitchen. The grape juice—or any excuse, to get away from the lights in other parts of her home.

He hurled the brush down, stood up and stepped on a tube of burnt sienna. It burst and oozed richly in an oily spreading glob.

The phone rang.

He stared at it. No. It wouldn't be her—she'd have enough sense.

It rang again.

He just stared at it. This was the extension, from the main house. As a rule, he let Louise just answer it, and the hell with it, because he didn't want to be bothered while working.

But now….

The ringing ceased. Louise had answered it. He picked it up, gently, carefully, trying to make no sound.

Somebody was breathing.

"Louise?"

"Oh, Bill?"

"Just heard the phone ring, thought maybe you'd rung me."

"I thought you'd rung me. Doesn't seem to be anybody on—wrong number, I guess."

"Yeah. Well—"

Louise hung up. He held the phone, sweat beading his forehead, waiting. He could still hear breathing.

"Yes?" he said quietly.

"Oh, Bill. It's all right. I mean, I wouldn't mess you up. Not yet, anyway."

"I told you never to phone."

"I just wanted to be sure you'll meet me tonight. Same place. I love you. See you."

"Karen. Wait."

She was gone.

He replaced the phone, and slumped into a straight chair. An odor of turpentine and oil paints, the pungent weavings of linseed, filled the single large studio room.

Go downtown, he thought. Hair of the dog. Then, start checking. This thing is going to cut your throat without leaving a trace of blood, Sommers.

Move. Tell Louise you've got to buy some paints.

5

He drank three double martinis at Casey's Bar and Grille, bought two fifths of Gordon's gin, and went on outside. He stood on the sidewalk a moment, lighting a cigarette. Glanced up and saw her.

Directly across the street.

Karen.

It was Karen, absolutely. She came out of a dentist's office. Hargraves. She wore a white nylon dress, white shoes, and she carried that transparent raincoat over one arm. In her other hand, she had a large manila envelope.

She must work there.

But seeing her had turned him to stone.

A yellow cab drew up in front of the office. She climbed in, her hair soft and beautifully highlighted with auburn. She looked terrific in that dress. The dress revealed her shape, and set her off, somehow.

The cab started away.

A young man, very well-dressed, wearing a brown straw pork-pie hat with a broad maroon band, ran across the street, dodging through traffic. The cab almost brushed against him.

Close one, Bill thought, seeing it.

Move, Sommers. Maybe she's going home.

He made his car, a shining black Porsche Speedster. He tossed the bottles in, stacked himself behind the wheel, and took out after the cab. He whirled in a U-turn, and passed the guy in the brown pork-pie hat, standing on the opposite curb, lighting a cigarette.

Bill glimpsed the cab about two blocks ahead, stopped at a light. He snaked the Porsche like a crazy drunken bomb through traffic, roaring, his hands sweating on the wheel.

The cab lurched away from the light, made a swift left turn.

By the time he reached the same street and turned left, there was no sign of the cab.

He cruised around, looking, his heart hammering. He saw another yellow cab, or maybe it was even the same one, pulling away from the Post Office. He should have checked what the driver of her cab had looked like.

Maybe she was at the Post Office. He hurriedly parked, and rushed inside. No sight of her. He wondered if she had vanished on purpose? Had she seen him?

He realized with an ache that he wanted to see her, badly. He couldn't go to the dentist's office; that would be stepping out of line.

Go home, he thought. Go home and paint that goddamned grape juice thing; necessary slug for the poor tired minds of America's tirelessly slugged.

He remembered the kitchen again. The grape juice of yesterday. One seldom loses memory of a taste.

Then Karen again.

And tonight again.

And April was "Lanvin"; France's, or now America's finest perfume.

Idiots, he thought. Idiot!

April had been wine, then.

Now they sup on perfume.

"The clothes you're wearing are the clothes you wore...."

1

April.

He tried to force it from his mind.

Swinging the small, black sports car around the block, he drove back to Casey's. He had to make some attempt to find where Jamais had gone when she left Allayne so abruptly—so long ago.

This thing had him now. He was torn inside. He knew he had to do something or just drown in a present that had suddenly become spring in nineteen thirty-seven.

At the bar, he ordered another double martini.

It was a good bar; bold, beamed, cool and dark, with fresh sawdust on the floor, no chrome, and a black cloth draped over the juke box until one PM every day except Saturday, courtesy of Casey himself, a two hundred and eighty pound ex-bookie from Jersey, who had once trained horses in Kentucky, and whose one ambition had been to be a jock. "I was always just too damned hefty and hungry to ride." With a pug nose, red face, and dour expression, ubiquitous white starched shirt open at the neck, and white apron.

The walls were hung with photos and paintings of horse flesh and woman flesh, mostly undraped.

One of Bill's paintings hung there, done on a day long ago, while refreshingly crocked during a battle with Louise. The painting was of a lushly put together, black haired traveling whore who'd been on her way to Detroit. She posed in a back booth early one morning, when no customers were around; posed on the booth table, a red blouse pulled wide over astounding breasts, tight black skirt roped around her waist, revealing large white mare-like thighs. She'd posed straddling the table, with a bottle of wine on her right knee, a finger stuck into the bottle's neck.

The gilt-framed painting hung in a dark corner. Customers were sometimes startled when they came upon it unaware; it had been stolen and forgivingly returned twice.

Bill had titled it *"Stranger's Delight."*

Casey had built a drink around the name.

Just now, no one else was in the place.

Bill went to the far end of the bar by the phone, picked up the directory, and began searching.

There had to be somebody left in town whom he could ask about Karen.

Ask: "What happened to Karen Jamais? Where did she go?" Trouble was, most of her friends would be gone.

Casey brought his martini. "You okay? Not to intrude, but you look pale."

"I am pale. But I'm okay."

Casey grunted, returned to the other end of the bar with his morning papers.

Sure, Bill thought, thumbing the phone book. I'm fine. They'd sure think I'm fine if I told them it was an April day in nineteen thirty-seven.

His hangover had subtly changed into a state of mild pie-eyed nostalgia.

Where had she gone? He sipped the martini, trying to recall names, but a picture formed in his mind's eye of Karen waiting for him on the corner by the mailbox, tonight. She hadn't gone anywhere. She was right here in town. Just like always.

He drank the martini, lit a cigarette.

God. It was nearly a quarter of a century.

Only it wasn't. Only it was.

He was a walking contradiction in the midst of a timelessness that was a contradiction of itself.

Mixed in with the thick emotion was a sense of doom; like approaching a walled street corner and knowing that around that corner something black and shrouded waited, had been waiting all these long years.

No matter what he did, he would round that corner.

Louise. Lolly. He thought of them now with a sense of anxiety, because what would happen to them if he allowed what he'd desperately wanted for twenty-two years to swamp him.

He couldn't comprehend Karen's death. It held no meaning because last night he'd held her in his arms and kissed her lips, heard her voice.

He glanced up. A young man had entered the bar, carefully dressed in a dark suit, a brown straw pork-pie hat with a broad maroon band. He sat on a stool at the bar, ordered a draft beer, and leaned with his back toward Bill, apparently looking out the front window, toward the street.

Karen. Those undead years.

Could thousands of nights of wakeful remembering be abruptly dismissed when the dream was again sudden reality?

He was not naive. If he was, it still didn't matter. Because she was real; what was happening was real.

"Casey. Another double."

If he could just find where Karen had gone when she left Allayne all those years ago, it might help.

He knew he grasped at tiny brittle twigs.

The drink came. "It's an okay day, right?" Casey said.

"Yeah."

He checked names in the book. Finally he found a woman who hazily recalled Karen, and she referred him to a Miss Sally Beachner, who had no phone. "But it seems to me she and Karen were friends. It's so long ago. What'd you say your name was?"

"Just a friend, passing through."

"Oh. Well, try Sally." She gave an address.

He vaguely recalled Sally Beachner; a freckle-faced girl with untidy rust-colored hair. He couldn't remember that she was a close friend of Karen's. But, then, when Karen and he had been together, back then, they'd had time for practically no one but themselves.

He would have to reveal who he was to Sally Beachner. Give her some excuse. He was in the neighborhood, thought he'd stop and talk over old times.

He left the bar, his heart rocking. As he passed the young man seated on the stool, it seemed he'd seen him somewhere before. It was a momentary thought.

He went on outside, slightly unsteady, and choked a bit because with every hour he was closer to meeting Karen again, tonight, on the corner.

Sally Beachner.

Then what?

Outside the bar, it was still April.

It might as well have been nineteen thirty-seven.

Maybe it was?

2

Walter Hogan watched Bill leave Casey's over the rim of his beer glass.

Damned if that wasn't the same joker who'd been with her last night. Swinging on the high side, too.

A kind of foamy laughter stirred inside him.

Crazy. Well, there was nothing to do but sit and wait for the tide to come in. He'd tried hard to catch what the guy was on the phone about, but all he'd managed was that he'd been trying to locate some dame named Karen.

Lining up some snatch? Probably not married. Still. He might be married; he'd had a worried look about him.

Just as long as nothing got fouled up with this mark. And her name wasn't Karen. Walter Hogan knew her name. Jean Brooks.

Jean, baby. If you only knew what you do to me.

Like a wild clarinet screeching down his backbone.

A smile twitched at his lips, but he forced the laughter inward, forced the smile away, and sipped at his beer. She was over in the dentist's office. He knew she wouldn't come out till noon. It was damned near noon already. Man, like it would be cool kicks, following her.

The thought wrung him deliciously.

He sat there, letting everything well and itch inside him, surge potently like a kind of hot oil within his loins, slow and certain. He thought about the big payoff, wondering when it would happen.

Like a movie. That was the scene. You never knew exactly when it would happen, if it was a good movie. Wow, he'd like to see this in a movie; what he had planned.

What a bitch.

Only not planned.

Everything was building just right.

Lawd, dad, how she did come on in those white nylon dresses.

He mused on that for a time with increasing excitement; how it would be if he could nail her in one of those tight white nylon dresses. Tight and white. Something about white. Just strip it off her a small piece at a time, after he'd really beat the hell out of her, maybe hurt her good again this time, like. Then kill her... then very slowly strip her, only remember, you cat, you, *explain* it all to her beforehand, so she'd be sure to know everything—so he could feel it right into the marrow, and see it—that real fear. In her. Chills swept through him. He took out a sparkling white handkerchief, and patted his moist brow.

Dig, the ultimate.

Oh, yes, that was the way. Never take even a single mother's thread off her till....

Mother's thread.

He had to force himself to think of something else, because mother had to know, only you shouldn't think about it. Because she'd know.

Pow. He'd go straight through the wall, like a goddamned torpedo. Wham. Crash.

"Bartender? Another beer."

His voice was strong, well modulated, and there was that something in the voice that suggested this young man was accustomed to excellent service, to people who obeyed when he spoke. He knew about that, too. He'd worked long enough at it, hadn't he? For a Bunkie, Louisiana farm boy, he hadn't done so bad. And he'd do better. He would always get by and have his kicks, too. Yes. And one of these days, maybe a year or so, he would have taught certain people enough of a lesson. Then he'd find some nice girl and settle down, have a family, take a steady job, become something.

He always avoided exactly what that steady job might be.

But it would be something great, all right, with visions of charming girl secretaries, and soft-napped thick carpets, and a large polished desk with two or three phones, and a big intercom blinking away, and an immense picture window looking out on tall sleek buildings shining against the sky, a private bar in the wall, all you did was press a button, and the whole wall swept out, gleaming and shining. Certainly not like this crumby joint, here. A real full-time bar, right in the big plush office, and always a special girl, hired to tend bar, so when the bar swung out slowly—to music maybe Garner's *Caravan*—the girl would be seated on the bar. And she would say, "What's your pleasure?" No special type of girl, just so long as she was beautiful. He'd pay her a fabulous salary to do anything... anything... God, yes....

Even play dead, sometimes.

Because by then, he knew, there would be sometimes when he'd want to look back on this terrific scene.

This was a perfect spot to wait, though.

It surged inside him like a sea. But none of his emotion was revealed in his frank, tanned face, the frank open, clear eyes.

Hey, now, that bartender was sure a big son of a bitch.

"Thanks," he said, paying for the beer.

Casey yawned, rang it up, and retired to his papers.

Walter Hogan drank some of the beer, and got a tingly feeling in his hands, his knuckles. All through him, in fact.

Think of something else, he told himself desperately. You'll ruin everything, damn you!

There was a mirror on the backbar, behind some bottles. A small strip of mirror, but sufficient. He checked his face, and felt relieved. The All-American boy, yessir. All he had to do was go along, and select the one he wanted. He didn't have to worry about anything else.

Well, ma, she'd know, goddamn her. A dirty whore, she'd been, by God; screwing every man-jack she could; locking the bedroom door when they came to the house, thinking he couldn't hear the bed springs and the moans; what she said. He'd got hold of a stethoscope and used that, holding it against the wall, and he got everything. Liked to be mauled, did she? *"Pinch me, Jack pinch me—harder!"* And then every time he was with a girl, spying on him, and beating him with that broom handle. All the goddamned time. And just as he was getting ready to cream with Sally Laboire, that time, out behind the old pig-pen, how she'd come down on them, beating his back, cursing him, and Sally had run, and he'd just stood there like a goddamned dope, taking it and taking it, till he was bloody, the way she beat him; the things she called him. He still had the scars, and it had finally been the first time—*the first time*, with Sally Laboire. Man, she never even spoke to him again, and it could've been so beautiful, so perfect. He could still remember Sally Laboire, and her tenderness, how she'd said, "D'you really love me?" All that time ago, when he was twelve. Yes, his mother beating him with that broom handle. And she didn't have to tie him to the bed in his room like that. *"I'll tie you up, son—I'll tie you up. You're going to be a clean boy, a clean man!"* And, even then, he'd started asking her about his father. Where was he? *"He's dead, boy—dead. A wonderful man. You'd of been proud of him. He'd of whacked some sense into that thick skull of yours."* Sure. A dirty whoring waitress, she was, in those white dresses, and telling him how wonderful his daddy had been—father he'd never seen, even a picture. Always a good looking bitch, ma, too; sexy as all hell, and taking them into her bedroom, one after the other. *"Jack! Just rip it off!"* So, he wasn't enough of a man to be going with girls, what she said, right? A clean boy, and these girls you see, they're no good—no good. You've got to do better. And her in the bedroom, merrily screwing away. *"Son, I want it to be right for you, and I'll just tie you to the bed till you're big enough to know, so you can learn what's right. When you're big enough."*

And along in that time, he'd realized that's what she wanted; somebody big enough, so by god when he was fourteen, and one day tied to the bed, and suddenly not scared of her any more—that day when something clicked into place. *"You're my hope. You'll study and be a big man—really big. That's what I want. I want my son to be big."*

So she'd untied him, that day, and he even thanked her. Then he got the broom handle and went to her bedroom, and called her, just as she came home from work in her greasy white waitress' dress. She wanted things clean and she wanted them big, did she?

Okay. Well, he'd taken a bath, hadn't he? And then he gave her a bath and showed her the broom handle. *"Is this big enough for you, ma? Is it?"*

Well, they never performed any autopsy. They'd just buried her, and she had died just because people die, that's all. Because he gave her another bath afterward, and got her dressed in a clean white dress and laid her on the bed.

She had looked happy.

So, that wasn't bad, was it? That's when he'd cut out, at fourteen. That's when he'd begun his education.

And, dig, he didn't use a broom handle any more. But he was a clean cat. He had at least three or four baths a day, didn't he? And she knew. He knew she knew.

Because that's what she really wanted, didn't she? A big clean man. He was a big All-American clean man, wasn't he? He sure was. And he knew what she really liked, because he'd had a stethescope. She hadn't been able to tell him those things, but he knew. So, by hell, he'd give them to her. Like this Jean. Sometimes Jean even looked like her, the way she turned her head, sometimes. And....

Like, the way things happened. He'd never expected to be here in this town, Allayne. He'd been headed for New York from Chicago; he'd had the big city itch, and it hadn't worked right this last time in Chicago. He'd gone and planned too much, trying to make it perfect. He'd even had a broom handle, yes, and stood it in the corner by that dame's bed.

But it all went wrong.

Don't plan, you fool.

The slightest little thing goes wrong, and it's no good. Like that one in Chicago saying, *"It's what I like, you honey—how'd you ever know? But be careful!"*

Because they couldn't like it. And she'd actually asked him to sock her. Imagine.

It was like a scream inside him. They couldn't like it, because that was the big part. Them so nutty scared, it was just....

All that crazy stuff gets riled inside you then and you can't get it out any way—except....

He was on the train, and she came and sat in the same car, and he knew. Man, he'd developed that sense, hadn't he? He knew. He could tell, she was right. And that was it. She never saw him, not really, and right then he let it start building, and that had been over three months ago.

A long run. Just right.

But it couldn't be much longer. Allayne wasn't that large a town. He didn't have so much patience, any more.

He was running low on money, too. Bread, he thought, bread, you cat. And he'd have to steal some, some way. But never in the town where he had a thing going. Never.

Who would ever suspect him? Walter Hogan. Expensive luggage, good clothes, carefully selected and with real taste. Hadn't he read everything there was to read about how to act, how to dress? How to speak? All the subtleties; the humble, yet not humble; chin up, carelessly aggressive, a gentleman at all times, everywhere—and never a Crazy, man, like dig this scene; none of that hip life-talk he thought; never out loud. Except, maybe—that would be a good idea, when this one was flushed. San Francisco, and dig these beat characters. Give them something really beat.

But, Jean.

This time, looking out the window, and thinking of her, it was so abruptly strong, so powerful it almost swept him up. He actually had a violent impulse to run right across the street, break into that dentist's office, and let it happen.

Off it, man. Something else. Quick.

He sat there in a desperate state for a long, long moment, fighting like a maniac to overcome a compulsion that was like a savage pile-driver, a cannon, ready to shoot him straight across the street.

But, like it could get better than this.

It passed, and perspiration pricked him all over his body. That guy. That guy on the phone. Who was he?

If—well, you couldn't tell. There were lots of games to play, and he needed some good money. That guy looked as if he maybe had some good money.

"Bartender?"

Casey looked at him.

"Don't want to trouble you. Listen, that guy who was in here just a few minutes ago. I keep thinking I've known him someplace. Probably not so, but I can't get it off my mind. What's his name?" Not smiling, but very serious, with the brow wrinkled just exactly right the way he practiced it in the mirror all the time, intelligently inquisitive. A very faint tensing of the lips, a subtle lift of the hand. Just exactly right. He knew how. And they always answered right off; all you did was accommodate yourself to whatever environment, whatever type mentality, because they were all types in a slot in Walter Hogan's mind.

"Bill Sommers," Casey said.

He moved his head slightly from side to side. Deep thought, mistaken. "No. I'm wrong. Thinking maybe it was the army." He lifted his glass. "Just passing through, here for a few days. Well." He gave a shrug and drank. Now, inconspicuous through action; "You can fill that up again."

Casey did so. Walter Hogan paid.

"You certainly have a nice place, here."

"Thanks."

Walter Hogan slipped off his stool, strolled around, carrying the beer with him. Time to waste. He came around a corner of wall and saw a painting and the word "Jesus" slipped quietly between his lips.

He tightened his teeth, experiencing a violent surge.

The painting was of a well-built girl with an open red blouse and black skirt, one finger stuck into the neck of a wine bottle, straddling a table.

He stepped closer. What a bitch!

A lot like Jean. An awful lot like Jean, except she wouldn't act like that. But there was something about the look of her, the sort of sexy sadness in her eyes, the way her mouth curved.

A name was scrawled on the painting. Bill Sommers.

Jesus, he thought. Bill Sommers.

An artist. Well, I'll be damned.

He turned suddenly.

Instinct, dad, instinct.

She was coming out of the dentist's office. He walked slowly over to the bar, drank the beer to the dregs.

"Well, better be moving."

Casey said nothing.

Walter Hogan went outside, watching her across the street. She turned to the left. He cut across and started following. By hell, if it steamed up much more inside him....

3

Bill left Sally Beachner's place on Park Street. She'd been of no help whatever.

"Why, Bill! I haven't seen you for ages—simply ages!" And, after a while, with the freckles obscured beneath pancake thick enough to carve bas-relief in, the rust-colored hair blonde, now, and the odor of her sick father in the house, which she explained about, she answered his questions. "Karen? Lord, you two were like glue, weren't you?" Then the still sly, sickening, trite, "Bill? What do you want to see her again for? Eh? Eh?" The sly laughter that sounded as sick as the house smelled. And he had pressed, he'd had to, helplessly hoping. But, "I sure don't know and that was so long ago, Bill. Why, you old Bill, you! We were kids, then—just crazy kids. And I remember—say, you two had a fight, or something, didn't you? We all thought you and Karen'd get married; a sure bet. Remember in the school papers? All that? No, she just went away—I thought she went to a relative's or something. Something must've come up." She went with the sly line again, "Or did you break her little sweet heart, did you? Huh? You old heartbreaker. You know, I used to have a crush on you—imagine that."

And somehow he'd got away, wishing he'd never gone there. Somehow it faintly touched the wondrousness of Karen. Not really. But, people like Sally Beachner—oh, get off it, Sommers. She's just a poor kid who never will get herself straight, taking care of her father, that way. Lonely. Unwanted. Straining all the time. Wishing, hoping, dreaming.

He breathed deeply of April, and drove toward home.

Well, he'd have to keep trying.

A kind of terrific anxiousness was building inside him now. Strong and overwhelming. He shouldn't see Karen tonight. He fought against even thinking about it.

He wouldn't see her. That's all there was to it.

The only way.

Go home and paint that glass of grape juice. Be kind to Louise. She must never know. Suppose Sally Beachner, but, no. He'd explain, some way.

Something wrung inside him with sudden nostalgia; very strongly. Karen... Karen....

The street blurred slightly through the Porsche windshield. You crazy stupid sentimental nostalgic jackass, he thought.

But what the hell good did it do to call yourself names. There it was. Growing stronger all the time.

Karen.

Rise above it, Sommers. Rise above it.

Karen Jamais.

4

Dr. Hargraves had kindly given her the afternoon off, and it was a good thing. She had so much to do in preparation for tonight.

Sometimes, thinking about what she planned to do, it occurred to her it was rather sneaky. When she revealed the outcome to Bill, she knew it was quite possible he wouldn't at first understand.

She would make him understand.

He loved her just exactly as much as she loved him.

And since this was true, it was the only way.

The terribly intense feeling she held for him sometimes threatened to overcome her completely, to such an extent she wondered whether she would be able to go on.

It had been so long.

Since way back in the late thirties.

But when she told him everything, he would have no choice. And having no choice would help that poor weakness within him; he could overcome things more easily then. They could have each other, the way it was meant to be, for always. A rush of emotion threatened her.

She was in her room.

It was a single, large room, with an adjoining bath, decorated with an eye to cleanliness, but with rather old furnishings. The bed, for instance, was an old iron, double bed, dating from almost any early period of the century, and covered with a patchwork quilt. The carpet was something the landlady had purchased for next to nothing from a hotel when it had redecorated; once-maroon, and so thoroughly walked on, it was almost of a metallic texture. A tall Chinese screen enclosed the corner of the room opposite the head of the bed; black, with enormous green and gold and red dragons painted on it. The landlady had told Karen a painter had made that screen; he had lived in this very room for a time, some years ago.

This was nice. For though the painter hadn't been Bill, it served to further the wonder of her love. It could remind her of Bill. Though she needed no reminding.

She had taken down the three pictures that had been on the sad blue walls, because they were such poor pictures.

There was a small couch, a straight chair, and an over-stuffed old chair that smelled faintly of moth balls, but was comfortable—if you avoided the lumps. And she had a small table, and a hot plate, for what little cooking she did.

And her closet, with the clothes he liked. She knew exactly what he liked; she remembered so well. He had always told her what he liked best. For instance that Scotch plaid thin woolen skirt; sort of dull, really, she thought. But he liked it. He liked it best when she wore a nylon half slip under it, so it kind of slid along her body when he held her in his arms, when his hands moved over her.

She had to stop thinking like this. At least, until tonight., And she mustn't think too much about tonight, either.

The things they'd done. The things they'd had. The love that had been theirs. They would have it all again, now.

She glanced toward the phone by the head of the bed, on the rickety nightstand. Not yet. She had to be very careful, for his sake. Yet, she must phone him, because there was no other way of helping him have strength enough to meet her tonight.

This room really was drippy. She frowned, then shrugged.

She had to get out of her dress. Then she would just lie on the bed a while and dream.

She took off the nylon dress. Dr. Hargraves kept his office so hot, she couldn't bear wearing anything under the dress except panties and bra. The nylon was so hot, yet he insisted on it. Dr. Hargraves was a good dentist, and it had been terrific luck, landing that job as quickly as she had.

She stood in the middle of the room, took off her shoes and stockings and stretched and yawned, feeling a thrill. She possessed a beautiful young body and she knew it, and just exactly the way Bill liked, too. A bit on the plump side, but not too much, with nice full breasts, and well curved thighs... and everything....

She went into the bathroom, washed her hands, then padded softly over to the bed.

It would be so nice to finally get away from this room, and be in Bill's house, with him. She would do everything for him; cook all the things he loved to eat, and love him to death... and... just everything.

She'd been a drip to have waited this long, sorrowing over something that could so easily be righted. Just a jerk, that's all.

Leaning, she brought a small phonograph from under the bed, and laid it on the bed. Then, the records. She plugged the phonograph into the wall socket, then lay down on the bed.

Her brassiere felt uncomfortable, so she took it off, then lay there for a moment, revelling in the silence, and the deep promise of what would come.

Such an old house. Such high ceilings, and with those old black iron ventilators in every ceiling and floor. There was one in the ceiling right over the foot of her bed. Anybody could look right down, but she had checked about that. They must have come into style around the turn of the century, and at least this one was no longer used. She'd stood on tip-toe at the foot of the bed, and looked. It was all black, plugged up, like the one in her floor. You couldn't see a thing.

Somebody lived up there, a nice looking boy. She'd seen him. And sometimes she heard him moving around up there. It was very silent now, though.

She opened the phonograph.

Just think. Soon Bill could take her, and they'd go maybe to Syracuse and catch Bunny Berigan, and hear him play and sing *I Can't Get Started*; it was so out of this world, the way he did that. And *Let's Do It*. She liked that. And *I'm Happy Darling Dancing with You*, and *In a Little Spanish Town*, and *But Definitely*, and *That Foolish Feeling*, and *Skylark*. And T. D., too—especially doing *In The Still of the Night*, or *Night and Day*, or *I May Be Wrong*. Or one she really got a kick out of, *The Dipsy Doodle*.

And maybe, even, Bill might be able to ask Bunny to do their song, like that time in Rochester. *Where Or When*.

She got goose pimples, just remembering.

She put a record on the phonograph.

Their special song. And she didn't really know why, either. Just something about it.

Oh, Bill... now we know where and when, don't we?

She lay there, listening....

"The smile you are smiling you were smiling then...."

1

Well, darn! She'd dozed off. She'd slept over an hour. The record was scratching, so she fixed it and it began to play again.

It played very softly.

She lay there, listening, her eyes closed.

She and Bill mostly liked the slow tunes. Real dreamy. But sometimes she liked to swing it. Only, neither of them were Jitter-Bugs, really. Sometimes, though. But the way even some of their friends blew their tops on the dance floor, you'd think they were just a bunch of twerps.

Then she remembered the definition for twerp.

Who was it told it to her, just a few days ago. Oh, yes, Sally Beachner. She smiled, thinking about it. What a thing to say. But, really, it was kind of funny. A twerp was somebody who went around smelling girl's bicycle seats.

It had kind of surprised her, that coming from Sally Beachner. She was so, kind of all, well—drippy, really. Sally was. Of course, Sally didn't have a steady, or anything. And she tried hard to look glamorous, and how could anybody look glamorous with that kind of hair and those freckles, the way she had.

Of course, it would only be boys who were really twerps. But. Well, certainly girls didn't go around smelling... only somehow Sally just fitted into that category.

That was an awful thing to think.

Right after study hall, that was when Sally had told her. Just then, she remembered, she'd have to check her camera equipment. Well, there was plenty of time.

How she'd like to hear Bill walking by the house again, whistling *Moonglow,* or something. So she'd know he was there. Even if she couldn't come out, because her step-mother wouldn't let her. And she couldn't go to her father, because he was dead. And there was only her grandfather, and he was all the time drinking that dandelion wine, he made. And her step-mother didn't like Bill, and sometimes after they were together, her step-mother would say awful things to her. Once she called her "whore."

When she'd told Bill, he laughed. Anyway, she wasn't, because there was only Bill. Nobody else got anywhere, though she recalled many tried. She began remembering....

Suddenly she felt funny, kind of sick in the head; a sick headache, and it seemed for a moment as if she didn't know where she was. She thought of Grace Adams, and remembered writing her a letter. The room seemed foreign to her. Then she stared at the Chinese screen, and something began to feel good again, and she remembered Bill, and what she'd been thinking about and she felt all right again. But there was something black and balled-up, like a big ball of black yarn, or black spider webs inside her. For a time she couldn't rid herself of it because it was a guilty feeling about something she knew she'd done, and thought of a moment before, and now she'd forgotten.

Then she felt fine again. Perfectly fine.

Bill was jealous, terribly. That was supposed to be bad. Sometimes it was. He didn't want her to go anyplace even with her girl friends. He was curious. He had to know everything, and even sometimes it got her sort of irritated. It was as if he had to know every move she made.

Only she had never really disliked this, not really. Because, she loved him so much sometimes she couldn't even stand it. It was those darned mothers of her girl friends who kept snidely saying it was wrong, the way they were always together, every minute. Who were they to know? They were married, and they'd look out the window, and then say those things, damned well good and satisfied themselves, one way or another—but always butting in.

When she and Bill weren't together they were thinking about each other and writing notes back and forth, hundreds of them. She glanced toward the Chinese screen again, and her heart bumped and rocked hard inside her.

She was always being told by some buttinsky it wasn't right, the way she and Bill were so close all the time. If they only really knew!

She recalled with a kind of fever, the first time they'd done it. It had been coming for so long. She'd held off, and now she knew they were both like a couple of animals, denying themselves something they had to have to be complete. Until, one night at Bill's house, he was half crazy, and so was she and nobody was home for hours, and they hardly even spoke. They just had what they wanted like regular fiends, for hours.

After that, it was pretty regular. And they felt much better, too. It made them feel perfect, and nobody mattered; not even her damned fool of a stepmother. Plenty of times they were almost caught red-handed.

Just remembering set everything afire. It was so wonderful, sometimes she'd cry and her heart would actually ache with it.

And now, it would be all the time again. And she would have to shock Bill, hurt him, even, so he'd snap out of it. Not that she held anything against Louise, or little Lolly, his wife and daughter. But when something was like Bill and herself, it just had to be, because anything else was wasting your life. And she could tell how Bill felt, from last night.

He'd wanted her so bad it was terrible.

Just like on the porch after a basketball game, or something, maybe a movie, so long ago. Because they couldn't go inside. Trying to be very quiet, whispering on the porch; summer, spring, autumn, winter. He'd say, *"I just want to devour you, eat you up. I'll never get enough of you."*

They always took precautions, except a couple of times, when they just couldn't stand it.

She began feeling funny in the head again. Sickish... because, getting knocked up would be a real drag, and kiddo if you didn't dig that you'd better come by a dildo some crazy way, or else you'd wig over snappy triangles, or get eyes for a keen knife man. And fast.

She sat up in bed. She thought for a moment she would be sick, right there. Those words. What was she saying? Because when she sat up, she heard the record, singing beside her and immediately sank back with a deep sigh, forgetting she'd even sat up.

Don't let anybody ever tell you you can't do it standing up.

Yes. That time she'd kidded him, just to see what he'd do—told him she was going to have a baby, that something had slipped. Right away he was filled with plans; they would go to some other state and get married. Not a moment's hesitation. That's when she'd really known how much he loved her. She never doubted him again. Never. Not once. Not even after that terrible day when he'd told her he was through, finished, done....

That awful day.

Don't think of it. Please, God, don't let me think of it.

But now she knew he loved her. Not that she'd ever doubted. She hated to hurt him, now. But she had to. She had to arrange things, because he'd just go on suffering and dreaming about her for the rest of his life.

It was silly. That's what it was.

She'd just have to go through with it—tonight.

What was that boy doing upstairs? There was a regular thump-thump-thump on her ceiling, or somewhere, up there. Maybe he was hanging a picture.

It didn't matter.

Pretty soon, she'd call Bill. Be real careful, so Louise wouldn't answer, or ever get wise.

Wow, she'd taken some real creepy chances, sneaking over there. She'd been to his home maybe twenty or thirty times, since she came back to Allayne. She knew everything about the house; where he worked and slept and everything. Once, they'd gone out and left the door open and she'd entered the house.

It had been wonderful. She'd lain on his bed, and kissed his photographs, and done just everything. She'd touched every single piece of his clothes;

everything, so she'd know, and maybe even he'd know. She had found the album with the *Where or When* records, and she could remember the simply groovy thrill when she'd discovered that snapshot of herself, the one he'd taken of her in the skirt and sweater on the lawn in front of her home; she found it in his studio, under the big brass ash tray in his tobacco stand, beneath a sheet of protecting cardboard; she had inadvertently bumped the stand, jarred the tray, and explored. He'd been hiding it from Louise.

Some time she'd make him another copy of the photo; it was so badly worn, and he'd obviously liked it a lot.

That delicious summer, so long ago. The grass lush and green, and their loving, too, and the elms and pines, like warm scent drifting through the streets, across the nights.

They were together now. The past was gone.

The record played softly.

It was nearly time to phone him.

For a few seconds more she drifted upon vagrant memories.

The things she remembered. The endless things.

Then: I have to call him now, she thought.

Just a few days and we'll be together again.

For good.

2

She dialed his number and waited. If Louise came on, she'd just wait, or hang up. But Bill answered.

"Tonight," she said. "Same time. Eight-thirty. Everything's arranged, almost."

"I told you never to call here."

His voice was very sharp.

"Is Louise nearby?"

"No, she's not. That's not the point."

"I won't need to call again."

"What d'you mean, 'everything's arranged'?"

"I'll explain later. But—you come, or I'll go to Louise and tell her everything."

"Karen!"

"I mean it."

She hated doing this, and this was the least hurtful part.

"I've decided something," she said. "You come and I won't bother you any more."

He hesitated. She knew he wanted to say she wasn't bothering him.

"All right," he said.
"Bring your car, this time, Bill. The Porsche. I have something worked out."
"Tell me."
"No, darling. I love you. See you."
She hung up.
Tonight, she thought. Tonight is the beginning of the beginning.
She looked upward.
Did God know how much she loved that man?

3

Overhead, Walter Hogan lay stretched on his bed. He had showered and felt clean again. Clean and big. For the moment, now, he had no need to watch her, down there.

He'd caught something when she'd called over the phone, though. Sure as hell it was that Bill Sommers guy, and especially since he drove a Porsche.

They were going somewhere.

Well, he'd have to rent a goddamned car, that's all.

It wasn't going to be a foot job. Well, sometimes the other paid off still better.

That's why never plan, he told himself.

There was something working in his mind about this Sommers joker, but it hadn't come to the surface. An angle of some kind. He could sense it. What was it? Maybe this Sommers had a lot of loot, hey? Maybe there was some way... like two birds with one stone... something.

He got off the bed in the dark room. The window was covered with the shade and a blanket. He looked down the ventilator. Oh, Jesus, oh, baby, what you do to me, to me, to me. I just can't stand it. I could come right down there, right now.

"Only that would ruin everything," he whispered softly. But the way she lay spread out there on that bed, listening to that stupid record that didn't make it, not once; a stupid damned record, with no beat—or a lost beat. Why, good Christ, man. She needed a lay, that's what she needed. Then maybe she'd get with Stan, or Garner, or Bird's records. At least something. Something good. Billy Taylor, or Monk, some of them. Christ, she was digging herself a mouldy hole in a graveyard, listening to that kind of crap.

He stared at her.

Take your panties off, you sweet baby, you, he thought. "Take 'em off!" he whispered savagely.

She was twisting faintly on the bed. Suddenly she reached down and stripped her panties off. It almost knocked him out. Imagine! Talk about extrasensory perception; the strong wills of some people.

Now, he thought. Go to it, baby. I want to watch.

He waited. She just lay there playing the same record over and over again until he thought he'd go crazy; even some of this stupid rock 'n' roll would be better. At least those cats lived a little once in a while. If they were high on weed or shit or something they'd really wail, just for the sake of playing. She had on an Art Tatum record now, and well that man could blow when he liked, but he'd be better if he'd lost a couple fingers, only he didn't really make it with this tune. Nobody could really do up this number. Too bad Tatum was dead. Once she'd played Berigan's *Chicken and Waffles*, and *You're My Everything*; good stuff, but 'way yesterday, and you couldn't make a scene like that any more. Berigan had been good, before he'd pooped himself and croaked. A lot like Bix. And Prez, too. Jesus. Walter Hogan shivered faintly. It hadn't been too long ago he'd seen a picture of Young before he died; in a New York paper. Lester Young, that tremendous driving horn. Him sitting on his bed in Queens, with his axe on his lap. Really his axe and executioner. Man, he'd never forget that picture. It would haunt him forever. The absolute gone look of that cat who used to cock his sax at a forty-five degree angle and let them hear sounds like they never heard before. Never. That was before everybody.

He watched her. He couldn't watch her much longer, he knew that.

She lay there.

Maybe she's a passive lay, he thought. No sock at all. The thought excited him. Maybe he could go a before and an after. He'd never done that before. Maybe it'd be worth trying.

Oh, you bitch… put your hand there, so I can see.

She lay placidly on the bed, listening to an old, slow tune… a tune more and more forgotten… a tune with dust on it, that once lazily drifted through summer nights.

If he heard much more of that fucking tune, he'd flip.

For Christ's sake, what kind of a dame was she.

Her brain, her brain, man—dig the cerebral context, and then dismiss it. Because you can't care less, really.

What you looking at, man?

It's just that goddamned tune, over and over again.

Say, this Bill Sommers. Going someplace tonight, and it sounded as if she were on the make. But hip. Real nutty. Well, he'd have to snap out and dig a used car lot, or a Hertz joint.

And this time, tonight, take the binoculars.

He clenched his teeth. He'd like to get her to dance for him, you know? Yeah. Then give it to her solid. Then the rest. And when he was really pumped up, give it to her right.

What a blast of a programme, Jack. Why hadn't it occurred to him before? He'd have to watch out for these passive kittens. Maybe it was new kicks.

With her, though, down there, it was going to be absolutely the most.

Man, get out—get away!

He pushed the rug over the ventilator.

Wow. Pow. Bam.

He took down the blanket, and upped the shade on the window. Man. A little more, and he'd scratch himself right through the floor, like a deadly rat.

Okay. Get dressed. He checked himself in the mirror over the bureau. He needed a little trim. Had to look just right. And act just right. Cool it, cool it.

Let's move. And watch it.

He wondered if she'd heard the noises he'd made when he'd nearly flipped there, a while back? Out of control, just seeing her lying down there asleep, or half asleep, all alone, and quiet.

Just like she was dead.

Only her eyes weren't open.

The eyes should be open. That was important.

He recalled a certain graveyard episode, and a cool—cool, man! Cold! Frozen!—blonde, but forced it from his mind. That had been a long damned time ago, so flush it, Jack.

But it was there.

And he remembered the time working for that undertaker. Things were pretty much in the open there. Even the old boy himself; he could get pretty worked up... only all of that was long before he'd learned how to operate; before he'd learned the real need. How it had to be. The need to do the whole thing himself... just himself.

Yessir, Walter Hogan, he thought, gazing into the mirror, arranging his fresh tie exactly perfect, checking those collar wings. You're a real cat.

Just a question of time.

When would it happen?

Now wouldn't it be a drag if it happened in broad daylight on a main street? Keep it real cool.

He moved softly into the hall and his door closed with a barely perceptible click.

4

Bill stared at the white expanse of canvas board.

It was no use.

Ever since Karen had called, he'd felt dazed.

He kept lightly tapping the bottle of gin by his feet. It didn't help much. Louise and Lolly were on his mind. Yet, he knew he would meet Karen tonight.

It was just too damned much.

What had she meant when she'd said she wouldn't bother him any more after tonight? Could she have really meant that?

He should feel good about that.

He didn't.

It troubled him, and because it troubled him, he felt still worse about the whole thing. The fact that she had perhaps come to her senses, and would actually leave him alone was only frustrating. He experienced the same feelings he'd felt over the years, not having her, never being able to explain.

It was a mess. It tore at him, inside, and he couldn't do anything about it. Logic did no good. Knowing she wasn't really Karen did no good. Nothing did any good.

He was faced with something he didn't know how to deal with. Maybe the reality of it was that people never lost that adolescent sentimentality, or whatever it was. He'd always considered himself as completely unsentimental a person as existed anywhere—except for this one thing.

And maybe this wasn't sentiment.

What the hell could he do!

Whatever it was, it had him spinning.

There was Louise and Lolly, everything they had, everything he'd built, on the one side—and Karen on the other.

The hellishness of it was, that he'd never expected to see her again. He'd given himself over to the memory itself, sometimes wallowing in it; knowing it would have made his life complete. That without Karen, he would never be complete.

He'd thought this for a long, long time.

But he'd never expected to see her. He'd relinquished the hope.

And now, for Christ's sake.

Yet, she wasn't even Karen.

He drank again, straight from the bottle.

All he could think about was Karen. The way she'd been last night. The sound of her voice, everything. And he wanted her. He wanted her so bad, it was close to some kind of mania.

He got up and paced the floor of the studio.

All right. Face it. She said she wouldn't bother him any more after tonight. If she meant that, then that was it.

He looked out the studio window and saw Lolly playing in the yard. He flung himself on a battered couch. And he knew the fool he was being, too. She wasn't even Karen, and he knew it, yet he clung to the thing like a blind idiot.

Maybe if he went out and found a whore, really tied himself up for a few days; maybe that would get it out of his system. But the recriminations, the attempts, were futile.

He knew he'd make some damned excuse to Louise, and meet Karen in the car tonight, just as she'd asked.

Much more of this and Louise would get suspicious. That would be all he'd need.

He realized he was a bit tight. He intended to stay that way. He sat on the couch, lifted the large metal ash tray off the top of the smoking stand, removed a piece of thick cardboard, and brought out a snapshot.

He lay back again, staring at the picture.

All right, he told himself. Admit it, you fool. You want it this way. You don't care if she really isn't Karen. She's exactly like her in every respect, and that's enough. It's what you've wanted. What you've wanted for twenty-two years. Now you've got it.

5

"Kiss me, then, darling."

He had picked her up on the corner by the mailbox. The streetlight shone in on her face, where she sat in the small sports car, hunched around on the bucket seat. Even being here with her, it seemed somehow dreamlike. There was trepidation inside him. He didn't want to go through with it. Yet, he knew he would. At the moment, he found it difficult to define his feelings, save that he did want to be with her.

There were so many contradictions.

"You're terribly quiet, Bill."

He said nothing.

"You'll feel better later."

"What makes you say that?"

He had half a moment's desire to ask her to get out of the car, because he thought of Louise, Lolly. Yet, the moment was too strong. He had waited, dreamed upon this moment much too long to dismiss it.

Her voice reached him, soft, assured. "It was such a long afternoon, waiting for now. But now we'll really be together. You will feel better. Now, give me a kiss, and let's go."

"Go where?"

He still refrained from the promise.

"Well, we can't go where I'm staying. I've found a place."

"You've what?"

"I've found a place where we can—where we can be together."

"Listen, Karen...."

"It's all right. I took care of everything. We can always meet there, go there. They think you're my husband."

He didn't like it. He knew he was weak. Yet, he'd been over all the self-recriminations a hundred times and none of it did any good. He had to be with her. He was hazy from alcohol. It was the dream. Karen. The years. Nothing else mattered.

"Let's go," she said.

He could at least play along, see what happened. He didn't have to do anything, not really. But every moment with her only increased the voltage of the magnet.

"I'm known around here," he said. "Don't you realize that?"

She laughed softly, moved swiftly, and her lips brushed, his jaw. "C'mon, now, Bill. We've got to rid you of these thoughts. It's silly."

"Why can't we go where you're staying."

"Maybe sometime. Not yet. Not till everything's settled, don't you see? I live right in town. Somebody might just see you. I don't want to start anything."

"Start anything—!"

"Please, darling. Drive North out of Allayne. I'll show you where."

April winds blew gently through the car, and he knew he would go. He looked at her, and something tugged inside him, and he wanted her. She looked lovely. It wasn't raining, but she had brought along the transparent raincoat. She wore a dark skirt, a light blouse and sweater, her hair brushed to a sheen. He knew what it would feel like in his hands, and he suddenly wanted to bury his face in it.

Bury himself in the dream.

The unreal dream.

He cursed silently. It did no good. It changed nothing.

He felt as before. This was Karen.

Crazy or not crazy, he couldn't help himself.

He could sense her eagerness.

"Why did you want me to bring the car?"

"We're going someplace. I told you that."

"Where?"

"You'll see."

A car drew slowly past them, a dark sedan. It seemed to hesitate opposite them, then drew swiftly away, and turned a corner. Why it was he didn't know, but the thought came to him that it might be somebody who knew him. That could be bad.

6

They drove out of town. Karen was silent. He was left with the usual thoughts, and a mounting sense of something akin to recklessness.

He realized he was going along with something that could bring evil repercussions. It didn't trouble him as much as it should. There was still plenty of alcohol in his system, and he supposed that had a lot to do with it.

Just the same, he shouldn't be here.

Only he was.

Only he couldn't rid himself of the desire to hold her in his arms, and with every moment, he sensed the night would bring exactly that. It tingled inside him, now. It was like holding his breath. He forced himself to dismiss all thoughts of Louise, or tried. Still, Louise was there.

He wished he had another drink. He needed it.

He wanted to ask Karen a lot of questions. He couldn't bring himself to. It was a culmination and he knew it, and couldn't avoid it. It was just too damned much to contend with.

He loved this girl beside him.

That she wasn't even truly Karen no longer troubled him. He had somehow accommodated himself to the dream. He knew a big share of it had to be because of the alcohol, but just the same, here he was. Here they were.

In this muddled state of mind, he heard her speak.

"It's not much farther."

"What?"

"A place where we can be together, undisturbed, Bill."

In the back of his mind, it kept returning to him that he should laugh this whole thing off. All right, go through with it tonight. Nobody need ever know. Then laugh it off. Tell Karen Jamais he would never see her again. Even take Louise and Lolly away on a vacation, anything. But put a stop to this fantasy.

He knew he would do nothing of the sort.

He couldn't.

The quickening within himself at just being with her, hearing her speak, being able to touch her, was so much as to destroy whatever qualms he had at the moment.

"Turn off here."

A narrow macadam road led to the right off the main highway. He took it, and they drove through the night.

"I'm very well known around here," he said.

He sensed conspiracy now. For some reason he also sensed a kind of fear in himself. He rejected the fear, but it didn't go away. It was an attempt at mental rejection, and it didn't work; the physical sensation remained. He had to attach it to something; he attached it to the moment.

He knew why she was doing this.

He knew what would happen.

He wanted it to happen.

His heart beat sullenly, heavily, quickly.

"Bill, this is heaven."

"Yes."

He had heard the breathlessness in her voice. And through it all, he sensed disaster. Only disaster could come of it, yet he had to go through with it. Where was it leading. She wasn't Karen, the Karen he had known. Who was she? He did care. Maybe he was insane. Maybe it was all a dream, a real dream.

He knew it wasn't.

And there were sharp moments when he wanted to pound his fists against the steering wheel, not alone because of his weakness, but because he knew nothing of her, really.

Yet, he couldn't prevent himself going through with it. With catastrophe looming at every point, directed toward him, he was still unable to take action. Conventional action. He tried to think of other things. He could think only of her; the sound of her voice, the feel of her when he reached out and took her hand, the look of her seated there in his car, waiting.

He was wronging Louise.

What they don't know can't hurt them.

Only that didn't suffice.

Yet, it must suffice.

He wished he had a drink.

Artificiality again. Yet, what he felt for the girl was anything but artificial.

"Here we are," she said. There was a strong excitement in her tone.

This moment had been building to a crescendo. Now it was close. Reality was dimmed even more than it had been. Instinct and the desires of years was taking over.

She had him turn off the road toward a group of cabins; a small out-of-the-way motel of sorts, set among pines and elm. The place was backed by a small lake.

The cabins were in a semi-circle. The place was old, dating perhaps from the late thirties. The owner obviously did little business; just enough to get by on. Bill recalled that this road had once been the main highway, and he supposed he should remember the place, though he didn't.

"They might ask questions here," he said.

"No reason, darling," she told him. "I rented a cabin. You're my husband.

We had to move from our home, because we sold it. Meanwhile, we're staying here while we look for another place."

"That's what you told them?"

"Yes." She pointed. "Ours is the last one, down by the lake. Set back in the trees, there. See? We won't be bothered at all."

The main house, with the office, was dimly lighted, he noticed as they drove by. He didn't like any of it, but was completely overwhelmed in this thought by her immediate presence, and by the soft sound of her voice.

He drove past other cabins, only one of which had lighted windows.

The place was called Pine Lake Lodge.

He parked the car.

"Karen. You really want to go inside?"

His voice sounded foreign.

"What do you think?"

She had arranged all this. Why had he asked such a stupid question.

She was already out of the car. Her door closed.

He hesitated. But his feelings were uppermost. It was what he wanted. He couldn't deny it. Again, he wished he had a drink. He got out of the car.

She waited as he came up to her. Even in the dim moonlight that shone through clouds that raced across the dark skies, her face, turned toward him, seemed to glow with everything he felt for her.

When she spoke, her voice was subdued.

"Shall we go in?"

He said nothing. But close to her, now, his emotions were very strong. They moved toward the door of the cabin. A car moved slowly past out on the road.

He couldn't speak to her properly, for some reason. Something he couldn't put his finger on made the scene faintly unreal. Out of the past; of memory. It seemed almost as if he were acting a part.

In a moment they were inside the cabin. It was better furnished than he'd hoped. The room was large, with a bedroom off to one side, revealed through a draped archway. The main room was furnished rustically, and there was a fireplace. She commented on this.

"The only one with a fireplace. It's not cold enough for a fire, though. Just the same, I like it."

He said nothing, looking at her.

She moved close to him, said, "Oh, Bill," and was in his arms. Once again he was swept up. There was nothing he could do, and this woman was more than wine.

His mouth was on hers, and he felt the way she breathed. Outside, a wind keened through the pines, softly, distantly. He wanted to ask again who she was.

He didn't. The feel of her body close to his was more than he could stand.

A kind of Niagara of emotion swept through him, and he sensed the same thing in her. Her breasts thrust against him, and he felt the stirring movement of her thighs. His hands ran along her back, and she pressed against him tightly with a little moan, her mouth open. And something happened to her. She became breathless, wanton, seeking him as much as he sought her.

A compelling wildness came into them both.

"Bill, how I've dreamed."

"Yes."

Any remaining shred from the world of reality vanished. Abruptly Karen broke away from him. There was something sly in her glance, her face was flushed.

"Come," she said.

One light was turned on in the living room, a pale suffusion from a small table. She moved beyond the rust-colored draperies through the archway into the bedroom, and a light came on in there. He saw it was a bed light, at the head of a large, comfortable looking double bed.

"Bill?"

The cabin was quite warm.

She stood just beyond the archway in the bedroom, watching him. There was something shy in her glance, but her gaze revealed a boldness that cut into him. A smile played across her lips, and again he felt that twinge, because there had always been a boldness in Karen that he had ever remembered. He stepped toward her.

Again she was in his arms, moving her hips excitedly.

"Bill. I can't wait."

Her words were whispered against the side of his jaw, as her firm young body pressed against him.

For a moment, he felt a sense of disturbance. He shouldn't be here. Then her lips wiped that away, and he held her tightly, wanting her. It was all the nights and days, the years, of recollection, swamped into this single moment, and he couldn't control himself.

He never experienced such sudden savageness as she revealed, then. Her fingers gripped him, and their teeth clicked in the kiss. She was panting, worming herself against him, lacing her body against his.

"I've waited," she said between tiny gasps. "So long. Let's lie on the bed."

"Karen."

Somehow, they were on the bed, and nothing mattered. He buried his face in her hair, inhaling the smell of her, needing her perhaps more than he had ever imagined and at the same time realizing in the back of his mind that he was still quite drunk. But he thought of nothing other than Karen, then. His hands sought her out, and she came more alive than ever, whispering things to him, trying to get closer to him, and there was something almost frantic in her. Somehow, the thin sweater was off, the blouse unbuttoned, and she wore no brassiere. His lips were on her breasts. She moaned, arching her back, whispering his name with her eyes clenched tightly shut.

"Karen."

He felt no sense of guilt, then—only a wildness that pervaded them both, sending him down and down into a kind of maelstrom, filled with dreams and nameless things. He wanted to rip the clothes off her. He wanted to tell her a thousand things, things that had been in his mind for years and years, reserved just for Karen Jamais.

Everything about her was familiar to him. The past was the present. There was no need to speak; they had simply been apart for all these years and now they were together again. The drive was tremendous.

Each time they kissed and touched, now, the intense pleasure was renewed with force, and he knew he was drowning. Her skirt was up to her waist, and his hand moved along bare white thighs, beyond the rims of her rolled stockings. They clutched and clamored at each other, and outside the April winds purled through the pines.

"Bill," she whispered hurriedly. "I didn't—I didn't wear any pants."

And the winds purled through the pines. Leaves and twigs rustled. Branches scraped against each other.

The wind was rising.

A branch scraped lightly against the side of the cabin.

"I love the wind," she said. Her voice was a moan.

"Yes."

7

Only it wasn't the wind.

Walter Hogan crouched by a window directly beside the bed. He peered between a voluptuous open fold in the curtains, and his view of the two people inside the bedroom was unobstructed.

Have to be more careful, he thought desperately. He'd lost his balance in his eagerness, and scraped the side of the cabin with his hand. Wow. If they ever knew he was out here.

Crazy. Dig it—dig it.

He stood like stone, a black figure, pressed tightly against the side of the cabin, worming in a cocoon of almost fiendish glee. It was more than he could have hoped for, and it was all he could do to contain himself. His breath came in sharp gasps, and he was perspiring heavily beneath his topcoat. His head was wet under his hat.

If he could just last through all of this. If he could just stand it. This one would be the end. He knew he'd explode when he finally got her. But he had to last, and it would be a fight, he knew that. It was all he could do to restrain himself from bursting through the window into the bedroom.

Window, hell! The way he felt right now, he'd smash straight through the wall. Nothing could hold him.

You're my baby.

Pow. Wham. Bam.

And something else ate at him. More than ever. More than usual, and he couldn't help but think of his mother with her men, because this babe was working things her way, too. Maybe she wanted a clean one. A big one. Big and clean. Yeah. Wow. Sweat trickled down his face, stung his eyes, and for a long moment he was back in a Bunkie, Louisiana farmhouse, thinking, listening, thinking what he would do with the broom handle.

He fought against something then that welled inside him; something that came up like rich vomit, scalding his throat with bitterness. He had to wipe it all out. He had to forget, somehow. He had to. It would drive him nuts.

But he couldn't forget.

And them, in there, on the bed....

He was clenched tightly within himself, watching. A shadow was spread over him, so he was almost invisible, like some devil perched on the rim of a dream.

Ah, God.

He strained against the rough side of the cabin, hearing the winds through the pines overhead, staring with a hot intensity into the cabin, at the bed where the two figures lay entwined. He wished he could hear what they said.

They weren't speaking much, though. And damn, it couldn't be much longer, the way he felt. He knew he couldn't wait much longer. It had to be soon, or he'd just fly apart, disintegrate. And if he weren't careful, he might do some fool thing, and blow the whole game. And wreck everything.

Sometimes when he thought like that, he had flashes where he half wished he could be caught. He often pictured himself telling the officers what he'd done. The police. He fought wildly against this vision, but sometimes he couldn't help himself picturing it in his mind, no matter how hard he fought. Because he knew the consequences. It would appear and he'd curse and try to quell it, but nothing helped. There was this crazy feeling inside him; that if he could just tell them, then maybe it would all go away.

Sure. Away it would go, all right. And you'd burn, Hogan, you cat. You'd burn.

Look at her. Wow. Pow. Just like... he's kissing her right on the... and then Hogan stiffened.

What the hell was she doing, there?

She was on her back. Her left hand was feeling around over the edge of the bed, on her side, clawing almost. What the hell was she trying to do?

Hogan strained. He tried to see in the dimmer shadows at the edge of the bed. He could see, all right, because the edge of the bed was very close to the window, and his round eyes.

Some kind of black cord. What the hell was up?

A black cord, pinned to the side of the mattress, with something on the end. She kept working it, punching it with her thumb.

Her skirt was up to her neck and she was all undone. The cord. What was it?

There she was, loving the hell out of this poor dope, and fooling with that black cord. It reminded him of a girl he'd known in Florida. She would suck an orange all the time, right while they were doing it in bed. Sucking an orange, and sometimes even humming to herself.

But this one.

What went with that babe?

Then he just forgot everything for what he could see.

He thrust his face against the window, and his hat fell off. He didn't even know it fell.

"Jesus," he whispered. "Jesus, God. Oh, man. It's crazy. This is the best yet!"

He whispered it, his mouth pressed against the window, his lips, his eyes burning and his whole body palpitant with crazy desire.

Christ, if he could only be in there instead of that poor old bastard.

Wait, you sweet bitch. Just wait.

He'd play her like a bongo.

8

She entered her room back at the rooming house, turned on a light and moved dazedly to the bed. She sat on the edge of the bed, holding her purse, a small black one, in both hands.

She didn't want to hurt him.

But it was the only way, for them both.

The night had been marvelous. It hadn't gone exactly as she'd planned, but all of that could come later. Maybe, maybe she even respected him more for the way he'd acted, finally. Maybe it meant more to her.

She fell back on her bed, eyes closed dreamily.

Oh, how she loved him.

And now, she had to run back out there. Right away.

She'd take the rented car, and run back out there, and pick up those things. She hated to go. She just wanted to slip into bed now. It would be so nice.

Just to lie here, and dream; relive every precious moment.

Oh, Bill— Bill, I love you so.

She lay there.

And I have to hurt you, Bill. But you'll get over it. And then everything'll be fine. Maybe—maybe….

Yes. Maybe he would understand right away. Because he loved her, too, she knew that. That was how she knew she was doing the right thing, even if it did take every speck of nerve she had. She glanced over toward the Chinese screen.

She forced herself to her feet, and left the room. The door closed softly.

Overhead, another door closed softly.

The room waited. It waited for perhaps thirty-five minutes, and then the door opened, and she entered again.

This time, she carried a small black bag. She came to the bed, dropped the bag, and just stood there for a time.

She had returned the car to the agency. She would have no further use for it. Her eyes seemed to still look inward, and she still was experiencing the sweetness of the evening.

What was he doing now?

She'd taken a terrible chance. If he'd ever caught her doing what she'd done, it might have ruined everything. Because, that way, she might not have been able to explain. He might not have believed her. But, after she finished with everything, then he'd believe. She could make him believe then, and they'd be together forever.

He was in a rut. He was filled with the rules of convention, and she didn't blame him for that. So she had to jar him out of the rut, that's all.

Well, she had things she must do. She couldn't wait.

The sooner, the better.

She picked up the black bag and moved into the bathroom.

9

Overhead, Walter Hogan lay stretched on the floor, watching through the ventilator.

What the hell was she up to now?

This one was real crazy. All the way.

He stood up, shook his head, and moved over to the bureau, feeling his way in the moonlit dark. He stood before the bureau and stared at the reflection of his face, faintly revealed in the mirror.

Then he silently slid a drawer open, felt around, and brought out a soft, slightly oiled flannel cloth, opened it.

Moonlight shone upon a .38 belly gun. He hefted it, liking the feel of it in his palm. He heard movement down there. He quickly but carefully re-wrapped the revolver, placed it in the drawer among shirts, closed the door and hurried silently back to the ventilator.

A real crazy kitten, down there. Out—'way out.

"But I can't remember where or when...."

1

Louise hurried up the front walk, opened the door, went inside, closed it, and stood there.

"Is that you, Mommy?"

"Yes, dear. You get on up to bed."

"But where were you?"

"I just took a walk."

A walk. It had been some walk, all right. She leaned against the door, feeling strange inside, and somehow ashamed.

Lolly was halfway down the stairs. She watched her mother, dubious.

"Up to bed, now," Louise said.

"You've been gone awful darn' long," Lolly said.

"Yes. Never mind, honey. I'm here, now."

"You left me all alone. Daddy isn't here, either."

"Please, honey—" Louise moved over to the stairs. She wore a tight woolen skirt, a heavy white cardigan. Her hair was snarled, her face flushed, and there was a worried, strained look in her eyes. She knew her garter belt was twisted, and hoped her panties weren't hanging out of her small handbag. "Please, trot on up to bed, now. It's getting late."

"Gimme a kiss."

Mother and daughter moved to each other on the stairs. Louise patted Lolly's shoulders, and kissed her brow. The child turned and moved upstairs, one of these black balloon Hong Kong dolls hugging her leg.

Louise stood in the hall, experiencing a sense of shame, and wishing it would go away. Whatever had gotten into her? Why had she acted as she had? That Dan Walters, from Tonawanda had dropped by, asked her to go out for a walk with him. He'd been staying over at the Thomases for a few more days then he'd planned. It had been some walk.

She lifted her skirt to her waist, revealing twisted nylons, and smooth thighs. She straightened the stockings, and the garter belt, then nervously smoothed her skirt down.

How had she ever agreed to go with Dan? How leave Lolly all alone in the house, with no notion when Bill would be home.

Bill.

It was just Bill's fault, that's all!

She almost stamped her foot. She knew it wasn't true.

But what was the matter with him? Why had he been acting so damned strange? He'd been half bonged all day, and hardly spoken two words to her. He'd been brusque with Lolly. He'd tried to cover it all up by saying he was terribly busy with a painting. He'd rushed out of the house early in the morning with the flimsiest excuses; had to run over to Rochester. An art exhibit he positively couldn't miss. Also, he hadn't asked her to come along, which was unusual.

Where had he gone? Why?

Yes. Only she knew it had been coming to something like this. They had been growing further and further apart. Still she didn't know why.

He'd been in an abstract mood all day. Jumpy, too. And that guzzling. She hadn't seen him put away liquor as he had today for years. What was the matter?

But. Her expression changed. Dan Walters.

Her face flushed with memory of "the walk."

They had walked as far as his car, a gleaming black Queen Elizabeth, which just happened to be moored down the street. He had "happened" to notice Bill drive away.

"Purely by accident, baby. I was driving by your place. I figured you might be lonely." How he had chuckled over that, winking slyly.

She knew his type well. Yet she agreed instantly to accompany him, to walk, to climb into that veritable bedroom of a car and be whisked away into the April night.

And then....

She felt she'd rather avoid the "thens." Was she a complete fool? He'd even had a miniature bar in the car. They had parked by the lake, under the willows, and he fixed martinis—in the car.

That wasn't all. There was a button. He pressed it and they were in bed together. She didn't want to think of it. She didn't know what to do. How could she face Bill, because, she'd just said to hell with everything, and she could still hear Walters' hoarse hot voice. And he was staying at the Thomases. Suppose he said something, tossed off a crack, to them. It wouldn't have to be much. Next thing, Nick might let a hint drop to Bill. Panic began to nibble and gnaw.

The feel of his hands, his lips—the whole engulfing episode swept through her.

She wouldn't forget easily.

Suppose he called her and Bill answered the phone?

She didn't want any further part of Walters. He'd been like a fiend. He'd even... she tensed, then shuddered.

She stared at the frill of lace pants in her purse.

Suppose he called her and Bill answered the phone? To spite Bill?

She didn't know what to do. She felt a sense of sudden shame. Goddamnit, she thought.

Yet she still experienced deep disturbance over the way Bill had been acting. There was abrupt, painful conflict, consciously within her. What was going wrong?

She heard the Porsche coming down the street. She couldn't mistake the irate roar of that engine as it turned quickly into the drive.

She put one hand to her mouth and tears sprang to her eyes. Almost wildly, she turned and rushed up the stairs.

2

Bill climbed out of the sports car, walked halfway toward the front door of his home, then just stood there on the lawn. He'd been a fool.

There was the first touch of real guilt inside him now, for the first time since meeting the girl. He didn't know what to do about it. Laugh it off. But he was still pent up some from what had happened out there in the cabin, with Karen. Pent up? Christ.

As young as she was.

It burned inside him, sent the blood into his neck and shoulders. He felt hungover from all the booze. This added to his confusion. It was a mess. So what was he going to do about it? Obviously, never see her again. She was just a teen age kid. A little girl. And he didn't even know who she really was.

She'd said she wouldn't bother him again.

But many of her remarks had been contradictory. Such as, "Now we'll have this place to come to." Meaning the cabin. Did she expect him to keep up the rent? Next thing, she'd want him to fix her up with an apartment in town. Young as she was, she was also plenty wise.

Still, there was the memory of her—the memory of Karen. Something that has been with one as long as this had been with him wasn't dismissed so easily.

Confusion reigned. He knew it.

And now, he had to go in and face Louise... and lie to her.

He wished he were drunk.

What good would it do?

He moved to the front door and went inside. Lights were on, but there was no sign of Louise.

"I'm up here, Bill."

She spoke softly from the head of the stairs.

They looked at each other.

3

Walter Hogan lay on the floor of his bedroom, and watched the room below through the ventilator.

He lay there, waiting.

The girl came out of the bathroom, took off her sweater, and tossed it over the back of a chair. His mouth was dry, watching her. He knew he couldn't stand this much longer. He knew the moment was rapidly approaching, that no matter what happened, he'd have to go through with things—soon.

God, what a choice piece.

Now, what the hell?

Back into the bathroom. Then out again, and over to the wall switch. The room went dark. The bathroom light was on, though, so he could still see her. Something new, all right. She'd never turned out the room light before, just to enter the bathroom.

He lay there, squirming inside.

She closed the bathroom door. Crazy. But a streak of light showed from the bottom of the door. He heard clinks and rattles coming from down there. Then she began running water in the sink. What the hell was she doing?

The bathroom light flicked out.

He waited.

Why had she gone all the way back to the cabin? He had followed her in the rented car, but had been unable to get close enough to the cabin in time to see what she did inside. What was she up to?

Then he recalled the black cord, and how she'd kept punching the end of it with her thumb. What had that been for? A crazy kid, that's all. Really wailing.

Man. He lay there, thinking about her. Actually he thought around the edges, now. He didn't dare really concentrate on her as he had before, and he was afraid that tonight he'd be unable to watch her take off her clothes and go to bed, the way he always did.

Things were too close. He wouldn't be able to stand it. He knew this well enough. He didn't want to tear everything now. First thing, he'd be down there, right here in this house. And that would be bad. Because things could get out of hand—very much out of hand.

Besides, he wanted to know what she was doing. What sort of game was she playing with this guy Bill Sommers?

He'd been a little disappointed with what went on out at the cabin between the girl and Sommers. Not really, though—not too disappointed.

Get off it, Hogan!

He began to writhe slightly on the floor.

Sounds came from down there, from the bathroom. Clinks and clanks. Then silence. The lights came on. They were on for a while, and the door opened. She came out into the bedroom, went over to the bed and sat down. She was thinking about something.

She began taking off her stockings.

He couldn't stand it. His face became taut, and a touch of saliva showed at the corners of his mouth. He felt his insides move as he watched her lift her skirt carelessly, and slowly roll the stockings down her fine white thighs and calves.

It disturbed him more now than ever before.

She lay back on the bed, staring at the ceiling.

She closed her eyes.

Her skirt was rumpled up, rather high.

He rolled swiftly away from the ventilator, panting.

Finally he rolled back and began watching some more. A new feeling was in him now. He recognized it immediately. The girl lay that way for a long time.

A terrific urgency was building inside him. It was no longer mere tantalization. It was mingled with a frustration, now. It was ignition, and all he could bear. He could actually hear the pound of his heart, his blood, at the side of his head. His palms were soaking wet against the floor.

Do something, you crazy bitch!

He knew he would lie here all night, if she didn't move. He would lie right here on the floor forever—or until he just went down there and....

Cut it out, Hogan.

He had to quit thinking. Just watch and don't think.

She moved faintly on the bed. Her every movement drove wild heat through him. His body was so alive, he could feel every faint indentation of the floor.

He lay there, listening to the thrust and pound of his blood, watching. He could hear a trickle of water running in her bathroom.

She remained stretched out on the bed for a long time, perhaps twenty minutes. Then she began to stretch. He watched this, actually trying not to watch, but unable to prevent himself. And all the time this bright new thing inside him boiled harder and harder. It was no longer in control. He bit his lower lip, and his fingers trembled where they were outstretched on the floor.

Calm, Hogan. Stay calm. The longer you wait, the better it's going to be. Hang on, somehow.

Experience. That was it.

Abruptly, the girl turned, sat up, and swung her feet to the floor. She rose and moved to the bathroom. The trickle of water ceased. Walter Hogan gasped. He had been holding his breath, and his entire body was covered with a fine film of perspiration.

He could hear her humming, now.

She came out of the bathroom again, and went to the dresser, over near the door of the room. She opened a drawer—still humming happily—and brought out a wide red scarf. It was made of thin material, Hogan saw, judging from the way it hung in her hands. Then she stepped over, and leaned down almost directly beneath the ventilator in his floor. She was spreading the red scarf over a floor register. The scarf moved and bulged slightly, from the rising gush of heat.

Back to the bathroom. She returned almost immediately with something in her hand. Pieces of paper. Four of them; two in each hand. They dripped water.

She went to the register and carefully laid the pieces of paper on the red scarf. The scarf fluttered. She picked up her shoes, and weighted the scarf down on either side with the shoes.

Hogan strained, peering down as she moved back toward the bed.

They weren't just pieces of paper. They were photographs. Startled, he stared at them, trying to make them out. They were very small, but he was directly over them, and he began to see what they were.

That little minx!

Photographs.

Photographs of herself and Bill Sommers on the bed, out there at that cabin where they'd been. And the poses were plenty compromising.

Crazy, man.

Dig that little witch. And Hogan knew then what the black cord had been. Somehow, she'd rigged a camera, and she'd been taking pictures right while she was on the bed.

Wow.

She had developed the film and the prints herself, in her own bathroom. Dig that, will you! Now she was drying the prints on the scarf over the register.

He kept straining his eyes at the pictures. They were good ones, all right. She was all spread out on the bed, with her skirt up to her neck, and that Sommers guy was loving the dickens out of her. And you couldn't mistake his features, either. In one of them, he was kissing her breasts, and his face was almost full toward the camera.

The girl was stretched out on the bed again. A smile shadowed her red lips, and she looked very happy, lying there.

An itching was all through Hogan. There was the overwhelming itch and ache for her, for what he knew he would do. And there was another itch, now. An itch to know what she planned do with those pictures.

Blackmail?

It had to be something like that. Good Christ, you'd never think it to look at her. But it had to be something like that. It had to be that. What else?

All the time—just think of it!—all the time, she'd been working some damned kind of a game of her own.

And all the time, he was playing a game, too.

Now, he could nail two birds with one....

Hogan didn't even realize he was thinking for a moment. then it came with a rush, all of it. Money and the girl, too. Because this Sommers guy would have money. Maybe not a hell a lot, but plenty. Plenty so he—Hogan—wouldn't have to take a job and save, the way he sometimes had to; so he wouldn't have to plan a robbery, anything like that.

The more he thought about it, the more excited he became. It promised untold variations.

Calm. He had to stay calm.

He could blow this thing easily. Play it cool, man.

But when he glanced over toward the girl, he knew he wasn't going to be able to play it too cool. Not with what she did to him. Not with the way he reacted now at the very sight of her.

He rolled away from the ventilator again, breathing heavily, trying to level off his thinking.

Jesus. Think of it.

Then, he remembered. No plans.

Plans invariably went awry. And, besides, what was the main object of *his* game? without which he knew he would go berserk.

Take it easy, that's what. Never mind scheming. See what happens, and stand it as long as you can. That's all you can do. He rolled back and stared down at the girl.

She was smiling quietly at the ceiling.

Several times during the next hour, the girl rose from the bed, and checked the photographs lying on the scarf over the register. Finally, they seemed to satisfy her. She put them in a red purse, and began to undress.

Hogan ceased watching. He went over and sat on the edge of his bed and listened as she bathed. He felt a fine trembling all through his body, and his mind was a gallery of swarming images—all of the girl. He could no longer put them from his mind. He fought against it, then finally relinquished himself to thoughts of her with a kind of voluptuous abandon.

Let it be, then. It could happen any time. He wanted to know exactly what she was going to do with the pictures, but, either way, knowing or not knowing, he was certain he could hold out little longer.

He looked down into her room again. She was in bed, with a dim bedlight turned on. He watched her shut that off, and sighed to himself. At least, he could lie down himself now. He was exhausted; the fierce play of emotions held him tense all over.

Undressing, he slipped into bed.

He knew he would not sleep tonight. It would be a night filled with waking nightmare, and he would approach daylight with flaming desires that could not be denied.

He knew this well.

Yet, all the time, another plan half formed within his mind. It had to do with the photographs. Why should he concern himself with what she was scheming? What matter? The course of her life was now in his hands.

The more he considered it, the more eager he became. He could have his cake and eat it too.

The sky was filled with pie.

He could go through with whatever happened, let it go, the way it wanted. All he had to do was somehow get hold of those photographs for himself.

With what he knew for certain must happen, he would have this Sommers character right in the palm of his hand.

But more and more the overwhelming urgency drove into him. He kept seeing the girl before him in his mind's eye, frightened, as he moved toward her.

4

The following day was worse.

He did not sleep all night. He waited on his bed for the first sounds of her stirring. He knew what the day would be like. There had been others. And he knew the time had come.

A wildness was inside him. It contaminated him. He was unable to think logically now, and his mind was a hurricane of promise. He smoked chain fashion, littering the floor beside his bed with butts. Time and again he left the bed, turned on the bathroom light, and stared at himself in the mirror.

Nothing much showed on his face. He was practiced enough for that. It wouldn't do to go wandering around with his features revealing what went on inside him.

What a bitch she was.

It sent him crazy, just thinking of her now. Of everything about her. Her body turned and twisted voluptuously within his mind, and he ached for her—for what he would do to her.

He could almost hear her screams.

And that was one thing that troubled him. Some time he wanted one that would really scream out her fear. He would have to have her someplace where she couldn't be heard. It always worked out that he had to silence them before enjoying the promise of the screams.

A fiendish rat, he thought. That's what you are.

He grinned at himself in the mirror.

If they only knew.

He visioned it all now. He went over it time and again; the act itself, and then the days following when he would rest and wallow in the newspapers, following the stories, the lurid details.

The thing that *he* would do.

He. Himself.

That she was playing this Sommers bird for something, in some way, had suddenly enhanced the matter. The thought of it sent Hogan's pulses racing. It was the needed dash of bitters. It degraded her, dirtied her, and that was what he wanted. Because in his mind were memories of what he termed hypocrisy; the evil inside them that did not show on the surface. Because—the white dress.

Maybe that was why they wanted them big and clean.

He was hungry, now, but she hadn't moved from the room. He watched her through the ventilator, stretched out on the floor. He watched her leave the bed, go to the bathroom, and return. She opened her purse and regarded the photos for a time, then sat on the edge of the bed, apparently brooding about something.

Maybe waiting.

As a rule, she hurried with her dressing. Now she just sat there in a pink shorty nightgown with ribbons at the neck, her white thighs showing, the burnished glow of her hair sparkling in the morning sunlight that splashed through the window.

She finally made coffee on her hot-plate, and sat sipping it on the bed.

5

As she sipped her coffee, she wished she could just go see Bill, rather than call him and force the issue. But she had to call him first.

How would he react?

She'd promised him she wouldn't bother him again. But, of course, he loved her. He wanted to be with her as much as she wanted to be with him. She knew this, and it sent a tingling feeling all through her.

Last night had been simply super, being with him.

But the days to come would be better.

Probably he'd get awful mad at what she had done, when he learned about it. But he'd get over it.

Should she call him yet?

Maybe she'd better wait a little while. At least till she was sure he had a chance to be in the studio. Then she could listen to the phone clicks, and be certain Louise wasn't on the line.

Not that it mattered.

Louise would know about her eventually.

Well, anyway, she had the day off. Hargraves had been nice enough about that. By rights she shouldn't be working at all. She should be with Bill, making him happy.

It thrilled her to think of it.

The thing was, he had to agree to see her. And it had to be today. She couldn't bear waiting any longer.

She put the coffee cup down. By gosh, if he refused to see her today, she'd just go over there—right to his home, signal him some way. Because she couldn't stand it... she simply couldn't. And—once she made him understand, then everything would be all right.

She felt a faint sense of shame, and it worried her slightly, too; what she was doing, what she planned. But it couldn't be helped. Maybe it was a dirty trick.

But he would get over it.

Yes—but suppose....

She didn't want to suppose anything.

She didn't dare suppose anything.

What time was it?

Nine o'clock. Surely, he'd be in his studio by now. And he'd be thinking of her, too. She knew it. But, thinking it over, she decided to bathe and dress first, before she called. It would give him a little more time. Just in case.

So many calls to his home would make Louise suspicious. And he'd told her never to call again.

Well, what of it?

She bathed and dressed, then sat on the bed again, and stared at the telephone. She picked it up.

Just then she heard the sound of footsteps overhead.

That young man. The one who lived over her, walking around. The one who dressed so neatly. Didn't he work anyplace? Rather strange....

She dialed the number.

Bill answered almost immediately.

"It's me," she said. "Should I call later?"

"Karen!"

"Can you talk?"

"I told you not to call—you said you...."

"Can you talk, now?"
"She's gone to the store."
"Good."
"Karen—"
"It's all right. There's something I've got to tell you. Were you thinking about last night? Did you think of me?"
He didn't answer.
"Bill—did you?"
"You know I did."
"Me, too."
"What do you want?"
"I've got to see you."
"That's impossible. Karen, we agreed…."
"I know. But things are different, now."
"How—what do you mean?"
"You love me, don't you?"
He did not answer.
"You know how much I love you, darling."
"Karen, this has got to…."
"I want to see you, today. As soon as possible."
"No."
"Why?"
"We agreed."
"Bill, we can't live without each other."
Silence. She waited, but he didn't speak. She said:
"I have something to show you. You'll have to see me."
"I can't."
"We'll meet at the usual place."
"No, Karen."

He was weakening, though, she could tell. He'd been thinking of her, and he wanted to say yes. He wanted to see her, she knew. She had to break through that stupid wall of convention. "Is it you can't get away?" she said.

"Yes. That's right. Louise will be here, and I can't keep going out every night. There's no excuse—listen, Karen. All right. Tomorrow night. I'll see you, then."

"I want to see you today."
"Tomorrow night."
She hesitated. How could she possibly wait that long?
"All right. Bring your car again." She lowered her voice. "We'll go someplace."
She sensed the emotion in his voice, now. "All right."
"You do love me, don't you."

"Karen, for God's sake. Listen, I've got to hang up. Louise is coming in the drive."

"Tell me you love me."

"Tomorrow night."

"All right. Tomorrow night."

"Yes."

He was gone. She sat in the silent room, staring at the silent phone, the sound of his voice still in her head, thrilling her. The day paced itself slowly. She went out for lunch, then hurried back to her room. There was nothing to do. She listened to records, but they didn't help the ache inside her. She was very nervous. She wanted to see him, hold him, talk to him, love him—and show him the pictures.

She was anxious about his reaction.

The afternoon waned. She didn't know what to do. Occasionally, she heard the young man moving about overhead. Maybe he had some sort of problem that troubled him. But nothing could be as soul-tearing as her own.

She had waited so long.

Then, finally, she knew what she would do. It would help some, and it wouldn't be the first time, either.

When it got dark, she would walk over where Bill lived. If she could just catch sight of him through a window, it would help. Just to be able to see him.

At once, she felt better.

6

As she left the room at seven-thirty that night, the door of the room above her also opened and closed. But she did not hear it. She did not hear Walter Hogan come silently down the stairs and follow her from the house.

7

She took her time, moving slowly through the April night, crossing streets, headed for the Sommers' residence. She felt curiously strange, yet was unable to explain it to herself. True, she was faintly excited at the prospect of seeing Bill through a window. She knew that would make her feel better, help her to bear the hours between now and tomorrow evening. But that wasn't it.

There was an unrealness about things that troubled her. Yet she couldn't say exactly what it was. There were remnants of persons' voices echoing in her mind: "You mustn't live in a past that didn't exist for you." Things like that, and it bothered her, especially because she was certain now that she had dreamed this. She felt mixed up, and unable to concentrate. It had happened to her before, but it was more forceful now, for some reason.

She didn't like it.

She wanted just to be with Bill; to love him. She wanted nothing else. Above all, she didn't want to hurt him. But what she planned wasn't really wrong. The fact was, she couldn't really understand what she was doing. It was more something that had to be done.

Her mind was hazy.

She kept walking, dwelling on the possibility of just seeing Bill through a window. She had done this before she had contacted him, and someday she'd tell him how she'd even been inside his home.

The streets were dark. There was a mild wind. The scent of rain was in the air.

She was carrying the red purse with the photos in it. If she could only see Bill, be with him.

But she would have to wait until tomorrow night.

She turned down the street where he lived, excitement picking up inside her now. She walked faster, and she felt a warm glow come to her cheeks. She tried to remember how she'd come to be here, in Allayne, but it was all rather hazy. She would much rather just think of Bill, of what the future promised for them.

A few heavy drops of rain touched her heated face. She moved swiftly along, under the gesticulant branches of tall elms. The rain smelled so fresh, the winds. And it was April. Her heart was light with a continual twinging of emotion that made her faintly breathless.

She neared the house.

Her lips kept forming his name: "Bill. Bill."

8

To Walter Hogan, the time had come.

It wasn't a thought.

He was a moving thing of pure instinct now. He breathed in gasps, watching her as she walked along the street under the trees. There was something about all this waiting, and then suddenly the way she walked, and the smell of rain and freshness that triggered everything.

He did not think.

The gap between them on the sidewalk was perhaps half a block, when he saw her slow and pause. Where was she going?

He had no idea. It didn't matter. His heart was pounding inside his chest and he trembled all over with wild anticipation. He wanted to yell.

He increased his pace. He didn't think of the photographs now. Only of the girl, of all the memories of her undressing, of the way she lay naked on her bed. His palms perspired.

He kept whispering it, now:

"You bitch! You bitch! You bitch!"

She was staring at a house, set well back on a broad lawn. He recognized it as one she'd walked past other times.

He moved off the walk, close in against the shadows of the trees now, panting, thinking, "You bitch! Oh, you bitch!"

Insane flashes of what he would do to her passed through his turbulent mind, and his body seemed to stream toward her like fire, throbbing with a savageness that blotted everything else out....

He ran toward her. There was a single tiny warning flash at the back of his mind: "Don't get caught!" But that was all.

For the rest he was a raging animal.

9

The girl heard something behind her. Just took little note; somebody coming along the sidewalk. What concerned her was the house itself. It was dark. Nobody was home. She hesitated by the driveway, then turned in along the edge of lawn by the gravel, moving toward the garage. The garage doors were open. She could see no car.

She felt a strain of excitement. Maybe she could get inside the house again. For certain there was nobody at home. No telling when they would return.

But the thought of once again being inside the house, among Bill's things had her very excited.

She neared the garage, looking toward the house.

She heard the pound of footsteps coming toward her across the lawn, and whirled. He leaped at her, grabbed her by the shoulders. Light from a streetlamp garroted his features, twisted, maniacal.

"It's you!" she said sharply, recognizing the nicely dressed young man who lived above her at the rooming house. "Stop. You're hurting me."

"Don't make a sound," he said. It was more a nearly inarticulate gasp. "Get in there—" He yanked her toward the open garage doors.

10

"You bitch!" Walter Hogan said.

She started to cry out.

His fist slammed against her face, again and again. Fury possessed him. He didn't even really know he was striking her. He was simply silencing a sound. A kind of throaty, choked giggling burst from his lips as he struck and struck again, dragging her into the garage.

A saffron shaft of light from the streetlamp illumined the corner of the garage, and now the garage had become the bedroom of a house in Bunkie, Louisiana.

"Speak!" he said, ripping her clothes off, seeing her through a red whirling frenzy of mind, an insane excitement that threatened to abolish him. "Say something!"

He didn't want her dead. Not yet.

She sagged in his arms, the last shredded remnants of her clothing gone, and suddenly there was a knife in his hand. Laughter came brightly from his open mouth. He struck. He struck again.

"Clean!" he said, choking. "Big and clean!"

He flung himself on her, there on the dusty cement floor of the garage, weeping with fits of laughter, knowing someplace within the maelstrom of his diseased brain that it had all gone wrong again, striking again and again with the knife... and then....

"Some things that happen for the first time...."

1

Lolly was in the jump seat of the Porsche, among the bulging paper bags from the grocery store.

"I wish you'd hurry," she said. There was petulance in her tone. "There's something on TV."

"Okay," Bill said.

Louise hadn't spoken much. There was something on her mind. It had been his idea that they all go to the store together. He knew he had wanted to avoid any possible phone call from Karen, but, too, it was more than that. He felt almost heroic. The effort he was making.

They came down the street, and he whirled the sports car in the driveway.

The headlights slashed across the lawn and into the garage and he cut them almost immediately, and stopped the car in the drive.

"Let's unload here."

He didn't know how he'd managed to speak. He'd seen something in the garage, on the floor. He wasn't certain what it was, yet something horrible registered.

"You may as well take the car into the garage," Louise said.

"No. Just remembered something. I forgot cigarettes. After we take the stuff in, I'll run down to the corner."

"I thought you had plenty."

"Just remembered. All out."

The garage was gray-black. A thin stream of light from a nearby streetlamp lit it up faintly in there, but he could see nothing. He would be wrong, he knew. Yet, he couldn't trust in possibilities. He'd seen something, and it had registered as awful.

Lolly was trying to get out.

A few minutes later, they were in the kitchen, loaded with groceries. Louise looked tired.

"Be right back," Bill said. "I'll just run to the drugstore."

He didn't like the way Louise watched him. She nodded. "All right, Bill."

Lolly was already in by the television set.

He hurried through the house. Suppose Karen called, now. Damn it.

What was it he'd seen in the garage. Something.

There was something in the pit of his stomach, too.

Imagination. All this strain.

2

Only it wasn't imagination. It was worse.

There was plenty of light from the streetlamp to see all he needed. He wanted to turn and run. He saw the torn clothes, the white body that was almost not a body now—and the blood. It formed gleaming pools on the cement.

He gagged, turned away.

Everything struck him with a crash.

Fear stood rooted within him, growing gigantically, like something red and terrifying in a movie cartoon.

It was then he saw who it was. Karen Jamais.

It was like being struck across the head with a brick. He knelt quickly.

She was dead. A constriction was in his throat, around his heart, all through him. He couldn't move. He knelt and stared and for a brief instant did not believe. It wasn't true. It couldn't be true.

Questions thronged his mind, mixed with the growing fear. Anxieties knifed him. Strangeness enveloped him; he could not understand what had happened. It was a horrible thing; something he could not as yet contain, comprehend.

He didn't know what to do. The word "police" had already flamed through his mind. Everything was jumbled.

His mind worked overtime.

Any moment, Louise might come running out of the house, wondering why he hadn't left for the drugstore. He ached with a sudden need for help. But at this instant he felt no loss. It was as if he had awakened from a turbulent dream. This was Karen. Yet, it was no longer the Karen that had caused him havoc. It was a very young girl, murdered, cut down, in a terrible fashion.

By whom?

His foot was by a purse. It was a red purse, though he couldn't see the color.

What should he do?

The torn body was at the very back of the garage, the clothes lying around in heaps.

He found himself standing toward the door of the garage, opening the purse.

Junk inside. His hand grasped something stiff, they felt like photographs. He was dazed. He didn't know what he was doing, what he would do. He hardly knew anything.

He stared at the pictures. It was difficult to make them out in the light from the streetlamp. Two people on a.... He moved swiftly across to a small workbench, picked up a flashlight, and blinked it on.

What he saw frightened him with new agony.

He shoved them into the purse, snapped it shut and hurled it from him.

He stood in the semi-dark.

Destroy the pictures.

Things were forming. Then, all at once, he realized his guilt—his guilt in the eyes of the law. It came with a burst, the way his mind was working. If there were photographs, there were negatives.

Had she taken them? This young girl?

"Bill?"

It was Louise.

He almost wept.

He ran from the garage.

"Just getting something. Going right down to the store." She was at the side door. Light streamed over her shoulder, chewed along the edges of her blonde hair.

"Toothpaste," she called. "We're out. Can you remember?"

"Sure. Yes. Going, right away."

"All right."

She went inside. The door closed.

He stood there. Abruptly, he was violently sick. He moved into some shrubbery beside the garage, stumbling, gagging. His hands sought the side of the garage, and he leaned there, shaken, soaked with perspiration.

What could he do?

Everything swirled within his mind, contaminated awfully by fear and guilt.

He retched, stumbled back toward the garage entrance. It was a near scream within his mind.

What should he do!

Catastrophe loomed all around, closing in, ready to explode. Desperation drove through him.

Faintly, from the house, he could hear the TV, and he pictured Lolly, on the floor with her pillows, watching the bright screen.

Odd how rapidly his mind worked now. Moments before he'd been stunned to near immobility. But now.... He felt like the general who leaped on his horse and rode off in all directions—only without humor. He didn't know what to do first.

Items ticked off and his anxiety rose.

He had to act, and fast.

But in what way? How?

Even the idea of the photographs was bad. What had she planned to do?

He'd been a complete fool. How could he have been so stupid? Riding on a dream, a memory. But where had she come from? Who was she? These questions were still with him.

He didn't dare think too much. Not now. He had to act now. And he didn't know what to do. He should phone the police, immediately. He should have done it before now.

Yet, somehow, standing there, he knew he wasn't going to call the police. He couldn't do it. The fantastic guilt in which he was standing was enough to send him out of his mind. He saw no escape.

There was the one single thing he was avoiding.

Get rid of her. Take the body somewhere.

Louise....

Any moment she might come out of the house to see what he was doing.

Suddenly, he began to act with instinct, driven with fear. As he acted, he worked faster and faster, sweating, and trembling with the thought of what he was doing.

What he had to do.

Almost blindly, he'd rushed to the far side of the garage. He hauled out an old, stiff, dusty tarp. They had used it once on a camping trip some years before, and it had lain in the garage ever since.

He worked as fast as he could, in a kind of angry dream, hardly conscious of what he was doing, trying to think of anything but this. He spread the tarp, began throwing the torn clothing on it. Then the body. He dragged and fumbled, until it lay on the treated canvas.

He started rolling it up.

Destroy the evidence, get rid of it. This was the only thought in his mind now.

He opened the purse, took the photographs, rammed them into his pocket.

3

Walter Hogan stood with his hand on the doorknob of his room, ready to enter, when he came out of the daze and remembered the photographs.

For a moment he thought the world rocked beneath his feet. He felt dizzy. He was still foggy. He hardly recalled everything that had happened, though he knew it had happened. It was always this way. His mind did not clear for some time.

But he recalled the photographs.

Turning, he raced down the stairs and outside to where he had parked the car he'd rented, a black, gleaming Ford sedan.

In the car, he drove fast across town toward the Sommers home.

As he drove, small tendrils of what had ensued came shred by shred into his mind. He gloated on them, but at the same time his content was marred with the fusion of the thought that he must get back there before anybody found her—he must get those photographs.

4

Bill stopped abruptly.

He'd have to get into the house quickly, give Louise some excuse for his not leaving for the drugstore as yet.

He left the grotesque hump of the dark tarp there on the garage floor, and started toward the house. He was drenched with perspiration, breathing heavily.

He wanted to tell Louise; with all his heart he wanted to tell her, to share this thing. He couldn't.

Luckily, she was upstairs. He called up:

"Louise? Anything else you want at the drugstore?"

"Haven't you gone yet?"

She was coming toward the stairs.

"Just leaving. Had to tighten the bracket under the radio on the car. It was loose. Anything else you want?"

"No."

He turned. She was coming down the stairs. He saw himself in a mirror in the hall. He looked wild, crazy.

"Daddy? You should watch this," Lolly called from the living room.

He didn't answer. He left the house, went back to the garage.

A car slowed out on the street, then passed on by.

He went to the Porsche, drove it up to the garage, and halfway in, refusing even to think now, wishing he had a drink—a long drink.

Quickly, then, he dragged the tarp with its contents, over to the car. It was a struggle. The tarp was rigid, and the body heavy. Finally, he managed to jam it into the car. He slammed the door, panting.

The side door of the house opened.

"Bill? Aren't you ever going?"

There was still blood on the floor of the garage. It would have to wait.

"Just leaving."

He climbed beneath the wheel, backed swiftly out of the drive, and into the street. He drove down the street, passing a gleaming black sedan that was parked nearby at the curb. From that instant on, confusion within him mounted. He had never realized such desperation existed. He drove with all sorts of wild things streaming through his mind, utterly unable to cope with any of them.

He knew he was doing the wrong thing. He couldn't stop. One thing at a time, he kept telling himself. But he didn't even really think.

He came through the outskirts of town, driving as fast as he dared, and headed into the country. In the small sports car, the bulky tarp and what was inside it, seemed huge. The eagerness to rid himself of it was immense, a torture.

But where?

Then he knew. Just anyplace. It didn't matter.

But the photographs.

The negatives. She must have taken the pictures herself, when they were at that cabin. Somehow she had rigged up a camera, and snapped those ruinous photos. It sickened him. Maybe she had an accomplice.

It meant he had to find where she lived.

How?

His head throbbed and he felt very ill. Thoughts of what could happen to him began to come to him now. It grew worse and worse.

Where could he hide the body? Where?

Suppose somebody saw him?

What if the law—anybody—found the body before he located the negatives of the photographs. Because he was certain now. Those negatives existed. Had she been going to blackmail him? He would never know the truth.

The dream of Karen Jamais was gone now. He was left only with an awesome horror.

He had turned off onto a seldom used country road. The Porsche swept through the April night and there was the smell of rain in the air.

Cigarettes. He had to remember to stop and pick up cigarettes. And toothpaste. So Louise wouldn't be suspicious.

How could he find where this girl had lived?

It was a terrible thing, the way it ate at him now.

He dwelt momentarily on last night, with her, at the cabin, and he remembered her voice.

Just then two cement blocks showed, one on either side of the humped macadam road. He passed them quickly, but they registered. A culvert.

Why not? He slammed on the brakes, backed up and over on to the shoulder of the road. There seemed to be no houses around. This was as good a place as any. The quicker he rid himself of the gruesome package, the better he would feel.

Or so it seemed.

Out of the seat, he went around, opened the opposite door and began dragging the bulky bundle from the car.

He knew what he was doing was wrong. But what else could he do? There was Louise—and Lolly. He kept thinking of the police. He couldn't get them out of his mind, now. The blood on the garage floor. Suppose Louise saw that—somehow. Suppose she went into the garage and turned on a light. She couldn't miss seeing....

He struggled, sweating, stumbling down off the shoulder of the road to the rutted ditch. Half frenzied, sweat stinging his eyes, he shoved and worked the heavy bundle into the mouth of the culvert. He was weeping inside. A sense of doom was all through him. He wasn't guilty of this thing. Yet, he would appear guilty if found out. He knew that. Those photographs told a story.

She would be missed from where she worked.

At the wherever-it-was she lived. Where? Where?

What had she planned to do?

Did anybody else know about her? About him? Them?

He had to do something. He couldn't do it tonight. How could he find where she lived? The dentist's office. It was the only place he knew of, the only thing he knew that was associated with her.

A drop of rain struck his face.

He hurried back to the car.

He should have searched the purse. He couldn't do it now. He couldn't go back and open that tarp. The one thing now, was get away from here. Figure a way to find her.

Who had she been?

It was like rising from one fog into another that was still worse. How could he have been such a fool?

In the car again, he turned it swiftly, and drove back toward Allayne.

It was beginning to rain much harder now, the water drifting from the skies, caught in an April wind, driving in sheets across the countryside. Then, slowly, it began to settle into a steady downpour and from the looks of things it was one of those spring rains that would last for some time. The winds ceased. The water streamed from a still, dark, sullen-looking sky.

Bill stopped and picked up cigarettes and toothpaste, then drove on home. The way it was raining, he doubted that Louise would come to the garage. It was his chance to clean things up. Disregarding the gushing water, he hooked up the hose, and hosed out the garage, sweeping it carefully with an old broom. Behind the garage was an old sandbox Lolly had once played in. He carried shovels full of sand into the garage and sprinkled it around, then dribbled some oil on the sand from an open can he used for the lawn mower.

Shining the car's lights into the garage, he felt satisfied with how things looked. Then he parked the car, and headed for the house with his package.

Inside the door, he felt as if he might collapse. He was breathing heavily, soaked through, a mess.

He started for the kitchen.

Louise stepped out of a doorway.

"Good Lord, Bill. Where have you been?"

"Flat tire," he said. "Wouldn't you know it?"

"I'll bet you forgot the toothpaste."

"Nope."

He started for the kitchen.

"Oh, Bill. By the way, somebody just called on the phone. They asked for you. A man."

"What did he want?"

"Wouldn't say. He hung up rather abruptly."

5

At Police Headquarters in Allayne, a phone rang. Lieutenant Avery, who was on night duty at the desk had just left for the washroom.

Detective Sergeant Ed Burke, a heavy-looking man, with bull-like shoulders, and a sunburned square face cursed lightly. He was seated on a low bench, leaning back against a row of lockers, smoking a cigarette. He was alone in the small room. Through an open door could be seen a long row of cells, dim lights glowing along the corridor ceiling.

Burke stood up, dropped the cigarette, and stepped on it with a quality of deliberation, then, with another curse, went over to the desk on a small raised platform, and picked up the phone. His voice was low, but it carried, and sounded hoarse.

"Yeah?"

It was a man named Crawford who lived out on County Road Number 2. It seemed that several cars were lined up where the road was badly flooded. "Something's got to be done. Way it's going, I'll have water in my front yard in a half hour—and by morning it'll be up over the porch."

"That's not our problem," Burke said. "Have to contact the County Highway Commission, tomorrow morning."

"But it is your problem," the man said. "It's just inside the city limits. Something's got to be done!"

Burke stared at the phone.

"Will you please take care of it?" the man said. "There's a culvert. But it's plugged, or something. The way it's raining, it's really bad. Traffic's lining up to beat hell." The man cleared his throat. "I never seen such rain, the way it is."

"See what I can do about a crew," Burke said.

"Better hurry up," the man said. "Cars stalled, everything. It's getting bad. Real bad."

"Hold your water," Burke said.

"Are you kidding?" the man said.

Burke hung up.

Lieutenant Avery came back into the room just then, a tall, mild appearing man, in uniform, with a thin, knife-like nose. Burke told him about the flooded road.

"What do they expect us to do?" Avery said. "At this hour? For God's sake."

"That's your problem," Burke said.

He turned and headed for the washroom. The door slammed behind him. He leaned against a sink, lit a cigarette, and frowned heavily.

Everything was wrong. Every goddamned thing. He needed something good to get his hands into, something that would brighten his relations with Chief Rodgers. This was a small town, and the police force was small, and Burke had it made if things went right. But some son of a bitch had reported him drunk on duty. Rodgers was teed off plenty. Things had to be smoothed over, and quickly. Christ, if he could only get his hands on something ripe. He had so much going, and he damned well wasn't going to lose out. That cathouse run by Marie, over on Radial Avenue was paying off good. He would lose that. He would lose his chances with the girls. He would lose every damned thing, unless he could latch onto something that would make Rodgers look up to him again, and this was his last chance in any town with the work he knew—and the ancient dream of making it big in a large city had long since gone.

He paced the small washroom in front of the two stalls with animal-like impatience, smoking. His tread was silent for such a heavy man. There was something about every movement he made that was brutal. Brutality, and reined energy was revealed in his pale blue eyes, the set of his jaw, the impatient movement of his heavy shoulders under the hardcloth gray suit jacket. He took off his snap-brim gray felt hat, revealing thin reddish hair, and scratched his head with blunt fingers.

Every damned thing was wrong. Wrong.

Every goddamned thing.

He hooked the hat back on again, still smoking.

If only something would open up. If he could just set his sights on somebody, anybody. The way he felt, he'd railroad his own mother. And why not? What had the world ever done for him? It had urinated on him, that's what.

Well, he'd damn well urinate on the world.

Now, take this damned silly flooded road.

Why the hell didn't somebody kill somebody?

Burke flipped his cigarette into a urinal, and stared at his knuckles. He needed a drink. He needed one bad.

Forty. He was forty years old!

Burke struck the open palm of his left hand with his right fist, whirled and left the washroom.

"Seem to be happening again…."

1

All Bill Sommers could see in his mind was how she had looked, lying on the garage floor.

He sat in the living room, staring at the image inside his head. Louise was very quiet. Lolly was in bed. Whoever the man had been who had phoned earlier, he hadn't phoned again as yet.

Knifed, bleeding, dead. Lying there. God only knew what had happened to her. Who had done it? Why?

What had she been planning to do with those pictures. They burned in his pocket, felt as big as a book.

How could he keep all this from Louise? He wanted to tell her—tell somebody. How could he contain all this, and stay sane?

And look what he'd done. Taken her out there and stuck her in a culvert. It wrung him.

He got up, went to the kitchen, poured himself a stiff drink of gin, drank it down, then mixed one with tonic and carried it back to the living room.

"You're awfully quiet," he said to Louise.

She was reading, or apparently so, seated on the couch. When he spoke, she jerked around, eyes wide. Then she smiled. He sensed it was forced. Or was it just that he'd become oversensitive to things?

"Didn't mean to be. You're no loudmouth," she said.

They watched each other. She fingered the pages of her book.

"Nothing on TV?" he asked.

"I didn't check."

He turned with his drink, and sat in a chair and stared across the room at the painting on the easel. The image of Karen Jamais stared back at him. Her face hadn't been harmed. Just her body.

He drank.

"You might have asked if I wanted a drink," Louise said.

"Sorry. Did you?"

"No."

The phone rang.

They both came to their feet. Louise's face was flushed. Her book fell to the couch.

"I'll get it," Bill said. He was already halfway there. He set down his drink, picked up the phone.

"Sommers?"

"Yes."

It was a strange voice. He'd never heard it before. A man's. Louise stood by the couch watching him. Her fingers plucked at the side of her pink skirt.

"Who is this?" Bill said.

"Never mind. Just something I want to tell you."

Whoever it was spoke carefully.

"Well, what is it, then?"

"I know all about it," the man said. "I know all about everything. What was in your garage, what you've been doing—and I know where you hid her. I watched you do it."

Bill stood there. He had heard what the man said, but he didn't react at all. At least it seemed. But when he tried to speak, nothing came.

"Just think about it," the man said.

"What?" Bill managed.

"Think about things," the man said. "Think about how you wrapped her up in a bundle and took her out there, and stuffed her into that culvert. Think about it."

"Who are you?"

"Never mind. For now. I just want you to think about it, that's all. Because I know. I know everything. Even about the cabin, last night. See? I know everything. You dig?"

Silence.

"That's all for now," the man said. "Just think about it."

Bill heard the click of the phone as the other hung up. He stood there. "Hello?" he said. He was sweating all over. He finally put the phone down, started back to his chair, turned and picked up his drink and drank it and headed toward the kitchen.

"Who was it?" Louise said from the couch.

"Wrong number."

"Been an awful lot of wrong numbers lately."

He said nothing. He went into the kitchen and stood in the darkness. It began to get through to him, and he experienced fright beyond anything he'd ever known.

Who had the man been?

He'd been seen.

What did the man want?

He poured himself another drink in the semi-dark of the kitchen. The neck of the bottle clinked against the glass. He drank a half glass filled with raw warm gin.

The pictures, the pictures, the pictures.

He felt as if he were tumbling into a dark, bottomless pit. He didn't know what to do. With every moment, things became worse—and this was the worst of all. Somebody had seen him.

The man who had done *that* to her? Could it have been?

Questions thronged his mind. He felt lost, and terribly alone. He felt a desperate need to go to somebody, to tell them.

He stood in the kitchen, hearing the ceaseless drum and pound of the rain. Even the gin wasn't helping now. He knew nothing would help.

He should have gone immediately to the police.

Sure. Then what?

He put his hands over his face and stood there. He had never felt so alone. He kept seeing how she had looked. And hearing the man's voice over the phone. The sense of being completely trapped was overwhelming. He saw no way out.

"Think about it," the man had said.

Who had he been? Would he go to the law?

He poured more gin, mixed it with a little water from the tap and drank it down.

What could he do?

Think, he told himself. Think rationally.

The negatives of those pictures. The man who had phoned. There was only the one link to the pictures, the dentist—Hargraves. Instantly, he started across the kitchen, thinking of the phone book, of calling Hargraves, right then.

He stopped. He couldn't. It would have to wait till morning. At least, the man on the phone hadn't mentioned the pictures and they were utter condemnation.

Who had she been? Where did she live? He knew nothing whatever about her. How could he have been such a complete fool?

Would the man phone back. What did he intend to do?

2

He didn't sleep.

Louise and he had spoken maybe ten words. He didn't want to talk. He was happy she didn't bother him. He lay in bed, in a kind of swarming horror.

He was up before dawn, watching the clock. The first thing, he would get to Hargraves and ask him about Karen; find out where she lived. It was taking a terrible chance, but he had to do it. There was no other way.

It was still raining, a steady fall from the graying morning skies.

All night long he had cursed himself about Karen Jamais. She wasn't even

Karen. Not the Karen of his memories. And he had gone along with it.

He opened a fresh bottle of gin, and was having one when Louise came downstairs. He felt guilty about that, too—and it was then he recalled the garage. But she wouldn't be going out there.

Only she might.

And he might have left some trace, overlooked in the darkness.

"You're up awfully early," Louise said.

She wore a pink housecoat, and her eyes were sleepy. But there was something that troubled him about her silence, even through everything else. He couldn't think about it, though.

"It's that painting I'm doing," he said. "Can't hit on the right gimmick."

"Oh."

She began pouring fruit juice. He watched her, then went into the other room and stood staring at the wall.

Everywhere was doom. He heard Lolly upstairs, running along the hall. He felt a sudden sharp pull of need for Louise. It was the first real feeling he'd had for her in a very long while. He turned, took a single quick step toward the kitchen, then stopped. He couldn't go to her. He couldn't tell her anything. And it was at the precise moment when he wanted to, with all his heart.

He went into the hall, took his raincoat from the closet, slipped it on, and called:

"I'm running downtown. See you in a little."

He heard her coming from the kitchen. He made it to the front door, had it open, when she came into the hall.

"What about breakfast?"

"Eat when I get back. Not very hungry, anyway."

"Oh."

"I won't be long."

She said nothing. Lolly came running down the stairs.

He went out into the rain.

The only thing he saw ahead of him was disaster. It glowered at every point, impending and certain. Yet, he knew he must keep trying. Maybe not even for himself, now; maybe for Louise and Lolly.

The body would be found eventually, and there would be an investigation. Whoever Karen Jamais was would come to light. That was certain. If he could just get hold of those negatives, find out if there were any more pictures, it might help some. He had to try.

But there was the man who had telephoned.

There it was. At every point. There was no real way out of this. The only thing he could do was attempt to prevent the worst from happening.

The guy had said he'd known about the "cabin." That meant he knew

Karen and he had been at the cabin together. How? How could he possibly know?

The terrifying aspect of the thing pounced down on him again just as he reached the garage. It was difficult to comprehend how bad it was. It came in waves, the realization. It was kind of numbing, almost a blank moment of awful anxiety that he couldn't put his finger on. Momentary loss of any reason for his being in this position.

Then it only became that much worse again.

No way out. Absolutely none.

He could easily be accused of murdering that girl.

Only it wasn't even just murder.

He opened the garage doors, backed the Porsche out, then went back into the garage through the falling endless rain and inspected the floor carefully. The rain had taken care of whatever stain might have remained on the gray gravel of the drive outside the garage.

He found no trace within.

Why had she come here?

He went back to the car and drove downtown. The pictures still burned in his pocket. He had to do something with them. He should have destroyed them already.

It was still quite early. Just a bit past eight-thirty. Hargraves might not be open as yet; probably didn't appear until somewhere around nine. He didn't know Hargraves, had never met the man. How long had Karen been working for him? In what capacity?

How in hell was he going to approach the man?

He parked the car a few doors down the street from the dentist's office, and sat there, trying to think. Rain drummed against the leaking top of the sports car. He lit a cigarette. The windshield clouded. He tried to think.

Matters only became worse.

Suppose she lived with her family, and it was very likely that she did. But, then, how had she found out about him? All the things she knew?

It was crazy. The whole thing was maddeningly crazy.

"Louise," he said softly. "Louise."

He couldn't recall ever having wanted his wife as much as he did at that moment.

Finally, he left the car, and went to the door of the dentist's office. It was locked. A small sign said: "Walk In." But office hours hadn't begun as yet.

He returned to the car and waited.

He sat there until after nine, but saw nobody enter Hargraves' office. Then it occurred to him. Probably the dentist parked his car behind the building someplace, and entered his office through a rear door.

He found the man there this time.

He tried to appear calm, nonchalant. It was near impossible to even stand there and face the man, knowing what he knew. The way he felt, he expected people could read on his face, see in his eyes, what had happened.

The waiting room of the dentist's office was quite clean, almost plush; red leather, stacks of the latest magazines, fine looking draperies, mirrors, and a canary in a cage.

Hargraves was just feeding the bird as Bill came into the room. A small, rotund man, with pale, blunt features, and a thick mop of jet black hair, well-oiled, the dentist wore a kind of cream-colored smock. He turned, scowling and half-smiling at the same time with a packet of birdseed in his hand.

"I'm not here about my teeth," Bill said. He felt immediately foolish, and on the defensive. "Something I wanted to ask you."

Hargraves stood quite still with the birdseed. Rain drummed against the windows. The canary flipped about yellowly in its cage.

"You have a girl working for you, Karen Jamais, her name is."

The dentist was shaking his head. Bill paid him no attention, plunged on.

"I'd like to contact her. Is she here yet?"

The dentist's eyes were as dark as his hair, but very small under puffy lids the color of bread dough. There was no expression in those eyes, none whatever. The man said nothing.

"If she's not here, I'd like her home address. Something I have to see her about. It's to her interest...."

He suddenly realized he was saying too much, and he realized all too forcefully that he was speaking of a person whom he knew was dead, murdered, rammed into a culvert.

But he had to know where she lived.

"Who are you?" Hargraves said. He had a mild voice that had a trimming of suspicion around the edges. He was the type who, if buying a pound of butter at a market, would reveal suspicion about the clerk, the butter, the store, everything. One of those to reckon with, and stay away from.

"Salter," Bill said. "James Salter." It came out very easily. "I have to see Miss Jamais. If you'll just give me her address...."

"I have no one working for me by that name."

"But—"

Hargraves stepped across the room, set the box of birdseed on a window sill. "Now, if you'll excuse me?"

"I know Karen Jamais works here."

Just then the waiting room door opened and an elderly woman, obviously a patient, entered. "Hello, Doctor."

"Yes, Mrs. Eberhard. You can come right in, now. If you'll just take the first chair, please." He turned to Bill. "Sorry," he said. "You're mistaken."

He held a door open. The elderly lady went through, and Hargraves followed her. The door closed. The canary flipped about. Rain drummed against the windows.

For a moment, Bill didn't know what to do.

Then he did know. Obviously Karen worked here under a different name. Momentarily, he felt a terrific helplessness. Contact with the world vanished.

The canary chirped desultorily. The cage swung. The bird scraped around on its paper floor, rattling seed.

A picture. He would have to see Hargraves again, with a picture to identify Karen. He knew he shouldn't. He wished he were someplace far away. The desperation was bad. He had to return here, expose himself again—somehow insist.

Those negatives.

He left the office, almost running.

Out on the sidewalk, it struck him. Where could he get a picture of Karen Jamais to show the dentist?

3

Walter Hogan was so nervous he couldn't stand still. Links in the chain of near perfection that he was fashioning, had parted. He had to seal them up again.

Crazy.

The damned photographs. He'd gone and left them in her purse. He had seen her put them in that red purse. She had taken it with her. Through the throbbing haze of memory left over from the moments he'd spent with the girl in the garage, he even recalled the purse. He remembered it tumbling to the cement floor. He knew the photographs were in that purse.

And he knew the photographs were with the body, wrapped in canvas, stuffed into a culvert on a lonely road near the outskirts of town. But dragons couldn't drag him out there.

Besides, it was raining.

Dig that. It broke him up for a moment. He lay on his bed, muffling laughter that threatened to burst from his constricted throat.

He calmed. He had to condition himself to the belief that this Sommers character, in his immense fright, hadn't bothered to look into the purse—hadn't discovered the pictures.

Jesus.

All of which meant he somehow had to get into the girl's room, directly below his own, and find the negatives for those pictures. And—more... more!

He writhed on the bed, not liking it now—not liking the things that flashed through his mind. The landlady would find the girl missing. Surely.

It always worked that way. So there had to be an explanation, at least to cover a certain time interval. And he had to take care of that.

He had to get into that room.

Either that, or run—leave town.

And lose out on everything. Never. It was too big! By God, the way things were, he wasn't losing out on anything. Dig that, you bastards—and dig it right.

He writhed some more on the bed, remembering.

How she had looked. Her fright. That fear. It shot through him again, torturing him with a kind of luscious agony, almost orgasmic. If they only knew, the sods. They'd never know.

And now, he was going to clean up. Really make a pile out of this Sommers character. The phone call had been a beaut. He kept picturing Sommers in his mind, the fear in the man. Too bad he wasn't a woman. Wouldn't that be rich?

He dwelt on that for a while, wallowing in it, along with the memories. What he remembered frightened him, too; that was a part of what made it so good. Nobody could identify him. He was clear again. And clean. And filled with a gigantic relief. He knew he could go along now, for a good long time, before another spell began to settle in on him. Live normally, not obsessed. Even when he thought of a woman, of scaring the pants off her—and then doing what he did, it wasn't anything much. It didn't drive him crazy with a wild tingling.

Not only that, he wouldn't have to start searching for a job this time; wouldn't have to set things straight again, go through all the normal worry that usually happened after he'd done something like this.

Because everything was set up for him. He'd simply get all the money he could out of Sommers, and then take off for some place. Maybe the Southwest. Relax. Play.

And wait. Wait for the next time.

It was perfect.

All he had to do was get into that room.

He wished he had the money, now. He wished everything was taken care of. He wanted to leave this town, this state. It was always that way. He didn't like hanging around, after something like this.

But he had to, this time. For a little while.

The bitter with the sweet.

He lay there, thinking back to the garage, how it had been, the girl's eyes, the feel of her body—and how she had felt—all limp and lifeless.

If he could only have allowed her to scream.

He'd have to work on that angle.

The negatives.

Imperative.

He thought for a time.

Yes. The best plan would be to find some of the girl's writing in her room, then compose a letter of some kind, a note, to the landlady, explaining that she—the girl—had to leave town for a time, and to keep the room for her return.

This would give him plenty of time.

He could leave the letter on the hall table, downstairs.

It meant, now, he'd have to work when the landlady left the house, which she did each day. He'd have to watch her. Because otherwise, he might be caught trying to get into that room. The house would be empty, then. There were only two other boarders, and they worked. So, that left just the landlady, Mrs. Delters.

He had to get into that room. Somehow.

Everything depended on that.

And he had to talk with Sommers again.

Dig that guy! How scared he must be. Taking the body out, like that, and hiding it. Keeping things from his wife. Man, he had Sommers right by the balls.

He slipped from the bed, went over to the ventilator, yanked back the rug, and looked down into the room below. For a moment, he experienced a small pang of regret. The girl was gone. She would never return. Gone for good, this time.

And he had done it.

Wow. Pow. Bam.

Elation spread through him. Calm, fine elation. He felt perfect. Then he recalled all that he had to do. He couldn't allow himself all the good feelings as yet. That would have to wait.

Maybe he'd make the scene at San Francisco, after all. Like he'd planned. Really blast it. Or, Jesus—maybe, maybe he'd have enough loot to ball it all the way to Paris.

All of Europe waited. Hip in Hipville.

Wow.

The negatives. Mrs. Delters. The note. Sommers. Money, money, money... what a wailing time money could make it. Dollar bills. Sometimes he called them Bollar dills. It made for sounds, man.

He wished he could hear some music. Good music.

He would have to wait. He hated waiting. He wanted to take off right now. Normally, he would. He couldn't.

All right, then. Mrs. Delters, the landlady.

He went and looked at himself in the mirror, and giggled with amusement at his features. Slightly flushed, healthy, happy—All American. Dig that, you crazy cats!

How to get into that room?

He couldn't break in. He couldn't shinny down the side of the house, there was no fire escape. He mustn't leave any trace. He was The Shadow, wasn't he?

Mrs. Delters.

He remembered the keys she carried. They would be keys that fit all the doors. And they would be downstairs in her apartment, someplace. Certainly, she didn't take them with her, did she? When she left the house?

That was it, then.

He went out of the room, stood at the landing. There was no sound, save for the faint gusting of wind and rain. Maybe she was out already. He had to know.

Everything always worked perfectly for him. Didn't it?

Check, then.

If Mrs. Delters only knew what she had in her house. Wouldn't that break her up, though?

He went quietly down the stairs, and came to the second landing, where the girl's room was. He stared at the door. Christ, a goddamned door. Goddamnit, anyway.

Now. Think how that Sommers must be suffering. Sneaking tail on the side with that young meat, and with a wife and a kid, like that. Imagine. No sense, that was all. And the girl, Jean, working something with those pictures. Imagine.

He went on downstairs. The girl and he would have made some pair, all right. She could have set him up—things like that.

Only he knew that sooner or later....

Well. Anyway.

He stood on the last step, staring into the dim hallway on the first floor. Stagnant air washed around him, tinged with odors of ancient meals. A thread of old boiled cabbage was strung in a layer about nose high.

He had to know if Mrs. Delters was in the house. She had the entire downstairs floor.

"Mr. Hogan?"

Inside, he nearly came unfastened. But he had long ago trained himself for shocks of this sort. Not the slightest sign showed on his face. He didn't move.

It was Mrs. Delters. She stood in the deep shadow of an open doorway, to his right.

He smiled easily. "Hi. Didn't want to disturb you. Just trying to make up my mind." He held the smile, knowing quite well how it worked on lonely landladies. "I've got some shirts that need laundering. Wonder if you know a good place? Laundry I've been using ruined three the last time."

She stepped into the hall.

Man, if she only knew what he'd done last night! If she only dug what these hands of his had done….

"Why, Mr. Hogan. Lucky you caught me. I was just going to the store."

Man, you're with it. How neat can you get?

"That's good," he said.

Mrs. Delters smiled wanly. She was a wan person, pale, and though rather thin, at the same time flabby. Her skin was grayish. The bright red dress she wore sagged about her figure, hung down in back, up in front, and the color was a bad choice. She carried a big black purse, a green shopping bag, and some sort of colorless coat over one arm. Her face was square, with sagging jowls, washed-out brown eyes, wisping pinkish hair. When she wasn't smiling, or speaking, her thin lips worked continuously.

She told him the name of a laundry.

"That'll do it, then," he said.

"They do a wonderful job," she said in her thin voice. "Just wonderful. You can trust them implicitly." She paused. "You always look so neat, so nice. No wonder you want a reliable place."

He smiled. She nodded, rustled her shopping bag. He watched as she moved on down the hall to the front door, the fact that she hadn't locked the door leading into her apartment registering. Then she was gone. He was halfway up the stairs. He turned and raced down.

Once inside her smelly apartment, he had to consciously prevent himself from lingering over things. There were kicks to be had in roaming a foreign house, unknown to the owners. He'd have to look into it. But right now, the thing that mattered, was the key to the girl's room.

He searched quickly, thoroughly, looking in all the obvious places, knowing she wouldn't hide the keys—and came up empty handed.

God damn it! She must carry the keys with her. A rotten trick. It irritated him badly, and he was in a sweat anyway, knowing all the things he had to do. He couldn't just break into that room; couldn't jimmy the lock. It would show. It had to be done right.

Damn.

Mrs. Delters' apartment smelled badly. An odor of urine clung to the area around the bathroom, and for the rest of it, it was old meals. She obviously never opened a window. He hated Mrs. Delters suddenly. He wished he could do something to show his hate. He couldn't. He'd better get on upstairs, and try to think, before he fouled up.

He felt more frustrated than he had in some time.

He had to get in that girl's room.

He left the apartment, raced up the stairs to the second floor landing. There was the girl's room, over there. He walked over, and stood before the door.

A large, heavy, gleaming old oaken door, with panels. Damn that Mrs. Delters.

He seized the knob, twisting it.

The door came open.

He stood there. It had been unlocked all the time.

Twenty minutes later, the note written and on the downstairs hall table, addressed to Mrs. Delters, Walter Hogan sat on the edge of his own bed with the negatives of the condemning pictures in his hands, softly giggling.

By Jesus, he had that Sommers right by the balls.

Now. There was only the one thing that troubled him.

The police wouldn't find the body—maybe not for a long while. And that had always been one of his happiest times, too; lying around after he had done what he had done, reading about it in the papers—and sometimes there were pictures, too. It all depended on the newspaper's policy.

That was when he was very happy.

He would lie and read and look and smoke and say to himself, "Me. I did it. Me. Don't you wish you knew?"

But—not this time....

4

Walter Hogan was wrong.

Detective Sergeant Ed Burke stood in the pouring rain on the muddy bank above a culvert out on County Road Number Two, and stared at the body of a dead girl crumpled on a dirt-streaked, wet tarpaulin. The body, wrapped in the stiff canvas had been discovered jammed into the rather small opening of the drainage culvert. The fields and road had flooded, but now the water had quickly receded when the blockage was removed. Some stalled traffic still lingered. Police urged those whose engines would start to get on their way. Other cars waited for garage help. Spectators lined the road, necks craned, trying to see what was on the bank above the culvert. Everybody was getting soaked.

"Why the hell don't they go away?" the coroner, Jed Martinson, said to Burke as he rustled down the bank in a heavy green raincoat.

"It's a good show," Burke said. "If her head was cut off it'd be a better show. Don't you understand those things."

Martinson, blinking behind rain-freckled steel-rimmed glasses, eyed the people who pressed closer down from the road shoulder. Uniformed officers were trying to get them on their way. Many were in shirt sleeves, disregarding the rain, the mud, the wind, for a look at the pitiful bloody bundle.

"They call it morbid curiosity," Martinson said. "I call it human nature. Human nature being what it is." He was a man nearing fifty, clean shaved, harried looking. He slid on down the bank, carrying a small black bag, and halted by the canvas. "Well, who found this?"

Burke heard him, yet didn't exactly hear him, didn't reply immediately because he was thinking. A killing, a murder. And a good one. A juicy one. A young girl, raped without a damned doubt; cut plenty. A fiend is loose in the area.

It excited him. He'd been hoping for something like this. That he might never find out who had done the killing didn't enter his mind. It was all satisfactorily filed away. He would find who had done it. It was just what he needed to get back into the good graces of Chief Rodgers. The excellent graces.

"What say?" Martinson said.

Not only that, Burke thought. But I've been assigned to the damned case.

Then he said, "Guy named Crawford. This whole area was flooded. Went down quick enough, once that was pulled out of the culvert. Listen, Jed. Let me know everything, fast as you can. The quicker you act on a thing like this, the better it is."

"Well, she's been murdered," Martinson said. "And that's a fact."

"Your deductions amaze me, and that's a fact," Burke said.

"Didn't you go through her purse? It's right here."

"You came along too fast," Burke said. "I haven't had a chance. Let's see it."

"You just hold your horses."

"She was raped, wasn't she?" Burke said.

Martinson looked at him.

Burke said, "What's the matter? You getting weak-stomached? Bet she was a good piece, by the looks."

Martinson picked up the red purse, opened it, and began going through the contents. "We can't do a hell of a lot here. Where the hell's that ambulance. I want to get her back to town. The way this rain keeps up."

"What's her name? Let's see her ID."

"There's no identification," Martinson said. "Not a thing."

"There must be. There's got to be."

"Well, there isn't."

A car, a sedan, came slithering along the slimy shoulder of the road and stopped. Two men got out. One carried a camera. Burke recognized him. Greene, from the evening *Herald*.

Things were moving fast.

Burke didn't like it. Things could get out of hand, when they moved this fast. He'd hardly gotten here himself, and one of the two newspapers in town was already on the job. He'd have to stick with Doc Martinson, all the way. He had to have a lead—any damned lead. But something. Christ, he hadn't even had a chance to talk with that hick, Crawford, really.

"Crawford!" he called. "Get over here."

A raw-boned, overall-clad man moved closer.

Greene, from the *Herald*, began taking pictures. When he discovered the dead girl hadn't been identified as yet, he asked Martinson to move the body.

"I want a good close-up of that face."

"Rain's washed it clean, all right."

"Yeah."

The camera clicked.

Burke began questioning the farmer, Crawford, who had called in about the flooded area, and then discovered the bundle plugging the culvert. Burke wore a hat which dripped water, and a heavy trenchcoat, belted tightly at the waist, buttoned securely around the neck.

Jesus Christ, he thought. I've got to get a lead. None of these stupid son of a bitches know what it's like. This Crawford, for instance. What a stupid looking son of a bitch he is. Jesus Christ, Rodgers might even take it into his head to bust me back to uniform. Just when I'm getting things cozy, too.

The thought of going back into uniform, walking a beat, maybe, appalled Burke.

It couldn't happen. By God, it just wouldn't happen.

He turned on Crawford, and there was something doglike in the way he shoved his face out toward the wet, shivering farmer.

"Well," Burke said. "I want to hear it. I want to hear every word of it. Start talking."

Crawford looked at him as he might look at a sudden stranger from Mars.

5

"Aren't you going to eat anything?" Louise said.

She stood by the kitchen table.

"I had some coffee and rolls downtown."

Bill moved on through the kitchen, dripping water. He hoped she couldn't read his face, the way he felt. "And, damn it," he said. "I've got to run downtown again. I forgot half the paints I went after."

"Bill. Why don't you take today off. We could just sit around…."

"Sit around?" He looked at her, troubled. "I've got to get that fool painting done."

"Oh. I forgot."

He went on outside, and cut across the back yard to the studio. He felt kind of crazy inside.

He crossed the studio floor, sat on the couch, lifted the big ash tray, the cardboard, and brought out the old photograph he'd kept for so damned long.

A fool. A fool.

He sat there staring at the picture. It just didn't look like that girl. It didn't look like her. A little bit maybe, but not much. And it had to look like her. It was the only thing he could do. He'd thought of it suddenly, on the way home. He'd take this picture and show it to Hargraves, and maybe the dentist would tell him something. He had to tell him.

He realized now how truly little the girl did resemble the real Karen Jamais whom he hadn't seen in some twenty years. Good Lord, had he been absolutely mindless?

But it resembled her a little bit.

He would force it out of Hargraves.

He put the picture in his pocket and stood up. He recalled the other pictures, the ones that had been taken out there at the cabin. He felt the blood hot all through him. Christ. Hargraves would recognize those quickly enough. He'd have to burn them, get rid of them some way.

The phone rang. He picked it up and heard Louise say, "Hello?" He heard somebody breathing heavily, and then a definite click as somebody hung up.

"Hello?" Louise said again. "Hello?"

He stood there.

"Hello?" Louise said.

He wanted to yell at her, scream it at her to hang up and leave him alone and let him work things out, somehow.

Silence. He could hear her breathing. He supposed she could hear him breathing.

"Who is it?" Louise said.

He held his face in a tight grimace, teeth clenched together as the rain drummed against the windows of the studio.

Finally she hung up.

So did he.

He knew it was the man who had called him the evening before. The man wanted to speak with him again.

He knew he had to get downtown and question Hargraves. But he had to answer the phone, too.

He stood there, staring at the phone.

The phone rang. He grabbed it up. So did Louise, and she said, "Hello?" She must have been standing right by the other extension, as he had here.

"I've got it," he said. "It's for me, Louise."

"Oh. All right."

He waited until he was certain she was gone.

"Okay," he said. "Who is it?"

"And so it seems that we have met before...."

1

A man spoke.

"You know who this is, Sommers."

"I damned well don't."

"You want me to explain? I've been rather decent not speaking with your wife. You rather call her to the phone and have me explain to her? You want me to explain?"

"Yes. Go ahead. Explain."

"You get gay with me, you'll know it, Sommers."

Bill said nothing.

"All I need's some of your stupidity, right now."

Bill still said nothing.

"You'd move damned fast, if I get your fancy little wife on the phone, and tell her you've been shacking up with a teen age broad." The voice became sly, then. "And, naturally, that isn't all. I could really lay it on the line, Sommers. I could really make you move fast, couldn't I? Killing a sweet little teen age broad, and wrapping her in some canvas, and stuffing her in a culvert...."

"Shut up!"

"Get you? Bother you, Sommers? Say, maybe you'd like to have me explain it to your little girl there, your daughter? About how you get in bed with other dames and suck their tit-ties, stuff like that—then kill them?"

"God damn you—" He didn't know what to say. It was beyond him. There was something terrifyingly vicious in the man's voice; something depraved that showed through, that was revealed in how the man spoke and the way he dwelt on certain words, phrases—as if he....

"You like that, Sommers? I could tell everybody plenty, believe me—plenty. How's about my telling the cops where to look for a real fancy package, and who put it there? How's about that? You beginning to get with this yet? You been doing some thinking and remembering?"

He had no words. He could not speak, reply. There was nothing to say. It was a horrible futility. At this moment, listening to the man speak, myriads of things flashed through his mind, ways to deal with him, methods of escape, ways and means to combat whoever it was—but nothing was any good. It was the futility of doom, like the complete hopelessness of trying to explain some simple thing to an ignorant person, or trying to make sense to a psychopath, or a maniac. This was a true horror, an obliterating futility.

He saw there was no way. He could see absolutely nothing to do.

"How's about this, Sommers?" the man said. "How's about if I show some pictures around? Pictures of you and that little teen ager, in bed together? You like that? Say, maybe you'd like to have some? Huh. You dig something like that, Sommers? Sure, you do. You're an artist, you paint, don't you. You could have some nice hot pix. Hang 'em on the wall. Maybe your wife'd like some, too? Huh? Could pass them around town, huh?"

Bill was surprised to hear his own voice, tight, but calm, modulated: "What do you want?"

"You're not very hip, are you, Sommers?"

He did not answer.

"Actually, you're square. As square as they come."

"Let's not argue about who's the square in this party," Bill said, surprised again at how he was speaking, because inside he was a turmoil of confusion, and fright. "What it is you want?"

"Money."

Pictures, Bill thought. It was all he could think. It had to mean that this man had pictures, perhaps copies of the same ones? He didn't know. He did know he had to find out immediately where Karen had lived, and try to find the negatives. He had to do this, and as fast as he could. There might be ways of dealing with this man after all. If he had pictures, he might be able to get them from him. This was as far as he got in his thinking.

"So," the man said. "Think about it some more. It'll be plenty of money I want. All I can get. You'll be buying your life—freedom from guilt. That's what you'll be buying, so I'll let you think about that, let it sink in your square head. It'll cost a lot. It'll be worth a lot. Your life, actually your wife's life, your daughter's life—your family's happiness, your reputation—not that it would mean anything if I decided to make a move."

Bill stood there.

"Think about it. And, say, if you knock off a piece of tail—off your wife, there, think of me. Give her a few good jabs for me. Okay? Fine. Till then, then."

The phone went dead.

He'd have to get down and see Hargraves immediately. Suppose the dentist wouldn't tell him anything, just on general principles. Then what? Because Hargraves had appeared to be exactly that type person.

There was the compelling desire to tell Louise everything. He took the picture out of his pocket and looked at it again. It was an old snapshot. You could tell that. But it had to do. It was right then he fully realized how bad things were for him. He was on the spot. He felt confused; doom seemed to spread all around him.

He slipped the photo back into his pocket and headed for the door.

2

The desk clerk at the Hotel Wynant glanced up as a tall, tired-looking man cleared his throat. The clerk was short, round, with a pale, ubiquitous smile, and oiled pinkish hair.

"Oh, Mr. Dederich," the clerk said. "You sure didn't get much sleep." He glanced at a large Western Union clock on the wall. "By gosh, you just went up to your room a half hour ago." The clerk shook his head and clucked his tongue. "You look tired."

"Yeah," the tall man called Dederich said. "I am tired. I'm beat. I feel as if I've been shot out of a cannon. Say, how do I get to police headquarters?"

The clerk looked at Dederich. "Police headquarters?"

"Yeah."

The clerk told him. "Outside, turn left. Just walk six blocks. Can't miss it."

"Thanks," Dederich said. He turned and started across the empty lobby of the hotel, taking long, lazy strides. He wore a light gray suit that obviously had just been unpacked from a traveling bag, though it was of good material and in maybe ten to fifteen minutes all packing wrinkles would have vanished. His white shirt was very white against the dark tan of his face. He wore a dark gray knitted tie, and a pearl gray lightweight felt hat.

Pausing midway along the lobby, he snapped his cuff back, glanced at a gold wrist watch. "Nearly one," he said softly. Then, still standing there, he reached into the breast pocket of his jacket and brought out a white envelope, opened it, and pulled out two photographs. He scowled at them. They were of a young girl with dark hair and a rather serious-looking expression on her face.

He put the envelope away, and stood there, frowning. He rubbed his eyes. They were muddy-looking, faintly bloodshot. He stifled a yawn. In his every move, there was a strong hint of strength leashed down, a tiger-like quality.

He reached for his shirt pocket, scowled, snapped his fingers and turned across the lobby toward the cigar counter.

"Cigarettes," he said to the lush, young girl with silver blonde hair standing behind the counter.

She eyed him soberly, then shot him a smile. She had seen something she liked. She wore a very soft golden sweater that outlined her breasts with intriguing tightness. She heaved a sigh. Her breasts heaved a sigh.

"What kind?" she said.

"Surprise me," Dederich said.

"I don't know if I could surprise you," she said, obviously baiting a hook.

"You couldn't," Dederich said. He spoke flatly.

The girl's smile turned into a red smudge. A pink blotch appeared on the left side of her nose. She scratched it with a long red fingernail that she'd purchased in some five and ten and painstakingly glued to her own well-gnawed nub. Meanwhile, she was unconsciously performing an interesting masturbatory bit of action with the corner of the cash register that thrust out toward her beyond the edge of the counter.

"Habit, I suppose?" Dederich said, lifting his brows.

She opened her mouth.

Dederich grinned, started to speak again, but just then a chunky young man in work pants, and a ragged sweater half ran into the lobby and over to the counter. He swung a bound bundle of newspapers to the floor, grinned maniacally, and said, "Hi-ya, Selma, baby. How's about tonight?"

The girl glanced at him with a touch of disdain.

"Dig that!" the young man said, pointing toward the bundle of newspapers. "Hot off the press." Then, in a hoarse whisper, shielding his mouth with an ink-stained hand so Dederich wouldn't hear: "You still look good enough to eat, baby."

He turned and jogged from the lobby.

Dederich stared at the torn front page of the top newspaper on the bundle. He stared at a large blow-up of a young girl's face.

"Jesus Christ," he said softly.

"I'm very sorry," the girl behind the counter said. "I never heard of that brand. Are they king size—filter tip?"

A large streamer read:

MYSTERY GIRL
BODY FOUND IN CULVERT

Dederich bought a paper and moved swiftly away.

3

April was a gentle mist as Bill drove downtown. There was something soft and breathless about the air outside the car. Maybe tomorrow the sun would shine. Maybe it wouldn't. But at any rate, it was very much April; very much the month of love, of change, of memory. It was in the air. It was a time when girl and boy, strangers on the street, exchanged glances and lingered, compelled by marvelous chemicals that might precipitate marvels.

Too, it was a fine time for death.

In the small sports coupe, Bill suffered plenty. The drag to return to

Louise and tell her everything was so strong he had to fight it with all his volition. He wanted somebody, anybody—no, specifically Louise—he wanted Louise to hear him out—hear everything.

Too much to ask.

She couldn't possibly understand. How could he expect her to understand a thing like this? It was crazy. He didn't understand it himself. He'd drowned himself in a swamp of nostalgia. He'd lost his mind, for a time. It had to be that. So how could he explain it to her.

And yet, he felt as if he were on a treadmill, rapidly losing ground.

Karen....

He gripped the steering wheel viciously.

That man on the phone. Demanding money. Letting him wait—letting him think about it. And with nobody to go to. Absolutely nobody. He couldn't go to the law. He'd be behind bars in a matter of moments. They would haul the body out of the culvert. They would discover everything. Only a matter of time, and very short time, too.

Everything depended on his getting those negatives, and—the photos from that man, too.

A kind of fury was inside him. A terrible helplessness. If it were only something he could fight. It wasn't. It was a miserable intangible thing—until that moment when it could become very real.

If he could only tell Louise. Just that much.

But they had grown so far apart of late. He didn't know how to approach her. There had been a time when he might have drawn her aside, and explained the whole thing to her.

He relished thinking about that for a minute. How good it would be. He visualized her, listened to her words, heard her tell him not to worry.

Sure, he thought. You son of a bitch. Only it doesn't work that way. You're in it right up to your neck. He could lose everything. No way to explain. They could probably even trace that damned tarp straight to him. They had ways.

He parked directly in front of the dentist's office, and wondered if Hargraves was there. He had to be.

He sat there a moment, tight in every muscle.

Imagine. Imagine trying to tell them. He could almost feel their disdain, their rocklike disbelief. A girl he'd known years and years ago. Trying to tell them he'd known it couldn't be her, but that she had been exactly like her; she had known everything about him, about how it had been so long ago. Explaining that to them. He could see their faces in his mind's eye. Not only that, they'd have him in the booby hatch. Psychiatrists would examine him. He would be one of these case histories in a book. Because how could he explain what he had done?

He had done it. Wasn't that enough? He'd gone along with it. Because she had been Karen and all through the years he had wanted Karen, loved her, dreamed of her—and she'd returned. The rest didn't matter. It had happened.

He no longer felt the same.

That didn't matter either.

God damn them. Let them explain. Where had she come from? Who was she? How had she known so much? Even she had admitted she wasn't the real Karen of his memories. But that didn't matter, either.

He'd swallowed it all.

He was breathing harshly, sitting there.

Abruptly, he got out of the car, slammed the door, and headed for the front door of the dentist's office. All he could do was try. Nearly to the door, he thought how it would be if he ever actually did have to try to explain.

It would be impossible.

That was when he recalled again that she was dead, murdered, stuffed into a culvert.

And in the eyes of the world, he would be guilty.

The situation was agonizing. It was so bad for a moment, he almost slumped down on the steps in front of the office, it was so overwhelming. No escape. Only a matter of time. And someone knew—someone knew. A man possessed pictures and words.

Kill the man.

A snag of black laughter burst past his lips.

He stepped through the doorway and into the waiting room. He pressed a small bell marked, Please Ring, and waited. Footsteps. Then Hargraves showed, round and inquisitive in a cream-colored jacket, his eyes owlish. The canary chirped and rattled in its cage.

"You again?"

There was a middle-aged woman seated at the far side of the waiting room, reading a movie magazine. She kept shooting glances at Bill from under her brows.

"I'd like to see you a moment, Doctor Hargraves."

"I'm busy."

"It won't take a minute." He was fishing out the picture. He felt foolish. He didn't like the way the woman with the magazine kept watching him.

"I'm much too busy. You'll have to make an appointment."

"I've got to see you."

Hargraves abruptly ignored him and turned to the woman. "Only be a few minutes, Mrs. Lowell."

"Thank you, Doctor." She smiled knowingly.

Hargraves turned back through the doorway and the door closed.

Bill stood there a moment. The woman rattled her magazine. Why in God's name did the man have to act like that? Why couldn't he be a human being? Or, maybe that was what was the matter.

Bill went to the door with the picture in one hand and knocked. He could hear a machine going from someplace behind the door. It sounded like a dentist's drill.

He knocked again.

No results.

He opened the door and stepped inside. A strange odor, not exactly unpleasant, but different than that of any dentist's office, reached his nostrils.

"Doctor Hargraves?"

He could see nothing. A hallway. The machine ceased.

He started down the hallway.

Hargraves appeared through an arch. Bill caught a glimpse of a dentist chair, various instruments of torture, someone, a man, seated in the chair with his mouth agape.

"I don't tolerate this," Hargraves said.

"Just a second. It'll only take a second."

"You heard me," Hargraves said. His voice had a brittle, antagonistic quality. "Get out—make it snappy."

"Please," Bill said. "Look at this—just look—please—"

He held the picture in front of Hargraves.

"Jean," Hargraves said. "So—who are you?"

"That doesn't matter. I merely wanted her address, that's all."

"But, I—" Hargraves' manner had changed, now. "Are you from the police, or something?"

"Call it what you like."

"This is a picture of my receptionist."

"I know."

"Jean Brooks."

Bill revealed nothing. He might have known nothing could possibly work out simply, not in this situation.

"Where does Miss Brooks live?" he asked.

Hargraves blinked at him. "She didn't show up for work today. Is something the matter? What's all this about?"

"Maybe I can explain later," Bill said. "Meanwhile, if you'll just get me her address?"

Hargraves chewed his lip, finally consulted a small steel filing cabinet, and showed Bill a card with Jean Brooks' address written across it in a bold hand.

"Thanks." He knew the street, he almost knew the house; one of those big old places that probably would never get torn down.

"What's all this about?" Hargraves said again.

"Sorry. Maybe later."

"Has something happened?"

Bill wanted to get out of there, now. He didn't like Hargraves. He held quick visions in his mind of talking Louise into leaving Allayne, moving someplace else. Because sooner or later—and this was just another thing, added to everything else. He should never have done it like this. But there had been no other way.

"Anyway, thanks," Bill said, moving toward the door.

"Are you certain there's nothing the matter?"

"Quite sure."

Hargraves frowned. Bill let himself out. The woman in the waiting room rattled her magazine. The canary rattled in its cage. Bill went out onto the street. It was raining very lightly. He ran for the car.

He sat tightly behind the wheel. Jean Brooks.

Karen Jamais.

He had to get right over there, fast.

No. It wouldn't work. He sat there and pounded the wheel with his doubled up fists. How the hell could he go to the address, it must be a rooming house of some sort, and demand to see Jean Brooks' room? And—if she lived with her parents, it was still worse.

He clenched his eyes shut, biting his teeth together.

What the hell to do!

Because now Hargraves could say things. He might even go to the address himself. He could say things to the wrong people: "Man stopped in, very forceful—demanded my receptionist's address. Acted damned strange. Why?"

He could feel the thick walls of a new world closing in. It was a bad sensation. There was no way to fight it.

There was urgency, too. A kind of bright urgency that he had never experienced before; something that got into his vitals, and ate away like rats.

Did the man who had phoned him know her name was Jean Brooks? Did he know where she lived?

He wanted to give up, collapse. He thought of running; just turning the car and taking off. He didn't know what to do. All sorts of wild things passed through his mind. He knew how truly desperate men must feel, when things began to close in. Kill the ones who know too much. Kill Hargraves. Kill the man on the phone; make a meeting, and kill him. Wipe the slate clean. Do away with evidence, those who could talk.

Only he couldn't do any of these things. All he could do was try the little things.

And meanwhile, the walls closed in—tighter all the time.

He knew it now—he knew he would have to take Louise and Lolly to some other town. They couldn't live on in Allayne. Not if he managed to get away with things.

And how could he even do what he had to do? He had to get to wherever Jean Brooks had lived, and search for the negatives to the photographs. How? At night. It would be the only time.

Meanwhile?

Suddenly, he had to see Louise. He had to talk with her. He couldn't help himself. Somehow she had to listen to him....

4

Louise wanted to hang up, but the damned fool from Tonawanda, on the other end of the line, was persistent.

"No," she said. "I don't care what happened. You're not to come around here. And don't call again, either."

"Now, baby—this isn't like you. Not like you at all—the other night...."

"Drop it," she said, feeling sick inside. "Don't phone again, and don't come around." She hesitated, then forced herself, "Listen, Dan—it was one of those things that happen. Let it go at that."

Silence. She expected him to come back fast with another relay. Instead, he said, "Okay. That's how you want it. But, I won't forget you, honey."

She said nothing.

"Couldn't we just—?"

He was coming on again. "No."

"Okay, okay. I got a family, too. I'm heading home, tomorrow."

"Good-by."

"Baby?"

She hung up.

The phone rang again, almost immediately. At the same instant, she heard the sound of the Porsche turning in the drive. It was Walters, again. "Listen," he said. "I could get a motel room—just for tonight. Just happy good-bys, y'know?"

She wanted to yell at him. "We've had it," she said. "Will you let it go at that!"

Hesitation, again. "Okay, but listen...."

She made herself speak as levelly as possible. "Bill's coming," she said. "Please, go home—forget the whole thing. Please?"

"Okay."

She hung up, her hand trembling faintly. Would he call again? He might. But he had sounded as if he understood. A lot of good that did.

She'd been a crazy damned fool.

She stood up, wearing a fluffy aqua dress with a tight white belt, and black thonged sandals. The rich blonde hair was tied in a pony tail with a bit of black ribbon.

She chewed her lower lip. She felt rotten inside.

Bill opened the side door.

She moved away from the phone, started toward the kitchen. Something was the matter with Bill—and plenty was the matter with her, now, too. Could Bill know something about what she'd done?

He came into the hall.

5

He had to tell her. It was wrong—he shouldn't; it would only hurt her. Yet, he knew he had to tell her. If he didn't, he'd explode.

He didn't like the way she looked at him.

"Your face is all red," he said. "What's up?"

"Nothing."

"Where's Lolly?"

"At school. You know that." She stared at him, turned toward the kitchen, then back toward him again. "Have—have you eaten anything?"

"No. It doesn't matter. Louise." He stood there. His speech faltered, but he pressed on, forcing himself. "Can I see you a minute? You have a minute?"

"You're soaking wet. You'll catch cold."

"Never mind that."

He brushed past her into the kitchen. "Go into the living room, Louise." He tried to make his voice imperative, without being too obviously brusque. "I want to talk with you."

He turned and looked at her. She watched him, chewing her lower lip, scowling, the fingers of one hand plucking at her dress.

"Go on," he said. "I'll fix a couple drinks. Be right with you."

"I don't want a drink, Bill."

"Okay. But I need one. Be right with you—"

"What the devil's the matter with you?"

He moved into the kitchen. "Just do as I say!"

He fixed two drinks, regardless. He took two long pulls at the bottle of gin, then went into the living room. She was standing by the couch. He sensed something stiff about her; he didn't like the look in her eyes.

"Sit down," he said. He spoke quietly.

"But—"

"Please, Louise."

She didn't move for an instant, then abruptly sat down. He dropped down in the middle of the couch, a foot away from her. He felt the keen palsy in his hands; it didn't show, neither did the turmoil inside. He didn't know how to begin. He had no idea how she would take it. He could only hope. His mind was fuzzed with alcohol. He wasn't certain of his decisions, now. Was he doing the right thing? He was. He had to tell her—tell her... abruptly, he handed her a glass.

She regarded him silently.

For an instant, he couldn't speak. Then a curse burst from his lips. "God damn it!"

He saw her teeth sink into her lip.

He emptied his glass, turned on her suddenly, and began talking. "Louise—I'm in hellish trouble. I want you to listen, and try to understand. It's nuts—but you've got to try!"

She stared, her glass gripped in both hands on her knees.

"It's the damndest thing you'll ever hear," he said. And then it began to spill from his lips in a torrent of words that was scalding to him; watching her reactions, and at the same time experiencing something kin to purge that slowly whittled at despair. He listened to himself telling her, as if he were standing off—and he felt a growing build-up of agony, now. The name "Karen" came from him, over and over and over again, and he stood there—sitting there—hearing himself, knowing he was tearing the hell out of his wife—and more and more conscious of how horrible the whole thing was; even the twenty years of dreaming. And it was then, too, that he became conscious, or half conscious, of Louise. She sat very stiffly, holding the brimming glass on her knees, knees tight together, lips faintly apart, eyes wide—and blank.

He became more and more excited. What was happening now—the girl, dead, everything; Louise—became stronger and stronger, worse than ever. There was a complete cessation of relief. The true sharp horror of what he had done came home with a brick-like shock.

There was no relief even in knowing he had not killed the girl.

He might just as well have killed her.

All the time, Louise said nothing. She sat there. She stared, wide-eyed, at him, the drink untouched while a gradual film of something like confusion showed in her eyes.

"I couldn't help myself," he said with a gasp. He hesitated, tried to drink from his empty glass, took Louise's from her hands and emptied that, the ice cubes rattling against his teeth. He put both glasses on the floor.

"I couldn't help myself. I'm a fool—a stupid ass. But it doesn't change things. That girl's dead, murdered, and I might just as well have done it. I stuffed her in that culvert, out there—like a—like a monster. I've been crazy."

He paused, sitting there.

"Louise," he said. "I don't know what to do. I've got to get those negatives.

Louise, I couldn't help myself. God damn it. How the hell can I ask you to forgive me? But I had to tell you. I wanted you to know."

She stared, but said nothing. She looked strange.

"It's something's been on my mind for years, that girl. And then she... only it wasn't. But, Christ, what the hell could I do? Can you understand that part—that part, at least? Can you understand how it is?"

He reached for one of her hands.

She did not speak.

He thought she seemed to pull away from him.

"Can't you understand?" he said harshly. "Louise, she was Karen. The Karen. I knew she wasn't. You understand that, don't you? But it didn't matter. I was nuts, see?"

He heard her say something, but didn't distinguish the words.

"Here," he said, groping. "Here—here. Look at this. This was Karen Jamais. The real one."

He hauled out the old snapshot and put it on her lap, so she could see. She glanced down at it, then up at him again. He said, "Well, this kid. God damn it. She was just a kid. Not much more than a damn' nymphet, you might say. But she knew everything about me. So help me, everything. Knew about the old days. Everything. I couldn't help myself. It was like...."

"You were a kid again."

"Yeah. And—something'd been happening to us, Louise. I don't know. I thought—I don't know. Anyway, it's a mess. It's a terrible mess. I had to tell you."

He ceased.

She handed the picture back to him, her mouth sober. "I've seen this."

"Seen it?"

"I clean up in your studio sometimes. I always wondered." She shrugged. "It's not important. I'm not the kind that—is she the one?"

"One what?"

"The one about the album? The song, there? *Where or When*?"

"Oh, Christ, yes. I might've known you'd—sure, you'd know." He kept looking at her. Her face was very sober. "How can I ever explain to you?" He stopped. "But that's not it, either. It is, but it isn't, not right now. Right now, I've got to act. And fast. Or else—"

She watched him. "Bill?"

She was watching him tightly.

His head was a-swarm with everything. With how he was hurting Louise, and with the diabolical trap he was in. The man on the phone, telling him to think about it. He hardly knew what was going on. And there had been no real relief. But as he looked at Louise, he seemed to sense something that looked like relief in her eyes.

"Bill?"

"What?"

She suddenly seemed to go tight all over. A strained expression came into her eyes, and around the corners of her mouth. Her hands were clenched in her lap and she looked quickly at them, then at him again.

"What is it?" he said, feeling, knowing, Here it comes! And no way to divert it, either.

"I don't know how to say it," she said softly.

"It's all right. I can't blame you. Say what you want."

She spoke quickly. "No. It's not you."

He frowned. "Then—what—?"

Again she looked down at her hands, twisting them tightly in her lap. "You're in a terrible jam," she said. "I want it to be us—but—" she paused—"how can I tell you?" The last words seemed wrung from her.

"Tell me what?"

He felt exhausted from explaining to her; now what was she getting at?

"Bill—" She turned on him, moving her knee up on the couch, facing him—"I've been as bad as you—almost. I mean, maybe now it's your turn to understand something." She spoke rapidly, and abruptly was telling him some crazy stuff about this bird Dan Walters. He very faintly recalled the man from the Thomas' party the other evening. But the stricken way Louise went at it reached him. Her eyes were damp, red lips sharp with revelation of what she said. It all came out, and it was a shock to him.

Her voice was tight. "We'd worked at our marriage—then we began to take it for granted, or something. Anyway, I didn't care what happened. Not until afterward."

He began to understand.

"There was a wall between us," she said. "Something I couldn't understand. But, now it's all so plain. And—I—I don't know what got into me."

They stared at each other.

"God," she said. "What a mess."

"What about now?" he asked.

"I'd never want to even see him again. I told you, it was crazy to begin with."

He thought she might begin to cry. Her chin trembled. He took her quickly in his arms, kissing her hair, holding her tightly, and remembering her clearly again; the shape of her body, of her love, of everything that truly excited him the most.

"Louise," he said. "Things like this happen to everybody."

"But not to us."

"Yes. To us. To everybody with active glands. Now, forget it. If you can forgive me and understand—I'm telling you, I understand what you did. I would understand if I'd done nothing."

She couldn't seem to hold him tightly enough, worming against him, her lips moving along his jawline.

Abruptly, she ceased.

"Bill!" Her face was pale. "What are we going to do? I mean, about that girl?"

Again, he held her tightly, needing her.

"I don't know what to do," he said.

Her voice was strained. "It's just touched me. I've been selfish—just thinking of myself. Now that doesn't matter."

"You say, 'How awful,' and I'll hit you."

She smiled. There was this much between them again, now, and it was good. He had somebody. Only it didn't really change things. He was still in the same spot as before. It was a bad one. Karen Jamais-Jean Brooks still was bundled in a stiff tarp, rammed into a culvert—she was still very dead, and it had happened in his garage. He had still been at that cabin with her. There were those pictures to prove it. There was still that man who knew, who had some of the pictures. There was still Hargraves. The law. The urgency. The desperation. And so little time—time pressing in from all sides.

He got up, went to the kitchen, half filled the glass with gin, shot in some water from the tap and came back drinking from the glass. He looked at Louise. She wasn't smiling now. He emptied the glass, set it on a table, and lit a cigarette.

"What the hell am I going to do? I've got to find her room."

"I don't think you should wait. But—listen, Bill. Why not go to the police?"

"They'd slaughter me. They wouldn't believe this thing. Not the way it is, not the truth of it. Would you, if you were the police?"

"Maybe not. It's not TV, where you maybe get a guy on your side, all that. Can't you talk to this man—the one who called you?"

"He wants money. That's blackmail. It can go on forever."

"You can't tell the police that, turn him in?"

He sighed with irritation. "No."

Just then something whipped with a slap against the outside front porch.

"The paper," Louise said.

"The hell with the paper."

Funny thing. He couldn't feel the gin. Nothing seemed to touch him. Just the downright horror of everything, the futility of his trying to do anything, the absolute necessity of his doing something, and right away. As soon as possible. As soon as it was dark. He couldn't act till it was dark. And the phone might ring at any moment. The man might demand a meeting. Anything could happen.

Louise got up, came over to him, pressed against him. It felt good. She had a harsh way of doing it, and it was good and he remembered it through all the mess, liking it.

"It'll all work out," she said.

She didn't understand. He knew that. How could she, really. All he'd told her was words. She'd had her own concerns, this Handsome Dan. The hell with it. What could he expect. He was alone in this. But he had Louise back again, that was for sure. That was a mighty big something.

She kissed him. He felt wooden, unable to respond. She grinned. "I'll go get the paper. We'll think of something. Lolly'll be home soon."

She vanished toward the front door.

He stared at the telephone, expecting it to ring.

He heard the door open, heard the rustle of the paper, and the door closing—then it slammed.

"Bill!"

She came running to him. She looked scared to death, gesturing.

"Bill—look!"

She thrust the early edition of the evening paper before his eyes. He stared at the black headlines, the huge picture of Karen Jamais' dead face. The eyes were open, but dead.

DO YOU KNOW THIS GIRL?

"Bill. Is that her—is that the one?"

He could barely speak. "Yes." Panic flashed brightly.

It was then everything came tumbling into his mind.

Hargraves. The dentist would get the paper. He would call the police. The police would go to where she had lived. The man who had called, demanding money, would see the paper. A moment ago, there had at least been a little time.

Now there was nothing.

Nothing but act. Act now. Move.

"I've got to go."

"Not now, Bill. Wait."

"I've got to go. Got to get there."

Everything swamped his mind. He cursed himself for being so stupid as to put the body into that small drainage culvert—during a rainstorm. A fool. Idiot.

"Bill."

He looked at her. "There's not a damn' thing I can do, Louise. I've got to go. I've got to try and get there first, beat the police."

The paper fell from her hands. "But—even then. You may not find the negatives, Bill. Don't you see?" She was touched with the fear, the excitement, now. She was beginning to realize what had happened. "There's that man—the one you said knows everything."

For an instant, he just stood there, rooted to the floor, unable to think, to move. Then, "I've got to try. You sit tight."

"Sit tight? Jesus!"

He turned and ran from the house.

It was starting to rain again, harder, heavier, now. He slogged across the wet lawn to the Porsche, in the drive. For an instant the engine wouldn't start. He cursed it, feeling suddenly the passage of time and how precious moments could be. It ground and ground. Then it caught.

All the time, words kept streaming through his mind: Fool, fool, you're a fool... stupid fool.

Only it didn't help. He knew what his chances were.

Practically nil.

Suppose she'd lived with her parents.

That thought struck with a kind of physical pain now. It hadn't been foremost. Now it was. Her mother, father. They would see the paper. The whole goddamned thing would be out. The police might know at this instant.

He had to take the chance.

He didn't know if he could stand much more of it. He wanted a drink, and didn't have one. What was the guy like? the guy who'd phoned? Where did he live? How could he contact him, find him?

He backed the small car viciously out of the drive, and swung off through the April streets.

Nostalgia was a slow disintegration, something like the ponderous loomings of white dangerously poisonous fogs, mushrooming after an atomic blast.

Bill felt himself snared in the blinding sear of the blast itself, the rainbowed fires below the fogs, deep in the ultimate reality.

"And laughed before... and loved before...."

1

It would have to be done in broad daylight.

The house was a rooming house. The sign, "Guests," told him that. And so did the house itself, a monstrous, gingerbread horror, gabled and latticed, a broken-backed red-painted fire-escape crawling up the side, all shaded, darkened by several ancient elms, and surrounded by a black iron spike fence with a gate.

The gate would creak. He was certain.

Apprehension was a dark cloak under which his raw exposed nerves screamed soundlessly, because it was broad, though clouded, daylight. He had counted on at least the dark. He'd felt he had half a chance in the dark.

He parked the car down the street three houses, close to some heavy bushes, behind a black sedan.

How to get inside, to find anything....

To even get to her room.

He had to. That was all.

Jean Brooks.

He left the car and came up along the sidewalk, tense inside. He'd never done anything like this. He'd never done any of the things he'd been doing, and he approached the house through thick apprehension.

The place looked quiet, almost as if nobody were around. Maybe nobody was. Stupid thought. Of course somebody'd be around. Whoever took care of the place, registered "guests," though he wondered at anyone selecting such a place to live.

He didn't want to pause in front of the large house. It would make him conspicuous. He looked quickly around, saw nobody, pushed the spiked iron gate open. It creaked. He hardly heard it now. Already he was pent up. He couldn't miss, that was the thing. He had to win out. There was no second chance. No way of coming back again. Second attempts were out. He was on his way.

He moved purposefully up the broad front porch steps, wishing he could ignore, wipe out, the sickness inside. He came across the porch. There was a small, open vestibule.

It was ridiculously simple. This far.

He wanted to laugh.

For an instant he felt a lightheartedness, like freedom. Knowledge. It was sweet. He would recall it, because it was sharp and momentary.

But, there it was.

A row of black, partly rusted mailboxes, with nameplates. Some written on. Some scratched out. Some typed.

He looked nervously.

The name Miss Jean Brooks slapped him violently. Written with blue ink, in a slanting hand, though decidedly feminine. The mailbox was empty. But there was a number after the name. "2-B."

For a moment he had wild visions of climbing the side of the house, on the rickety fire-escape—reaching her room. But he didn't know where the room was.

The next step.

The next normal step was to ring the bell.

He didn't. He tried the door. It opened. He went immediately inside, closed the door as quietly as possible, and stood in the dusky old hall, sniffing ancient meals. Onion soup? Cabbage?

The key to her room.

He was beginning to perspire now.

He listened.

There was no sound at all in the big old house. Just the almost articulate odors.

He noticed the doors at the sides of the hall, stairs leading upward.

He started toward the stairs, expecting any instant to be stopped. His mind focused on those negatives, the girl's room. All of it intermingled with the man's voice on the phone. All of it tightening him up.

How to get into her room? For Christ's sake, find it, first.

He went up the stairs, fast. An instant later he stood in the shadowed hallway before her door. He thought of her, the newspaper pictures. The urgency was powerful. For a second he thought of breaking the door down, that close to panic.

He tried the knob. The door opened. Something crazy happened inside him, a rush of wild urgency.

The room was dim. He took it in at a glance, then closed the door and stood there silently staring, sopping it up.

So this was where she'd lived.

Had anyone heard him? He couldn't comprehend the silence.

2

Walter Hogan heard the noise below. He went fast to the ventilator in the floor, yanked back the rug, and looked.

Jesus Christ!

Dig that!

He stared, disbelieving, unable to comprehend what he saw. It's him—it's that flack, Sommers.

It wrung him. He stared down there, breathing heavily, wondering, gnawing the inside of his cheek. How the hell had Sommers found this place?

Splinters came off the main timber. The whole damned thing would blow up any minute, unless he thought of something. Inside his head it was one long curse.

He had to do something.

He had to do something.

It was like a scream inside him. The scream was like countless roaches gnawing frantically at the stale crust of his soul. He stared.

He stared. Sweating.

There was blood in his mouth.

3

Bill started around the room systematically, but working fast, looking for signs of photographical equipment. All sorts of stuff streamed through his mind. Memories of Karen, from 'way back; the reality. And all of the present, scorched like a brown stink across the white sheet of embalment that had been precious flesh. Memories.

The old Chinese screen kept taking his attention.

It seemed to enclose a very small corner of the room.

He gave up, went to the screen, yanked it awry.

He stood there, staring at himself.

From somewhere: "In every house there should be an ikon."

O.K.

Here he was, it—enshrined?

No candles, though. And what else.

In an ancient gold frame, the photograph of himself, very young, obviously re-photographed and cropped and blown up for large framing. On the wall, above a small, carefully arranged table....

He faintly recalled the photograph.

Two gold boxes on the table, arranged so one was on either side, beneath the framed picture.

For some reason he felt a sense of shame, and of helplessness. He was sweating now. It was hellishly quiet in the house. It came to him hard that that photograph, old as it was, would definitely attach him to Jean Brooks if and when the police found it. He grabbed one of the boxes, opened it, and stood still. It was packed with folded papers, envelopes. They looked very old. He took one up, opened an envelope. A letter. "Dear Karen...."

It was from him. He'd written it those many years ago. It was real. He read rapidly, feeling crazy rushes of emotion. He didn't know what to do. He grabbed up other letters. There were high-school notes. They were real. They were ones he'd written to Karen Jamais, so long ago. There were snapshots. Of himself. Of Karen. Of both of them together—so long ago.

It was absolutely nuts.

He flipped open the other box. The same thing. Packed. But what about those negatives?

He was reeling now. Inside he was a mess. He started jamming the letters, old folded notes, photographs, into his pockets, cramming them in every way he could. He snatched the big framed picture off the wall, tore off the back and took out the photograph. He creased it and stuck it in his pocket. He couldn't carry all the stuff. He'd have to take at least one of the boxes. Everything had to go.

The negatives!

Where in hell had she got all this stuff? How?

He heard the door open, behind him.

He turned, touched with panic.

"Hello, Sommers."

He stared at a neat young man. The neat young man was smiling quietly, with a show of arrogance. But there was strain behind the façade. Bill spotted a tense quality around the eyes, a soft sheen of sweat on the brow.

It was the voice of the man on the phone.

"You're looking for something that isn't here," the neat young man said. "I've got those negatives, see? So what is it you found?"

Bill said nothing, staring. The man gripped a revolver in his fist and the hand was quite steady.

"C'mon—" the voice urgent and sharp now, demanding—"what'd you find, Sommers!" There was threat there, too—and worry revealed tiny white fangs.

"Who are you?" Bill said.

The young man continued to grin but it was like a paper cut-out. "Name's Hogan."

Bill wanted to stall him. There was something wrong with this Hogan. His stomach constricted as he looked at the gun, knowing surely Hogan would use it. The thought was in the young man's eyes, and everything was at stake now. There couldn't be any mistakes. Not now. Not any more.

"I'd as soon kill you," Hogan said quietly. "It doesn't matter. There's nobody in the house."

"The shot would be heard."

"I don't think so. What'd you find, Sommers?"

"Nothing."

"You're a liar, Sommers." Hogan made some kind of a high note in his throat, something distantly related to laughter, and Bill suddenly knew he was facing some sort of a maniac. He had to move—and fast. Then, Hogan said, "So, you're going to pay, Sommers. Because I've got all the dirt on you. You'll pay—and pay—and pay!" The young man cleared his throat. "Because otherwise, that sweet little wife of yours is going to know everything."

"She already does," Bill said.

Hogan's face changed. "Don't you dig, Daddy? I know when you're lying." His eyes were almost blank, yet Bill knew they took in everything. "What you think'll happen to you if I phone the cops? Tell them your name? What then? That you killed that broad, and stuffed her into a culvert. You're going to pay. I can see it on your face."

Bill held a card.

"You read wrong."

"Don't bug me. I read right."

"You see the evening paper?"

"No. What would I want with the evening paper?"

Bill thrust his jaw forward slightly. "Because, Hogan. It's all over—only a matter of time. They found the body, Hogan. How long will it take for the cops to get here?"

"Don't give me that."

"It's true," Bill said. And he knew Hogan knew it was true. "It's been quite a while since they found her, Hogan. Time for the story to be written, photographs—and the paper's gone to print—and it's on everybody's doorstep. So, it's out. You get what I mean?"

The gun in Hogan's hand did not move. But something came into his eyes, across his face, now.

"The cops'll be here. They'll find her room, the same way I found it. See? I didn't know her under the name you knew her. You'll never know the real story, Hogan."

They watched each other.

Bill listened intently. He knew that what he spoke of the law was true, too. Somehow, he had to get those negatives from this armed man, and also gather up the remainder of the letters he'd written to the real Karen, so long ago. His body was charged with energy now.

"You're lying," Hogan said. "And—even so—"

"Even so, what?"

The door behind Hogan swung open, and a tall man in gray stood there, wearing a felt hat, and a gun in his right hand. "Drop it, kid. Right where you stand. It's all over." Neither Hogan nor Bill moved. "Drop it!" he snapped. "Neither one of you move!"

But Hogan moved. It was incredible. Like a flash, he was on the floor, flat out, and the revolver fired twice.

The tall man in gray fired his gun once, into the floor, grasped at the doorjamb, turned, took a step, and fell out in the hall. At the same instant, Bill leaped at Hogan who was already rolling toward him, bringing up the gun, his eyes crazy now.

An envelope slid from Hogan's pocket, and black slippery negatives spread in a fan on the thin, maroon rug.

Bill drove directly at the gun itself, at the wild eyes.

"Up your—!" Hogan gasped.

Bill caught the gun in both hands just as it fired. Something plucked at his shoulder, but he held to the gun, and he was fighting as he'd never known anyone could fight. It was for his life, and he knew it. He knew his condition. And he immediately felt the hard strength of the young man; a maniacal strength that with the first moment threatened to demolish everything in sight. Hogan struggled and fought like a madman, cursing and grunting.

"You killed her!" Bill said.

Hogan brought his knee up. Bill fell back, but forced himself to cling to that gun hand. He released his right hand and swung with everything he had. It caught Hogan in the gut, and the young man laughed. The laughter was hysterical.

Hogan ripped his hand free of Bill's grip. Bill saw the gun come toward him. He heard no shot—there was only a quick obliterating haze.

He wasn't unconscious. He was just unable to move. He saw the shadow of Hogan move fast through the room's door, through the red haze beyond his eyes. He couldn't move. He heard Hogan running down the stairs of the rooming house.

He fought to rise. His head was an explosion of pain.

Why hadn't Hogan killed him?

He'd just pounded him on the head with the gun. Bill didn't know how many times. By rights, he should be out cold. He wasn't.

He was on his knees, scrambling amid the few slippery black negatives on the floor with both hands, thinking, trying to think, to know what he had to do. Evidence. Destroy the evidence, for Louise and for Lolly. Somehow.

He got to his feet, reeling.

Hogan. He would have to catch Hogan. He knew that. Otherwise....

He turned, lurched to the Chinese screen, grabbed up the other gold box full of letters.

Downstairs, he heard the front door slam. Glass shattered and fell tinkling. He rushed into the hall.

The tall gray man, lying on the hall floor, stared at him. "Wait!" the man said. It was a gasp, dry—a harsh whisper. All he could think was, I've got the negatives—the notes—the letters....

"Wait," the man said again. He had both hands gripped into his mid-section. Dark blood seeped between the clutching fingers, staining the white shirt. The man's face was a lonely winter of gray pain.

Bill hesitated. His head was an awesome red blotch of stabbing aches.

"Name's Dederich," the man said above a cough. "Get that kid—get him. Police'll be here—" He grimaced with inner horror, and a rush of blood started from his mouth. Eyes frantic, he swallowed it back, his lips frothed with a macabre scarlet against the gray pallor. "Burke," he said. "If I last—I'll try to tell 'em. No time—just get that kid!"

Bill saw the man's sick eyes flick to the gold box in his hands. "What y'got there?"

"Nothing—nothing."

Dederich lurched to a half sitting position. His gun lay several feet away, and he tried for it, lunging grotesquely. "Son-bitch," he gasped. "You—you, too!"

He collapsed, cursing hoarsely.

Bill whirled. An elderly woman stood at the head of the staircase. Very pale, she wore a red dress and carried a large green shopping bag, and a black purse dangled from her other hand. As Bill moved toward her, she dropped the shopping bag. It opened, and cans of food, a loaf of bread, bottles, and other things clattered banging down the stairs.

The landlady. He knew it.

She stood there with her mouth wide. She saw Dederich, and then Bill coming toward her, and she began to scream. "Please," Bill said. "You're wrong—don't—"

She fell back against the wall, one veined hand clutched into her lumpy bosom, screaming. The thin, wattled throat, vented a sound something like chalk scratched in long dashes against a blackboard.

As he rushed past her and down the stairs, she flung the black purse at him. He dodged cans of tomatoes, beans, onion soup. His foot squashed into a loaf of bread. He took the last four steps in a flying leap to avoid several bottles of beer.

She screamed up there. And Dederich slowly inched, bleeding, toward his gun.

Outside the house, Bill was in time to see the black flashing sedan that had been parked in front of his car, roar off into the street.

He headed as fast as he could for the small sports car, tossed the box of letters in the rear, and started out after Hogan in the black sedan.

He could barely see, hardly control the immediate and violent rush of speed of the small car.

The black sedan vanished around a corner, and even above the maniacal wail of the Porsche's unleashed engine, Bill heard the scream of fat tires across the April afternoon.

5

Hogan's mind was really a blank, because so much streamed through it, every bit of it greased with terror, sending him wilder and wilder, he could at first contain nothing.

He drove the car savagely; first with the gas pedal flat to the floor, leg-strained, then driving that same foot against the brakes. No in-between. Just go. Tires smoking, engine agonized.

He had to go.

He knew this.

He had this rented car. His mind swarmed with unrelated cursings. The girl. That bastard he'd shot in the guts. Fear squatted groaning in his bowels.

He had to go as he'd never gone before.

It had never been like this. This was a first time.

It was all blown to hell.

All shot.

He'd lost everything. Go. Just go.

Only—where?

He fought for control of his thoughts. Cool it—cool it. Crazy—man, it was mad.

Why hadn't he shot that guy, Sommers? He should've done that. He knew it. But—he was out cold, really out; the way he'd hit him with the gun. Maybe he was dead.

His room. He thought of his room, of everything he'd left there. Sure, but not a trace of anything that could lead to him. Except fingerprints.

And that was okay.

Yeah—unless they got him.

He drove with complete abandon, with utter disregard for everything; stop-signs, cross-walks, people... and still, in the dark recess of his turbulent and disordered brain, he knew he must take the back streets—get out of this raunchy town before goddamned lousy cops stopped him, just for speeding: "*Officer, I was just....*"

Wouldn't that be a blast?

He had to have another car. Clout one. Money. All his money except for a few bucks was in his room. He had to catch a plane, a train, a car—and fast... a rocket; Superman.

He had to stop thinking like this. He'd always played it cool, and the image was there—only everything was cockeyed, off-kilter.

Something inside him kept screaming. It was as if he were driving through a long dark tunnel. He was lost. He realized that with a flash. And his fool mind wouldn't work right. He had to find a route out of this town—go somewhere—get away. But he was in a seemingly endless maze of residential streets and he recognized none.

It was then he looked in the rear view mirror and plainly saw that bastard Sommers in his sports car, racing after him. He slammed the accelerator to the floor.

There was something behind his eyes. It was something he remembered, from a long, long while back. It was a sensation of tears.

But he didn't cry.

Nor did he smile.

He laughed.

6

Following the black sedan, Bill felt pain in his left shoulder, grabbed with one hand. Blood. It was obviously just a nick, because his arm moved all right—but he recalled the fight with Hogan, and the blast of the gun, the quick tug at his shoulder.

This angered him all the more. Yet at the same time, wave after wave of remorse swept through him, mingling with his hate for Hogan; remorse over what he'd done to Louise, and his daughter; all these years, dreaming to himself as he worked and lived, dreaming a senseless dream that had walked in on him diabolically. It was so comic as to be horrifying to him. Now it was as if he'd leaped from some darkened hole toward light, only to discover the light was burning, painful, relentless.

He shifted down violently as the sedan ahead of him took another corner. The sports car drifted wildly toward the larger automobile... but what could he do?

Where was this kid Hogan going?

Probably trying to get out of town. But Hogan seemed lost. It was only a question of moments, Bill knew, before police would be on their tail. He didn't want that. He wanted Hogan to himself.

Who was the man, Dederich? What was going on?

His mind was a dizzy throng of unanswered questions.

At the same time, he was aware of everything, and of the driving package of guilt he would appear to be to the law. His car filled, his pockets loaded, with letters, photographs. The man, Dederich, and his words, *"You—too!"*

Who was "Burke"—the man Dederich had mentioned when he'd first seen him. And, distinctly, Dedrich had seemed to trust him when he'd first bolted out of the room after Hogan and seen the man on the floor, fingers stained with blood over his stomach. Yet, the instant Dedrich spotted the gold-flaked box, he'd changed. Why? He'd tried to get to his gun, across the floor.

By now the alarm would be all over town. He knew that. And it was all just a question of time.

Identification of the tarp.

Louise, breaking down, confessing to the story he'd told her. And Bill could hear the laughter, too, even if the law didn't so much as smile, when his wife repeated what he'd said. They would disbelieve, perhaps, even with such a dream dwelling within their own minds. Memory was a damned queer thing. It could play hell.

The intangible, reluctant growing apart of Louise and himself had thrown him into memory; he'd dwelt on the one thing he thought had truly meant something to him in his life, denying the actual truth—that he loved his wife, and child. He'd been half drunk and still was. He had grasped crazily at something he knew wasn't even true.

Self-pity. He hated it, yet couldn't avoid it, now.

Because it hinged to everything. Maybe it wasn't self-pity. He did know he had a crazy hate for the man, Hogan.

Throat constricted, arm muscles taut, his head a throbbing thing that still forced a reddish haze across his vision, he again realized how simple it was to catch Hogan, with the small fast sports car. Time and again, he rode the bumper of the car ahead.

But—what then?

There was nothing he could do.

They swerved wildly through traffic, and came into the largest business intersection of town. Cars, people, a sense of near insane dreaming; red lights, a cop's shrill whistle, a woman's scream as she ran dodging and sprawled across a curb, barely avoiding the careening black sedan, with Hogan at the wheel.

Abruptly Bill saw Hogan turn left, straight up the main street of town, whirling through traffic and people.

A stranger kind of madness came over him.

He gunned the Porsche and rammed it into the back of the sedan. It did nothing. If he only had a gun.

The sedan turned right, on a street that led to a highway leading out of town. In the distance, above the sound of the engine, he heard the first siren.

He drove to the left, and came spinning up aside the other car. Hogan laughed out at him. Bill slammed the Porsche against the black sedan. The sports car leaped back and away as the other car went on. Bill fought for control, up across the curb, a lawn, around two trees, and back bounding into the street again. He spotted the black car as it took a corner to the left, headed off from the highway again; headed once more into residential streets, and Bill knew Hogan was lost.

What could he do? How could he stop the larger car?

He roared after it. Approaching, catching it, was simple. Stopping, something else again....

He realized suddenly that they were nearing the vicinity of town where he lived.

A police cruiser appeared directly ahead, between himself and Hogan. The car lurched violently from an alley. Bill drove directly toward it. For an instant the two cars sped side by side, the sound of the siren violent and inexhaustible. He turned the Porsche directly into the cruiser. The police car whirled to the right, lost control, leaped the curb, cut up across a lawn and smashed into the side of a house.

A cop came out of the car, firing at the fleeing sports car. Then Bill was again behind the black sedan.

They were only blocks from his own home now.

The sky was darkening rapidly, and the first splats of April rain struck the windshield.

He slammed the sports car up beside the sedan again, and kept slashing it directly against the larger car. The Porsche wove dizzily down the road. Hogan was having all he could do to keep the other car under control now. They were approaching a section of narrow, winding streets, above a canal perhaps thirty feet wide.

A narrow bridge loomed into view.

Bill again came to the side of the sedan, and slammed the small car against it again and again. He saw Hogan look at him, and suddenly the other car seemed to leap.

They had reached the bridge. For a moment, Bill fought brutally with the steering wheel, tires sliding on wet brick, the rain falling slowly, a mist with sparse heavy drops.

He straight-legged the brakes, and came to rest against a wall, looked around.

The other car was spinning in the middle of the small bridge area, lined with white-painted cement guard rails.

He knew they were only a block and a half from his home.

He heard Hogan yell something, and in the falling dark glimpsed the other man fighting with the steering wheel.

The car shot through the right guard rails, catapulting down into the shallow canal. Water founted as it struck. Bill was already running. He saw the rise of flashing water subside.

Maybe Hogan had been killed.

"Hold it!"

It was Hogan. Bill kept running. A gun fired, and brick chipped at his feet. He saw Hogan standing on the far wall of the canal, soaked with water, the gun in his hand.

"You haven't got me, Sommers. You'd better quit. I'm heading for your place, see? And I've got this!" He waved the gun. "So, don't try anything."

He turned and ran directly into a landscape of trees and shrubs that would carry him through the block. Another half block and he would be at Bill's home, and Louise and Lolly were there. He knew Hogan was cracked. He didn't know what to do, except that he had to stop him.

He made the opposite bank and started out after Hogan.

It was direct brutal pain inside. He had to catch that man and make him tell the truth.

He had to stop him, before he reached Louise.

7

Hogan felt something inside him that was like a machine. It was the machine of fear, and he recognized it, but refused to acknowledge it as his own personal catastrophe.

He turned, running up sloping lawns away from the canal, at an angle that would bring him to the street, behind one of the row of houses that loomed against the pink-gray April skies, and then across the street. Only a couple lots down and he'd be in Sommers' back yard.

It was a crazy thought, but the way he felt, it seemed the one out. He'd have to get a car. But he'd take the wife—or the kid—with him. He hadn't made up his mind as to which one would come with him. If necessary, he would kill Sommers. But, with the wife or the kid with him—and a car, any car, he'd stand a chance. A hostage was a chance.

He ran, panting raggedly, plunging through deep shrubbery, his feet sliding on the dampened grass. It wasn't raining hard, and it might even stop. Dig, it didn't matter. Not to him.

Everything ran swiftly through his mind, all jumbled. The loss of the other car was maybe a good thing. Lucky he hadn't been hurt. The police would be looking for that car. Sure.

But—he should have killed Sommers.

The bastard. The dirty bastard. He'd fouled everything up.

It was a kind of sob inside him, a sob that never reached his throat, or his being, truly. Loss.

He didn't even really know what he was doing.

Only—now—that he was scared. Nothing like this had ever happened. He'd never even had a really close brush. This wasn't a brush. This was the real thing. Who had that character been? The one he'd plugged, back there at the boarding house? My Christ, he'd killed him; aiming for the man's guts, too.

A shrill series of giggles burst from his throat.

He raced across a lawn, behind a house, stopped, and turned to glance back. He thought about his clothes, all ruined. All the petty little things touched him; thinking, what'll I do! What'll I do! My clothes are ruined—it's all his fault... his fault....

His breath racked in his chest.

He'd lost everything—lost out on everything.

He saw Sommers running toward him, crashing long-legged through the shrubs, like an animal, lunging—and damned close, too.

"God damn you!" Hogan screamed.

He lifted the gun.

8

The sound of the shot rattled like a cannon across the still, peacefully misting evening, bouncing from side to side of the small, shallow valley above the canal.

Bill sprawled as the slug socked him.

"There, by God!" Hogan yelled.

He turned and ran again. Bill watched him. For an instant he thought he was hit badly, that it was all over. The bullet had struck his thigh.

But he moved his leg, looked at the spot searchingly in the dim light. It was nothing more than a nick again.

The next time, he'd get it. He knew this in his mind. He came to his feet, running again, pushing with everything he had. A stitch of riotous pain tore in his left side, now.

There wasn't far to go. Hogan would reach his home. He ran as he had never even tried to run before in his life, knowing he had to stop Hogan, no matter what. He recalled there couldn't be many shells left in Hogan's gun, but he had no idea how many. He knew the calibre of the man, now; knew Hogan was out of his head. At bay, he would shoot to kill. He had already tried. He had shot that Dederich. But—in his own home... Louise and Lolly....

And running along with him, captured in the pit of his mind, was the picture of Karen Jamais, on the garage floor, as he'd found her.

With him ran those moments of wrapping her body in the old tarp, then the culvert... and sickness was deep within him.

He couldn't continue much farther. The pain in his chest was a stabbing thing, like a live animal biting—a knife grinding.

Panting, fighting for breath, he saw Hogan cross the street, the younger man running like a flash through the saffron splash of early lamplight; the fading sky touching him, twinkling on the gun in his hand.

Bill hit the street, running.

He sensed other movement. He sensed more light than usual beyond the lots, to where his own house was.

Springing beneath an elm's shadow near the sprawling rear patio of a neighbor's home, he saw Hogan stop dead.

The young man stood half in Sommers' back yard, by a hedge. He was in a half crouch.

It was his chance.

He took it, running and leaping. Hogan turned and brought the gun up, but Bill was on him. Again he sensed the intense, wild strength of Hogan. But there was something inside him that refused to acknowledge anything now.

"You killed her, that girl!" he said.

"Yes!" Hogan screamed it, kicking, fighting.

They sprawled on the damp ground, fighting. Bill kept trying to get the gun from the other's grasp, and at the same time hurt the man.

He managed to grab Hogan's wrist, twisted with all his might, and brought a right into Hogan's mid-section. The gun fell to the ground. Bill kicked at it violently.

Hogan's breath rasped.

For an instant, they fought like animals. Bill saw the young man's eyes and a spike of fright drove into him; he'd never seen anything quite like it.

They stood and slugged.

Suddenly, Hogan broke clear, running toward the house.

"Stop!" Bill shouted. He started after him.

Instantly, he ceased running. A bright spot of brilliant white light came from the side of the house, and engulfed Hogan, and at the same instant, a shot rang through the evening.

Hogan plowed the back yard with his face.

"Police!" a man called. "Just hold it!"

The light buried Hogan.

For an instant, Bill stood there, by the hedge, staring. The law was there. At his home.

And in that instant, he remembered everything. He turned, without even thinking, and ran blindly back the way he'd come. Through the neighbor's yard, across the street. He plunged down the sloping lawns—racing with an awful fear inside him—racing toward where he had parked the Porsche.

9

He could barely stand. He choked for breath, kneeling beside the sports car on the wet brick. Fumbling, cursing without sound, rasping for air, he ripped his pockets open, bringing out the crumpled letters, the negatives, pictures, emptying the gold-flaked box from inside the car.

A match. A lighter.

He'd lost his lighter.

He heard a siren. 'Way up on the hill, he heard a scream of tires. There was the distinct sound of pounding feet, still some distance away. But those feet were nearing him, coming toward the canal.

He heard his name called, shouted in the tiny valley. "Sommers! Sommers—"

He staggered lurching, and ripped open the glove compartment of the car, searching for a match. He had to burn those things. It ripped at him. He had to do it. There would be enough for Louise to bear—without that.

There could even be the knowledge; just so long as there wasn't the reality.

There were no matches in the glove compartment.

The pounding feet came nearer, faltered. There were several men. He knew that. Then they came on with a rush. He heard the siren again.

He found a pack of paper matches on the floor of the car, grabbed them. They were damp. He crouched over the pile of letters, and suddenly the heap of memories blazed before him.

The fire licked at the paper. Abruptly, it caught healthily, sprang up.

He knelt on the wet brick, staring into the flames.

They found him like that. He said nothing.

Crisping black flakes of burned paper floated in the April evening, and pulsating red embers gradually popped out, like life-snuffed fireflies.

Only then did he look up at them.

"Sommers?"

"Yes."

"Name's Burke. You'd better come along, now. We're the police, Sommers."

"All right."

The burly, red-faced man, Burke, turned to a uniformed man who held a .38 in his hand.

"Mosher? You bring his car along. Got it?"

A string-like thread of smoke puffed amid black chips on the damp brick.

"What were you burning?" Burke said.
Bill looked at him and shook his head.

"But who knows where or when...!"

1

The house was rather quiet now. There had been a lot of noise, talk, but it had died now. There was no Hogan. Bill sat on the couch with Louise. Lolly was upstairs in bed. Bill stared at the woman and the man who sat across from them, each in a large easy chair.

There was little left to say.

He could see a police cruiser, waiting out at the curb in front of the house. He heard a uniformed cop in the hall. At the archway stood the red-faced, burly man in plain clothes; the man called Burke. He stood with a kind of leashed nervousness; tight, trying to reveal nothing. Only the ridge muscles of his jaw showed his impatience.

Bill ached all over.

But that didn't matter.

They had told him Dederich was in the hospital, he would pull through. Hogan was dead.

He stared at the woman across from him.

He could hear Louise breathing.

Beyond the woman and the man was the painting he'd been working on; not the one he was commissioned to do, but the other one; the crimson flashes of dream.

"You see," the woman said. "We came as soon as Mr. Dederich wired." She hesitated, half-smiled. There was something not quite calm about her.

"I see," Bill said.

"We understand," Louise said.

Burke cleared his throat. Nobody glanced his way.

Bill felt Louise's hand touch his. Her fingers gripped his hand. The woman's eyes across from them flicked quickly, then away. The man moved heavily.

The man was large and silent, pale. He had very black hair, and he was dressed in expensive clothes that even so could never conceal his immense weight. It was not the weight of muscle, bone; it was fat. It thrust and bulged at neck and wrist and ankle and gut. It was revealed in the balloon-like, rubber-like tautness of cheek and jowl and bulge of eye... in the protruding pouting puff of lips. A fat gold ruby ring was on the ring finger of each of the man's hands. On his left wrist was a fat gold wrist watch. On his right wrist a heavy gold chain of some sort. His eyes were like black October late over-ripe grapes, ready any instant to bead with sweet sugared juices. He breathed through a tiny hole between his lips, and the breathing was extremely rapid; something like a bird's might be. A pigeon? Bill wondered.

"Charles and I came immediately," the woman said.

Bill could sense Louise's reasonable uncomfortableness.

The two across from him were not uncomfortable.

He finished with the man, and looked at the woman, something inside him trying to find something, searching, while all the time he knew it was gone forever. Yet, still he searched—for what, he didn't know... something, anything. Any remaining speck of what once had been. He searched and searched and found nothing.

Yet he looked. Wonderingly.

All he found was a comely-appearing hunk of ice.

There was no point attempting to find the bright young fire-like streaks of auburn in her hair. The hair was yellow-blonde, and he knew if he touched that hair it might break brittly between his fingers. Yet, he searched.

"Of course," the fat man said. "Karen and I must make that plane back to the coast." He checked his wristwatch. A gesture. He did not see the watch. His arm moved in a fat arc, then descended to the chair's arm, both possessing an immediate similarity. He spoke lazily, with a strange accent; aloof, supercilious, Harvard, faked, Madison Avenue—yet none of these truly. "I've already arranged about the—ah, child's...." He made a soft sound in his throat and glanced from the corners of his eyes toward his wife. "We don't have long."

"The lawyer?" the woman said.

"I discussed this with him on the phone, as I told you," the man said gently, easing the words from between his lips. "We won't be hook—that is, we must make that plane." Again, he nearly lifted his arm.

Nobody spoke.

Burke cleared his throat, from the hall archway.

The fat man spoke again. "The airport limousine won't wait out there forever."

"Yes, dear," the woman said.

Bill kept looking at her. Was she, too, searching? He saw no sign whatever. None.

Everything was out, now. All in the open. There were only little details he wanted to know.

She wore some sort of black and gold dress under a snow-white coat. She wasn't heavy. She wasn't a lath. Her mouth was still. Her eyes were simply eyes. She moved seldom. Her legs were neat in nylon, her feet fine in black, glistening pumps.

"Then," Bill said. "Your daughter—wrote this friend of hers? Grace

Adams? And Miss Adams told you? And that's how you came to employ Dederich?"

"He worked from the agency. He was assigned to the case, really," the woman said.

Karen, he thought. This is Karen. It was her daughter. There wasn't much room for any more emotion in him. He just asked and received, and occasionally glanced over at Burke, who raised his eyebrows in return.

The fat man nodded.

The Lakewoods. Charles and Karen Lakewood.

Karen Lakewood.

"We'd already had him working," Karen said.

He remembered not a single nuance of her voice.

She said, "As soon as she ran away from the—" she paused.

"Broke out of that mental hospital," Charles Lakewood said smoothly. "Mr. Dederich was immediately in our employ. Then Gracie told us about Karen's letter, and it was simple enough, actually." He sighed. "The postmark." He shrugged. "And, of course, my wife knew, then."

"Yes," Karen said. She shook her head, glanced lightly at Louise, then looked at Bill. For an instant, their gazes held. Then it broke. "Really," she gave a light laugh. "All my fault."

No feeling. Nothing.

"Of course, it's a terrible thing," Charles Lakewood said. "We..." he ceased. He looked at his pudgy hand.

"I don't like to embarrass you," Karen said to Louise. "But you do know now how Bill and I used to know each other. And—it was a lark sort of. I just saved every fool thing, you know. Everything. I kept them in boxes, all his letters, pictures. They got stuck away in the attic, and somehow—for years, Charles and I never knew—our Karen—" she glanced at her husband — "was playing in the attic." She paused again. "It was an extremely difficult birth."

"They thought she would die. My wife, I mean. They thought the child was dead. It lived," Charles Lakewood said, tightening his lips. "But something was wrong."

"I lived, too," Karen said. "We gave her everything. Then we found out. The doctors, that is—she'd assumed she'd decided to become...." She paused for a long time. "Become me. In every respect. It's a difficult thing. Living with those letters of yours—Bill, I mean. Your writing, those old snapshots—everything. I was a sentimental fool. But I'd forgotten. And when the doctors got some of it out of her, she'd already hidden the things—the boxes—everything. And she'd asked about you." She hesitated again. "Oh, I've told Charles everything—and I guess Louise understands, don't you, honey?"

Bill felt Louise nod. "Yes," she said. "Of course."

Karen Lakewood said, "She was terribly retarded, you see. She even looked it. She was twenty-four, you know, and she... well—" She shrugged. "It's a terrible thing."

For an instant, he thought she was going to cry. He saw the fight, then. It registered in her eyes. She won. Her eyes remained clear.

"You really have to think about it," she said, looking at him. "Imagine, even dressing like that—using those old words, like 'droop' and like that. Remember them?"

Nobody spoke.

"I was a fool," she said.

"Cease the flagellation," her husband said smoothly.

"Yes." She was quite still. "Karen had an obsession, that's all. She was compulsive—she was very, very ill. We did everything we—but, what can you do?"

"Yes," Bill said, still searching.

Burke said, "Think you'd better cut it short."

They all stood up. Charles Lakewood made it first and fast. Somehow, Charles Lakewood and Louise moved ahead of Bill. For an instant, he stood there, looking at Karen.

She stared at him. He thought she moved her head, but he couldn't be sure, and then she dropped her gaze, and stepped toward the hall.

"I'm—sorry," Bill said.

She turned again, and looked at him.

Something passed between them. Something that was there like the flicking touch of a bird's wing, then gone.

"Yes," she said. "I am, too."

They all converged in the hall, moving toward the front door. Bill was completely exhausted. The police knew about almost everything, and had a complete run-down on Hogan, whose real name was Ledly Jeffers.

Charles Lakewood went out the open front door and walked quickly to the large car that waited to carry them to the airport. He stepped inside and motioned toward his wife.

A thought touched Bill. He shoved it away. It came again. If the girl had been twenty-four? What then? Could it be? Could she have been....

"Good-by, Bill—Louise," Karen said. She smiled at Louise, and Bill took her hand.

For another instant they regarded each other, and he desperately wanted to ask her. Had that girl been their daughter? Because—it must be. It had to be.

"Good-by."

He stood there, with Louise, watching the car drift down the drive. He wanted to run after it. He had to know.

"You okay?" Louise said.

"Yes."

He would never know.

Not ever.

Burke's voice was heavy, yet somehow tentative.

"We'd better get down to headquarters now, Sommers. Lot of things to take care of."

"I'm coming with you," Louise said.

She bent and kissed his jaw. He leaned toward her and watched the red taillight of the airport limousine vanish down the street.

And he knew.

"C'mon, Sommers," Burke said. "Move it."

Louise was at the hall closet. "Bill?"

"Yes." He looked at Burke. "Will it be bad?"

"It won't be easy," Burke said.

Bill stood there another moment, staring into the April dark. He had his wife. He had his daughter. He deserved them.

And he knew.

THE END

Made in United States
Troutdale, OR
06/23/2024